The Harrison Duet

Two Novels in One Volume

SYRIE JAMES

songbird

This story is a work of fiction. Names, characters, places, and incidents either are a product of the author's imagination or are used fictitiously. Any resemblance to actual persons, living or dead, events, or locales is entirely coincidental.

Copyright © 1986 by Syrie Astrahan James

All rights reserved.

No part of this book may be reproduced, or stored in a retrieval system, or transmitted in any form or by any means, electronic, mechanical, photocopying, recording, or otherwise, without express written permission of the publisher.

propositions

This story is a work of fiction. Names, characters, places, and incidents either are a product of the author's imagination or are used fictitiously. Any resemblance to actual persons, living or dead, events, or locales is entirely coincidental.

Copyright © 1987 by Syrie Astrahan James

All rights reserved.

No part of this book may be reproduced, or stored in a retrieval system, or transmitted in any form or by any means, electronic, mechanical, photocopying, recording, or otherwise, without express written permission of the publisher.

ISBN-13: 9781495952869

Also By Syrie James:

The Missing Manuscript of Jane Austen
The Lost Memoirs of Jane Austen
The Secret Diaries of Charlotte Brontë
Dracula, My Love
Nocturne
Forbidden

PRAISE FOR THE NOVELS OF SYRIE JAMES

Nocturne

"You will love this beautiful and mysterious story, full of love and longing, but with a passion that sizzles through the pages. The characters are bold and imaginative, and our hero Michael is everything a woman looks for in a man, but just a bit more."
—*The Romance Reviews*

"Lyrical, lush, and intensely romantic, this infinitely touching, bittersweet story will weave its way into readers' hearts, with its complex characters and compelling emotions sure to linger long after the last page has been turned." —*Library Journal*

"Brilliant, couldn't put it down...a wonderful read with a beautiful romance that pulls at the heart strings. A must read for any romance fan." —*Book Chick City*

"What could be more romantic than getting snowbound with a dark and mysterious stranger?...*Nocturne* is the kind of book that makes you want to turn off the phone and the television so you can do nothing but read."
—*Barnes and Noble.com*

i

The Harrison Duet

Dracula, My Love

"Syrie James weaves a tale of quite a different Dracula: a mouth-wateringly handsome, powerful, cultured, and passionate one. And...I...Loved...It! This is a gripping story, infused with passion, excitement and emotional turmoil. It sheds a whole new light on Count Dracula. In true über-vampire style, he completely outdoes Edward Cullen and Buffy's Angel in the sexy tortured soul stakes. This vampire can bite my neck any time!"" —*American Book Center*

"Only Mina Harker, who once fell under the seductive spell of literature's most famous vampire, knows Dracula's true story. James gives readers an intriguing alternate theory as to the events that occurred in Stoker's classic horror tale while at the same time delivering a spooky yet thoroughly romantic love story." —*Chicago Tribune*

"Rich with emotion, feelings, and passion...a page-turner of a book...You come to crave the heat of Dracula and Mina's passion while shivering from the cold and lonely torment of Dracula's eternal existence." —*Suite 101 Book Reviews*

"Extremely romantic! A truly beautiful story of love, deception, obsession, survival, and sacrifice. I was riveted, and could not put it down!" —*That Artsy Reader Girl*

The Lost Memoirs of Jane Austen

"This fascinating novel will make readers swear there was such a man as Mr. Ashford and that there is such a memoir...

Tantalizing, tender, and true to the Austen mythos...highly recommended." —*Library Journal, starred review*

"The reader blindly pulls for the heroine and her dreams of love, hoping against history that Austen might yet enjoy the satisfactions of romance... offers a deeper understanding of what Austen's life might have been like." —*The Los Angeles Times*

"Syrie James is a fine story-teller, with a sensitive ear for the Austenian voice and a clear passion for research. The result is a thoughtful, immensely touching romance that does justice to its subject and will delight anyone who feels, as Syrie James does, that Jane Austen couldn't possibly have written with such insight without having had a great romance of her own." —*Jane Austen's Regency World Magazine*

You don't have to be a Jane Austen expert to enjoy this book. You just need to be in the mood for a page-turning, romantic story filled with warm characters, great passions, enjoyable language, and a terrific plot. And it's to James's credit that her novel reads a lot like—what else?—a classic Austen novel." —*Goodreads*

The Secret Diaries of Charlotte Brontë

"For fans of biographical tales and romance, Syrie's story of Charlotte offers it all: longing and yearning, struggle and success, the searing pain of immeasurable loss, and the happiness of a love that came unbidden and unsought. I did not want this story to end." —*Jane Austen's World*

The Harrison Duet

"James takes the biography of Brontë and sketches it into a work of art…specific, passionate details give the book its main pull…A can't-miss novel for Brontë fans and historical fiction buffs alike." —*Sacramento Book Review*

"Through Charlotte's diary, the reader is privy to her inspirations and heartaches, her secret jealousies, and more importantly, her muse. . . The revelation of Charlotte's romantic relationships—her shocking infatuation with a married man and the evolution of her relationship with her father's curate and future husband, Arthur Bell Nichols—is fascinating. A must-buy!" —*Romance Junkies*

"I was swept away. James's book provoked tears at times, and a delicious romantic shiver at others. It's truly masterful." —*Meditative Meanderings*

The Missing Manuscript of Jane Austen

"A novel within a novel honoring what we love most about Austen: her engaging stories, her rapier wit, and her swoonworthy romance. James's pitch perfect, brilliantly crafted prose will have you enchanted and in awe of her mastery until the very last page. 5 out of 5 Regency Stars!" —*Austenprose*

"A literary feast for Anglophiles… [with] an Austen-worthy ending." —*Publisher's Weekly*

"This richly imagined Jane Austen 'road novel' is such a page turner…A standout addition to the crowded archive of Austen homages."—*Kirkus Reviews* (starred review)

"Syrie James has surpassed herself...She did a brilliant job both at delivering a well-designed plot echoing Jane Austen's voice— but modernizing it for a present-day audience—and at enclosing it in an intriguing frame of quest and romance... an incredible gripping story...it'll be one of your favourite reads in 2013!"
—*My Jane Austen Book Club*

Forbidden

"Hands down the most fascinating book I have read in quite a while... As the characters develop and the story unfolds you will find yourself wrapped up in their world, indulging in every kiss and holding your breath with every twist."
—*Luxury Reading*

"A YA novel that hits all the right notes... If you enjoy angels, 'forbidden' romance and dashing heroes, then this should be added to your TBR." —*USA TODAY*

"A YA paranormal fantasy gem! I LOVED IT! Young adults who enjoyed the Twilight series will be just as intrigued."
—*Book Reader's Heaven*

"Full of intrigue, romance and humor …[and] very much about trust, discovery, and love… I was entertained by the inspired prose, witty dialogue, the humorous actions and reactions, and of course, the honest, pure character development…This may be written for Young Adults, however, might I also suggest, for the young at heart?" —*Austenprose*

songbird

BOOK ONE

THE HARRISON DUET

AUTHOR'S FOREWORD

Dear Reader,

It is with great pleasure that I share with you this newly edited edition of my very first published romance novel.

This story is especially meaningful to me because it was inspired in part by my relationship with the man I love. Just like Desiree and Kyle, Bill and I had a whirlwind courtship. But we lived in different cities and were faced with the challenges of a long-distance relationship. From the very start it was difficult, and when he moved many hundreds of miles further away, it became more difficult still. I'll never forget how devastated I was each time he or I had to get on a plane and leave. But from the moment of our first meeting, we each recognized our missing other half. We've been married now for thirty-seven wonderful years, and I am grateful for every minute.

I wrote *Songbird* in 1985. This gently edited version better reflects my current sensibilities as a novelist, but the story remains unchanged—and it is like a little time capsule. While re-reading it, I couldn't help but smile fondly at the descriptions of clothing, songs, popular recording artists, and at every mention of technology. Car phones? Phone booths? Who can even remember such things?

The Harrison Duet

No matter how much the world changes around us, however, the fundamental things in our lives do not change. We work hard. We have dreams. We fall in love. We experience the joys of a new relationship, and risk our hearts on the road to happiness.

I hope, as this story takes you back to an earlier time and place, that it will touch your heart and make you smile.

Happy reading!

Syrie James

1

The song ended. Desiree leaned forward on the high stool, bringing her lips close to the padded microphone. "That was Rita Coolidge singing the hit from her new album, 'Be Mine Tonight.' Before that we heard from Johnny Mathis with 'So in Love with You.' "

She checked the pie-sized clock on the wall above the console. "It's twenty-five past three here on this hot and sunny Wednesday afternoon in June. You're listening to KICK Anaheim, 102 on your FM dial. This is Desiree Germain keeping you company for that long drive home."

Right on cue, the first soft notes of the next song began to play. Desiree removed the massive black headphones and lifted her toffee-colored curls off her shoulders, letting the cool air from the overhead vent flow freely around her neck. A fire-engine red bumper sticker affixed to the window above the console caught her eye: SPEND THE NIGHT WITH DESIREE...KICK 102 FM!

Time for a new slogan, she thought, carefully peeling the length of vinyl off the glass and tossing it in the trash. Seven years of working evenings and nights, and she had finally made it: Prime time, daytime radio in Southern California. So whatever you do, she told herself, don't blow it.

She turned up the volume control, leaned her head back, and closed her eyes, hoping the mellow tune's soothing rhythm would help calm her senses. *It's the same job as before, only the time has changed.* Forget about Arbitron and shares and rating points. Forget about the hundreds of would-be deejays standing in the wings, chomping at the bit, just waiting for you to mess up. Put it out of your mind. You're good—one of the best jocks this station has—or Sam wouldn't have given you the afternoon drive. Just relax and enjoy yourself.

She heard the studio door open and straightened up. Tom, the station's part-time gofer, rushed in, his forehead perspiring beneath a tangle of wiry red hair.

"Man, it's hot out there," he said, fanning his youthful face with a stack of small newsprint sheets. "The air conditioner can barely keep up. You're lucky—your cubicle is nice and cool."

"I know. I am lucky. And cubicle is right." Desiree glanced about the studio with a smile. It was tiny, the equipment was out-dated, and dog-eared posters of Elvis, The Beatles, Kenny Rogers, and Streisand were plastered across the dingy beige walls. She knew that some people got claustrophobic in elevators, yet she was stuck in this microscopic space for four straight hours every day—and she loved it.

"Here's the latest, fresh off the wire." Tom handed her the stack of newsprint.

"Anything good?"

"What do you think this is, *Sixty Minutes?*"

Desiree leafed through the pile of news briefs, reading some of the titles aloud. "'New smoking control law giving people nicotine fits.' Cute, but no cigar. 'Millionaire owner of laundromat chain taken to the cleaners in palimony suit.'" She winced. "Why do we do these, anyway? We're not a news station."

"Don't ask me." Tom shrugged as he turned to leave. "Sam likes this kind of stuff. And one must never argue with the P.D." Before shutting the door, he scrunched up his face and mimicked their program director's gravelly voice. "Above all else—*Be Entertaining.*"

Desiree laughed as she slipped on her headphones. "I'll give it my best shot. Today's news can use all the help it can get." A familiar refrain signaled the end of the song. She pushed the start button on the deck to the left of the console. A glance at the digital countdown timer told her she had fifteen seconds. Just then Tom pressed his face up against the glass of the window above the console, staring in at her with distorted fleshy lips and huge bug-eyes.

She smothered another laugh, dropping her voice an octave as she said into the mike, "If you're sitting in traffic out there right now, feeling that tension creeping up your spine, here's the perfect way to get rid of all that stress. Just imagine that I'm sitting right next to you, giving your shoulders a nice, long, intimate massage." As soon as she said the words, she cringed inwardly. *Nice, long, intimate massage? Good grief! Did I really just say that?*

The commercial break began. Desiree again plucked off her headphones and glanced up at Tom, who was rolling his eyes as he walked away, mouthing the word "outrageous" at her through the glass.

Outrageous. That's what the reporter from the Los Angeles Times had written about her in this morning's review of her new afternoon show. "One outrageous, sexy woman, whose luscious, lusty voice could, with one well-placed sigh, bring half the male population of Southern California to its knees."

She laughed softly to herself. Luscious? Lusty? Hardly. She believed she was reasonably attractive. Steve, her ex-husband,

The Harrison Duet

had once told her she had eyes like molten gold and a face like a cameo. Her hair seemed to match her personality. It brushed her shoulders in unruly waves, a blend of vibrant shades from light brown to red to dark mahogany. But somehow, she'd found, her deep voice led people to expect someone entirely different: a tall, voluptuous blond bombshell who walked, talked, and breathed sex. No way on earth could she ever hope to fit that image.

She was petite in every sense of the word. She possessed curves in all the right places, but no matter how hard she tried, she didn't quite reach the five-foot-one-inch mark. Thirty years old, she had endured a lifetime of jokes about the discrepancy between her voice and her looks. She'd seen the disappointment in people's eyes too many times when they met her and discovered she wasn't the sex symbol they'd imagined.

Still, her voice was her biggest asset. Sam insisted that teasing banter meant higher ratings. The listeners couldn't see her, after all. What harm could there be in playing along?

She scanned the news brief she'd selected, waiting for the commercial break to end, then threw the mike switch to program and turned up the volume.

"Here's an item of interest for all you soda-pop guzzlers out there. Looks like the new diet soft drink, Sparkle Light, is losing steam. In an unexpected move yesterday, the parent corporation, privately owned, multimillion dollar Harrison Industries, announced plans for Sparkle Light Bottling Company to go public." She went on to read the experts' analysis, which pointed a finger at a suspected drop in product sales, then laid the news bulletin up on the counter.

"If you've always wanted to own stock in a soft-drink company, this might be your big chance. But let's hope Sparkle Light picks up in a hurry, or you may find yourself making a big deposit, no-return investment on a warehouse full of pop without any fizz."

She played a groaning sound-effects tape. Next, grabbing a large pink index card from the board above her console, she announced it was time to play the Trivia Game. "I hope you're all next to your phones. The number to call is 555-KICK. I'll take caller number twelve."

All five lines on the multi-tap phone in her studio lit up with magical precision. Desiree smiled. The immediate response to contests on the afternoon drive never ceased to amaze her. This was the time of day to be on the air!

"The caller who can answer today's trivia question correctly will receive a complimentary dinner for two at Maximilian's in Huntington Beach." She read a blurb about the restaurant, then punched the buttons on the phone one at a time, counting out loud and disconnecting each line in sequence.

"Hi, you're on the air," she said when she reached the twelfth caller. "Who's this?"

"This is Kyle Harrison." The voice, obscured slightly by faint background noise, sounded low, smooth, and deeply masculine. She found herself sitting up straight on the stool, listening attentively.

"Hello, Kyle." She conjured up a quick mental image to fit the voice. Tall, athletically built, thirty-five, and devilishly handsome? *No. People never look the way they sound. And you ought to know that better than anyone.* Odds are he was old and fat, with bad teeth. "Did you know you've got a terrific radio voice, Kyle?"

"Thanks. Yours isn't bad either." He sounded irritated. "Listen, I'm calling—"

"Are you as good-looking as you sound?" she teased.

A split-second pause. Then, he replied curtly, "Are you?"

The Harrison Duet

Oh, God. Open mouth, insert foot. She glanced down at her worn, tight-fitting cutoffs and clinging pink T-shirt. What kind of woman was he imagining? A gorgeous blonde in a sexy billboard or magazine cover shot? Think fast. *Be Entertaining.*

"Just let your imagination go wild," she said in her most velvety voice. "If only you could see the wicked little dress I've got on today. Electric-blue silk. Open in the back. Cut just off the shoulder. Terribly chic. And these silver spiked heels are positively sinful."

"I'll bet." He laughed suddenly, a deep pleasant sound which set her spine tingling.

What a gorgeous laugh, she thought. Maybe he isn't quite so old or so ugly after all. Get to the trivia question, an inner voice warned. You've talked to him too long already. But instead, she leaned forward on the console, resting her chin on her hand. "Where are you from, Kyle?"

"Seattle."

"Seattle! That's a thousand miles away. KICK'S coverage must be even more widespread than I thought."

He laughed again. "Sorry to disappoint you. I'm only about thirty miles away, near the L.A. airport. At this moment I'm crawling along on the San Diego freeway, bumper-to-bumper, at the incredible speed of three miles per hour."

"A car-phone executive!" she announced with delight. "My very first one on the air. You just made my day." Mobile phones cost thousands of dollars. A new image of the man formed in her mind: a cigar-smoking corporate executive in a dark blue suit, three diamond rings flashing on each stubby hand. Age: sixty. Eyes: watery-gray. Hair: none. "Well, Kyle, I hope you can think trivia and drive at the same time, because—"

"Hold on," he interrupted. "I know this is a contest line, but I called for another reason—to comment on a news item you gave about a company of mine a few minutes back. Sparkle Light."

She opened her mouth to reply, then froze. *Sparkle Light.* In a flash of belated understanding, she realized the significance of his name. Kyle Harrison. Harrison Industries—the privately-owned parent corporation. Desperately, she began to riffle through the stack of newsprint on her counter, her mind racing, trying to remember what she'd said about Sparkle Light. Something about a no-return investment, the product losing its fizz. Had she sounded overly sarcastic? Defamatory? If only we had a seven-second delay system, she thought, so I could bleep out his comments if he starts to get nasty.

"The information you gave was essentially correct. Sparkle Light *is* going public. But the so-called expert analysis you read was completely off base. Since you popped up with your phone number so conveniently, I thought I'd call and set the record straight."

"Thank you, Mr. Harrison," she said, hoping her voice sounded as light and sparkling as his product. "We always welcome a little inside information from the business world." Why did she suddenly feel as if she had to call him mister? From now on, she told herself, I'm going to start screening calls. To hell with spontaneity!

"We're going public to raise capital for other investments. It's that simple. The move is no reflection on the sales record of Sparkle Light. In fact, the product has far exceeded our sales projections, and—"

"That's wonderful," Desiree cut in quickly. "I apologize if I gave out any information that was incorrect or misleading. Our news comes straight from UPI in New York, and we can't verify every—"

"Your commentary doesn't come from New York."

The Harrison Duet

Her stomach tightened into a knot. Sam would kill her for this. Absolutely kill her. "True. Thanks so much for calling to straighten that out." She cued up the next song, struggling to keep her voice calm. "And now, we—"

"I'll take that trivia question now."

"What?"

"This is supposed to be a trivia contest, isn't it? Something about a free dinner for two?"

"Oh. Yes..." Quickly, she reached for a small box with the words THE TRIVIA GAME emblazoned across the lid. He really got a kick out of putting her on the spot, didn't he? Well, she'd give the jerk a hard one. Taking a deep breath to steady herself, she pulled a bright green card from the game box. "Are you ready, Mr. Harrison?"

"Ready."

This'll get him, she thought. "What was the name of the first successful helicopter, and in what year was it built?"

Without a moment's hesitation, he said, "The FW-61. Germany built it in 1936."

Desiree's mouth dropped open. How did he know that? The damn obnoxious man had to be a trivia king on top of everything else. "That's correct! You're our winner for today." Trying to sound enthusiastic, she added, "Congratulations. If you'll stay on the line, I'll have someone explain where you can pick up your prize." She punched the hold button on the phone. Play the next song, she instructed herself, going through the motions mechanically. And for God's sake, don't try to say anything cute. "Okay, coming up, three great tunes in a row from KICK 102 FM, your mellow music station."

Blowing out a relieved breath, Desiree punched another phone line and called the receptionist in the front office. "Barbara? The contest winner's on line one. Would you take care of him, please?" She hung up without waiting for a reply. The radio broadcast was piped throughout the building; she could count on Barbara to assess the situation.

Just then the studio door burst open. It was Sam.

"Since when did you become a stockbroker?" he bellowed, eyes blazing in a tanned face surrounded by thinning, dark hair. "No one asked for your advice about Sparkle Light. We play music around here, not the stock market!"

"I know. I'm sorry. I just—"

"Stick to sports and the weather, and leave Wall Street to the experts. Got it?" The door slammed.

Terrific, she thought.

The door opened again. "And another thing!" Sam yelled. "Don't chitchat with people on the air. We're a music station. If you want to do talk radio, get a job at KTLK. "

She sighed deeply as the door slammed once more. She should never have commented on the news release. And she certainly shouldn't have talked so long on the air with Kyle Harrison. Whatever had possessed her? She was lucky Sam hadn't fired her. One false move and a deejay was usually out the door. It's going to take a lot more than one rave newspaper review to keep me on the afternoon drive now, she thought with a frown.

Dejectedly, she studied the rotation chart taped to the window above the console. A hit tune—or type "A" song—was next. Reaching aside to the revolving music rack, she pulled the next cartridge in sequence from the row marked "A" and slipped it into the deck. It was a new Anne Murray hit—a real heartbreaker, and one of her favorites.

Suddenly the lyrics of the song on the air caught her attention. The tone was tender, with an underlying melancholy.

Desiree's eyes crinkled with a familiar pang of sadness. She felt an affinity with the singer, as if the words about long and

The Harrison Duet

lonely nights were being sung solely to her, about her. She heaved a little sigh. Her career demanded that she be self-sufficient and independent, and over the past five years she'd come to terms with that. In fact, she now preferred being on her own. So why was she partial to these tear-jerking love songs? Why did they always bring a lump to her throat?

She grabbed a pencil and scratch pad to jot down the titles of the songs coming up, so she could list them later on the air. But for some reason her pencil stood poised and motionless as a smooth, deeply masculine voice drifted into her consciousness. A voice that set her spine tingling. A voice that a prince would be proud of. Too bad he'd turned out to be such a toad.

Several minutes later, a tall brunette in a gaily striped sundress hurried into the studio, waving a candy bar. "Sugar break. I know you like peanut butter cups, but the machine was out." Her nose was slightly crooked, her accent unmistakably Brooklyn. "Hey, what's the frown for? Did Sam read you the riot act?"

Desiree shrugged as she slid off her stool, grabbed the candy bar, and tore off its wrapper. "Yeah. But apparently I'm still employed. For today, anyway." She knew she shouldn't be eating this, but after what had just happened on the air, she needed something to cheer her up. She took a bite of the chocolaty goodness and smiled with pleasure. "Mmmm. Hits the spot. Thanks, Barb. I've been eating celery all week. Another piece and I'd probably turn green."

Barbara pursed her lips in mock irritation. "As if you need to watch what you eat, you skinny thing."

"I do. Constantly. It's a cross all short people must bear. You Amazons don't know how lucky you are."

Barbara laughed and handed her a phone message. "Listen, I just got a call from a lady at Barney's, a new restaurant in

Orange. They want to know if you'll host their opening-night party next month."

As she stared at the note, Desiree felt a stab of disappointment like a knife between the ribs. She couldn't do it, of course. It was impossible. "You gave her the usual polite refusal, I hope?"

Barbara shook her head. "No, I didn't. I told her you'd think about it."

"What's there to think about?" She handed back the note. "Just thank her and tell her I'm busy."

"You've got to stop hiding from your fans, Des. The lady raved about your voice. It'd be great publicity for you."

"Some great publicity. They're expecting Candice Bergen and instead they get Shirley Temple."

"Would you come off it? You might be short, but with your hair up, in the right kind of dress, you'd look glamorous as hell." She gestured emphatically with both hands. "And besides, you're gorgeous. I'd give a million bucks for a face like yours."

"For this face?" Desiree thrust out her front teeth and wiggled her jaw in chipmunk fashion. "Well, I'd give a million bucks to be about seven inches taller, have your tan, and wear your bra size."

Barbara laughed. "Desiree, you're so dense. You don't know a good thing when you've got it. Plenty of men go gaga over petite women."

"I don't want men to go gaga over me. I'm perfectly happy the way I am."

"The hell you are. Only a nun would be happy living the way you do. When's the last time you went on a date? Two years ago? Three?"

"What's the point? You know what happened to my one attempt at marriage. Look at Dave. Look at Mike and John.

Divorced, every one of them." Desiree finished the last bite of the candy bar and sighed. "Relationships and radio don't mix."

"Who's talking about relationships? I'm talking *date* here. A simple night out with a guy." Barbara shook her head in disgust. "Just because that husband of yours was a moron doesn't mean you should swear off men for the rest of your life. The other jocks sure haven't sworn off women."

Steve wasn't a moron, Desiree thought. But there was no sense arguing with Barbara about it. She glanced back at the digital countdown timer on the console. "I hate to eat and run, Barb, but I'm on in thirty seconds."

"Okay. Bye." Barbara backed up and paused in the doorway. "By the way, no matter what Sam said, I think you handled the guy on the phone like a pro."

"Thanks a bunch."

"No, I mean it. He pulled a dirty trick, calling on the contest line and springing all that stuff on you over the air. When he comes in to pick up his free dinner pass tonight, I promise I'll be as nasty as possible."

Desiree grinned as Barbara pulled the door shut. "Do that."

Five-thirty. Desiree began to hum to herself. A half hour more and I'm out the door, she thought. And I know exactly what I'm going to do when I get home. Take my phone off the hook and curl up in bed with a glass of wine and a good book.

She waited for her cue, then said into the mike, "That was 'Songbird,' by Barbra Streisand. It's always been a special favorite of mine."

Behind her, she heard the studio door open quietly and thought, Barbara again? Didn't she see the red warning light? She knows better than to come in while I'm on the air!

"I hope you're taking advantage of the beautiful weather we're having this evening." The door clicked shut softly behind her. "The summer equinox is next week, the longest day of the year. So take a walk on the beach with your loved one this evening. Enjoy all those extra hours of daylight. And tell him…or her…that Desiree sent you." She took off her headphones as the commercial break began. Three more tunes, she thought. Then the traffic report.

"You do that well."

The voice from behind startled her so much that she jumped up from her stool. Instinctively, she knew who it was—there was no mistaking the deep, resonant Radio Voice. But what was he doing back here?

She whirled around and froze, clutching her headphones. Surprise rendered her speechless. This was Kyle Harrison?

2

Where was the fat, balding business executive she'd envisioned, the man who smoked cigars and wore half a dozen diamond rings? Desiree had been certain Kyle Harrison would look exactly the opposite of the way he sounded. But even in her wildest dreams, her most outlandish fantasies, she would never have imagined anyone quite *this* handsome. Simply put, the man was…devastating.

He stood with his back against the closed door of the studio, his arms crossed over his broad chest, studying her through dark-green eyes twinkling with what seemed like mingled curiosity and amusement. He must be in his mid-thirties, she decided, incredibly young to be the sole owner of a multimillion-dollar corporation like Harrison Industries.

At first glance he seemed tall, at least six feet. But then, judging the difference in their heights to be closer to nine inches, she attributed his apparent tallness to the way his chest tapered to a narrow waist and hips, and to the slim fit of his light grey dress slacks over long, well-proportioned legs. The short sleeves of his white dress shirt exposed muscular fore-arms. His conservatively cut, rusty-brown hair fell in thick, natural waves. An upturned nose reigned over lips which, at this moment, were twitching slightly, as if he was enjoying some private joke at her expense.

14

"I'm glad to see there really is a beautiful woman behind the beautiful voice."

She saw a curiously stunned look in his dancing green eyes as they traveled the length of her slender figure, from her bare legs to her tight-fitting cutoffs and T-shirt.

"I was afraid I was going to find an old man operating some sort of electronic synthesizer," he went on, "like in *The Wizard of Oz.*"

Desiree felt herself blushing under his scrutiny. Funny. She'd expected him to be an old man, too.

"Thanks for letting me come back here. I wasn't sure if you would, after what I said on the air a while back. I wanted to apologize in person for getting you in trouble. Your receptionist told me what happened."

She tried to speak, but her tongue had uncooperatively glued itself to the roof of her mouth. Say something, you idiot, she screamed silently. Tell him you *didn't* let him come back here. Tell him it was clearly Barbara's idea—*the traitor.* Tell him to get out! Instead she found her eyes drawn to the riot of curly brown hair peeking out above the open neck of his shirt. A tie should be there, she thought. A monogrammed silk tie.

"I know you talk. I just heard you." His eyes seemed to search her face for an explanation of her silence.

What had he called her before? A beautiful woman? Hah! He's just being polite, she thought, to mask his disappointment on seeing the real me. If he said one word about the electric-blue silk dress and the silver spiked heels, she'd kill him.

But he didn't. He took a step forward, smiling warmly. He leaned one elbow on the high counter running the length of the small room.

"I understand your boss had a minor coronary after my call, and threatened to transfer you to Siberia."

She felt a smile start and fought to tighten her lips into a firm, straight line. I'm angry with this man, she reminded herself. He embarrassed me on the air and caused my employer to scream at me. I will not let him charm me. I will not smile.

"But I understand there are a few radio stations in Siberia, so you should be all right. If they're enlightened enough to hire female deejays in Russia."

Against her will, a small laugh bubbled up from inside her chest. She curbed it, shot him a wary glance. "I'm afraid I'd be out of luck in that market. I don't speak Russian."

"You never know. There are lots of English speakers in Russia. Maybe you could convince them to start an English language radio station."

"May be." She studied him for a moment. When he smiled, his eyes twinkled and lit up his entire face. It was a nice smile.

"When do you have to go back on the air?" he asked suddenly.

Oh God, she thought, whirling back to the console with a rush of panic. To her horror, the commercial break was nearly over—another three seconds and she'd have had dead air. She was in enough trouble already without *that*. Quickly, she turned up the volume in the studio and made a smooth transition into the next tune.

She sighed with relief. "That was a close call." Lowering the volume again, she pulled out two cartridges from the music rack, feeling extremely self-conscious as she set up the next songs. What was this man doing, standing in her booth and talking to her? It was totally against the rules! She ought to be furious with Barbara for sending him back here.

"I'm sorry if I'm distracting you." He still leaned against the counter, gazing at her with a compelling warmth. "I suppose I shouldn't be in here."

"No, you shouldn't." She ought to tell him to get out. Now! Instead, for some reason she heard herself say: "But it's okay—I don't have to talk for a while."

"That's too bad." His voice was deep and soft. "I like listening."

As his eyes locked with hers, a strange, inexplicable heat coursed through her body and she backed up into the stool, almost knocking it over. *What* was happening to her? She'd never reacted so strongly to any man before, not even when she first met Steve.

Apparently misinterpreting the cause of her confusion, he said with sudden concern, "Hey, if you're worried about your job, don't be. I just spoke with your manager, and I think you're off the hook."

"Off the hook? What do you mean?"

"I just bought a sizeable advertising package for Sparkle Light. It blankets the next three weeks and continues well into next year. I gave strict instructions that our spots run only during your show."

She stared at him, astonished. As the impact of his words filtered into her brain, she swallowed and said, "That ought to make Sam dance in the aisles." And it certainly wouldn't hurt her standing there, either. She cocked her head, eyeing him curiously. "Why did you do that?"

"It seemed the least I could do, after getting you in so much hot water. I know I shouldn't have called when you were on the air. But it hit me wrong when you read that news release, and I—" He shrugged, running a hand through his hair. "Sometimes I do impulsive things."

The Harrison Duet

So do I, Desiree thought. How could she possibly be angry with him now?

He glanced around the small control room with obvious interest, appraising the equipment. "I haven't been in a radio station in years. This is fascinating. All right if I stay for a while and watch?"

Vigorously she shook her head, and was about to speak when he raised one large palm as if stopping traffic.

"Okay. I understand. But before you kick me out, let me ask one favor." He reached into his shirt pocket and pulled out a white card. "I just happen to have a pass for a free dinner for two at—"

"Maximilian's," she finished for him with a laugh.

"Will you have dinner with me tonight?"

"What? No...sorry, I can't." Long years of refusing invitations conditioned her response. The words escaped before Desiree could stop them.

"Why not?"

"Because I..." she began, then hesitated.

He's a rich entrepreneur from Seattle, she cautioned herself. You're a deejay from Anaheim. He's only asking you out because you're convenient, and he has a free dinner and no one to share it with.

"I..." She'd always been the master of the instant, fabricated excuse. Why couldn't she think of anything? "I already have plans," she finished lamely.

"Oh." He nodded slowly, gazing at her. "I guess I shouldn't have expected you to be available on the spur of the moment. But I had to give it a try."

Inexplicably, a wave of disappointment welled up in Desiree's stomach. Was he going to give up so easily?

"Still, maybe we can work something out. These plans of yours. Tell me about them."

18

"Well—" *Don't you have eyes?* a small voice taunted in the back of her mind. The man's an eleven on a scale of ten. What are you thinking? Go out with him!

"I promise you I'm harmless." He flashed her a boyish grin, raising his right hand in the traditional Boy Scout salute. "Trustworthy, honest and obedient. Scout's honor."

She couldn't stop her laugh. His smile radiated warmth and friendliness. You'll like me, it said. I already like you. She paused a moment, admiring his high sculpted cheekbones and the fine laugh lines at the corners of his eyes. When her gaze rested on the gracefully angled bridge of his nose, she fought a sudden urge to run her finger down its narrow slope to the place near the tip where it dipped and turned up just the tiniest bit.

"Is it anything of critical importance?" he persisted. "Or could you get out of it?"

She considered. She hated to play right into Barbara's hands, but maybe her friend was right. She ought to enjoy some male company for a change. Since he lived so far away, it would be all on her own terms. Dinner only, with no danger of involvement, and no strings attached.

She looked him straight in the eye. "I was going to fly to Washington for a late supper with the President, but I suppose I could call and cancel."

"Dinner at the White House? Is that all? And here I was afraid it was something really special."

She shrugged, smiling. "That kind of invitation *is* rather run-of-the-mill. And let's keep our priorities straight. How often do I have the opportunity to dine with a soda-pop king?"

The Harrison Duet

Kyle waited for her in the lobby until her shift ended at six o'clock. Fortunately, she found Barbara had gone for the day. Questions would certainly come tomorrow, but for now she was spared the embarrassment of a confrontation.

Since Desiree needed to change her clothes before dinner, Kyle followed in his car while she drove to the small house she rented in Garden Grove.

As he stood behind her on the front steps, Desiree unlocked the door and pushed it open a crack. She peered through the small opening into her living room, unsure in what condition she'd left the place. Cheeks flaming, she whirled around, yanking the door shut behind her. Her body collided with his in a sudden sharp impact, completely knocking the breath from her.

"Oh! Sorry!" Kyle grabbed her by the shoulders, not retreating an inch.

"You can't go in there," she gasped, pinned between him and the door.

"Why not?" His hands gripped her shoulders firmly as he looked down at her.

"It's a battlefield."

"I'm sure I've seen worse. Don't worry about it."

He stood so close she felt the warmth emanating from his body, and felt his breath, warm and sweet, on her cheek. She pressed her back against the door, tilted her head back slightly, and looked up at him. "Trust me, you don't want to see it. Several people died there this morning, and the bodies haven't been cleared away yet."

He laughed. "It doesn't matter." His eyes roved slowly over her face, lingering for a long moment at her lips as if they were a mouth-watering dessert just out of his reach. His voice was somewhat rough when he spoke again. "I don't care, really. I didn't exactly give you much warning."

Her shoulders, under the pressure of his fingers, began to tingle, sending magnificent shooting sparks throughout her body. She was aware for the first time of the faint scent of a very pleasant masculine cologne. She closed her eyes, enjoying the feel of his hands, the sense of his nearness. If only her living room wasn't such a mess, then he could come inside. She'd like to have him in her house. In her living room. In her—

No, Desiree! she cautioned. He's gorgeous and witty and incredibly sexy, but for God's sake, don't get carried away. Tomorrow he'll fly back to his work and his life in Seattle, and you'll be back to your comfortable, uncomplicated...boring...lonely...routine.

She took a deep breath. "The thing is, there's...the dog."

He relaxed his grip on her shoulders and stepped back. "The dog?"

"A vicious Doberman. Trained to attack strange men on sight."

He studied her for a moment with narrowed eyes, clearly aware that she was vamping. "Would it really embarrass you that much if I saw the way you keep house?"

"It really would."

"Why?"

"Because..." She hesitated, her shoulders still tingling from the remembered pressure of his fingers. "I don't want you to think—"

"Think what?"

She sighed in resignation. "That I'm a slob."

"I won't think that. I won't pass judgment, I promise."

"Okay. But remember: I warned you."

Gritting her teeth, her stomach quietly tying itself in knots, Desiree turned the knob, pushed the door open, and stepped inside.

The Harrison Duet

She could have died. She wished she wasn't so disorderly. She preferred tabletops and counters to be clear and things to be organized and put in their places. She just couldn't seem to get herself to do it on a regular basis.

Various items of discarded clothing lay draped across the back of the flowered chintz sofa. A wing chair in a French blue-and-apricot print held a basket of clean laundry waiting to be folded. To her mortification a pair of panties and a lacy bra peeked out noticeably from the center of the pile.

Numerous pairs of shoes and sandals lay under the antique mahogany coffee table and at either side of the couch and chair. Magazines and books lay scattered on every surface, and partially filled water glasses on cork coasters seemed to be everywhere—on the ornate carved credenza, on the end table, even on the mantel over the brick fireplace.

When would she grow out of that habit of taking a glass of water with her everywhere she went? And when would she learn to stop taking her shoes off and leaving them wherever she happened to be sitting? What was this man going to think of her?

Kyle took a step inside and paused, his lips set in a non-committal line. But the expression in his eyes as they swept the cluttered room could only be called mild dismay. When she saw his gaze drift to the kitchen, where she'd stacked last night's dinner dishes and pots on the counter, the color rose in her cheeks.

"I'll bet you're a neat freak. One of those folds-his-under-wear-in-the-drawer types."

He nodded silently.

"I was afraid of that." She wanted to disappear into thin air, to start the day over again. Why had she ever agreed to this dinner date? It was madness! She scooped an armful of clothes off the sofa and crumpled it into a tight ball against her thudding chest.

Any kind of relationship, even a short-term one, wasn't supposed to begin this way. A man, on seeing a woman's home for the first time, was supposed to be overwhelmed by its charm, impressed by her impeccable taste in furniture and decor. Well, she'd certainly impressed him...he was speechless!

"I told you it'd be a disaster," she said. "I'm sorry. All I can say in my own defense is...it's not always this bad."

His smiled returned and he glanced at her with contrition. "Please, don't apologize or feel embarrassed. It's my fault. This has all been very impromptu. You weren't expecting visitors, and I shouldn't have been so pushy. But...truth be told, this makes me feel right at home."

"Really?"

"I have five sisters. To this day, every one of them is a bit... relaxed about keeping house, you might say."

"Five sisters? How on earth—" did you ever turn out so incredibly, indisputably masculine, she wanted to say. Instead, she finished quickly: "How did you ever survive?"

"Being the only son, I got royal treatment. My own room. Special outings with my dad. It was great."

She was grateful for his easygoing manner and apparently intentional effort to change the subject. "I just have one brother. Growing up in a big family must have been a lot of fun."

"It *was* fun." He sat down on the edge of the couch and absently arranged the scattered magazines and books into neat stacks. "I enjoyed playing Big Brother to a house full of beautiful women. My sisters are terrific. All of them, especially the twins."

"Twins! How wonderful. I used to dream I'd have twins of my own some day." Unintentionally, her eyes swept to his chest. Firm pectoral muscles rippled in sharp relief beneath his white summer dress shirt. Despite herself, she found herself imagining what that chest might look like without a shirt to cover it.

"Maybe you will." His voice brought her eyes up to meet his with a guilty start. Maybe she would what?

She stepped over to the credenza and turned on her stereo, letting the soft music of KICK-FM fill the room. "I hope you like mellow music."

"If I don't, I'm taking out the wrong girl."

"You have a point."

He studied the carved legs of the coffee table appreciatively. "Your furniture is beautiful. Is this an antique?"

"Yes. It belonged to my great-grandmother. All of this did. Do you like antiques?"

"I usually go for the more modern stuff, but I admire the craftsmanship on these old pieces. Especially the hand carving."

"If you like carving, you should see the detail work on the headboard of my four-poster bed. It's—" She broke off, blushing. Why did she say that? It almost sounded like an invitation.

"I'd love to see it."

"No!" She realized she had shouted the word, and softened her voice. "The bedroom's even more of a disaster than the living room." She took several steps backward. "I'll go and change. Oh, can I get you something to drink?"

"No, thanks." He indicated two half-filled water glasses on the coffee table. "I'll just help myself to some of this if I get thirsty."

She choked back an embarrassed laugh. "I'll be back in three minutes." Turning, she fled down the hall. If she survived this evening with her sanity intact, it'd be a miracle.

I'm only going out with this man once, Desiree thought, as she fastened the tiny buttons up the front of her lavender cotton sundress. So I might as well do it right.

What was it Barbara had said? In the right dress...with your hair up...you'd be as glamorous as hell. Well, the dress was far from glamorous, but it was the best she could do. The flared skirt, trimmed at the hem by a long ruffle with matching crocheted lace, made her feel dainty and feminine, and the form-fitting bodice accentuated her tiny waistline. The deep orchid color contrasted with her fair complexion and seemed to bring a healthy glow to her face.

She pulled on high-heeled white sandals and picked up her brush, running it fiercely through the curls that cascaded over her shoulders. She never wore her hair up. How would it look? She threw her head forward, grabbed the thick mass of hair and twisted it into a bun on top of her head. Holding the bulky knot in place with one hand, she pulled a few wispy tendrils of hair down around her forehead and ears. Standing up, she surveyed the effect in the beveled mirror above her dresser.

She looked ridiculous. Like a midget balancing a ball on her head.

Sighing, she shook her head vigorously, letting her hair fall into place in its natural side part. On a sudden impulse, she pulled out a delicate gold pendant from her jewelry box and fastened it around her neck.

The Harrison Duet

When she returned to the living room, she found Kyle thumbing through a magazine, one arm draped across the back of the sofa, his legs stretched out in front of him. He'd buttoned his shirt and had put on a grey-and-blue-striped tie, which he must have brought in from his car. The last beams of fading sunlight streaming in through the front window burnished the gleaming bronze and copper highlights in his hair. He looked totally natural and completely at ease, as if he made a daily habit of waiting in strange women's living rooms while they dressed for dinner. As she wondered if that was true, she thought he looked right somehow, relaxing there on her couch, as if he belonged there.

She smiled. "Glad to see you made yourself at home."

He tossed the magazine aside and looked up at her, his eyebrows lifting in admiration. He let out a low whistle. "Wow! You look terrific. I like your dress."

"This dress?" She felt her cheeks glow with pleasure, but couldn't quite bring herself to meet his gaze. Fingering a corner of the long ruffled hem, she said, "It's just an old thing. I'm sorry I don't have anything more chic, but—"

"You mean something in electric-blue silk, open in the back, cut just off the shoulder?"

The color in her cheeks deepened. "Something like that."

"I prefer what you're wearing." He sprang up off the sofa with an athletic grace and covered the distance between them in a few quick strides. Tilting his head to one side, he regarded her the way an artist might study a painting. "That's a beautiful pendant."

"Thank you." She fingered the golden charm at her throat. Her favorite piece of jewelry, it depicted a tiny robin perched on a branch, singing its heart out to the sky. A small diamond twinkled in its eye.

"A songbird," he said. "Just like you."

His admiring gaze sent warmth spiraling through her and she couldn't help but smile. "It's over a hundred and fifty years old."

"From your great-grandmother?"

She nodded. "From my great-grandmother. I was named after her, and was lucky enough to get some of her prized possessions."

"Well, she had excellent taste in furniture and jewelry. And in great-granddaughters."

He lifted one hand to the slope of her neck, sifted his fingers through her hair, and held it up to the light, watching as the gleaming strands fell softly back to her shoulders. He stared down at her for a long moment, his hand poised in midair, fingers tense and contracting.

Adrenaline pumped through Desiree's body as her eyes locked with his. What was going on in his mind?

A shiver tiptoed up her spine and her pulse quickened, as if anticipating a plunge into deep, icy waters. She blinked and lowered her eyes to his full, beautifully shaped lips. For some reason her thoughts scattered like petals in the wind and she struggled to reorganize them.

He lowered his hand and took a step back. She sighed with relief. Or was it regret?

"What do you say we go eat?" he said. "I'm starving.

3

They sat at a window-side table, overlooking the wide expanse of white beach and rolling surf one flight of stairs below. Desiree had never been inside Maximilian's, although she'd often admired its stunning blend of plate glass and California redwood when she passed by during an evening walk on the Huntington Beach pier.

The interior was both comfortable and sophisticated with its nautical theme, tables draped in royal-blue, solid oak chairs, and vases of chrysanthemums scattered about.

She'd noticed several women's heads turn as she and Kyle made their way through the crowded restaurant to their table. No wonder. Kyle was easily the best-looking man in the room.

Their conversation flowed as smooth as the wine. The waiter, when he stopped to take their order, apologized for intruding, which made them laugh. Kyle seemed to want to know everything about her, and she was equally fascinated by him, each new and exciting detail of his life only whetting her appetite to learn more.

"How long have you been working at KICK?" Kyle asked after the waiter had served bowls of thick clam chowder.

"Two years."

"I read a review of your show in the *Times* on the flight down this morning. You're quite a celebrity."

"Not really." She shrugged. "It's a pretty small station. Few people recognize me by voice, and nobody knows me by sight. Thank goodness."

"What do you mean, thank goodness?" Kyle sipped his wine. "I thought all performers liked to be recognized."

"Not me. My voice—I'm sure you've noticed. It's so... throaty and low. It doesn't match up with the rest of me. People have kidded me about it since I was twelve. My listeners seem to expect some tall, curvaceous beauty. You can imagine how disappointed they are when they meet me."

He fell silent, watching her. "I wasn't disappointed," he said softly.

She felt a flutter in her stomach and wanted to look away, but couldn't bring herself to break their eye contact. "You weren't?"

He shook his head. "I think your voice fits you perfectly." He seemed to want to say more.

She held her breath, waiting, wondering again what he was thinking. How would she respond if he told her she was beautiful? Would she believe it if *he* said the words?

He glanced away. She swallowed her disappointment.

"While you were getting dressed, I took a look at your library," he said, picking up his knife and spreading sweet butter on a chunk of crusty sourdough bread. "Very impressive."

"My library?" She let go a short laugh. "You mean the books piled on the coffee table, or the ones stacked three-deep on the shelves?"

"Both. I saw quite a few of my favorite contemporary authors and titles. And you have all the classics that I love and re-read all the time: Shakespeare, Austen, Dumas, Dickens, Twain, and Carroll."

The Harrison Duet

She smiled with delight as she took a spoonful of chowder. "I ran out of shelf space long ago, but books are like best friends. I can't stand to part with any of them."

"Me neither. My whole living room's lined with bookshelves. Reading's the best kind of company for someone living on their own."

"I know what you mean. Reading keeps me from noticing how lonely I am. I read while I eat, before I go to sleep—"

"It does get lonely, doesn't it?"

She froze, her spoon halfway to her mouth. His eyes locked with hers across the table.

"Do you like living alone?" he asked softly.

A current of awareness seemed to travel across the space between them. She lowered her eyes, toyed with the blue linen napkin in her lap. "I don't mind it. I've been alone for five years. I guess I'm used to it by now." She laughed lightly. "I'd better be used to it, anyway. I tried marriage once. It didn't even last a year. I'll never try it again."

"Never say *never*. Maybe you just married the wrong man."

"I don't think so. The divorce was inevitable, no matter who I'd married." She hoped he wouldn't pursue the subject further. She considered the last months before the divorce to be the lowest point in her life. She preferred to forget them.

"How about you?" she asked. "Have you ever been married?"

"No."

"Really? Thirty years old and never been hitched?"

A smile tugged at the corners of his lips. "Thirty-five. But thanks for the compliment."

She expected him to add more, to explain that he, too, was against the idea of marriage. After all, she reasoned, a man this handsome, this charming and successful, could hardly have

30

escaped marriage unless he had an aversion to the institution in general. But he said nothing for several heartbeats, just continued to look at her over the rim of his wineglass.

She felt her skin grow hot under his gaze and she glanced out the window beside them, where the setting sun painted a watercolor wash of purple, pink, and gold across the sky. A few hardy surfers still sat astride their boards, rising and failing on the water's dark surface like bobbing ducks.

"I guess we can't get married, anyway," he said.

Her eyes flew up to meet his, astonished by the stab of disappointment those words had brought.

"We'd have two copies of every book in the house," he teased.

She laughed. "True. It'd be so...redundant. And since I can't throw anything away, it'd create quite a storage problem."

He grinned in response but didn't comment. She had no idea what to say next. To her relief, the waiter chose that moment to arrive with their dinners. For Desiree: a platter of mesquite-broiled halibut, with wild rice, French-cut green beans, and honeyed carrots on the side. When the waiter placed Kyle's meal before him, she felt a pang of envy rise in her chest. He'd ordered lobster. Fresh American lobster, flown in that morning from Maine.

"Ahh. Look at this beauty." Kyle spread his cloth napkin across his lap. The lobster reclined on a bed of rice in reddish-orange splendor, head and tail intact, arched shell up. The detached claws, already cracked, were arranged beside a cup of melted butter. She could smell its rich scent across the table.

She watched him pierce a wedge of lemon with his fork and squeeze it into the butter. Her mouth watered. He used the fork to scoop a large piece of white meat from one claw,

The Harrison Duet

dipped it into the lemon butter and lifted it to his lips. He caught her eye and stopped, the fork poised in midair.

"I *told* you to order the lobster," he said.

It was true. The waiter had also highly recommended it. But the complimentary dinner pass stated plainly that lobster was not included. Favorite food or no, they came for a free dinner, and she insisted that at least one of them should take advantage of it. Besides, she could eat for half a week for the same price.

"This is fine," she said. She quickly tasted a piece of halibut. Firm. Meaty. Mildly flavorful. One hundred and ninety-four calories per four ounce serving. The healthier choice. "Delicious," she lied.

"Try this." Kyle extended his forkful of lobster across the table.

"Your first bite? No, I couldn't—" Before she could protest further, he popped the morsel into her mouth. She closed her eyes and chewed, savoring the moist, buttery flavor.

"Oh, yum," she said. "A rare treat. It's been ages." She heard his laugh, followed by a scraping sound. When she blinked open her eyes, the lobster stared back at her. Her own plate sat in front of Kyle.

"I got a sudden, uncontrollable craving for halibut." He picked up the plastic bib the waiter had brought, leaned forward, and tied it around Desiree's neck. "This looks better on you than it would on me, anyway."

Her eyes widened. "No, Kyle. I wouldn't dream of taking your dinner."

"Go ahead. Enjoy."

Hesitantly, she added, "Are you sure you don't mind?"

"I'm sure."

She pounced. Picking up the lobster's steaming shell in two hands, she turned it soft side up and arched it until the tailpiece pulled loose from the body. With one deft movement she bent back the tail flipper section until it cracked off. She lifted the tailpiece downside up, expertly inserted the lobster fork through the hole left by the flippers and pushed the tail meat out through the open end.

"I can see," he said, watching her, "just how rarely you get lobster."

"It's only been rare recently." She took a bite, pausing for a moment of appreciative silence as she chewed and swallowed. "I lived in Maine for a year and a half. Every chance I got, I'd buy a lobster or two at the wharf. Three dollars a pound, plucked right out of the tank, and cooked while you wait."

His eyes never left her face. "No wonder you can't stand the prices here."

She broke off one of the lobster's legs, softly closed her mouth around the open end. With lips and tongue she slowly and gently sucked out the contents. Across from her and watching, Kyle drew a single breath that was out of rhythm with the others. His green eyes glittered with sudden brightness, and a smile lingered on his mouth.

All at once aware of what he might be thinking, Desiree felt her cheeks flush red and hot. She swallowed hard. Picking up one of the legs, she held it out to him. "Would you like to share?"

He shook his head. "Not just now." Finally he picked up his knife and fork.

As they enjoyed the meal, they talked. Desiree found herself relaxing as the conversation moved from one topic to another. They discovered they liked the same movies, listened to similar music, and both enjoyed the theater. She told him about the wonderful Victorian house in Pasadena where she grew up, and how sad she'd been when her parents sold it and moved to Florida.

The Harrison Duet

Kyle had lived in Seattle all of his life, he said. His parents and most of his relatives still lived there.

"Washington's beautiful. Everything's green all year round. From my office window on the tenth floor I've got a fantastic view of downtown and Elliot Bay. When the sun shines, the sky is the bluest blue you've ever seen."

"Do you come to Southern California very often?" she asked.

"I've been down here a few times. But it's too hot for me."

"Not always. Today you could have fried pancakes on the sidewalk, but generally it's mild and wonderful—and at times, I'll bet our sky's as blue as yours."

"I've seen days where it comes close," he admitted. He folded his napkin on the table and sat back in his chair. "But I'd still never leave Washington state. I like having four seasons."

"Well, after a few summers in Tucson and winters in Detroit and Bangor, Maine, I'll take this weather any day. I don't know how long my gig will last, but I'm grateful to be here, especially since I finally got my own drive time show. Seven years of nights is enough for anyone."

"Seven years? Why'd it take so long to get a decent shift?"

"There's a built-in prejudice in this business against women. We're stuck with the worst hours for the least pay. Midnight to dawn—they still call it the Women's Shift. And that's one of the nicer names for it." Five years ago, she explained, you rarely heard a woman on the air during the afternoon, even in Southern California. "They're a bit more progressive here. Most deejays would kill for the chance to work in L.A. or Orange County. It's the hottest market in the country."

"Why? Because you're so close to the television and film industries?"

34

"That's a big part of it. A jock with a good voice can earn good money on the side in commercials, voice-overs, and animation—or so I'm told, I haven't explored that yet. But the biggest attraction here is the pay scale." She finished her wine. With instinctive awareness Kyle reached for the bottle and raised an eyebrow in her direction. At her nod, he refilled her glass.

"AFTRA, our union, takes care of us," she went on, "sees to it that we have decent wages and working conditions. Other markets aren't so lucky. Just a few years back, I was working ridiculous hours for starvation wages."

"Really? I imagined deejays were paid handsomely. Like television stars."

"Far from it. This might be show biz, but we're on the bottom rung of the ladder."

She reached across the table to offer him her last bite of lobster. He smiled and leaned forward, then closed his lips around her fork. At the same time his hand closed around hers. A spark shot through her veins at the warmth of his touch.

"Nice," he said, his eyes lighting up appreciatively. She wasn't sure if he was referring to the taste of the food or the feel of her hand. He took the fork from her and set it down, leaned her elbows on the table, and wrapped her hand in both of his. "Why have you lived in so many places? Detroit, did you say? Tucson? And Maine?"

"Change of jobs." His hands, she noticed, were large and covered with dark springy hairs. They felt warm and dry and wonderful against hers. "In this business after a year at the same station you're practically considered an old-timer. Unemployment's always looking over your shoulder."

"Why is it so hard to keep a job?"

The Harrison Duet

"Ratings."

The candlelight flickered across the side of his face and caught in minute flashes the reddish-gold of his day's growth of whiskers. She wondered if his cheeks felt smooth or rough to the touch. She wondered what color his beard would be. Brown? Or bright red, like the highlights in his hair?

"Ratings?" he asked.

She took a deep breath and continued. "If the station isn't doing well, the program director often wipes the slate clean and starts off with all new talent. Or he might decide to switch the format of the station from music to Talk Radio or All News, which also requires a whole new crop of people. And there are so many young kids, beating down the door to take our jobs. If we forget to play one spot or say one thing the P.D. doesn't like, he might decide to can us, try somebody else."

"Sounds too precarious for my blood."

"Not me. Once you're in the business, it's like a compulsion. Any other job would pale in comparison."

She watched, transfixed, as his fingers gently rubbed across the back of her knuckles. The tingling sensations that began there raced the length of her arm, down through her body. She wondered what it would feel like if his fingers were to touch her in more intimate places, in places that had been so long denied, and even now seemed to swell with—

She tore her eyes away and looked down at the table, drawing a mental curtain over the pictures forming in her mind. To her surprise, their plates were gone, replaced by steaming cups of coffee. When had the busboy stopped by?

"Cream?" he asked, letting go of her hand.

"Y…yes," she managed in a strangled voice. *Stop thinking of him that way,* she scolded herself. *You'll drive yourself crazy.*

She took the pitcher of cream from him and allowed herself a small dab. "We've talked far too much about me. Tell me, how'd you come to be such a power in the business world?"

He answered her questions simply, but with enthusiasm. He seemed proud of his achievements, and showed no trace of conceit or arrogance. He studied engineering in college, he told her, worked for a while at Boeing, and eventually decided to start his own company to manufacture tooling and parts for aircraft. The business mushroomed after a few years, and he invested in other companies, including an engineering firm. Sparkle Light was his latest acquisition.

"Why a soft-drink company?" she asked, after a rather bemused busboy had refilled their coffee cups for the third time. "Everything else is related to aerospace. It doesn't seem to fit in."

He shrugged. "It looked profitable. Keeps things interesting."

"And you started the whole thing on a shoestring." She shook her head in amazement. "I'll bet when the other kids were playing cowboys or cops and robbers, you were out learning how to close business deals."

He didn't answer right away. Instead, he gazed out the window at the midnight-blue sky, which descended toward the rippling dark water in gradually lighter shades of blue.

"To tell you the truth, I never intended to go into business at all," he said in a low voice. "From the time I saw Cary Grant in *Only Angels Have Wings,* all I ever wanted to do was fly. As a kid I was crazy about airplanes, helicopters, spaceships—anything that flew. I made models, read every book I could find on the subject. I vowed I'd someday be a commercial pilot or join the air force."

The Harrison Duet

"So that's how you knew the answer to that obscure trivia question about the helicopter. I thought for sure I had you stumped on that one."

He grinned and reached for her hand again across the table. "Lucky for me I got it right."

Why did she feel such a sizzling jolt each time he touched her hand? "Then why didn't you become a pilot? What happened to change your mind?"

"I didn't change my mind." To her surprise and disappointment he jerked his hand away. "Circumstances prevented me from becoming a pilot. I thought designing airplanes would be a good substitute for flying them, but..." He remained silent, staring moodily into his empty coffee cup.

She read resentment and suppressed frustration in his gaze. Her fingers ached to reach out and touch his cheek, to smooth away the lines of tension she saw there. As she debated the advisability of such a move, he abruptly pushed back his chair and stood up.

"Well, what do you say we go, before they start charging us rent for this table?" Kyle said as he paid the check.

Desiree fumbled for her purse and quickly followed Kyle out of the restaurant. Conversation was strained during the twenty-minute drive back to her house.

She sank back into the Maserati's deep leather-cushioned seat and watched the darkened rows of stucco housing tracts whiz by. What had prevented Kyle from becoming a pilot? she wondered. He'd been so free to tell her everything else about himself. Why did he suddenly become withdrawn when that subject was brought up?

He pulled into her driveway, got out, and walked her to her front step.

She considered asking him in, then thought better of it. She reached into her purse and rummaged for her key. "Well, good night, Kyle. Thank you for—"

38

"Wait." He placed one hand lightly on her arm. "There's something I want to say. Do you know why I came to the station tonight?"

Her eyes lifted in surprise. "To pick up the free dinner pass." As soon as she said it, she realized how ridiculous it sounded. What did a man like Kyle need with a free dinner pass?

"I came to meet you."

"Oh," she said, feeling flattered and flustered at the same time.

"When I heard you on the radio, I kept wondering what you looked like. I couldn't stop thinking about you. I wanted to know if there was a living, breathing woman behind the sexy talk and the sexy voice."

His reference to her on-air role made her blush. "It's not really me, you know. It's just a part I play. I do it because my program director likes it. It keeps the ratings up."

"No need to defend yourself. I think it's great. I'll bet every red-blooded male in Southern California is as curious as I was. You must get hundreds of calls every week—bags of mail."

"I do get my share. All kinds of men write me letters and ask me out."

His voice lowered as he studied her. "Ever take anyone up on it?"

"Never."

He placed his hands on her waist. "Never?"

She shook her head. He was standing so close. Her breasts began to tremble from the sudden erratic beating of her heart. The heat from his hands was a sizzling presence at her sides. She wanted to wind her hands around his neck and pull him against her, until she could feel the warmth of his body against hers. "Never," she repeated.

"Well, I consider myself very lucky then," he said softly.

She swallowed hard. "I still can't believe Barbara sent you back to my studio today when I was on the air. It is *so* not allowed."

"I thought it was a bit unorthodox, but I couldn't pass up the opportunity. 'If Desiree finds out you're here,' she said, 'she'll refuse to see you and won't leave until ten o'clock. So you'd better just barge in.' I hope you didn't mind."

"I didn't."

His hand slipped from her waist to the small of her back and drew her closer. A tremor ran through her as her softness molded against the hard contours of his thighs and chest. He lifted his other hand and gently grazed his fingertips up the soft whiteness of her neck to rest briefly on her earlobe. He held her gaze for a moment, his eyes smoldering in the reflected glow of a nearby street lamp.

Her heart pounded in her ears. She knew he wanted to kiss her. And she knew now that she'd dreamed of his kiss, hungered for it, from the moment they first met. But she shouldn't let it happen. The magnetic pull she felt toward him was overpowering. The very touch of his hand had caused fire to rush through her veins, threatening to consume her with need. Once she felt his mouth on hers, she knew she'd be lost.

He was only here for a day or two. There was no telling if he'd ever be back. And she couldn't get involved with Kyle, with any man, even if he lived next door. How long would she be at KICK? Another year if she was lucky? Then, as always, she'd have to move on. She could never stay in one city long enough to make any relationship last.

Kyle Harrison already lived more than a thousand miles away. No matter how strong her attraction was to him, she knew that long-distance relationships didn't work. She'd been down that road before with Steve, and her heart still hadn't quite mended. It would be emotional suicide to try it again.

"It's getting late." She tried to pull free of his embrace but his arms tightened around her.

"Is it?"

"I have to be at the station early tomorrow. And you must have a long drive back to your hotel."

His body moved against her as he shrugged. "That depends on where I stay."

"What do you mean?" She wrenched herself out of his arms and stepped back in sudden alarm. Did he think she'd let him stay here?

"I had reservations at a hotel in L.A. and was on my way there from my meeting when I heard you on the radio. I got kind of sidetracked."

"Oh. I'm sure the hotel held your reservation," she said quickly. "You can call them to see. And if not, there are plenty of other—"

"Relax." His eyes narrowed as he watched her. "I'll find a room somewhere."

She let out a relieved breath. "Okay. Do you want to use my phone?"

"No. Don't worry about it." He made no move to leave.

"How long did you say you're here for?"

"I go back tomorrow afternoon."

"Oh," she said again.

"Can I call you sometime? After I get back to Seattle?"

"Sure," she said, knowing he wouldn't.

"Good."

She climbed the step and unlocked the front door, her heart still pumping erratically. This is what she wanted, wasn't it? A quick and final goodbye?

The Harrison Duet

She turned back to face him, one hand on the doorknob. "Thank you for dinner."

"Nothing to thank me for. Your dinner was free." He smiled.

"The lobster was a real treat."

"I'm glad you enjoyed it. Thanks for going out with me. It's been a wonderful evening."

"Yes. It has." She wanted to tell him how much she'd enjoyed his company, that she'd like to see him again, even though she knew it would never happen and would be hopeless even if it did. All she said was: "Good night."

"Good night," he replied.

Goodbye, she amended silently.

He turned on his heel and was gone.

4

Desiree slept badly. What little sleep she did manage to catch was filled with dreams of Kyle. She went for her morning jog and then fixed her usual breakfast—half a grapefruit, a poached egg, a cup of black coffee—but she couldn't seem to get him out of her mind.

One date, that's all it was, she reminded herself. That's the only reason you went. No danger of involvement. No strings attached.

Hah, she thought as she rinsed off yesterday's dishes and slid them into the dishwasher. So much for not getting involved. So much for no strings attached. From the moment they met she'd felt a wild attraction to the man, and she couldn't do a thing about it.

Activity, she told herself. That's what you need. Anything to get your mind off Kyle. All at once the clutter in her house seemed a welcome challenge. She spent the better part of the morning clearing away the scattered books and clothes in the living room, vacuuming and dusting, and scrubbing the kitchen floor. The bedroom was still a mess, but it would have to wait. Shortly before noon, pleased with her accomplishments, she locked up and left for work.

She slipped through the side door at the station, hoping Barbara was too busy to bother her. No such luck. Desiree

43

The Harrison Duet

had just begun taping a routine for her Comedy Corner series when Barbara strode through the recording-studio door.

"Des! There you are. I've been dying to hear—" Barbara stopped short at the sight of Desiree's grim expression. "What happened? Didn't you go out with him?"

"Yes."

"And?"

"Leave me alone."

"What do you mean, leave me alone? I have to know! What happened?"

"We went out to dinner. Then he took me home."

"That's it?"

"That's it."

"Was he a creep or something?"

"No," Desiree snapped. "He wasn't a creep."

"Then why...? You're going to see him again, aren't you?"

Desiree let out a long sigh. "How do you suggest I do that? He lives in Seattle."

"So what? That's what airports are for. Des, the man is *gorgeous*. I thought for sure you'd go nuts over him. And he was so nice, the way he fixed things with Sam." She looked at Desiree anxiously. "You aren't mad at me, are you? For sending him back to your studio yesterday?"

"I'm not mad. I just don't want to talk about it. Okay?"

Barbara's hands flew up in exasperation. "You're impossible." She turned to leave, nearly colliding with a stunning floral arrangement carried aloft in the doorway.

"For me?" Barbara said with a teasing smile.

"Sorry, sweetheart." Tom peered around the flowers and grinned at Desiree. "They're for this lovely lady. Better tell me where you want 'em pronto, 'cause this thing weighs a ton."

Desiree stared at the brilliant red buds. A dozen long-stemmed red roses were surrounded by ferns and baby's breath in a tall, cut-glass vase. She squeezed in front of Barbara and grabbed the small, attached envelope. Turning her back, she pulled out the card inside. It read simply:

To the loveliest woman with whom I've ever shared a lobster. Kyle.

Her stomach seemed to trip over itself. She realized she'd been holding her breath and let it out in a long, deep sigh. Aware of Barbara's tall form peering over her shoulder, she clasped the card to her chest. "This is private, if you don't mind."

"Just went out to dinner, huh? Never going to see him again?" Smirking with satisfaction, Barbara tossed her dark hair and slipped out the door.

"If you don't tell me where to put these, I'm going to dump them right here as a doorstop," Tom said.

"Sorry. I'll take them."

Tom lowered the vase into Desiree's arms, and she inhaled the sweet fragrance of a perfect red bud.

"What happened, anyway?" Tom said. "Did somebody die?" At her withering glare he grinned and ducked into the hallway.

Desiree glanced up at the clock. It was 3:06 p.m. How could only two minutes have gone by since she last checked the time? The day usually zoomed by. Today time crawled. The roses' perfume filled the small studio, doing nothing to decrease the feeling of light-headedness that had descended on her the moment they arrived.

She wondered what time Kyle's plane left for Seattle. Was he still in the meeting? Had he already gone? Would he call before he left?

The Harrison Duet

She wanted to thank him for the flowers, but realized she'd never even asked for his home address or phone number. Should she call information or leave a message at his office?

It was impossible to concentrate. Memories of the way he had looked across the dinner table by candlelight, the intimate way he'd held her hand, the expression in his eyes when they'd stood on her front porch, played over and over in her mind like a movie on a continuous reel. Several times she found herself singing along with the music on the air. She'd forget to notice when a song began to fade and nearly miss her cue for the next tune.

She forgot to keep track of what she played and couldn't think of a single witty thing to say. The Trivia Game contest was completely lacking in excitement. She dutifully screened each call, her heart leaping with each punch of the button, hoping it might be Kyle. It wasn't. The man she finally put on the air stuttered and stammered and was about as lively as a dead chicken.

Somehow, she managed to finish her shift. At six o'clock, she strolled nonchalantly into the reception area and asked if anyone had called or come by.

"Sorry," Barbara said as she packed up to leave. "His Gorgeousness has not appeared within these four walls. Better luck tomorrow."

Disappointment curled inside her stomach like a tightly wound spring. He'd left without saying goodbye.

She retreated to the recording studio, began to dub comedy spots and humorous sound effects from albums onto tape. Between seven and eight o'clock someone dropped off a hamburger and fries, and she dug into them hungrily. By nine-thirty the effects of her long day had caught up with her. Feeling tired and dejected, she returned the albums to the station's library, grabbed her purse and sweater, and headed for home.

She parked in her garage and was in the process of yanking down the heavy, wood door when she heard the approaching roar of a car. Tires squealed. A dark-green Maserati turned into her driveway and stopped before her, engine humming, headlights glaring.

Kyle leaned his head out the open car window. "Just getting home?"

Astonishment and excitement tingled through her at the same time. She couldn't believe how glad she was to see him. Glad? she asked herself. Understatement of the year. Try ecstatic.

She locked the garage door and crossed to his car, fighting to hold back a smile. The smile won. "Broads in broadcasting are dedicated souls," she said.

"No kidding. Remind me to believe you if you ever say you have to work late."

She leaned on the window frame. In the glow of the street lamp she could see he wore a light tan suit, blue shirt, and matching striped tie. He looked gorgeous.

"Thanks for the roses," she said. "They're beautiful."

"My pleasure."

His rusty-brown hair was wind-tousled. She ached to run her fingers through it. He must like to drive with the window open, she thought, to feel the wind on his face. So did she.

"Why aren't you in Seattle?"

"My meeting ran later than I expected. Much later, in fact. Looks like I'll be here for another day. I was with a potential client and he insisted on wining and dining me. I couldn't wait to get out of there. Finally, I told them I had a date for tonight, and made my escape."

"Do you?" she asked.

"Do I what?"

"Have a date for tonight."

"That depends on your answer to my next question."

"Which is...?"

"Do you like ice cream?"

She laughed. "Do ballerinas wear toe shoes?"

His lips widened in a devastating smile. "Well then, hop in."

Hop in? Should she? She studied his face in the moonlight and decided he was too handsome for her own good. She'd love to go out with him. What sane woman wouldn't? But if she spent another few hours in his presence, she'd only make it harder for herself when he left the next day.

She swept a lock of hair behind one ear and gestured toward the cutoffs and T-shirt she was wearing. "My outfit may be fine for my job, Mr. Harrison, but I doubt if it's appropriate for a night on the town."

His eyes traveled the length of her legs with an appreciative glow. "As a matter of fact, I'm the one who's overdressed for the place I have in mind. As I recall, the sign outside said Shoes And Shirt Required. It didn't say a thing about long pants."

She laughed again. "I don't know, Kyle. I—"

"Come on, lady." He reached across the car and pushed open the passenger door. "Be daring. I promise you a good time."

Reason and caution deserted her. She circled the car and climbed in. "You're the last person I expected to find on my doorstep tonight," she said after he'd backed out and gunned the sports car through her quiet neighborhood onto Beach Boulevard.

He gazed at her briefly before turning back to the wheel. "I couldn't leave without seeing you again."

He asked about her day, probed with endless questions, and seemed to be fascinated by what seemed to her the most obscure details. He said he'd spent the day in boring meetings, and the high point of his day was dinner.

"You'll never guess what I ordered," he said.

Their eyes met. "Lobster," they said in unison. Their laughter was immediate and spontaneous.

"I hope your client didn't steal it away from you."

"No. But it didn't taste the same without you there," he said, his voice low and deep.

She felt that now-familiar flutter in her stomach and had to turn her face to the window to hide her blush and the wash of sexual desire she knew must be written there.

He drove to Huntington Beach and parked just a few blocks down from the restaurant where they'd eaten the night before. "I saw this place last night," he said, indicating the small ice-cream parlor in front of them. "What do you say to a double cone and a walk on the beach?"

"Fantastic." Desiree jumped out of the car and pulled on her lightweight sweater. The air felt cool and pleasant, with the sound of nearby crashing waves and the pungent, salty smell of the sea.

Kyle pushed open the glass door and they stepped inside the dimly lit interior of the ice-cream parlor. A teenage girl in a white smock smiled at them as she vigorously rubbed the long glass counter with a rag. "You're just in time," she said. "I was shutting off the lights. I'm about to close up."

Kyle stepped up to the glass display case and raised an eyebrow at Desiree inquiringly. "What'll you have?"

She pondered for a moment over the vast array of different flavors, finally tapping the glass above a container of mint chocolate-chip. "I could go more exotic, but I think I'll stick to my favorite flavor tonight."

He glanced at the barrel of pale green ice cream below the glass. "Oh? Strawberry?"

She stared at him, lips parted in surprise. Strawberry? Was he kidding? "Are you color blind?" she asked.

She blurted the question without thinking, presuming he was just joking. The look in his eyes told her it was no laughing matter. His face reddened slightly and he averted his eyes, his mouth drawn into a tight line. "Why? What'd I say?"

"Nothing, it's just that..." She could have kicked herself. Why hadn't she been more tactful? "This flavor. It's mint chip. It's green."

"Oh." He shrugged off his embarrassment. "Yes, I'm color blind." He turned quickly to the girl behind the counter, who was staring at them curiously. "She'll have two scoops. Mint chip. The green stuff." He ordered fresh peach, paid for the cones, and guided her outside.

"I'm sorry, Kyle," she began. "I didn't—"

"Forget it." His clipped tone warned her to drop the subject. But why? She was sorry she'd embarrassed him, but color blindness was no big deal. Why was he so touchy about it?

"Come on." He grabbed her by the hand, urging her to hurry.

His enthusiasm was contagious. She forgot everything in her sudden need to be closer to the lapping surf. They found a staircase at the end of the block and bounded down the concrete steps to the beach. They took off their shoes and left them on the bottom step. He rolled up his pant legs and she laughed, telling him he looked like a schoolboy in knickers. He threatened to capsize her ice-cream cone if she didn't behave herself.

They joined hands again and raced across the wide stretch of cool, gritty sand, which glowed pale grey in the moonlight. He slowed a few yards from the water's edge and they strolled along in silence. She enjoyed the feel of the cold, wet, dark sand beneath her feet and the sweet, frosty taste of the ice cream.

"Isn't this nice?" he grinned, squeezing her hand and swinging their arms.

"Yes." A laugh bubbled up inside her chest. "I haven't done anything this spontaneous—or fun—in ages."

"Why not?"

"I don't know. I guess because I've worked nights for so long. My social life has been pretty nil."

"Work is important, but you have to make time for fun." He glanced at her. "You don't strike me as an overly serious type. And from what I've read, people who are—people who create clutter—"

"Create clutter?" She punched him lightly on the arm. "How rude. Is it my fault if the maid decided to take the week off?"

"People who create clutter," he went on, his lips twitching with suppressed laughter, "are often marvelously relaxed. They don't need everything to be in order around them. They're imaginative, impulsive, open to new ideas. They respond to the moment. Is that true of you?"

"Sometimes."

A challenging look crept into his green eyes, and she sensed he intended more by the question than appeared on the surface.

"I just haven't been around many other crazy, spontaneous people lately," she added.

"It's time we changed that."

The shiver that ran through Desiree's body had nothing to do with the breeze that whipped her hair across her cheek. She pulled her sweater more tightly around her.

"Cold?" he asked.

"I'm fine."

"You can have my jacket if you'd like." He began to shrug out of the tailored suit jacket.

"No thank you, that's not necessary." She flashed him a grin. "Anyway, the sleeves would probably hang down to my knees."

"I'm not that tall. Only five-ten."

"You seem tall to me."

He finished the last bite of his ice-cream cone. "That's because you're such a tiny pixie yourself." When he saw her grimace at his choice of words, he stopped and slipped an arm around her waist. "Hey! What's wrong with being short?"

She almost forgot his question, she was so entranced by the feel of his body next to hers, and the sound of his voice against her ear.

"Being short is a pain. I can't reach the top shelves in my kitchen. I can't reach the dipstick to check the oil in my car. Clothes off the rack never fit me right. Every time I buy a pair of pants, I have to cut off at least six inches at the hem. And since I'm so small, it seems I've had to fight all my life to be noticed, to be respected."

"You didn't have to fight to catch *my* attention," he said softly. "I think you're the perfect height."

"Perfect?" To disguise her rising discomposure, she made a face and imitated Barbara's Brooklyn accent. "You think five-feet-and-three-eighths is perfect?"

Chuckling, he drew her closer. "Do you have any idea what a relief it is to be out with a woman who doesn't have to worry about whether or not she'll be too tall for me if she wears heels?"

She laughed, loving his ability to put her at ease. "That's one problem I've never had, no matter who I've gone out with. And thank goodness you're not any taller. I practically have to bend my neck in half to look up at you as it is."

"At last, a woman who can appreciate my height." He went silent for a moment, smiling, and then nodded towards her cone. "You know, except for the chocolate chips in your ice cream, the peach and mint chip look exactly the same color to me."

She searched his face, relieved at the lack of embarrassment she saw there, but unsure how to respond. The breeze had ruffled his hair and she stifled an impulse to brush the unruly strands off his forehead. "What do they look like to you?"

"Sort of a light beige, I guess. I assume they're completely different colors?"

She nodded. "Do you have trouble seeing all colors?"

"No. Mainly reds and greens. I don't know what purple looks like to you—to me it looks blue."

His nearness and the mild fragrance of his cologne were doing strange things to her heartbeat. She finished her cone, stepped back and knelt in the sand a few feet away and rinsed her hands in the gently flowing surf.

A sudden thought occurred to her. Last night, he said he'd wanted to be a pilot, but that circumstances had prevented it. With a jolt of painful awareness, she remembered reading somewhere that normal color perception was mandatory for air force and commercial pilots.

She stood up and shook her hands dry. Hesitantly she asked, "That's what kept you from becoming a pilot, isn't it? Being color blind?"

The Harrison Duet

"Yes."

"Why is color perception so important?"

"Warning lights, mainly. In military and commercial aircraft, each light in the cockpit conveys a specific message. Green is status quo. Amber's a warning. Low oil pressure, that kind of thing. Red's an emergency situation. There are lights on the wing tips, too. At night the color tells you if other aircraft are approaching or heading away. And if your radio should malfunction, the tower can signal landing instructions in code with colored lights. They can't take a chance on someone who might misinterpret the signals." He let out an ironic laugh. "I passed all the other tests with ease but..." He shrugged.

"If that's what you really wanted to be, I'm sorry."

"Don't be. I don't regret it, not anymore." He took her hand again and they continued on down the beach. "I've become successful at what I do, and it didn't keep me on the ground. I may not be able to fly for an airline or the air force, but I can still fly a private plane. I'm restricted to daytime flight, that's all."

"Really? You have a pilot's license?"

"I do. And a twin-engine Bonanza. I use it for pleasure outings, short trips. It's a great little machine." He gestured animatedly with one hand. "There's a special kind of excitement to flying. Up there you've got the entire sky to yourself, the world spread out beneath you. It's incredible. Have you ever been up in a private plane?"

A shudder ran through her body and she shook her head. "No. That's one subject we won't agree on—flying. I'm not a fan, especially of small planes. I have enough trouble getting myself to relax on a commercial flight."

He seemed disappointed. "If you're inferring that light planes aren't safe, they are. It all depends on the experience of the mechanic and the pilot. If you tried it, I guarantee you'd change your mind."

She shrugged. "Maybe."

After what happened three years ago, she'd vowed never to fly in a private plane. But she didn't want to think about that now. The night was too perfect, with the crisp evening breeze, the dark velvet sky, and the frothy tide softly ebbing and flowing just a few yards away. She turned her head, focusing on the perfect sets of twin footprints they'd left behind in the damp sand. His looked large and solid next to her smaller ones. She thought how wonderful it was to have a man at her side, to walk with, talk with, share with. If only—

Stop it, Desiree, she warned herself. *You know it's impossible.*

She searched quickly for a new topic to divert her mind. "What do you do about traffic lights when you're driving?"

"I can tell by position. Red's always on top. Green's on the bottom."

"I never thought of that."

"It's only a problem when there's a flashing light. I'm never sure if it's red or yellow, so I just plow right through."

She gasped, then saw his devilish expression and laughed. "You seem to have adjusted well."

"No, I haven't." He stopped and wrapped his arms around her, pressing her close to him. "As you saw yesterday, I'm still embarrassed about it."

Her pulse accelerated as she looked up at him and felt her slender body warm against the hard strength of his. It seemed only natural to slide her arms around his waist. "Why is it embarrassing?" she asked.

"It's a flaw. It means there's something permanently wrong with me. When the leaves turn colors in autumn, I can't see them. The trees all look the same to me. Just plain dull brown."

The Harrison Duet

She hugged him tightly around the waist, wishing she had the courage to rub her hands up across his back, to learn the feel of his contoured muscles against the palms of her hands. "It hurts me to think of all the beauty you're missing," she whispered.

He tilted his head back and looked at her, his eyes reflecting the moonlight's glow. "All the beauty I'll ever need to see is right here, in my arms." He raised his hand and she felt the rough strength of his index finger caress her cheek and trace the curve of her jaw. When his fingertip reached the corner of her lips, he paused, his eyes locking with hers. She read there his admiration, his desire, and his intent.

Desiree's heart seemed first to stop, then beat double time. She shouldn't kiss him. She should step back and deliver her friends-only smile. But just as moths are drawn to flame, she boldly followed the dictates of her instinct. She stood on her tiptoes, moved her hands to the back of his neck, threaded her fingers through his short silky hair, and offered her lips to him. Dazed by the fire of need blazing through her veins, she whispered, "Kiss me."

He didn't need a second invitation. His mouth came down on hers in a single expedient motion, the force of his lips matching the depth of passion in her voice. A moment later, they took a simultaneous, ragged breath, their eyes locked, glimmering with delight in the newness of what they'd just found. She felt his body tremble slightly against hers, as if he were struggling to contain the same impulses raging within her.

"Desiree..." he whispered.

It was the first time she'd heard him say her name. He whispered it reverently, with the throaty, sensual French inflection for which it was intended. It sounded like a prayer.

56

When his lips met hers again, it was with gentle persuasion. His mouth moved slowly, teasingly, as if savoring her warm softness. She felt her knees weaken beneath the feather-light contact, and he slid his hands tenderly up and down the length of her back, then pulled her more tightly against him. His tongue flicked back and forth across her lips, then delved into her moist mouth, hot and insistent. She arched against him, unsure if the rapid thudding she felt against his hard chest was the beating of his heart or her own.

Kyle drew back slightly, then trailed fiery kisses across her cheek and buried his face in her hair at the side of her neck. He heaved an uneven sigh, still holding her against him possessively.

"*You are Desiree*. Desired. Wanted. Longed for." He pulled his head back and brought his wide, firm hands up to cradle her face. "I've wanted to kiss you from the first moment I saw you, standing there like some enchanted sprite in your studio. And when I had you in my arms last night, before we said goodnight..." He paused, taking a deep breath as if to steady himself. "I could see you weren't ready, that I was going too fast. I can't tell you how hard it's been to wait, to force myself to keep my hands off you."

"You didn't have to wait long," she whispered.

"Wrong." His lips nuzzled her ear. "We met on the air, at three-forty-five yesterday afternoon. That was—let's see..." He raised his head, eyes squinting as he made the mental calculation. "Thirty-one hours ago. Believe me, it's been long enough." He kissed her again, harder this time, then drew back and moved his eyes lingeringly over her face, as if trying to memorize every detail.

A sudden rush of icy water raced up the sand and swirled about their ankles. Desiree squealed as the wave splashed their

The Harrison Duet

bare legs with cold salty spray and foam. Kyle grabbed her hand, and they made a dash for higher land.

"Let's go home." He said the word *home* as if it was his too, a place they both shared. For some reason, she didn't mind. They retraced their steps to his car and drove back to her house, their feet still bare and sandy.

When they arrived, she opened the car door and gestured toward the house with a nod of her head. "Come on in and get cleaned up. I'll make you a mug of Mexican coffee, my own special recipe."

"Who could refuse an invitation like that?"

They dusted off most of the sand from their feet, then went inside. His eyes widened when they passed through her sparkling-clean living room.

"What happened here in the past twenty-four hours? Did the maid get back from vacation?"

"Spring cleaning," she retorted, grabbing his hand and pulling him down the hall. "Out of season."

"Well, the place looks terrific."

"Don't get too excited. The back half of the house still thinks it's the dead of winter."

She tried to hurry him through to the master bathroom, hoping he wouldn't notice her bedroom's state of disarray. To her dismay, he stopped beside her unmade, four-poster bed, and wrapped one hand around a carved bedpost which reached his chin.

"You weren't kidding," he said. "You've really got one hell of a bed here."

Remembering her remark the day before about her antique headboard, she followed his line of sight. He was paying more attention to the thrown-back comforter and exposed rumpled sheets, however, than to the exquisitely carved mahogany.

She gave him a shove toward the bathroom. "You have no respect for antiques."

"I do," he said. "I have a deep and abiding respect for antiques." He yanked back the shower curtain over the porcelain bathtub. "I'm looking at one right here. A pink bathtub! Where would you find a pink bathtub nowadays?"

Her mouth opened and she took a sharp breath, watching him closely. Should she tell him? The bathtub was green. She closed her mouth again.

"You're right," she said. "You hardly ever see pink anymore."

He seemed unaware of his mistake or her reaction to it, and she was glad. Quirking a brow in her direction he asked, "Want to take a bath?"

"No!" She tried to sound irritated and failed miserably. She handed him a wash cloth and towel from the linen closet and turned on the water in the tub. "I'm going to rinse my feet off. Or do you want to go first?"

"No, please. Be my guest."

Standing alongside the tub, she dipped one foot under the running water. Bending forward, she washed the sand from between her toes and then switched legs. She was halfway through before she realized what a view her too-brief cut-offs must be providing Kyle. She jerked upright and whirled around.

"Don't mind me." The glimmer in his eyes made her cheeks flush red-hot.

"I'm done. I'll just wait for you in the other room." Desiree grabbed her towel and escaped out the door, her feet dripping as she ran.

"That was delicious," Kyle said, finishing the last of the coffee she'd laced with tequila and a generous helping of cream. "I don't get Mexican coffee too often up in Seattle."

She sat beside him on the living-room couch, her bare feet, now clean and dry, tucked beneath her. "A definite drawback to being a northerner."

"There are other drawbacks I can think of." Putting down his cup, he drew her into his arms, his lips against her hair. "I had a great time tonight."

"So did I."

He held her against him for a moment, then bent his head and pressed his lips lightly against hers. He smoothed her cheek with his fingertips and kissed her again, and again, lingering longer with each soft touch of his mouth on hers.

A cloud of desire enveloped her, wrapping her in its swirling depths. She wanted to give in to her body's yearning, to press herself against his hard strength and let his body imbue her with warmth. Instead, she gripped his shoulders lightly and whispered his name against his lips. "Wait," she said. "We should—"

"Should what?"

"Say good-night. You're going home tomorrow, and—"

"Am I?" He brushed his lips against hers. "That depends on you."

"On me?"

He nodded, drawing back slightly. "I'll be tied up in a meeting all day tomorrow, but the truth is, I'm in no rush to fly home. We've got Friday night and the whole weekend ahead of us. If you'll let me see you again, if you want me to stay—I'll be here until the last possible second—until Monday morning at dawn."

Surprise rendered her speechless. Her heart began to pound.

He searched her face for an answer. "Do you want me to stay?"

He took advantage of her moment of hesitation to lower his mouth to hers. His hands roved across her shoulders, then tenderly massaged her back before sliding around to brush the sides of her breasts.

She tried to resist. She couldn't. Melting against him, she lifted her arms to caress his neck, her fingertips lacing through the thick short waves of his hair. His mouth moved slowly, gently against hers, his kiss kindling a fire that burst into flame deep within her. His tongue circled hers, exploring, dipping deeper, deeper, as if searching for each hidden sweet taste.

He turned, lowering her gently onto the sofa. His hand caressed first one soft breast and then the other through the thin fabric of her shirt and bra. A thousand tiny explosions coursed through her. Her entire body began to throb with sexual awareness, from her breasts, so full and aching, to an exquisite hot wetness between her thighs.

A moan escaped her lips. He lowered his body on top of hers and recaptured her mouth in a deep burning kiss. She felt the evidence of his arousal, hard and insistent against her. It only intensified her desire. *Make love to me*, her body sang out at the same time as her mind shouted, *No!* With the last vestige of her self-control, she tore her mouth from his.

"Kyle, wait," she gasped. "This is...it's all happening so fast. I haven't known you long enough. I—"

"I feel as if I've known you all my life," he said huskily. His palm caressed her cheek, gently urging her to meet his warm gaze. This time there was another, more immediate meaning in the question he whispered feverishly in her ear.

"Do you want me to stay?"

5

"N-no." Desiree pulled herself out of his arms and jumped to her feet, her fingers trembling as they fumbled to straighten her T-shirt.

Kyle sat up on the couch and leaned forward, resting his forearms on his thighs, hands clasped together. For a while he stared at the plush area rug beneath his feet, taking slow, deep breaths, as if struggling to regain his composure. His words, when he spoke, sounded clipped, yet still congenial. "Do you mean *no,* you don't want me to stay the weekend, or *no,* you don't want me to spend the night?"

Desiree turned toward the fireplace and stared at the dark, lifeless hearth, her fingers tightly interlaced to stop them from shaking: What was she doing? She'd wanted to go out with Kyle, there was no denying it, but she'd promised herself not to get involved with him. How could she have let things get so out of hand?

"No... to both questions," she replied, her voice tremulous.

His head whipped up. "What?"

She faced him again. "There's no need for you to change your plans to go back to Seattle. I'm really sorry, but..." She swallowed hard, forcing herself to continue. "I won't be able to see you tomorrow."

His forehead furrowed in a puzzled frown. "Why not? Don't you get off at six?"

62

"Yes. But I have to work late."

"How late?"

"There are a bunch of commercials I have to produce. It might take hours. I have to put music behind them, do the vocals, cut them onto tape, record them on cart—"

"Cart?"

"Short for cartridge," she explained impatiently. "I should have done it tonight, but—"

"Okay," he conceded. "I get it. You're busy tomorrow night. What about Saturday?"

"I have to work all day. All weekend, in fact."

"All weekend?" He stared at her. "What kind of a schedule is that? You must get off sometime?"

"I just got this new shift," she said evasively. "The schedule's not final yet."

He stood up, shoved his hands in his pockets, the muscles in his forearms rigid and distended. "I see."

Guiltily, she lowered her gaze. Her hands wanted to touch his cheek, his neck, his arms. Her lips yearned for the feel of his mouth on hers again, the taste of his tongue encircling hers. But she knew if he took her in his arms again, if she gave herself up to the thrill of his tantalizing caresses, all her willpower would fly out the window. He'd end up spending the night. And she couldn't do that. Once she'd made love to Kyle, she sensed that her heart would never be able to let him go.

She took several steps back. An unpleasant shiver ran up her legs as her bare feet left the cozy warmth of the area rug and came in contact with the cold, hardwood floor. "Thank you for the walk on the beach, Kyle. It was wonderful. And thank you again for the roses. I—"

"Desiree." The deep, resonant timbre in his voice made her jump. "Stop talking as if this is goodbye. If you're busy this

The Harrison Duet

weekend, I understand. I'll call you when I get home. We'll pick another weekend. I'll fly back down."

"No." Her back struck the credenza and she froze as he took a step toward her. "I'm glad I met you, Kyle. I really am. But I think it's better if we end things here. I told you before, I can't get involved with you...with anyone."

He crossed the room in two strides and grabbed her gently but firmly by the shoulders. "We're already involved."

"We can't be—we shouldn't be. You live too far away. It's—" Her voice broke and she turned her head to avoid his heated gaze. "It's just going to cause a lot of heartache for both of us."

"What if it does? I can stand a little heartache, can't you? Isn't it better than not feeling at all?"

She opened her mouth to respond, then closed it, unable to utter her intended denial.

"Desiree, I've been alone a long time. I'm sick of it. There's something special between us—and I'm not just talking about physical desire. I felt it the first moment I saw you, and I'm certain of it now." One arm swept down to the small of her back and he cradled her against his chest, then lowered his face to hers. She stiffened slightly, struggling to maintain her resolve despite the warm glow of desire that rekindled within her body each time it came into contact with his.

"I felt you respond to me," he said. "I feel you responding now. You want me as much as I want you. Admit it."

She squeezed her eyes shut, trying to block out the fiery eyes and sensuous lips so dangerously close to her own. She wanted to say No, but all she managed was: "Kyle, I—"

He cut off her next words with the pressure of his lips. His hands traveled across her back, up and down her spine, sending rockets of desire shuttling to uncharted regions of her body. Desiree's mind reeled. The throbbing in her chest spread down toward her loins, where it pulsed a frenzied rhythm. The tiny part of her that could still think told her to break away from his embrace. But her body acted of its own volition. Her arms wrapped around his back. Her fingers grasped his shoulder blades, pulling him closer. She molded her body against his lean, muscled frame.

At her response he moaned, low and deep in his throat. Apparently sensing she'd resist no further, he relaxed his hold, took a ragged breath, and began to move his lips slowly, gently, persuasively over hers. His fingertips stroked through the silky hair at her nape. His warm, sweet breath fanned her mouth as his feathery kisses tickled and teased her lips, then brushed across her cheeks, nose, and jaw.

She felt her limbs melt like candle wax against a flame as he again lowered his mouth to drop a series of long, sensuous kisses along her neck and throat. Her breathing was short and shallow and she leaned her head back to allow him full access to her throat. She held him tighter, no longer certain her quaking legs could support her weight.

Ever so slowly he kissed his way back up her neck, across her cheek to her forehead. Then, tenderly, he folded her in his arms and brought her head down against his chest.

Silently, he held her.

Even if she had wanted to push herself away from him, there wasn't strength left in her limbs. Her cheek lay against the softness of his shirt, and she could feel his chest, moving up and down in an erratic rhythm against hers as they caught their breath.

He was right; there was no denying the attraction she felt for him, and it seemed that he felt the same way. But what

The Harrison Duet

exactly did he want from her? A weekend fling? Someone to keep his bed warm on his business trips down south? Or did he imagine there could be more to it than that?

She knew that any kind of future between them was extremely unlikely, if not impossible. His home, his work was in Seattle, and hers was here. She knew what it was like to be separated from the one you loved. She'd never forget the loneliness of those long months without Steve, longing for his company at the end of each day, reaching out for him in the empty darkness at night. No matter who was to blame, she'd learned her lesson. If she wanted a career in radio, she had to remain free and independent. She couldn't give her heart to any man.

"Kyle," she said, tilting her head back and fingering the lapel of his shirt as she looked up at him, "I can't hide the way I feel about you. But I tried to explain last night—there's no way a relationship can work between us."

"I heard what you said last night. Every word. Your lack of job security, the way you have to move every few years, all the excuses you've learned to cling to as reasons not to get involved with anyone. So you might get fired any minute, so what? We already live a thousand miles apart. What difference would another few miles make?"

All the difference in the world, she wanted to say. But she didn't want to dredge up the painful memories she'd managed to bury so deep inside her. Still, somehow she had to make him see.

"One of us will end up getting hurt," she whispered. "I know it."

"You can't know that." He kissed her again, long and hard. "I'm not trying to predict how things will end up between us, Desiree. But let's give it a chance. Let's take things one day at a time. If it's meant to be, it will be. I've waited a long time to find you, and I'm not about to give you up now."

A bird chirped outside Desiree's window. She opened her eyes and squinted against the first faint light of a grey dawn. She must have finally dozed off. How many hours did she toss and turn last night, thoughts of Kyle and his impassioned caresses burning into her mind, keeping sleep at bay?

Even now, her mind still spun with confusion. Why wouldn't he listen to her? Why, when he left, did he insist that she would hear from him again? Why did that make her feel like shouting for joy?

It didn't seem possible that they'd only met two days before. Nothing seemed the same. Her room, cast in shadows by the unfamiliar early-morning light, looked foreign to her. Her bed, which had always seemed so warm and inviting beneath the fluffy white comforter, had never felt so hard...so cold...so empty.

Her response to Kyle's embrace filled her with equal measures of fear and exhilaration. No man's touch had ever inspired in her such fierce desire. And what she felt was more than just a physical response. She enjoyed being with him, loved the sound of his voice, the knack he had of putting her at ease, the way he laughed at her jokes. In only two days he'd made her feel more beautiful, more feminine, and more desirable than she'd ever felt in her life. With the slightest encouragement, she could easily fall in love with him. And to do that...well, history had a way of repeating itself, and she knew *that* could only end badly.

What on earth was she going to do?

The Harrison Duet

With a sigh, she threw back the covers and climbed out of bed. For now, there was nothing she *could* do. He'd left without saying when he'd call, or if he intended to stop by. She'd told him she'd be busy all weekend, so presumably he'd return to Seattle tonight. Or would he?

She went into the bathroom, pulled her nightgown over her head, and stepped beneath the shower's warm, stinging spray. The morning sped past as she straightened up her bedroom, paid a few bills, and watered the flower beds in her front yard.

She showed up at the station with an hour to spare, produced three commercials in record time, and slipped into her seat at the console at precisely two o'clock. She was more than halfway through her shift and was standing by her counter logging promos when Barbara threw open the door.

"Hi, Des. What's new with my—" Barbara pulled to an abrupt halt in the doorway and stared at Desiree, her eyes wide. "What is that you're wearing?"

Desiree shot an impatient glance over her shoulder. "It's quite obvious what I'm wearing."

"But it's... a *skirt!*" Barbara uttered the word in disbelief, as if a skirt was the last thing on earth a petite, thirty-year-old female would wear.

Desiree smoothed the folds of her floral wrap-around over her knees, and fluffed the ruffled V-neckline of her turquoise silk blouse. She'd bought the outfit months ago, on impulse, even though she had nowhere special to wear it. "You act like you've never seen a skirt before," she said testily.

"I haven't—not on you. Since the day we met, you've worn nothing but cutoffs or jeans. What's the occasion? Come on, tell me! You must be going somewhere." Barbara's glance darted to the vase of roses which still graced the counter beside the console. "Ahh! You're seeing Kyle Harrison, aren't you? And you *do* like him!" She giggled loudly. "Far be it from me to say I told you so." She flounced out the door.

A moment later Tom poked his head inside. "I had to see it for myself—and it's true. You *are* wearing a skirt."

"Get out of here!" Desiree glared at him.

Tom shook his head, grinning. "For two years I've offered my body up on a plate, and who do you fall for? Some loser in a rented Maserati."

Desiree picked up a paperback and hurled it at him. The door slammed just in time.

She climbed up on the stool, put on her headphones, and drummed her fingernails against the console, waiting for her cue.

"102 FM, KICK on this Friday afternoon," she said into the mike. "That was Kenny Rogers with 'Why Was I So Blind?' from his latest album 'Cutting Loose.' The weekend's almost upon us now and we'll all be cutting loose. It's ten minutes before five o'clock."

She played three more songs, then ran a commercial break. She began to read a public service announcement about an annual aerobics dance for the National Heart Association when she heard the studio door open again. She froze, not daring to look over her shoulder. *No one* would walk in here while she was live on the air. No one except...

"You can win some exciting prizes," she said, trying to keep her voice steady as she read, "get some great exercise, and have a whole lot of fun." She heard the door shut.

"Sign up now. That's The Dance for Heart..."

Strong hands came to rest on her shoulder blades. Warm lips pressed against her neck. She stifled a gasp as a frenzied shiver traveled up her spine.

The Harrison Duet

"...at the Anaheim Convention Center..."

She felt his hands rove up and down her bare arms, his body press against her back. A heady languor descended over her, as if her veins were flowing with thick, sweet syrup. Her voice slowed and deepened with each touch of his fingers.

"...next Saturday, June twenty-seventh." Her chest rose and fell with increasing rapidity as his mouth nuzzled against her throat. Her ears began to pound. She strained to hear her own voice.

"For registration forms, call the National Heart Association at 555-3110, or stop by the studio here at KICK."

She flicked off the mike and punched a button on the cart deck to start the next song. Pulling off her headphones, she heaved a sigh of relief. He crossed his arms underneath her breasts and pulled her back against his hard frame.

"I missed you," he said against her ear, his voice soft and deep.

"Don't you know what a red warning light is?" She tried to sound indignant, but the words came out like a soft sigh.

"Yes," he murmured. "It's the signal that flashes in my brain every time I see you."

She leaned her head against his shoulder and closed her eyes, enveloped by his warmth and the spicy scent of his cologne. "I'm talking about the big red beacon on the wall outside the control-room door."

He lifted his head. "Red? You mean that green light telling me it's all right to come in?"

She gasped, remembering he was color blind. "Oh! You thought it was green?" But when she pulled out of his embrace to look at him, she saw a flash of devilment in his eyes. "Liar!"

70

He laughed. "I assumed it was red. I know what a warning light means."

"Then why did you—"

"Barbara said it was okay—just like last time—as long as I was quiet. And I wanted to surprise you."

"Well," she huffed, "you have to stop doing this. The mike picks up every little sound."

He leaned over and breathed close to her ear. "Every little sound?"

"Yes."

"Would it pick up this sound?" He wrapped his arms around her again and kissed the side of her neck.

Her head tilted upward, as if obeying a silent command. "Yes," she said huskily.

"And this?" He dropped kisses around the graceful curve of her neck to the hollow of her throat.

"Definitely."

"Then I guess I'll have to restrain myself while we're in here."

"You will." She sighed. "Otherwise I might make a mistake. Say the wrong thing. Sound...terrible." *"Au contraire.* I'll wager you've never sounded more sultry or sensuous in your life than you did on the air just now." His arms tightened around her from behind. "I only helped promote your image."

"I've been doing just fine on my own, thank you." Desiree knew she was playing with fire. This time her job, not just her emotions, were on the line. Anyone might walk by and see them through the high windows above the console. If Sam caught them kissing, or if she missed so much as one precious cue, his rage would be immediate and intense.

She squirmed out of Kyle's arms and slipped off the stool. "I guess you missed your flight to Seattle?"

The Harrison Duet

"Looks that way. Pity, isn't it?" He leaned back against the counter, his eyes sliding the length of her slim figure. He whistled. "Don't you look nice. Quite a change from your previous work attire."

Her cheeks grew hot. "I felt like dressing up a little today."

"Just in case I decided to stop by?"

"No!" She pushed him out of her way. "Because I felt like it." With a glance at the rotation chart, she cued up the next few songs.

"Whatever the reason, I'm glad you did. I figured we'd need time for you to go home and change, but now we can fit in a quick dinner before the show if we leave right at six."

"Dinner?" Her glance fell on his wrists, where square, gold cuff links glimmered in the cuffs of his long-sleeved dress shirt. He wore the light grey suit she remembered from the night they met, this time with a matching vest. "Show?" she asked.

He pulled two theater tickets out of his breast pocket and handed them to her. "I had a hell of a time getting these."

She stared at the tickets in astonishment. They were for a new musical that had gotten rave reviews. "This show has been sold out for months!"

"So they told me. I badgered them so long at the box office, though, they finally managed to find something. I hope you can go? Last night, I know you said you had to work late..."

She smiled sheepishly. "As luck would have it, my schedule just opened up." She slid the tickets back into his jacket pocket. "Thank you for getting these. I've been dying to see this show."

"So have I. It'll be even more fun to see it together."

She couldn't argue with that. Her attention returned briefly to her work as the song on the air ended with a cold fade. She expertly segued into the next tune, then sat back on her stool.

72

Kyle's eyes darted about the room, finally coming to rest on the row of knobs, meters, and buttons on her console. "Correct me if I'm wrong, but this equipment isn't exactly state of the art, is it?"

She shook her head and touched a hand to one of the black knobs. "No. Most control boards today have levers instead of pots like these."

"Pots?"

"Short for potentiometer. It controls the level of modulation. There usually are remote starts right in a row, so the operator doesn't have to go through as many motions." She smiled ruefully. "Lucky me. With all the modern equipment around today, I end up at a station with an ancient system."

"But this is a major market. From what I've read, you're a highly rated station in Orange County. Why doesn't the owner modernize?"

"This place is only a hobby for him. He owns several other companies that keep him busy, and he has some pretty definite ideas about what to spend his money on. The equipment works, he says. As long as we have an engineer who knows how to keep it running, he'll make it last for ages." She shrugged. "He'd rather spend his money on an air watch pilot, if you can believe that."

"An air watch pilot? You mean you have your own man in a plane up there?"

She nodded. "I'll show you. Traffic is next. Hang on."

She whipped on her headphones and turned up the volume inside the studio for Kyle's benefit, then switched on the mike. "It's five o'clock. You've got Desiree, and this is KICK-FM, Anaheim. Now let's hear from our daredevil in the skies, Deadly Dave Dawson." She punched a button marked Traffic on the control board. "Dave?"

The Harrison Duet

"Hi, Desiree. Hey, you were breathing pretty hard a few minutes ago. Who've you got in there with you? Some hot, young stud?"

She felt a blush start in her cheeks and spread to the roots of her hair. This was their typical daily banter; Dave was always kidding her about the sensual quality of her voice. How was he to know that this particular time his comment hit the nail on the head?

"The truth is, Dave, I do have somebody in here." She turned and met Kyle's amused gaze. "He's a top name in his field, incredibly rich, devilishly handsome, and he has a fantastic body and the most gorgeous eyes you've ever seen."

"Oh yeah? Who is it?"

"That's *my* little secret." Out of the comer of her eye, she saw the buttons light up on her phone. Don't miss a trick, do they? she thought with a grin. "Now what about that traffic? How's it look out there?"

A chuckle traveled the airwaves. "Things aren't looking *too* bad for a Friday night. The Golden State southbound is slow and go at…"

As Dave continued the traffic report, Desiree's earphones were plucked from her head and an arm stole around her again from behind. Quickly she flipped off the mike.

"Devilishly handsome?" he murmured, his lips against her ear. "Fantastic body? Gorgeous eyes?"

"I guess I did get a little carried away." As she sat on the stool, his chest pressed against her back, she couldn't stop her eyes from closing and her neck from arching back and resting against his shoulder. "As long as they *think* someone's in here, let's give them something to worry about."

"Great idea." He slowly rotated the stool until her side rested against him. Cupping her chin in his hand, he turned

74

her mouth up to his and tantalized it with light, soft kisses. His free hand roamed to her opposite hip, holding her captive against his chest as his tongue traced her lips, then slipped inside her mouth. She returned the kiss as it became deeper, locking her hands behind his neck and pulling him closer. In the back of her mind she heard a voice, distorted words, droning on in what seemed a foreign language.

"Stalled vehicle...605 northbound...no other problems..."

She felt Kyle's hand drift down her arm, brush the side of her breast. She was spinning, as if from lack of oxygen, as if he was drawing the breath from her body.

"That's about it for..." The voice hazily penetrated her dazed state. The words formed a familiar pattern, then began to flash in her brain like a neon sign. "...Dawson for KICK. Have a nice weekend."

She bolted upright, pushed Kyle away with a shaky hand and turned to the console, turning up the volume control. Her heart pounded in her ears as, with several instinctive, expedient motions, she started the next tune and sank back against the counter, arms hanging limply at her sides.

She glanced quickly out the control room window in both directions. Thankfully, there was no one in sight. She blew out a sigh of relief. "Kyle. How do you expect me to do my job, when you..."

"When I what?"

"When you hold me and kiss me like that!"

He lifted his palms, shrugging innocently. "Sorry."

She attempted to glare at him, but suspected she was failing miserably. "I can't concentrate with you in here. Go sit out in the waiting area until I'm finished. Go!"

With a smile, he moved to the door. "Six o'clock," he reminded her. "I'll be waiting."

Desiree relaxed against the contoured leather seat of the Maserati and closed her eyes. The engine hummed a soft lullaby, blending harmoniously with the colorful kaleidoscope of images floating through her mind.

"I didn't think anyone could tap dance so fast," she murmured.

"Neither did I," Kyle said, chuckling. "What a show."

She couldn't remember ever spending a more enjoyable evening. They'd feasted on a delectable *canard a l'orange* at a small, French restaurant near the theater. Kyle had ordered everything in advance, from the *salade Lyonnaise* to the delicious *tart aux pommes* for dessert. He'd arranged for the meal to be served with a minimum of delay, and they'd arrived at the Music Center just minutes before the show began.

The musical was an extravaganza of dazzling costumes and breathtaking production numbers. But even the star's spectacular toe-tapping could not compare with the thrill and pride she'd felt just being in Kyle's company. Other women had stared at him as they'd walked by, and no wonder. In his three-piece suit and silk tie, his hair carefully groomed, his face recently shaved, he looked handsome, sophisticated, and indisputably masculine.

The mind-stealing embraces they'd shared earlier in the studio, made all the more exciting by their illicit nature, never strayed from her thoughts. When his hand reached over to gently warm her thigh through the thin fabric of her skirt, it required rigorous self-control to keep her breathing steady and focus on the stage. But now, although he sat just inches from her in the cozy interior of the small sports car and his hand brushed her cheek tenderly, she felt too relaxed and content to be aroused.

"I couldn't believe it when he tapped his way up and down that entire staircase," he said.

Drowsily, she caressed his hand. "That *was* amazing. Like something out of a Fred Astaire movie." She opened her eyes and smiled. "Thank you again for getting the tickets."

He squeezed her shoulder. "Any time."

They drove along in contented silence. The effects of Desiree's sleepless night and hectic day finally caught up with her, and she drifted off to sleep. It seemed only minutes later that she heard the engine clicking off and the car's final shudder into silent stillness.

Disoriented, she tried to speak, but only managed a small yawn. All at once she felt herself being gathered up by a pair of strong arms as warm lips pressed against hers.

"Wake up, sleepyhead," he whispered. "We're home."

"Already?" She slowly opened her eyes. Moonlight splashed through the windshield, making her squint. The silvery beam that illuminated her face only touched the side of his cheek, emphasizing its smooth, angular planes.

"You've been asleep for half an hour." He leaned back slightly and threaded his fingers through her hair. "Did anyone ever tell you that you're beautiful when you're asleep? Even more beautiful than when you're awake, if that's possible."

"You're just saying that because it's true," she mumbled.

He laughed, his eyes inky-black in the darkness.

His nearness, his warmth, and his unique masculine scent enveloped her senses. Kiss me again, she wanted to plead. But as she lifted her hand to touch his cheek, a sudden, inexplicable shyness came over her. She lowered her eyes, let her hand fall away, and toyed with the edge of the smooth leather seat,

The Harrison Duet

struggling to make conversation. "This is a nice car. Where do you rent a Maserati?"

"There's a place near the airport." With measured slowness, his thumb traced small, sensuous circles at the side of her neck.

She caught her breath. Could he feel the erratic pulse beating beneath the pad of his thumb?

"They have every luxury car you can think of," he added, moving closer. "Rolls-Royce. Mercedes. Ferrari."

"What about…a Cadillac limousine?"

"One of every size and color—or so I'd imagine." His breath fanned her lips. "Limos are their mainstay."

"I've always wanted to ride in a limo. An incredibly long, plush limo, with a built-in bar and a TV."

"An intriguing fantasy. Just think what we could do in a limo."

His mouth pressed tenderly against hers, infusing her body with warmth. His tongue persuaded her lips apart, then probed her mouth, performing an intimate mating dance with her tongue. As his hands scaled her back, she locked her arms behind his neck, twisted her hands in his hair. She felt a thread of trust weave between them, through them, around them, as if entwining them together for eternity.

"Desiree, you taste so sweet…"

His hand traced up her side to lightly graze the side of her breast, and her head fell back. A sigh of ecstasy echoed in the night as his lips moved slowly, sensuously up her throat, then covered her mouth once more.

Suddenly he winced sharply and she felt him draw back.

"What's wrong?" she asked breathlessly.

"I think the stick shift's permanently embedded in my side."

78

"Oh. I'm sorry."

"And the windshield's all fogged up."

She giggled softly. No more than my brain, she thought. "I guess there's no point in kissing out in the car, is there? Would you like to come in for a brandy?"

He leaned his forehead against hers and smiled into her eyes. "I thought you'd never ask."

6

As Desiree retrieved a bottle of brandy from her credenza and poured two snifters, she watched Kyle take off his tailored suit jacket and hang it neatly over the back of a wing chair. His tie soon joined the jacket, and he opened the top two buttons of his shirt.

"That's better," he said, exhaling deeply as he sank back into the couch. "Ever try to kiss a woman with a tie digging into your neck?"

Desiree laughed. "Not recently." She handed Kyle his drink and sat down next to him.

"Thanks." He raised the glass in a toast. "To the loveliest deejay I've ever met."

"*The* loveliest? How many deejays have you met?"

His lips tilted up in a roguish grin. "Not many. And all the others were men."

"That's what I thought. Thanks a lot."

"Allow me to amend my toast. To my new favorite deejay. May she forever rule the air waves."

"I'll drink to that." She clinked her glass against his.

He extended an arm across the back of the couch, his eyes caressing her face as he slowly sipped his brandy.

"I hope you know..." his voice dropped to a husky whisper "You *are* truly lovely. I was proud to be out with you tonight.

Not just because you're beautiful to look at, but because you're...you."

Her heart hammered in her chest as she drank in his frankly adoring gaze for a long, heady moment. She'd been told she was beautiful before. She'd never believed it. Hearing the words on his lips made her *feel* beautiful for the first time in her life. Her heart soared. She wanted to respond in kind, tell him how attractive she found him and how much she enjoyed his company, but before she could voice her thoughts, he said:

"You mentioned that you were married once. Will you tell me about it? What happened?"

Tearing her eyes from his gaze, she stared into the amber liquid in her glass. "It's not a happy memory. It was over five years ago, but I still have scars. To tell you the truth, I'd rather not talk about it."

He took the glass from her hand and set it on the coffee table. The arm behind her dropped to her shoulders and his other hand cupped her face, tilting it gently up to his. "Did he hurt you?" His jaw tensed. "Because if he did—"

"No. Not in the way you mean. My scars are purely emotional. I don't blame him for wanting the divorce. It wasn't entirely his fault. Mostly it was mine."

"I doubt that. He'd have to be an idiot to give you up."

His lips met hers, both possessive and gentle at the same time. His arms wrapped around her tenderly, adoringly. Her arms encircled his back as she arched against him, joining in a sweet, insistent caress with his tongue. She relished the flavor of him, the heat of his skin, the silken texture of his hair.

"Desiree..." His lips now nibbled the length of her throat, then took small, teasing bites from her earlobe. "All night, I've been dying to hold you...kiss you...touch you like this."

The Harrison Duet

His mouth returned to hers as his hand closed over the round fullness of her breast. Slowly he rotated his fingers and palm until her desire bubbled within his grasp. His other hand pulled her blouse loose from the waistband of her skirt and slid up her back. His hand felt rough and masculine against her smooth, bare flesh, sending tingles up her spine. Slowly he stood up, pulling her with him, and held her against his chest.

His hand glided past her waist, to cup the soft swell of her buttocks. He pressed her body against his, making her aware of the throbbing hardness of his desire. Even through the layers of their clothing she could feel the rapid drumming of his heart, which beat in cadence with her own.

"You told me last night you didn't want to see me again, that you didn't want me," he whispered against her lips. "Did you mean it? Was it true?"

His eyes were shining with affection, alive with need. She tried to tell herself that this was wrong, that they shouldn't go any further, that she *didn't* want him; instead, she admitted, "No. It wasn't true."

Without another word, he swept her up into his arms. She felt his mouth against her forehead, her cheek, her hair. His footsteps echoed on the hardwood floor as he carried her down the dark hallway. Oh God, she thought helplessly, as she wrapped her arms around him and buried her face against his neck. *This shouldn't be happening.* But she didn't want to stop it. Did she?

He nudged open the door to her bedroom with his foot and strode inside, lowering her gently onto the bed. She heard him fumble with the bedside lamp, then a flick of the switch and the room was filled with soft, golden light. As if in a dream, she watched him shrug out of his vest and toss it onto a nearby chair, then sit down on the edge of the bed and take off his shoes.

Still wearing his shirt and pants, he turned toward her and grasped her foot, pulling off first one sandal and then the other. He cradled one of her feet in his hands, massaged the high arch, circled his thumb over her toes.

"Such tiny feet," he said with wonder. "So delicate. And your legs...they're beautiful." His hand slid up one bare calf, under her silk skirt to cup her knee. His touch sent flames licking up her thighs.

Don't do this, said a voice inside her head. She pulled herself upright on the bed, her body stiff with uncertainty, her pulse racing.

"Kyle, wait."

"Why should we wait?" He pulled her down on the bed next to him, held her against the length of his body. "You know how I feel about you. I've made no secret of it." His voice dropped to a husky whisper. "Am I reading something that isn't there? Or do you feel the same way about me?"

"You know I do," she whispered.

"Then let me show you how much I care. Let me make love to you."

"I'm not sure it's right for me, for either of us. This is all happening too fast."

"It *is* happening fast. I never imagined it could be this way. But that doesn't mean it isn't right." His hand stroked her cheek as he gazed lovingly into her eyes. "There's nothing more beautiful than what we feel for each other right now."

Right now. His words drummed in her head, bringing to the surface all her reservations, all her fears.

Right now. For the moment.

Temporary. Temporary insanity.

The Harrison Duet

Catching the look in her eyes, he whispered, "We can stop if you want. It's up to you. But help me to understand. What are you afraid of?"

Of you. Of me. That I'll fall in love with you, and when it's time to say goodbye, I'll never recover. She couldn't make love to a man without giving her heart and her soul, and she was already perilously close to giving both to Kyle.

Monday morning you'll be gone, she thought, and I'll be left empty and aching.

She wanted to tell him, to try to explain, but her throat felt so constricted she couldn't speak.

"You said the other night that you'll never get married again, that your divorce was inevitable. Aren't you being a little hard on yourself? Are you so afraid of failure that you won't allow yourself to love anyone again?"

She closed her eyes. "That's...part of it," she managed in a low quiver.

"Have you been with anyone since then?" he asked softly.

She shook her head. Unbidden tears sprang into her eyes. He smoothed her hair back and kissed away her tears. "Don't be afraid, Desiree. We can never be certain what the future holds for us. But don't let that stop you from living, from loving."

The tears brimmed over and trickled down her cheeks.

"Don't cry, my darling. Don't cry." His lips moved across her eyes, cheeks, and chin, and brushed away her tears, absorbing them into his own mouth. "Oh, God, Desiree, I'm sorry."

He stretched out on his side and cuddled her close against him, massaging her back and heaving long, steadying breaths as if fighting to regain control over his body. Finally, his voice deep and vibrant, he said, "I didn't mean to push you into something you're not ready for. I'm sorry.

84

I don't want to hurt you, my darling. I only want to love you."

My darling. A shuddering sigh escaped her control. No one had ever called her my darling. Not even Steve. Until this moment, she didn't realize how much she'd always longed to hear just those words, in just the way he had said them.

Her arms looped around his back. Her hands tangled in his hair. Oh, Kyle, she thought. I didn't want to need you. I didn't want to want you. But I can't help myself. I do. Her eyes met his with a wordless plea, revealing the depth of her emotions and desire as she tilted her lips up to his.

He read her assent in her gaze. With a low moan, he rolled on top of her. His lips touched hers again, with such sensitivity and gentle adoration it took her breath away. His tongue slid between her lips, then encircled hers with a slow, tender intimacy. His hands roamed over her shoulders, then down to caress her breasts through her silky blouse.

She felt herself relax beneath him. All her reasons to resist drifted away to some dark, forgotten corner of her mind. It's going to be all right, she told herself. Somehow, he'll make it right. His hand reached down to unbutton her blouse, and when he reached inside her lacy bra to cup her breast, a shudder of pleasure rocketed through her and she called his name out loud. He raised her up slowly and slid the blouse and wispy bra from her body. At his sharp intake of breath she felt her heart begin to pound.

"You're perfect," he said huskily. He laid her back down and kissed her as his hand covered one throbbing naked breast, fingers stroking gently, seeking to please. With slow, circular motions he kneaded the rose-colored nipple until it sprang to life beneath his thumb. His touch sent tiny jolts of

The Harrison Duet

electricity through her, like sparks on a live wire. Soft moans of desire escaped her throat.

Her hands roamed across his back, then tugged feverishly at his shirt until it pulled free of his waistband. She ran exploring fingers along the bare, smooth skin above his waist, then traced the distinct ridge in the center of his back.

"I want to see you," she whispered. With quivering fingers she reached around to grasp the placket of his shirt.

"Let me help you," he said softly. He sat up and quickly removed the unwanted barrier between them and let it drop to the floor.

Her heart beat faster as she gazed at his naked chest. Dark, curly hair covered the taut contours of his upper pectorals, then descended in crisp swirls down the center to a thin, tapering line that disappeared into his pants. She lifted hesitant fingers to his smooth skin, then plowed through his soft chest hair. She sensed a barely leashed passion burning beneath the surface of his skin, and it matched the fire raging beneath her own.

He slid down on the bed and enclosed the pink, pointed crown of one breast in his mouth. His tongue outlined her rounded nipple, stroked it, teased it. One hand pushed open the front fold of her wraparound skirt and his fingers glided up her slender thigh, massaging a path along its inner, most sensitive parts. Her legs began to tremble. His fingers reached the edge of her bikini panties and toyed with the lacy elastic.

"Yes," she breathed.

"Are you sure?" he asked softly.

"I'm sure."

"What about—do I need to—?"

She felt heat rise to her cheeks. "It's okay." She'd been on the Pill for years for health reasons, and she told him so.

He nodded. As she lifted her hips to help him, he slid her panties down along her legs, over her feet. He untied the wraparound skirt at her waist, then drew the folds apart to view her in her naked splendor.

"You take my breath away." His voice was sandpaper-rough. He stretched up over her and fastened his mouth to hers in a fiery kiss. The pressure and texture of his hard, wiry-haired chest against the sensitive tips of her breasts sent ripples of exquisite sensation throughout her body. His hand stroked up the inside of her thigh, ever closer to the center of her femininity. She—

The phone rang.

Their bodies stiffened at the same moment. He lifted his head.

"Don't answer it," he whispered.

She lay frozen beneath him. The ring persisted. She glanced at the bedside dock. It was almost midnight. "Who could it be at this hour?"

"Does it matter?" He softly trailed his fingertips along her collarbone.

She took a deep breath, trying desperately to think despite the fire raging throughout her system. "No one would call so late unless it was really important." She turned sideways and reached for the phone. With a groan he rolled off her.

"Hello?" Her voice was as unsteady as her hand.

"Desiree? Thank God you're home." She recognized the gravelly voice of Sam, her program director at the station. "The Board Op just called and got me out of bed. He said John's stuck on the freeway. There's a tow truck on the way, but he doesn't know what time he'll get there. Dave's already worked two shifts and can only stay another half hour. I need you to substitute until John makes it in."

"This isn't a good time. Did you try Mark or Wayne?"

The Harrison Duet

"Wayne's too drunk to stand up straight, and I wasn't able to reach Mark or anyone else."

"I'm sorry Sam, but I can't go in now."

"Dammit, Desiree, don't give me any excuses. If you don't do this, we're dead in the water. You're the only one I can depend upon."

She let out a deep sigh of frustration. "Okay. Fine. I'll be there as soon as I can." She hung up the phone and slid from the bed, her limbs still trembling.

"What is it?"

"The night-shift deejay has car trouble." She explained what happened as she quickly got dressed.

Kyle cursed loudly and sat up on the edge of the bed.

"I'm really sorry," she said sincerely. "I have no choice."

"I know." But his tone said, *That doesn't make it any easier to take.* He bent down and retrieved his shirt from where it lay on the floor. "Would it help if I drive you to the station and wait for you, so you don't have to drive home alone in the middle of the night?"

"Thanks, but I'll be okay." She struggled to steady both her breathing and her nerves as she fished in her closet for a pair of flip flops.

"Then I'll wait for you here." He put on his shirt and began to fasten the buttons.

"No." She swallowed hard, avoiding his gaze as she slipped into the open shoes. If not for the phone call, they would have made love. She felt certain it would have been wonderful… and she *had* wanted it…but afterwards…what then? Even if she and Kyle had the most romantic weekend on earth, he'd have to return to Seattle on Monday. How often would she see him after that? For a day or two every other week at the beginning, if they were really lucky? Or only once a month?

How long would that go on before they both realized it wasn't working, or he met someone else who lived closer to home? She didn't want to think about the wretched loneliness of those long months of forced separation from Steve. No. No. She couldn't do that to herself again.

Reluctantly, she said, "I think it'd be best if you went back to the hotel."

"What?" He was incredulous. "Are you serious?"

"Yes."

"You're going to kick me out now, after this—" he gestured toward the bed beneath him "—at this hour?"

"You have a hotel room in L.A., don't you?"

"No. I checked out this morning."

Her mouth opened in surprise. "Why? You bought the tickets for tonight's show...you didn't plan to fly home today." It was statement of fact, not a question.

"Right." He stood up and tucked his shirt into his pants. "I planned to stay here tonight. Maybe the weekend."

She stared at him, dismayed consternation prickling through her. "You *planned* to stay here?"

He blew out an exasperated breath. "Not *here,* in your bed. I was going to find a motel closer to your house."

She strove for a carefully controlled tone. "And when exactly did you plan to do that? After you found out whether or not you'd score?"

"What? No."

"Is that what the roses and dinner and show were all about—a perfectly-planned seduction? Do you play this little game on all your business trips? Pick up the first woman you find and see how long it'll take her to go to bed with you?"

As soon as the words left her mouth, Desiree regretted them. She wasn't sure why she'd said them. Was she trying

89

The Harrison Duet

to make him angry? In all fairness, she knew that she was as much to blame for what had happened between them as he was. She'd invited him in, had responded to his caresses, had urged him on even when he'd offered to stop.

But she was thinking more clearly now. Now, if she explained everything about her past, would he understand her feelings? She doubted it.

In her peripheral vision she could see a muscle twitch in his jaw.

"Desiree," he said quietly, "I don't make a game of seducing women, on business trips or anywhere else. I took you out the past few nights because I wanted to be with you. It's that simple. I planned to book another room this afternoon."

"Well, that phone call was a wake up call. It came just in time. It stopped me from doing something I think I'll regret." Avoiding his eyes, she added, "What happened just now was a mistake."

"Mistake? It was no mistake, Desiree, and you know it." He darted forward, his lips thinning in irritation as he stared down at her. "You've been running hot and cold since the moment we met. The last two nights you backed off like a scared rabbit. This afternoon you were only too willing to let me hold you and kiss you. A few minutes ago you responded to me like a woman on fire—you fanned every spark. And now you're telling me to get lost? What kind of game are *you* playing? What kind of woman are you?"

She opened her mouth to protest, but he went on:

"Don't tell me. I already know. When I first heard you on the air, I thought you had a cute radio act with your sultry voice and all those none-too-subtle sexual innuendos. Until a few minutes ago, I thought the *real* you was different: a warm, caring person, capable of honest emotions. But I see now it's all part of the act. You're just a clever tease."

90

She gasped, her cheeks stinging as if she'd been slapped. Tears stung her eyes, and she grasped for something to say in reply. But he continued:

"I've got to hand it to you, Desiree. You're a real pro. You've got this thing down to a science. You know how to lead a man on, get him breathless, and then cut off his air supply. Did you arrange for that phone call to come when it did? I wouldn't put it past you."

He flung himself away from her, grabbed his vest, then stopped in the doorway and fixed her with an icy, ironic stare. "It was nice knowing you, Desiree."

His footsteps pounded against the hall floor. Her stomach lurched as she heard the door slam with ominous finality. Then she buried her face in her hands and began to sob.

Desiree slammed down her ceramic mug on the kitchen table, causing hot coffee to slosh over the rim and burn her fingers.

"Damn, damn, damn!" She grabbed a sponge and cleaned up the spill, then slumped back in her chair, staring moodily at the arrangement of long-stemmed roses next to the open kitchen window. Sunlight sparkled like diamonds on the tall, cut-glass vase and burnished the perfect red buds to a velvety sheen. *Why did I bother to bring them home from the station?* she wondered. *I should have just let them stay there and wither.*

She hoped Kyle had driven straight to the airport the night before and taken the first morning flight to Seattle. *I don't need him to complicate my life,* she told herself. She was glad it was over before they'd had a chance to get too involved.

Yeah, right, she scolded silently. If she was so glad it was over, then why did it take fifteen minutes to pull herself together after he left, before she could trust herself to drive to the station? Why did she spend half of her time on the air in those early morning hours wiping away tears?

Because he wounded you, she reminded herself. You knew you were going to get hurt. It just happened a lot sooner—and in a different way—than you expected. She wrapped her arms around her chest, anger curling inside her as she recalled the cruel things he'd said to her last night.

You know how to lead a man on, get him breathless, and then cut off his air supply. Did you arrange for that phone call to come when it did? I wouldn't put it past you.

How dare he say that? He'd called her a tease! Incapable of emotion!

A sudden flush of guilt washed over her, causing her anger to waver. If she was honest with herself, in her private confusion with regard to her wants and feelings, she *had* given him very contradictory signals. His anger was actually very understandable. But still...

The now familiar sound of the Maserati engine pulling into the driveway made her jump. *He was here?*

Her stomach knotted with anxiety. In part, she was relieved that he'd come back; it would give her a chance to apologize for the way she'd behaved. Maybe he's come to apologize too, she hoped. But then she remembered the jacket and tie still draped over the chair in her living room. Of course. The efficient businessman wasn't here to say he was sorry—he'd had his final say last night. He'd only returned to wrap up all the loose ends.

When she heard his knock, Desiree crossed the living room and flung open the door, determined to hold onto her anger and let him speak first. But on seeing him, her heart went into a skid.

In no way did he resemble an angry entrepreneur come to retrieve lost property. In his present, casual state of dress he looked more like a handsome Olympic athlete, and his expression as their eyes collided was apprehensive, hesitant, contrite.

"Hi," he said softly.

"Hi." The raspy, high-pitched response didn't sound like her own voice. She couldn't help but stare at him, transfixed, one hand glued to the doorknob.

He wore a navy-blue polo shirt, open at the neck. The short sleeves stretched over his well-formed biceps. His legs, long and lean beneath crisp white shorts, were braided with flexible-looking muscles and covered with the same curly dark hair that graced his arms and chest. In one hand he carried a small, white paper bag.

"I'm glad you're up," he said. "I was afraid I'd wake you."

"Oh...no. I didn't have to work too late. John arrived about half past two." She noticed dark circles under his eyes and wondered if she had them, too.

Her pounding pulse told her how glad she was to see him. Suddenly, in her mind, they were no longer standing like statues in the doorway. They were back in each other's arms last night and he was saying, "You know how I feel about you...I don't want to hurt you, my darling. I only want to love you."

She'd wanted him last night. She still did. If he'd said some cruel things in the heat of anger, it was partly her fault. She had provoked him.

She swallowed hard and glanced down at the paper bag he was holding. "What's that?"

"A peace offering."

She took the bag he extended, reading his unspoken apology in his eyes. Her heart flinched when he quickly withdrew his hand as if afraid to touch her.

The Harrison Duet

"Croissants!" she cried with true delight when she looked inside.

"Freshly baked this morning. Okay if I share one with you?"

She stood back and opened the door wide. "Of course."

He stepped inside. "Should we put them in the oven to warm up?"

She nodded. He brushed past her to the kitchen and turned on the oven. She followed.

"Would you like a cup of coffee?" she offered.

"I'd love one. Thanks."

They engaged in small talk at the tiny kitchen table as they sipped their coffee and ate the hot, buttery pastries. He made no further reference to their argument, and she felt too uncomfortable to bring it up. She wanted to reach out and touch his hand, to tell him how sorry she was. But he seemed a bit distant, reserved. Was he still angry with her? What was he thinking? Why had he come?

When he'd drained his cup, Kyle sat back in his chair and gave her a small smile. "So. Do you have any plans for today?"

"Not really."

"Good. Because I've got a surprise for you."

"A surprise?"

"After last night—" He checked himself, frowning, then went on: "What we need is to get out and have some fun. And I've got it all arranged. I'm going to take you for a ride in the sky."

A stab of alarm pierced through her. "What do you mean?"

"I arranged to rent a plane from the Long Beach Pilots' Club." He grinned like a child who'd just gotten out of school for the summer. "I'm taking you to Catalina Island for the day.

7

"Catalina Island?" Desiree's eyes widened in dismay. She'd almost forgotten he had a pilot's license, that he liked to fly. "You're kidding, aren't you?"

"Why would I be kidding?" Kyle asked.

"Because I told you, I don't like to fly. Commercial flights are one thing, but I won't go up in a small plane."

"Desiree: you'll love it. I promise." He leaned forward, his elbows on the table, his face eager with excitement. "It's a thrill you can't even imagine until you've experienced it."

"Maybe for you. But not for me."

"You'll never know if you don't give it a chance."

"I don't want to fly to Catalina. I've read about the airport there. It's dangerous—it's on a high, remote hilltop with a precipitous drop-off. They have a lot of accidents."

"Don't exaggerate. They have more accidents on L.A. freeways in one day than Catalina Airport sees in ten years. Airplane crashes just make the front pages, that's all."

"Maybe. But still—I read that some pilots compare the Catalina Airport to landing on an aircraft carrier." She shuddered. "Too risky for my blood."

"Everything we do involves a risk of some kind," he returned softly. "What's the point in living if you never venture

The Harrison Duet

out into new territory, never take any chances? You might as well be dead."

She took a sharp breath but didn't reply.

"Look, there's nothing to worry about." He gestured with an open palm. "I've been flying for thirteen years. I know what I'm doing. The weather is perfect today. And I've made this flight before."

"I'm sorry. If you want to go to Catalina, that's fine, but let's take a boat. I don't want to fly."

He heaved a sigh, struggling visibly to keep his patience. "The cruises to Catalina are all sold out today—I already checked. We can fly there in fifteen minutes. I've been on the phone since six this morning setting this thing up. I had to pull a few strings to get the plane I wanted. I understand your concerns, and I know this is very short notice, but I made special arrangements on the island...I've got a whole day planned for us. I know you'll love it. I don't want to cancel it all now."

She stood and took a few steps away. "I'm sorry you went to so much trouble. For all I knew, you were back in Seattle by now. If you were going to make all these elaborate arrangements, you should have asked me first."

"Asked you first? How could I do that, after last night?" He took a deep breath, but it did little to calm him. "Anyway, this was supposed to be a surprise."

"I appreciate that," she said sincerely, "and the thought behind it. But it doesn't change how I feel."

"What is with you?" Kyle leaped to his feet. "Can't you meet a new challenge for once in your life? You're afraid to get involved with me. You're afraid to go to bed with me. You're afraid to ride in a plane. I'm surprised you have enough nerve to get in your car and drive to work every day."

"That's not fair," she said, irritation prickling through her. "My reasons for not getting involved with you have nothing to do with my fear of flying."

He braced tense fingers on the tabletop. "Then why are you so afraid?"

"Because my best friend was killed in a small plane crash! And I almost went with her that day!"

They stared at each other in silence across the table, his face frozen in shock.

After a moment, Desiree went on: "Her husband was the pilot. They'd only been married a few months. She was only twenty-five."

A flicker of anguish shone in his eyes. "I'm sorry," he said quietly.

"Pam was like a sister to me." Her voice cracked and she cleared her throat before continuing. "When I find myself feeling angry over what happened, when I think what a waste it was she died so young, at the same time I know how relieved I am that I didn't go with them. And that makes me feel guilty as hell."

In a few quick strides he circled the table and took her in his arms. "I'm sorry, Desiree. So sorry. I wish I could take back what I said. I wish I could take away the pain you must feel."

She released a wavering breath as her arms wrapped around his back. The hot tears that welled up in her eyes were tears of relief, not sorrow. It felt good to be back in his arms again.

"And I'm sorry about last night," he added, his voice thick with emotion. "Sorry about everything. I said some ugly things, things I didn't mean. I was frustrated out of my mind. I didn't want to leave. I didn't want to spend another minute without you."

She tilted her head back and met his tortured gaze. "It wasn't your fault, it was mine. I feel terrible about the things *I* said. I'm so, so sorry. Can you forgive me?"

"I already have. You had every right to react the way you did. Things have been moving at light speed between us. I've been all over you from the moment we met. I can only say again: I'm sorry. I've never felt or acted this way with a woman before—I don't know what it is about you, or about me when I'm around you—but I promise I'll be different from here on out. I won't try to persuade you to do something you're not ready for." He gave her a quick squeeze, then released her. "Okay?"

She smiled weakly, drying her tears as he stepped away, an irrational sense of disappointment flooding her at the brevity of his embrace. "Okay. Thanks."

"That said," he added, meeting her gaze, "I'll call and cancel my plans for Catalina today. Tell me what *you'd* like to do instead."

The large white bird stood at attention on the parking strip, wings spread high and wide. Turquoise racing stripes were splashed across the body, nose, and tail, and sunlight gleamed off the wings. A friendly looking plane, Desiree decided, trying hard to ignore the tense knot of anxiety in her stomach. *Maybe this won't be so bad after all...*

Once Kyle had left the decision up to her—after all the trouble he'd gone to in arranging this— she'd felt bad turning him down. She'd decided he was right: what *was* the point in living, if you never ventured out into new territory, never took any chances? And as long as she'd agreed to do it, she was determined to show him what a good sport she could be.

He'd spent a good half hour going over the safety statistics at the Catalina Airport, and reassuring her that the weather was in their favor, the plane was practically new, and he had all the experience required to land there safely.

She leaned against the corrugated aluminum building that housed the Long Beach Pilots' Club and watched Kyle as he checked over the plane, inside and out, in minute detail. There was certainly nothing glamorous about private flying. Unlike the sleek sophistication of a modem commercial airport, the Pilots' Club consisted of one small, stark office and a plane-filled parking lot of cracked asphalt, surrounded by a chain-link fence. She had to admit, though: the idea of hopping into one of these small craft and simply taking off into the air, the way she might take off down the street in her car, filled her not only with trepidation, but with excitement and anticipation.

Kyle attached a small metal tow bar to the front of their plane and signaled her to join him. "We need to tow her out of the lot. Grab hold of the wing and pull."

Not wanting to show her surprise, Desiree stepped nimbly up to the front of one wing and grabbed the edge with both hands. The rounded ridge of aluminum felt smooth and cool. As Kyle yanked on the tow bar she lunged backward and gave a mighty tug. To her astonishment the plane rolled forward almost effortlessly.

"Okay, you can let go now," Kyle called. "Just keep an eye on the wing tips. Make sure we're clear of the other planes." *No wonder they call it a light plane*, she thought as she watched Kyle tow the plane just past the parking area, her stomach re-knotting with apprehension. The thing seemed as flimsy as a child's toy.

"Let's go!" Kyle called a few minutes later.

The Harrison Duet

She ducked down under the wing and opened the cockpit door. "Are you sure this tin can will make it all the way to Catalina?" she asked, striving for a light tone.

"Trust me."

She smiled stiffly as she climbed up onto the smooth, leather seat and slammed the door. Settling back in her seat, she fastened her safety belt. Myriad gauges and switches, vaguely reminiscent of her console at the studio, covered the black panel before them. The cockpit was tiny, even smaller than the front section of a foreign compact car. Well, at least they'd be nice and cozy.

"Do you always do such a thorough check before you take off?" she asked.

"You bet. I'm not taking somebody else's word that this baby's fueled up and in flying condition. I want to see it with my own eyes." He consulted a small handbook on his lap, flipped several switches, and leaned out his open window. "Clear!"

A man working on a nearby plane stepped back and waved. Kyle kicked over the starter and the engine sputtered to life. A voice on the radio began to spew out information like a moderator at an auction. She only caught a few intelligible numbers and phrases.

Kyle picked up the hand microphone. "Long Beach Ground, Cessna nine three six five Uniform, Long Beach Pilots. Taxi to two five left with information Echo." After a moment's pause the voice on the radio replied with instructions in the same peculiar language. Kyle hung up the mike and grinned. "Funny. Somehow I feel like you should be talking on this thing."

She laughed, finding his relaxed manner a balm to her apprehension. "No way. You talk a different language than any deejay I ever heard. What did they just tell you?"

100

"The first part was recorded weather information," he said as they taxied toward the runway. "Winds, temperature, altimeter setting. After I identified myself, Ground Control gave me the takeoff point."

"Sounded like Greek to me."

"It's a phonetic alphabet. Helps distinguish one letter from another. Prevents misunderstandings. A is Alpha. B is Bravo. C is Charlie—"

"E is Echo and U is Uniform," she finished for him in comprehension.

"Exactly." He guided the plane onto the runway and pulled to a halt. As the engine hum increased to a fevered pitch, she stole a glance at Kyle. His mouth curved into a youthful grin and his eyes smoldered with growing excitement, an enthusiasm that was both pleasing to see and contagious.

He called the tower. Her palms began to sweat and her heart drummed with anticipation. It's going to be okay, she reminded herself. Don't think about what happened to Pam. It was a freak accident. He knows what he's doing.

A radio voice cleared them for takeoff. "Okay, here we go," Kyle said.

The plane moved forward slowly, then began to pick up speed. The cockpit vibrated. The hum became a roaring buzz in her ears. Vast open fields raced by on both sides. The tower shot past. The tension in Desiree's stomach heightened. Beads of sweat popped out on her brow. Then, suddenly, her stomach dropped as the plane lifted gracefully toward the sky. They were airborne.

"Yee-haw!" Kyle shouted with childlike glee.

"Wow!" Desiree heard herself shout. The anxiety that had built up inside her on the ground released itself in a roar of relieved laughter. The plane was buffeted slightly up and down

The Harrison Duet

and the engine continued its loud hum. Mingled with her fear, she felt an unexpected sense of lighthearted giddiness, as if she'd discovered a newfound sense of freedom.

"That wasn't so bad, was it?" he asked.

She turned to look out her side window. The plane's high wings allowed an undisturbed view of the ground. Familiar streets and landmarks flashed by, and all at once she felt a sense of smug superiority, floating so freely above all the people and cars stuck on the ground.

"This is great," she answered, much to her surprise. "It's almost like a ride at Disneyland."

He laughed with delight and gave her thigh an affectionate squeeze.

In what seemed like minutes they were over the ocean. The dark-blue water shimmered below them. "It's beautiful, Kyle."

He grinned, his hands on the controls. "I knew you'd like it."

When they reached the island, Kyle circled slowly around it and she held her breath in wonder. No Mediterranean island could be more beautiful than the sight of Santa Catalina as it rose majestically out of the sea. All dark browns and greens against the crystal blue ocean, the island's jagged shoreline was interrupted only by a few small harbors and scattered beaches.

After Kyle received his landing instructions, Desiree eyed the island's mountainous interior with concern. They swept past the island, over the ocean, then circled around the back again. "Where's the airport?" she asked.

"Right there." He pointed toward a high mountain plateau bisected by a ribbon of asphalt.

"That's the runway?"

"Yes."

Her mouth went dry. Even the reports she'd read hadn't prepared her for the sight of something quite so scary. The short, paved road began just beyond a sharp drop-off…and ended at the edge of another cliff dropping straight down to the sea.

The cliff loomed closer. The engine roar quieted to a low hum. The plane slowed, aiming straight for the cliff's top edge.

"Oh, God!" Desiree cried, leaning her head back against the seat and closing her eyes.

"Nothing to worry about," he said reassuringly. "I've done this before. We're fine."

She nodded mutely. *Nothing to worry about. We're fine.* She chanted the words over and over to herself. Suddenly she felt a lifting sensation, as if they'd floated up on a strong breeze. Then the plane drifted downward and touched ground more smoothly than she could ever have imagined.

Desiree could almost feel the brakes grabbing as the plane quickly decelerated, the vibration traveling through her body with blinding force. Her heart pounded violently as they slowed to a taxiing speed, then expertly turned and rolled on.

She opened her eyes and took a deep breath, noting that he had landed quite a distance away from the drop-off at the other end of the cliff.

"Nothing to it, was there?" he grinned.

She smiled, relief surging through her, along with a sense of admiration for his piloting skills. "Piece of cake."

"Everything's here, just the way I wanted it." Kyle tossed the beach bag they'd brought into the trunk of the waiting sedan.

"What have you got in there?" Desiree glanced curiously toward the back of the car but he shut the trunk with a clang.

"You'll see."

He opened the door for her and she slid into the bucket seat. At his direction, she'd put on her bathing suit under her shorts and T-shirt in the airport rest room. He now wore sleek navy-blue bathing trunks which matched his shirt.

"How did you manage to get this car?" she asked after he'd climbed in and shut the door. "I heard that they don't rent cars on the island."

His eyes glittered mysteriously. "They don't."

"You must know someone who lives here, then."

"I do." He started the engine and headed out of the airport lot.

Noting the direction he was taking, she said, "This isn't the road to Avalon, is it?"

She'd taken a one-day cruise to Catalina two years before, and had spent the afternoon with hordes of other sightseers, combing through the shops and museum in Avalon, the island's one and only small harbor town.

"No," he replied. "I can only take so much of that touristy stuff."

"So where are we going?"

"You'll see," he said again. "I have something completely different in mind for us today."

The narrow, winding road hugged the dry, desolate mountain on one side and dropped off sharply on the other. The terrain resembled a desert wilderness, mostly scrub oak, rock, and cacti. Soon, they rounded a bend and she caught sight of a small, lonely stretch of sand beach below rocky cliffs. He turned onto a bluff above the beach and parked next to the only other car there.

"Oh, Kyle, how wonderful."

She jumped out of the car, ran to the edge of the bluff, and gazed down with growing excitement at the sparkling white sand and gently rolling surf beyond. The hot sun blazed in a cloudless sky over an endless, shimmering blue sea. The only people in sight were packing up their things and heading up the winding path along the cliffs.

"I've never seen a beach so empty on a Saturday. Why isn't anyone else here?" she asked.

Kyle stepped up beside her and draped an arm casually across her shoulder. "Tourists can't rent cars, so the only people who can get here are the islanders, and there aren't many of those. This is the smallest beach, and the farthest from town, so I figured it wouldn't be too crowded." He raised an inquiring eyebrow in her direction. "Like it?"

"It's incredible. It's like being shipwrecked on a desert island. It's paradise."

He turned to face her. "I hoped you'd feel this way. I was here once on my own, several years ago. I've always dreamed of coming back, when I had someone special to share it with."

Yesterday, she thought, he'd have wrapped his arms around her waist and whispered those words against her ear. She glanced up wistfully at him. After the things she'd said last night, the way she'd run so hot and cold, he was probably afraid she'd shrink back again if he got too close—and she couldn't blame him.

"I'm glad I'm the special someone you chose," Desiree said softly.

She could tell he was pleased by the soft glow in his green eyes. "So am I," he answered.

The Harrison Duet

"Now *here's* what I call an ideal picnic spot." Kyle set down the ice chest and wicker basket next to the rocky cliff and pulled a folded blanket out of the beach bag.

Desiree helped him spread the large, soft blanket across the sand, then stood up to admire the spot they'd found. The hot sun baked the beach like a giant oven—but this little, sandy alcove at the far end of the beach dipped in under the shade of dark, overhanging rocks, hiding them from view of the bluff high above. Just a dozen yards away the surf lapped the shore, but here the sand was fine, soft, and white.

"I can't wait to try the water," she said.

Kyle peeled off his shirt. She couldn't resist a glance at the strong muscles of his smooth back as he raised his arms over his head. She had to restrain the urge to steal up behind him, touch the curved shoulder blades of his broad upper back, and curl her arms about his slim waist.

"How about if we eat first?" he said. "I'm starving."

Suddenly aware of a ravenous ache in her own stomach, she dropped down on the blanket, Indian-style. "Sounds great. What have you got in there?"

"Just a few odds and ends." He knelt and opened the lid of the picnic basket, then proceeded to lift out its contents: a small French bread, knives, a wooden cutting board, napkins, plastic plates, and utensils. From the cooler he produced three kinds of cheese, a salami, a tin of pâté de fois gras, green grapes, apples, a jar of black olives, and a relish tray. Finally he pulled out a frosty bottle of champagne and two stemmed glasses.

"Where did you get all this?" she said in amazement.

"I told you I was up at six this morning making phone calls." Smiling, he expertly opened the bottle and filled her chilled glass with the sparkling wine. "The owner of the Avalon Grand Hotel is a friend of mine. He had the restaurant put this together for us. Oh, and one more thing." He reached back in the cooler and lifted up a six-pack of Sparkle Light soda. "In case you're still thirsty after the champagne."

She laughed in delight. "Lucky me, to know someone with such terrific connections."

When he'd filled his own glass he raised it to hers in a toast. "To four unforgettable days, and many more just like them."

Desiree felt a little pang at that—this hopeful mention of the future—but tried to tell herself that anything was possible. She clinked her glass lightly against his with a facetious smile. "To the best pilot to whom I've ever entrusted my life."

She took a sip of the crisp, tangy wine and sighed in satisfaction as she felt the refreshing coolness revitalize her system. They feasted on the assortment of delicacies as they enjoyed the cool shade under the overhanging cliff, the sound of the rolling waves, and the pleasant, fresh scent of the sea air. After they packed up the leftovers, Kyle dipped back into the cooler, brought out two small covered bowls, and handed one to Desiree with a flourish.

"Ta da! La piece de resistance. "

"Chocolate mousse!" Desiree cried. "How did you know it's my favorite?"

"A lucky guess. It's my favorite, too."

Desiree picked up a spoon and dove in. A mesmerized smile crossed her face as she savored the cold, creamy chocolate. "Mmm, this is heaven. I've been *dying* for chocolate the past two days."

He sat up, scooted next to her, and slipped one hand around her to rest on her waist. "A bona fide chocaholic, huh?"

"In the worst possible way."

She felt herself tremble under the touch of his fingers, and briefly closed her eyes. *Desiree,* he'd said last night, *you take my breath away.*

To her disappointment—as if afraid he was getting too close—Kyle abruptly withdrew his hand and reached for the champagne bottle. "Shall we finish this off?"

All night I've been dying to hold you...kiss you...touch you like this. She swallowed over the lump in her throat. "You bet."

He emptied the bottle into their glasses. They sat side by side on the blanket, finished their dessert, and sipped the bubbly wine. Desiree glanced at his bare thigh, so close to her own. *There's nothing more beautiful than what we feel for each other right now,* he'd told her. *I don't want to hurt you, my darling. I only want to love you.*

The thought came unbidden, yet she realized, with a start, that it had been smoldering at the edge of her consciousness, just waiting for her to acknowledge it. In the short time they'd been together, she'd come to feel closer to Kyle than to anyone she'd ever known. Despite the brevity of their relationship and all her reservations about the future, she was, just as she feared, falling deeply in love with him. But somehow, the realization made her feel happy instead of worried or scared.

"Penny for your thoughts."

Her head whipped up. "What?" *Could she tell him? No—of course not.* "Oh, I was just thinking...how beautiful it is here. And how much I've enjoyed everything."

He drained his glass and set it back in the basket. "Even the flight?"

"Even the flight," she admitted. "It was a thrill—the biggest thrill I've ever experienced."

"*The* biggest thrill?" His voice had a teasing lilt to it.

She blushed. "Yes. I know—how lame am I? But it's true. It was *the* biggest thrill."

He smiled. "I'm glad. Now what do you say we go jump in that water?"

"All right." She shook her head to clear it, then pushed herself to a stand. As she shrugged quickly out of her top and shorts, she heard his soft whistle.

"Nice bathing suit." His eyes slid down her body, took in the rise of her breasts above the skimpy royal-blue-and-white bikini top, the soft curves of her waist and hips, the triangular wisp of fabric below.

"Thank you."

He cleared his throat and grinned devilishly. "But the truth is, you don't really need it. We're the only people here. There's no path at this end of the beach. And the only creatures who are likely to happen by from the ocean side are the feathered variety."

"No way!" she cried indignantly. "If you want to skinny dip, you can do it by yourself."

"You've got yourself a deal." To her surprise, he took her at her word. In one downward swoop he divested himself of his bathing trunks and tossed them aside.

She only had a brief instant to stare, breathless, at his perfect body, before he grabbed her hand and pulled her with him into the sparkling waves. She gasped as the cold water splashed against her legs, then enveloped her to the waist. She would have preferred to proceed more slowly, to take a few minutes to adjust to the water, but in typical Kyle fashion he plunged ahead, refusing to let go of her hand.

She couldn't prevent her eyes from darting toward the naked, virile man beside her. Were the sudden shivers travel-

The Harrison Duet

ing up her spine due to the brisk water temperature, or to the sight of Kyle's splendid masculinity so casually displayed?

Finally he let go of her hand and dove forward under a wave. He emerged a few feet beyond, spraying water and laughing. "Want to swim out a ways?"

"Yes." A strong swimmer, Desiree happily knifed forward through the water. Her body gradually adjusted to the temperature, which now felt delightfully invigorating. They swam side by side for a time, rising up to crest each gentle wave, and then turned to ride the tide back in. When he reached a spot where he could touch bottom, he stopped and pulled her into his arms.

"Fantastic, isn't it?"

In answer she wrapped her arms around his neck, laughing and nodding. Suddenly their eyes met and she felt his entire body stiffen, as if struggling to keep his emotions in check. Desiree's heart beat a jagged rhythm as they bobbed up and down together with the waves.

His eyes seemed to echo his words of last night. *You know how I feel about you. I've made no secret of it. Do you feel the same way about me?*

Yes! her mind cried. *Yes.* Can't you see? I adore you!

He brought one hand up to the nape of her neck and kissed her lightly. With a small moan she parted his lips with her tongue and deepened the kiss, sighing with pleasure as he wrapped his tongue around hers. A lightning bolt of desire flashed through her body, touching each vital organ, the tips of her breasts, the center of her womanhood. His arms tightened around her as he kissed her slowly, lovingly. He brought up one hand to cover her full, aching breast, kneading it gently, working his way to the crest, which strained toward his caressing fingers. The ocean lapped and rolled against them, a frenzied counterpoint to their mounting passion.

"You're lovely, Desiree. Every perfect inch of you."

He fused his mouth to hers once more and she lifted her legs to clasp tightly around his waist. She recalled the words he'd spoken the first time they walked on a beach, just one day after they met:

You are Desiree...Desired. Wanted. Longed for.

A shiver passed through her body as she felt his naked manhood, hard with desire, press against the very cove of her femininity. She might as well have been naked, too, for all the protection her thin bikini bottoms provided between them. *Let me show you how much I care. Let me make love to you,* he'd said last night. With sudden force he freed her mouth, and she felt rather than heard his passionate groan.

"Desiree," he whispered thickly into her ear. "I told you we'd wait until you were ready—and we will. But can you feel how much I want you?"

"Yes." *And I want you.* The acknowledgement came from deep in her soul and she wrapped her arms more tightly around him, as if by holding him close he could never leave her side. *What's the point in living if you never take risks?* They lived separate lives, could probably share no more than an instant in time together. But somehow it didn't matter anymore.

She'd spent far too long, she realized, avoiding the possibility of pain. All she had to show for it was years of loneliness. She knew what was to come would be sweet and precious, a treasure to look back on all the years of her life. They were meant for each other now; this moment was as inevitable as the ebb and flow of the swirling tide.

Her voice was a soft plea against his ear. "Make love to me."

8

She was glad that he didn't hesitate. He carried her out of the water and across the sand, laid her down on the soft wide blanket in the shelter of the cliff, and stretched out beside her. He held her for a long moment before he kissed her, his hands combing through the wet hair streaming across her shoulders.

She relished the feel of his cool, wet body against hers, drank in his clean scent, and savored the salty taste of his skin beneath her lips. She felt her heart drumming riotously beneath her breast and knew he must feel it, too. When he bent his head to kiss her, his lips moved softly, earnestly, slowly over hers. Each light touch of his mouth was like a mind-stealing drug, warming and soothing her already willing body and brain.

As she returned his kiss, her hands massaged the smooth, firm muscles of his slippery wet back, which flexed with each movement of his arms and body against hers. He ran his fingers the length of her slender back to the edge of her bikini bottoms, then up again, to the ties holding her top. With a single tug he untied the bow at her back. He kissed her once more leisurely, as if to savor each tiny moment and heighten their pleasure by prolonging the anticipation. At last he drew back and lifted the wisp of fabric over her head. He gently rolled her to her back, swept his fingers over her bare breasts and down the curves of her waist, then nimbly removed her bikini bottoms.

She lay submissive beneath him, marveling over her lack of embarrassment. Never in her life had she felt such pride in her body. A thrill raced through her under Kyle's impassioned gaze.

"You're a goddess," he whispered, eyes shining with tenderness and delight. With loving fingers he traced the inside of both her thighs, and she caught her breath as he ruffled the trimmed section of curls above.

She looked at his sleek masculine body, his powerful chest, his muscular legs, and the dusting of wiry hair over his smooth skin. "You're beautiful," she said. "All day I've wanted to touch you, hold you."

A smile twitched his lips as he lay suddenly still beside her, propped on one elbow. "Please. Feel free."

Hesitantly, she ran her fingers through the soft hair that covered his upper chest, then sifted down through the satiny trail toward the dimple of his navel and his hardened masculinity. She felt his stomach contract and heard his rapid intake of breath.

A sudden sound startled them both; they turned to find that a seagull had dropped to the sand a few yards away. Then, just as quickly as it had come, the bird spread its wings and darted away across the waves.

They shared a soft laugh. Kyle grasped her hand in his, turned it against his lips and kissed each one of her knuckles in turn. "Are you okay?" he asked softly. "Does it feel strange to be here with me, like this, on the beach?"

Did it feel strange?

No, she thought. *It feels right. Oh, so right.* His entire body spoke of his longing for her, and the fire burning within her

The Harrison Duet

told her how much she wanted him. The overhanging rocks sheltered them from view above, and the distant rolling surf played a melodious symphony beneath the canopy of the bright blue sky. It was as if this secluded, shaded alcove was meant for them alone.

"Do you want to stop?" His low voice was concerned.

She felt tears start in the comer of her eyes and a rush of affection welled in her throat. Twice now she'd told him to stop, forced him to leave when his desire for her was all too evident. Still, he was willing to call it off now if she was uncertain. She'd never met anyone so understanding or unselfish.

His eyes as they met hers were filled with a yearning that surpassed sexual desire. He wanted her. But not just her body. She knew he cared about her, that he was sensitive to her needs, her feelings. Her heart went out to him wholly.

"I don't want to stop," she whispered. "It's just been a long time. I think I'm a little nervous."

"Don't be. Relax. Enjoy the pleasure we can give each other."

Their mouths touched tentatively at first, as his fingers cupped one of her breasts and paid loving attention to its rose-colored peak. Her hands moved caressingly up and down his sides, acquainting themselves with the lean hardness of his hips and hair-roughened thighs.

Then their lips began to move faster, faster. Tongues delved, tasted, explored, driven by hunger and the need to fulfill their long-restrained passion.

Her hands roved down his back, cupped his firm buttocks and pulled him more tightly against her. She felt his urgent desire, like a shaft of velvet-covered steel, press hard against her thigh. He groaned low and deep in his chest as he kissed the corners of her lips, her cheeks, the length of her throat.

114

Their breath came in quick gasps now as their hands moved over each other without restraint, each caress becoming bolder, more intimate. His nibbling teeth against her sensitive neck brought every cell in her body to full jolting awareness. His mouth moved with seductive slowness across her shoulders, over the outer curve of her breast, then closed around the nipple aching with desire. She wound her fingers through his damp hair, held his head against her breast as he sucked sweetly, his tongue revolving tantalizingly around the taut bud.

His palm prowled across her ribcage and abdomen, then lower, and lower still. And then he was there. Questing fingers gently parted her thighs, sought, and found. Tremors shot through her as his fingers probed the pulsing source of her passion, mesmerizing her with their gentle accuracy. She writhed beneath him in ecstasy, a molten core of need, mindless to everything but the tributes his hands and lips paid her body.

I want you, I want you, her body sang. Now! Now!

With an impassioned groan, she curled her fingers around his hard biceps, pulling him up on top of her. There was no need to speak. Their eyes locked, communicating their mutual hunger more eloquently than words. With trembling fingers she reached down, encircled him, and guided him into the inviting silk of her body. She felt a sensation of piercing tightness, an injection of smooth liquid fire that blended with the flames raging within her, and she whimpered with joy and relief.

"Does it hurt?" he whispered against her lips, his eyes filled as much with passion as compassion. "Tell me."

"No." It did, but it was a welcome pain, and she knew it wouldn't last long. She moved against him, pulling him more

The Harrison Duet

deeply into her tight moistness. His body molded perfectly to hers, like two missing pieces of a puzzle finally joined.

"You feel wonderful," he whispered. "So soft. So warm."

The hurt gave way to a sweet, violent throbbing as she matched his body's rhythmic movements with her own, bringing him closer and closer to her center. She heard the call of a gull again, and the lulling sound of the waves seemed to surround her. She opened her eyes for an instant to glimpse the brilliant blue sky, then shut them again, nearly bursting with the joy of having him within her in this beautiful, magical place. Each thrust of his body sent her further and further into a realm of uncharted ecstasy.

Did it ever feel like this before? she wondered. Ever?

He moved harder, faster, until she felt her body tense with anticipation, vibrate with impending need. For an instant she froze, suspended in time, and then in a burst of light she broke free, her body pulsing with climactic shudders, which carried her high into the air.

She cried out, and moments later she heard his own soft moans, felt his entire body tauten as he gripped her and lost himself in his own release. She wrapped herself around him, her mind floating freely, her body reveling in his closeness and warmth. Then ever so slowly, they drifted together back to earth.

Many minutes passed as they held each other, panting to regain their breath. She opened her eyes and smiled into his. The corner of his mouth lifted up in a grin. He rolled them gently to their sides, bodies still clinging together, arms and legs entwined, tips of noses touching. She caressed his cheek lovingly with her palm, trying to memorize the texture of his skin, the exact slope of his nose, the angles of his cheek and jaw.

"I take it back, Kyle," she said at last, a teasing gleam in her eyes.

"What?"

"The plane ride today was only the *second* most thrilling experience of my life."

She felt her grin start just as his shoulders began to shake. Then, together, eyes shining, they laughed out loud.

Desiree awoke and stretched lazily. Memories of the night before filtered into her mind, filling her with a sense of complete contentment. A sleepy smile curved her lips as her eyes snapped open. To her dismay, the pillow beside her was empty. A sudden ache swept over her. Where was he?

A low, cheerful whistle and the smell of freshly brewed coffee drifted in from the kitchen. With a happy, relieved sigh, she relaxed beneath the covers and closed her eyes again.

It was a night she'd never forget. Just thinking about it made her pulse race with pleasure. They had returned from the island just before dark, still glowing from their passionate encounter on the beach.

"I could make love to you all night long, and it still wouldn't be enough," Kyle said later, after they'd taken a long, luxurious shower together.

She'd smiled alluringly. "Try me."

And so he did. They made love again and again, and each time was better than the last. He carried her to heights of ecstasy she'd never imagined were possible, all the while treating her with infinite tenderness and affection.

Sometimes, afterwards, they'd looked into each other's eyes and laughed, just as they had that afternoon, overwhelmed

The Harrison Duet

by the sense of pure joy that enveloped them. Other times they slept, enveloped in the warm cocoon of each other's arms, only to awaken in the moonlit darkness more filled with desire than before.

"How was I lucky enough to find you?" he'd said as he cradled her against his chest.

"I've never known anyone like you, Kyle. It's never been like this for me before."

"For me either. My lovely Desiree..."

Never in her life had she felt so cherished, so adored. He awakened desires within her she'd never believed existed.

"Touch me," he'd said. "There. Ahh, that's it. If you only knew how good that feels..."

Her marriage bed, she saw now, had been chaste and routine compared to the loving she shared with Kyle. It seemed there was no part of her body left untouched by the warm pressure of his lips, the magic of his fingers.

"Your skin is so soft. So smooth. So feminine. I love the way it feels here. And here."

"And you're so hard. Everywhere. Especially...here."

He chuckled softly. "Do you like...this?"

"Like it? Oh! Kyle..."

As she thought back over everything she'd said, every wanton thing she'd done, her cheeks flushed hotly. Was the woman who behaved with such unashamed abandon last night really *her?* Yes! And she'd loved every second of it.

Desiree threw off the sheet and darted into the bathroom. As she brushed her teeth, she grinned. She couldn't remember when she'd ever so looked forward to a new day. She'd slept very little; she ought to feel exhausted. Instead she felt completely revitalized.

Hearing footsteps in the hall, she returned to bed and propped herself up with her arms, watching the doorway where

118

morning sunlight filtered in through the sheer curtains. He stepped in quietly, wearing only his navy-blue bathing trunks and carrying a black leather garment bag. As she feasted her eyes on each well-sculpted muscle, each detail of the strong, masculine body she'd come to know so well, a shiver of pure delight ran through her.

All at once, it occurred to her that he was standing very still and was staring at her in much the same manner; and she blushed.

"Good morning," he said, his voice so low and rough she barely caught the words.

"Good morning." She glanced down briefly, suddenly aware of how she must look to him, with her tousled hair framing her face, her amber eyes still flushed with a sleepy-warm glow, and her naked body stretched out in full view. She reached for the sheet to cover herself, but he said:

"Don't."

His tone was soft, flattering, affectionate, disarming. She left the sheet alone.

He took a deep breath as if trying to reassemble his thoughts. Finally he said: "I hope you don't mind if I hang up a few things. This has been sitting out in the car for two days."

"Please, be my guest." She swung her legs off the bed and crossed the room to him.

He opened her closet, hung his garment bag inside. Unzipping the case, he moved two suits and shirts out onto the closet rod. They looked hopelessly wrinkled.

Her arms encircled his waist. "You can't wear those. We'll have to iron them."

"Don't worry about it. I have every confidence that they'll spring back to life by tomorrow."

"You think so?"

He drew her closer. "I do."

The Harrison Duet

"But what will you wear today?"

"The same thing you're wearing. Nothing."

"Nothing?"

"Absolutely nothing." He kissed her. "Mmmm. You taste minty."

"You taste delicious. Like coffee."

Kissing her again, he heaved a sigh of pleasure, then said, "By the way, I was right."

"About what?"

"We made love all night long, and it still wasn't enough." With an animal-like growl, he picked her up, set her down on the bed, and leaped on top of her.

"Wait!" she cried. "Kyle! We haven't eaten since lunch yesterday at the beach. I'm famished. I've got to eat something."

He smiled wickedly into her eyes. "I can think of something I'd like to nibble on right now. But...I'll settle for this." He pretended to take a bite out of her shoulder.

She writhed with laughter beneath him, finally managing to roll away and drop off the side of the bed. Taking a few steps backward, she grabbed her hairbrush from the dresser and brandished it like a weapon, her eyes flashing dangerously. "Come near me again and I'll strike where you'll most regret it."

He stood up and raised his palms. "Truce! I surrender. We'll take a food break. But first, I have to run."

"Run?"

He nodded. "*Run.* As in jog. You know, that's where you move quickly, one foot after the other, like this." He darted around the bed and grabbed her. Her scream ended abruptly as his mouth came down on hers. He kissed her soundly, then released her again. "Don't you ever run?"

"Yes," she said breathlessly. "Three mornings a week."

120

"So do I—at least I try to, but it rains so much in Seattle, I can't jog as often as I'd like. I want to make the most of your gorgeous weather while I'm here. Care to join me?"

His reference to his home town sent a stab of pain piercing through her, reminding her of how short their time together would be. Her smile wavered, but she resurrected it quickly. "I'd love to run with you. Let's put on some clothes."

They did warm-up exercises together on her living-room floor, then jogged through her neighborhood to a nearby park. She kept pace with him easily, enjoying the warm sunshine and the smell of the freshly mown grass. She gazed frequently at Kyle as they ran, trying to memorize the pleasure of this moment, to push the thought of his leaving out of her mind.

More than once during their lovemaking the night before, she'd wanted to burst out with a heartfelt *I love you, Kyle*.

She knew it now. She wasn't *falling* in love with him. *She loved him*. She felt it in every fiber of her being, knew it as surely as she knew the sun would set that night and rise the next morning. But how could she tell him?

His own whispered endearments had made her feel that she was as special to him as he'd become to her. But he'd never said he loved her—and why would he? They'd only known each other a few short days. As he'd pointed out, everything had happened at light speed between them. She didn't expect him to fall in love overnight, just because she had. Even so, that didn't make her feelings any less real, or do anything to soften the pain of their impending separation.

Let's just take things one day at a time, he'd said the other night. Was a few days together all he had in mind? After he left on Monday, would she ever see him again? *Of course you will*, she told herself. *Don't be ridiculous*. But when? How often? And for how long?

The Harrison Duet

It suddenly became a Herculean task to draw breath into her lungs as she ran. She wondered if he often spent weekends away from home this way. How many women had enjoyed the delights of his lovemaking, the passionate warmth of his embrace? *Don't think about it,* she cautioned herself. *Just enjoy the little time you have.*

After they returned and took a shower, they made breakfast together in her cozy kitchen. Kyle, his bare back magnificent above a pair of white tennis shorts, stood at the stove and cooked a fluffy omelet filled with mushrooms, cheese, and crisply fried ham. After throwing on a pale blue halter top and Hawaiian-print shorts, Desiree prepared freshly squeezed orange juice and toasted English muffins. They ate at her tiny kitchen table, crowded by the vase of red roses he'd sent three days before.

"Nice flowers," Kyle said as he speared a forkful of omelet. "Where'd you get those? Some love-sick fan?"

"Sick is not the word. The man's a maniac." She grinned at him across the table. "He hasn't let me sleep for the past four nights."

"Four nights?" His eyes narrowed with mock jealousy. "I can vouch for the fact that you didn't get any sleep *last* night. But what happened the three nights before?"

She reached across the table to caress his bare forearm. "Who could sleep after our first date, or after the way you kissed me the next night, when we got home from the beach? And on Friday, after our argument—"

"Let's not talk about that. It's past. Forgotten." He seized her hand in both of his and squeezed it. For a long moment he was silent, staring down at their interlocked hands atop the table. Suddenly he drew back with a frown, tapping his fingertips on the table. "Why do you have this awful table, anyway? What's it made of?"

122

"Formica."

"Why on earth do you have a Formica kitchen table? Everything else in this house is a beautiful antique."

He had a point. The table was stained, sported burn marks, and was cracked along one edge. Teasingly, she said, "You don't like my fifties-era pink Formica? What's wrong with you? It's a classic."

"Pink? What do you mean, pink? The table's white."

"It's pink."

He bent closer, staring at the tabletop. "Really? Pink?"

"Pink. Pale pink."

"It looks white to me." He shrugged, then shook his head. "Good grief, a pink Formica table. And I thought white was bad."

She frowned with feigned indignation. "This table's the height of chic. The epitome of class. Besides, it—"

"Was my great-grandmother's," they finished in unison. He rolled his eyes. She nodded.

"I think it's great you were named after her," he said, pointing his fork at her. "It's a beautiful name. But you didn't have to take every piece of furniture she had."

She laughed. "It *is* hideous, isn't it?"

"Why don't you get a nice table? Mahogany, to match your living-room set? Your dining room is practically empty."

"I never had any reason to buy another table. I don't have people over for dinner very often." She finished the last of her coffee and shrugged. "I've had to move so often, and I already have a lot of furniture. This table is sturdy, and I don't have to worry if it gets slightly banged up."

He frowned again, then said: "Does it bother you? Having to move all the time?"

"It comes with the territory. Radio's a part of me I can't give up. Moving is a condition I've had to accept."

The Harrison Duet

"What about now? They seem to love you at KICK. Do you think they'll keep you on indefinitely?"

"There's no such word as *indefinitely* in a radio station's vocabulary." She toyed with her empty coffee cup, finally lifting her eyes to his. "But I'm grateful to be here. I have a terrific job, and good jobs are hard to come by. I'll stay as long as they'll keep me."

He opened his mouth to speak, then seemed to think better of it. All at once he stood, walked around to her side of the table, and gently pulled her to her feet, holding her hands in his.

"What do you love most about being a deejay?"

"Everything."

"Everything?" He lifted one of her hands to his lips and kissed her palm. "Really?"

Considering, she amended her statement. "Well, admittedly, there *is* a burnout factor. After you've played and talked about the same song two hundred times, it's pretty hard to think up something original to say. Even so, it's—"

He dropped tiny kisses from her palm along the length of her arm, causing exquisite chills to shiver through her.

"It's what?"

She was finding it increasingly difficult to think. "It's... exciting, stimulating."

His lips reached her shoulder as he pulled her closer. When his tongue flicked over the sensitive spot at the side of her throat, she drew a deep, wavering breath.

"Stimulating?" he said softy.

"Yes. I can be beautiful on the air. I can stir people's imaginations."

"You don't need to go on the air for that. You're beautiful in person." He deftly untied her halter top at the nape of her

124

neck and tugged downward. The top dropped and her breasts flexed out to his admiring view. "You're stimulating," he added, pulling her into his tight embrace. With a gasp she felt the solid ridge of his masculinity burrow into her abdomen.

"And you definitely stir my imagination," he said as he covered her mouth with his.

"What do you do about clothes?"

"Clothes?"

Darkness had just descended. They'd spent the afternoon in and out of bed. Mostly in. They'd ignored the outside world, as if nothing existed but the two of them and the feelings they shared in this tiny, stolen moment in time. Since it had been too hot to cook, Desiree had made a chef's salad for dinner, which she'd served with the bottle of Chablis she'd put in the refrigerator that morning.

Now, their appetite sated, they relaxed together in the redwood swing on her back patio. The cool night air, perfumed with the scent of orange blossoms from the tree in her backyard, felt delightfully refreshing. They'd each donned shorts and a T-shirt, and Desiree wore the songbird pendant Kyle had admired on their first date.

She tipped the last of the ice-cold Chablis into the stemmed glass in Kyle's hand. "If you can't see certain colors, how do you know what clothes go together?"

"I don't. I have to rely on what the salesclerks tell me at the store, buy things as a set, and always wear them that way. I stick to gray, blue, and brown most of the time, so that even if I make a mistake about what goes with what, it won't look too horrendous."

The Harrison Duet

She was silent for a moment, savoring the wine's delicate aroma and dry, tangy taste as she pondered his dilemma. "It must be frustrating."

"At times." He grinned. "When I was a kid, my sisters used to laugh at me when I tried to adjust the color on the TV set. They'd mix up the clothes in my drawer so I wore things that looked ridiculous together. I still have a lot of trouble with socks, telling the dark browns from the blacks and blues."

"You need a wife to help you dress." The moment she said the words she regretted them. What a stupid thing to say!

His eyes opened wide. His eyebrows lifted. He studied her with earnest amusement. "Maybe I do."

She averted her eyes, cleared her throat. "It wasn't very nice, what your sisters did."

"I made up for it. One night when I was a senior in high school, the oldest four girls were sitting around the living room in bathrobes and curlers, with mud masks plastered all over their faces. They were in their teens at the time. I called a bunch of my friends and asked them to come over, guys they all had crushes on."

"Kyle! You didn't."

"I did."

Desiree burst out laughing. "They must have died of embarrassment."

"I was blacklisted for months."

"I guess they deserved it."

"I guess they did."

He sipped his wine, watching his fingertip trail along her shoulder and down her arm. A quiet sadness filled his eyes and his voice as he said suddenly, "I'm going to miss you."

His change of mood caught her off-guard and brought a lump to her throat. She looked away. Why was he bringing

126

it up now? She knew this was their last evening together, but she'd avoided thinking about it, the way one avoids thinking about the inevitable end of a wonderful vacation. You know it'll be over soon, and you'll have to go home. But you put it out of your mind. You don't let it spoil your fun.

"I'll miss you, too," she said softly.

"I wish things were different. I wish I didn't live so far away, that we could—"

"It's okay." Suddenly the wine tasted bitter. She set down her glass next to the swing. "You don't have to explain."

"I do. I want you to know how much this weekend's meant to me. You're a very special woman, Desiree. I care for you a great deal. It's not going to be easy going back, putting myself through the usual routine, knowing you're over a thousand miles away."

She pressed her lips together, not trusting herself to speak.

He drained his glass and set it down. Gently taking her into his arms, he caressed her shoulders and ran his lips over her hair. "I wish I could stay longer, but I can't. I've got an important meeting tomorrow afternoon. I have to leave first thing in the morning."

"I understand. I didn't expect you to stay longer." Her voice cracked and she inhaled a sobbing breath as tears welled up in her eyes.

"Don't cry, sweetheart. Don't cry."

"I'm not." She squeezed her eyes shut, swallowed hard, and willed the threatening tears to dissolve. "I knew we would only have a few days together. I tried so hard, at first, not to get involved with you because I knew it couldn't last. But I—"

He pulled back and stared at her. "Who says it can't last?"

"You know it can't. You said at the beginning, 'Let's take things one day at a time.' So I did. But let's be realistic. Where

The Harrison Duet

can it go from here? What kind of future could we build, with you firmly planted in Seattle, and me here?"

"We'll make it work," he said emphatically.

"How? How often could we see each other?"

"Weekends. Every single weekend. Plenty of couples who live in the same town don't see each other more often than that."

"Every weekend? How can we? It'd cost a fortune."

"Who cares? I'll pay for the airline tickets, the phone bills. I'll do all the traveling if you want."

"You can't fly down here every single weekend."

"I can and I will."

She shook her head. "We'll only make each other miserable."

"I expect to be miserable five days a week. But we're going to live gloriously on the weekends." He slid next to her, stretching one arm behind her along the back of the swing. Lifting the songbird pendant at her throat, he held it up to the moonlight and studied it appreciatively. "Nothing is going to keep me away from my beautiful songbird."

"Kyle—"

"By the way," he added, "I may have another excuse to come down here. Often."

"Oh? Why?"

"I flew down originally for a meeting with a potential client. While I was here, I took a look at a manufacturing plant in L.A. I'm considering buying it."

Her pulse quickened. "Really?"

"I expect to make a decision in the next week or two." He took one of her hands in his and squeezed it. "If I do buy the company, I'll be flying down for a week at a time, especially at first while things are getting set up."

128

A small flame of hope lit up inside her. Could it be true? A week at a time? Then the flame died down and a voice inside her cried, *What difference would it make? Someday you'd have to leave. Who knows where you'll end up? And you'll be back where you started.*

He cupped her cheek in his hand and caressed her with his gaze. "But no matter what happens, I'll be down here as often as I can to see you. Believe that."

A lone tear trickled down her cheek. "I do. I believe you mean it now." She grasped his hand, pulled it away from her face and held it in her lap. "But I don't see how it can last, Kyle. One of us will be hurt in the end."

He sighed in exasperation. "Desiree, didn't this weekend mean anything to you? Don't you care enough about me to even try to make this work?"

"Yes! I care about you!" she cried. "More than any man I've ever met. I wish more than anything that we could be together. I'll be miserable the moment you leave. But a long-distance relationship can't work. It's impossible."

"How do you know it's impossible? Have you ever tried it?"

"Yes."

"When?"

"When I left my husband!"

9

A tense silence reigned for several moments. Desiree stared straight ahead at the dark stretch of yard beyond the patio light's glow, unwilling to meet his gaze.

"Tell me, Desiree," he said finally, his voice soft and deep. "Tell me what happened."

She leaned her head back against the wooden swing beneath his outstretched arm. She sighed, then spoke in a low monotone.

"I met Steve the first night I arrived in Tucson to start a new job. He was an attorney, very smart, very successful. We hit it off right away, and before I knew it we were living together. One night, about six months later, we were out having a few drinks, and a friend of Steve's stopped by our table and asked us when we were going to get married. 'What's wrong with right now?' Steve said. I don't know when I've ever been so excited. I loved him, I really loved him, and he said that he loved me. He grabbed my hand and we got in his car and drove all the way to Las Vegas. We got married at one of those little chapels at two in the morning...you know the kind, where a justice of the peace reads a few well-memorized words, and his wife stands by in her bathrobe, smiling and yawning and wishing you luck."

She paused for a deep, trembling breath and pressed her palms together, bringing them up against her lips. "Anyway, things were great for a while, but then I lost my job. I applied at every station in Tucson but no one would hire me. Finally I got an offer from a station in Detroit. He didn't want to move, so...."

"You left," Kyle said softly.

She nodded. When had he taken her hand? She couldn't remember. But she realized he was holding it now, gently massaging her knuckles with his thumb.

"We tried to keep the marriage together. We visited back and forth on weekends every three or four weeks. Every penny we earned went to the airlines or the phone company. It worked out fine for several months, but then he missed a visit. Then another. He started having all kinds of excuses why he couldn't come, why I shouldn't come to see him. Business problems. This and that. Finally I discovered he was seeing someone else. It hurt so much—I was heartbroken. I was lonely, too, but I hadn't cheated on him. Then he called me one night...he didn't even have the decency to tell me in person. He wanted to marry her. He wanted a divorce."

"I'm sorry." A brief silence fell, then he said: "I understand why you had to leave, to go where the work was. But why wasn't he willing to move with you?"

"He was only licensed to practice law in Arizona. He'd built up a clientele. How could he leave? When it comes down to it, one person in a marriage has to be willing to move, to sacrifice their career if need be for the other. And I don't think that's fair to either one of them." *Which is why I can never marry again*, she wanted to say. But somehow she couldn't bring herself to voice the words.

His arms tightened suddenly around her. "I think when two people love each other enough, no matter what, they can always find a way to be together."

"It's not always so simple."

"It can be." He stroked her back and shoulders as he hugged her, while rocking the swing back and forth. She clung to him and buried her face against his neck.

"I don't want to go through that again," she whispered, knowing at the same time that she couldn't bear to let him go. "I'm not strong enough. It took years for my heart to knit itself back together, for me to realize I could survive on my own."

His lips moved over her shoulder, her neck, and she felt herself succumbing to his magic touch. "Desiree, you were hurt badly, I know, and I'm so very sorry. But you've got to let go of the past. What happened to you before isn't going to happen to us. It's not going to be easy...nothing worth having ever is. But we can't throw this away. Not before we've even tried."

He drew back and cradled her face in his hands, adding: "Give us time, sweetheart. Give us a chance to make things work."

Her eyes brimming with tears, she slid her hands around his neck and pressed her lips against his. His kiss was a warm, sure force. She felt his strength pouring into her body, filling her, making her new. Maybe, just maybe she was wrong. Maybe, somehow, they could make things work. At the moment she couldn't imagine how, but what did it matter? How could she possibly say goodbye to him, even if she wanted to?

"Sign here, please." The burly deliveryman extended a clipboard and Desiree dutifully signed her name.

It was Tuesday morning. Kyle had left before sunrise the day before, and Desiree had spent the day and night reliving their long weekend over and over in her mind, her body still tingling from the memory of his touch.

He'd called her at the station Monday afternoon, and again late that night when neither of them could sleep. They'd teased and tantalized each other over the phone with vivid descriptions of what they'd be doing if they were together. It had taken hours to fall asleep.

"You'd better let me carry this in for you," the deliveryman said. "It's pretty heavy."

A good five minutes later, she finally managed to pry open the top of the large, heavy carton. She turned the box to its side, pulled out the contents, and stood it upright on the hardwood floor.

It was a chair. A delicately carved mahogany chair with a straight back and steel-blue, floral tapestry seat, the kind that would be at home in a long line of matching chairs in an elegant, nineteenth-century dining room.

She loved it on sight. The smooth grain was stained a deep reddish color, the same shade as her credenza, the same shade as his hair. He must have seen it in an antique shop and known how much she'd like it. What a unique gift! How thoughtful! She ran her fingers along the highly polished rung across the back, touched to her very soul.

That afternoon, the hot line flashed in her control room at the station. Her heart leapt when she heard his voice.

"Hi, sweetheart. Miss me?"

"Yes! Oh, Kyle, the chair...it arrived this morning. How did you ever get it here so fast? I don't know how to—"

"Do you like it?"

"I love it! It's exquisite. Thank you."

"You're welcome. I wanted to make sure you liked it before I send the other one."

"What other one?"

"You can't just have one chair, for God's sake. It's a matched set or nothing." He chuckled. "I've got to run. I only had a minute between meetings. See you Friday night, right? Let's eat in. Can you cook?"

"What?"

"I asked if you can cook. The only thing I've eaten made by your two hands is a freshly squeezed orange, an English muffin, and a salad."

She laughed. "I can cook."

"Great. I'm dying for a home-cooked meal. And I'm dying to hold you in my arms. I'll see you at the airport. Bye."

She smiled at the phone long after he'd hung up. "He's crazy," she muttered to herself. "Absolutely crazy."

It took three-quarters of an hour for two deliverymen to set up the new dining-room table and five additional chairs Friday morning. The note that accompanied them read:

Hope your great-grandmother would have liked this. Love, Kyle.

Opened to its full oblong size with the two accompanying leaves, the gleaming mahogany table stretched majestically across the room. Everything about the table reminded her of Kyle. Its strength. Its beauty. Its polished sophistication. She knew she shouldn't accept such an expensive gift, but she couldn't send it back, either. It blended perfectly with her other furniture and suited the house as if made for it.

No wonder he wanted to eat in tonight, she thought with a grin as she frosted a dark chocolate layer cake later that morning. She popped a leg of lamb into the oven—his favorite food, he'd told her, lobster notwithstanding—and set the timer to start baking at four o'clock. After closing the table to a small oval, she covered it with a white lace tablecloth—the only cloth she possessed—and set out her best china.

When she picked him up at the airport after work, they flew into each other's arms as if separated five months instead of only five days. The aroma of succulent roast lamb enveloped her senses as they opened her front door, and he closed his eyes, savoring the delicious scent. When they finished eating, he proclaimed it the best meal he'd ever tasted, and promptly whisked the chef off to bed to show his appreciation.

The nights were long with loving, the days warm and fun-filled and far too short. Each morning they exercised and jogged. On Saturday they toured the immense *Queen Mary* and Howard Hughes's *Spruce Goose,* docked at San Pedro harbor. They wandered through the quaint Cape Cod-style harborside shops at Ports of Call Village, where Kyle bought her hand-woven Irish linen tablecloths to fit the table in two different sizes. They had dinner aboard the elegant *Princess Louise,* a cruise ship turned restaurant, and toasted a passing tugboat with raised glasses of icy champagne.

On Sunday they rented bikes and rode along the meandering paths at a large tree-shaded park a few miles from her house, then returned home with sunburned shoulders and noses. They made love in the hushed stillness of early evening, the setting sun glowing on their bodies through the open bedroom windows.

"I'm hungry," she said much, much later, as they lay face-to-face on the plush area rug in her living room, each wearing

The Harrison Duet

nothing but a smile. "I feel like I haven't eaten in four days." The brass table lamps on either side of her couch cast a warm glow on the frosty glass of iced tea they sipped together through separate straws.

"It's no wonder, after all the strenuous activity we've had this weekend," he said.

"Are you referring to daytime activity or nighttime?"

"Take your pick."

She laughed. "How many calories do you think we burned up last night? I should go check my scale. I've probably lost five pounds by now."

"Don't get too excited. You're going to gain it all back at dinner. What I have in mind is sinfully fattening." He kissed her, then jumped to his feet and disappeared into the kitchen.

"There's nothing decent in the refrigerator, unless you want leftover leg of lamb. We ate everything else for breakfast."

"I know," he called from the other room. "Let's order something in."

"Great!" A sudden craving seized her and her mouth began to water. *A thick, Sicilian-style pizza oozing with sauce and cheese, smothered with...* She frowned, shook her head. No. Not his style. A man who serves pâté and champagne and chocolate mousse on a beach picnic, who orders *canard a l'orange* and *salade Lyonnaise* in their native tongue, will not go for an everything-on-it pizza.

He returned with the Yellow Pages. Kneeling down beside her, he opened the book on the coffee table and flipped through the pages. "Is there a place around here that makes a nice, juicy pizza with a thick crust? I always go for The Works—but what do you like? Mushroom? Sausage? Olives? Pepperoni?"

136

At her astonished expression he added, "What? Don't you like pizza?" His eyes narrowed and he wagged his index finger at her. "It's un-American not to like pizza."

She burst out laughing and threw her arms around his neck. "I adore pizza! I was afraid to admit it. I thought you only liked gourmet food."

"There's a time and a place for gourmet food, and a time and a place for junk food."

"That is so profound." She kissed him, still laughing. "Want to hear a secret? I'm a closet junk-food junkie."

His arms glided around her waist. "Really? A chocoholic *and* a junk-food junkie? I'm impressed. What's your favorite?"

"My favorite what?" Her hands combed adoringly through the silky short hair at the back of his neck.

"Junk food."

"Oh!" Her lips followed the movements of her fingers. "Well, a Big Mac of course. They put the greatest sauce on those things. A Big Mac, hot salty fries, and a chocolate shake."

She spread kisses down his neck, across his shoulder. His breath hissed in through his teeth.

"That's your favorite?"

"Yes...no, wait. Big Macs are my second favorite. My first favorite are S'mores. How I used to *love* those. I haven't had one in years."

He pulled her more closely against him. "What are S'mores?"

"You haven't heard of them?" She settled against him, loving the feel of his strong arms around her, the warmth of his skin. "We used to make them on Girl Scout camping trips." His mouth and tongue paid an inordinate amount of attention to the soft skin behind her ear, and she gasped, arched her neck, and closed her eyes as she struggled to continue. "You...

toast marshmallows over the campfire until they're hot and gooey, then squish them between two graham crackers and a square of chocolate. The...hot marshmallow makes the chocolate melt...sort of like I'm melting right now..." She heaved a deep, ragged sigh. "They call them that because they're so good, you always want S'more."

"I'll bet." He cradled her back over his arm as his mouth charted a fiery trail down her neck to the valley between her breasts. "I'll have to try one some day."

"What's your favorite?" she murmured throatily.

His hand slid up the outside of her thigh, then swept over the curve of her hip to cup her bare bosom. "I always like a nice juicy...breast."

"I presume you mean...*chicken* breast."

"Presume all you like."

"That's not a junk food," she said hazily.

"It's not? What were we talking about? I got distracted." His lips closed around the object of his affection and he lowered her to the soft carpet.

"Kyle. Wait. The pizza...you forgot to order the pizza."

"The pizza can wait." He spread her thighs apart with his own and covered her with his warm, hard body. "Right now," he whispered huskily, "I want s'more."

Before sunrise Monday morning he sat on the edge of her bed, dressed in a dark blue three-piece suit as he kissed her goodbye.

"I wish you'd let me take you to the airport," she said as she held him fiercely against her chest.

"There's no point. You'd only be stuck in morning traffic." He stood up. "I've got a busy week of negotiations coming up. I may not have time to call every night."

"Okay."

"I'll miss you."

"I'll miss you." She couldn't stop the tears that trickled down her cheeks. Damn! She didn't want to cry every time he left, didn't want him to see her this way.

He leaned down and kissed her again. "I need you, Desiree," he whispered. She watched him go through a blur of tears.

It was the longest week of her life. She bought a stack of cards at a stationery store and sent him one each morning. Tuesday she sent him a cuddly, stuffed toy lobster of plush red velour, as big as a bread box, which she found in a children's boutique. *I'm hungry for you*, her note read.

She didn't hear from him all day. When she tried calling him at the office, his secretary said he was tied up in meetings, and he didn't return her call.

Wednesday she had a mixed flower arrangement sent to his office, with a note saying, *Let's do business together*. She called him that afternoon, but their conversation was cut short soon after he thanked her for the flowers.

"I'm sorry I haven't called, honey," he explained. "I've been wining and dining clients all week. I'm in the middle of negotiations for an important contract and I just don't have time to talk."

She sat on the edge of her bed Thursday night, fresh from a shower, about to apply polish to the second to last toenail, when the phone rang. She jumped to her feet and grabbed the receiver, the nail-polish brush still in her hand.

"Hi, lover." The deep vibrant voice never ceased to send delicious shivers up her spine.

The Harrison Duet

She smiled radiantly into the receiver. "Hi. I miss you. I can't wait to see you tomorrow."

"I miss you, too. And thanks for the stuffed lobster. Didn't do a thing for my appetite, but he's cute." He paused. "Listen, Desiree. I've got bad news."

Her stomach tensed. The radiant smile disappeared. "What's wrong?"

"I expected these negotiations to wrap up today, or by noon tomorrow at the latest, in time for me to catch my flight. But there's no way that's going to happen. The client refuses to budge on his price, and I'm not going to give this thing away. We need at least three, maybe four more days. They've got a bunch of guys here from Cleveland who don't want to fly home for the weekend and come right back. We've agreed to work Saturday and Sunday to get this thing done."

"Oh." She sank down onto the bed. A hot flash of disappointment coursed through her, touching every limb, every nerve. She tried to stab the nail-polish brush back into the mouth of the tiny bottle, missed, and stabbed again. The bottle tipped over and rolled off the nightstand, trailing Passion Pink along the hardwood floor into the bathroom. Tears of hurt and frustration burned behind her eyes.

"I'm sorry, sweetheart. The last thing I wanted was to spend the weekend locked up in a conference room, haggling with a bunch of cigar-smoking men. But I have no choice. I'd like to turn it over to my negotiating team, but I've got two new people and I can't afford any screw-ups. The deal's too important. Please don't be angry."

"I'm not angry." The words shot out sharply, like an expletive. Steve's excuses for not coming to see her were always just as crucial, just as plausible, and always at the last minute. She believed him right up to the bitter end.

140

In the past week apart, did Kyle come to see the futility of their relationship? Was this his way of letting her down softly? *No*, her brain insisted. He was telling the truth. He had to be. Two tears spilled down her cheeks and she sniffed.

"Hey. Hey," he said softly. "It's only one weekend. I'll be there next Friday, on the same flight I planned to take today. All right? You'll meet me?"

"I'll meet you."

They were silent for a moment. She clutched at one last hope. "What about the manufacturing plant you were looking at down here?" At least if he buys it, she thought, he'll have to fly down here once in a while. "What did you decide?"

"The prospects didn't look good. I decided against it. I'm looking at a company in Tulsa, Oklahoma, instead. I have to fly out there next week."

She stifled a gasp of disappointment. Tulsa. Would he meet another woman there, and spend the weekend the way he did with her? *Don't be ridiculous*, she told herself. *He cares for you!*

When he spoke again his voice was low, deep, rusty. "Desiree, I miss you. I can't begin to tell you how much. I'm sorry I can't be there tomorrow but I'll make it up to you. I promise."

They said goodbye, and Desiree knelt down, retrieved the half-empty bottle of polish, and began to clean up the spill. *I promise*. How many times had she heard those two words from Steve? Promises were so easily made, and so easily broken....

She shook her head firmly, determined not to let such gloomy thoughts take over her mind. It was just one weekend, not the end of the world. This was Kyle, not Steve. They would get through this. Everything was going to be okay.

She found solace and pleasure in reading and working in her garden, pursuits she had always thoroughly enjoyed on

The Harrison Duet

her own before she met him. But somehow, they were no longer quite as enjoyable. Each time the phone rang she jumped to answer it, disappointment piercing through her with razor sharpness when it wasn't Kyle.

You'll see him Friday, she reminded herself. *He will come.*

She got through the next day at work, and the next. Her calm voice and brittle smile masked the lonely ache that wrenched at her heart. Wednesday night he still hadn't called. She lay down on the bed and closed her eyes, her mind full of vivid memories of their lovemaking. The room echoed with remembered laughter, electric touches, softly whispered endearments.

She blinked open her eyes, wishing she could make him magically appear in the doorway. But the doorway was empty.

From that moment at Catalina Island when she'd first acknowledged her burgeoning love for him, the feeling had grown and blossomed until every filament of her being seemed to shine with newly found sustenance from within. She felt as if he was her missing other half, a part of herself she hadn't even known had been lacking. Could she ever again feel completely happy or whole without his warmth, his caring, his sharing? She doubted it.

Yet she still didn't know if he loved her. She could see deep affection in his eyes every time he looked at her, feel it in his touch every time they made love. But he'd never said the words.

Did he love her? Could there be any kind of future for the two of them? Or would it always be like this...a few glorious weekends, with long stretches of lonely disappointment in between?

Why? Why? she asked herself silently as she covered her face with her hands. *Why did I do this to myself again?* Why did

142

I let myself fall so deeply, so hopelessly in love with him, when I knew this would happen?

"When I said I wanted a hot and sizzling evening," Desiree said into the mike, "I wasn't referring to the temperature outside." She mustered every ounce of vigor to spice up her voice. "Let's hope the thermometer takes a nose dive in the next hour or so because this city is sweltering. Right now it's ten minutes before six o'clock on this Thursday afternoon and I'm Desiree, getting ready to sign off. Coming up is Dave Hamilton and thirty minutes of non-stop music on KICK 102. Catch you tomorrow, same time, same place."

Pulling off the headphones, she stood up and wearily shook out her long curls. She filled in the broadcast log with all the promos she'd played and did a little end-of-the-day housecleaning in the studio, then cued up an especially long, sentimental love song which matched her mood. Slumping on the stool, she toyed with the frayed white edge of her cutoffs and closed her eyes as the lyrical, feminine voice sang out softly, sadly:

"We're on opposite shores, but lover I'm yours, Come take me away...I'm lost in your arms, fall prey to your charms, when you hold me that way..."

The studio door opened. "Hi," he said softly.

"Kyle." She realized she'd whispered his name aloud, heard agonized relief in her voice as she jumped off the stool and threw herself into his arms.

Desiree opened her eyes. The room was as empty and lifeless as before. She breathed in deeply and shut her eyes

The Harrison Duet

again, losing herself in the scene that unfolded in her imagination:

He took her in his embrace, capturing her mouth with his.

"I've thought of nothing but you since I left. I could hardly eat. Sleep." He covered her face and neck with kisses. "I've missed you so much. I missed holding you, touching you. I couldn't forget what you feel like. It tormented me, day and night."

A delicious warmth penetrated her body. She hugged her arms to her chest as the soft, sweet words of the song swam around her, through her:

"I tremble like a child, a fire burning wild, you bring out the woman in me..."

His mouth feasted on hers. Their tongues met, skirmished. She tightened her arms around his neck and swayed against him. He reached down with two hands, undid the snap and zipper of her cut-offs. In a few swift movements, he removed the clothing between them and pulled her down to the floor with him. She gasped but made no move to protest. At his lightest touch she shuddered with desire.

"I want you so badly, I love you so madly, take me now and set me free..."

The studio door flew open. "Move over, gorgeous, it's my turn."

Desiree blinked, refocusing glazed eyes as she struggled to return reluctantly to the present. Dave, the slightly balding deejay on the evening shift, towered above her.

"Were you asleep?" he asked.

"No. Just...daydreaming."

"You've been off in a fog ever since the day that boyfriend of yours showed up in his fancy Maserati."

"He's not my boyfriend."

"No?" Dave peered at her, his forehead furrowed with apparent surprise and concern. "You didn't break up, did you?"

"No."

He shrugged, but seemed a bit confused. With a side glance at the promo log on the counter, he added, "Good thing you've been filling this thing in. Can't afford any mistakes now."

She slid off the stool, grabbed her purse, and leaned against the counter, her mind still in a daze. "Why? What do you mean?"

"Didn't you hear? Old man Westler's planning to put this place up for sale. Retire."

She snapped back to reality now with full force. "For sale? When?"

"Don't know. He hasn't made any announcements yet. It's just a rumor going around—but I've found *that* kind of rumor usually turns out to be true."

A wave of fear flooded her body. Was the station going to be sold? New owners were notorious for doing major overhauls, firing everyone and starting over from scratch. She bit her lip. "I was miserable enough without hearing that kind of news, Dave."

"Well, cheer up. It might not happen, and if it does, let's hope we both get to stay. Right now it's time for you to split, so git." He sank onto the stool and picked up the headphones. Jerking his thumb over his shoulder, he added, "By the way, there's something waiting for you in the parking lot."

She stared at him blankly. "Something waiting for me? What?"

The Harrison Duet

Dave waved an impatient arm, "Go see for yourself, woman!" He flashed her a knowing smile. "I'll give you one little hint. It's not a Maserati."

10

Desiree punched open the studio door. What was waiting for her in the parking lot? If it wasn't Kyle, then who or what could it be?

She raced down the hall and through the reception area, then threw open the double glass exterior doors. The dry heat seared her skin after the air-conditioned interior of the station, but she hardly noticed. She turned the corner of the building to the asphalt parking lot, then stopped dead in her tracks.

Parked across and in front of her car and three others, a sleek, white Cadillac stretch limousine gleamed in the late afternoon sun. A tall man in a dark suit stood beside it, his hand resting on the back door handle.

"Ohh!" she cried aloud. What did Kyle do? Send a limo to take her to the airport, so she'd fly up to see him? But…she couldn't go. It was only Thursday. She had to work tomorrow.

She took a few tentative steps forward.

"Miss Germain?" the man asked.

She nodded. He opened the door, gestured for her to step inside.

The hell with it, she decided. Be spontaneous. Respond to the moment!

She flew to the door, bent down, and slid inside onto a soft, leather seat. Long arms immediately scooped her up,

147

The Harrison Duet

drawing her against a broad chest, and warm, familiar lips came down on hers.

Desiree's eyes opened wide with surprise and met Kyle's twinkling green ones. She let out a cry of pleasure as her arms came up around his neck. Vaguely she heard the car door shut, another door open, and the motor start as Kyle hooked a hand under her legs, lifted her across his lap, and settled her between his thighs.

"What are you doing here, you crazy man?" she whispered against his lips.

"I couldn't wait until tomorrow." His mouth rained kisses across her cheeks. "I couldn't stay away another day."

They kissed long and deeply, holding each other tightly, drinking of each other as if dying of thirst. The car moved forward. She ran her hands across his wide shoulders, his back, his ribs, reacquainting herself with each hard, familiar muscle, bone, and sinew.

"I missed you," she whispered when she was able. "God, I missed you. I thought I'd die."

His hands roved her body, slipped under her snug-fitting T-shirt, to glide up the smooth, soft flesh of her back. "I'm sorry I wasn't here last weekend. I'm sorry I haven't called. I came straight from Tulsa. I've been there all week, negotiating a major contract. I barely had time to eat or sleep."

"I'm so glad you're here." She hugged him. Hard. "I'm sorry if I sounded angry that night on the phone. I was just so disappointed. I wanted you so much."

"I wanted you, too." He kissed her again, then cuddled her against him.

"How long can you stay?"

"Only tonight."

She tilted her head back, mouth opening in dismay. His reddish-brown hair was brushed back from his forehead in neat waves, and he looked even more handsome than she remembered. "You flew down here for just one night?"

He nodded. "I left the negotiations to the rest of the team this afternoon. Looks like things will wrap tomorrow in Tulsa, so I'm heading back to Seattle first thing in the morning."

She sighed sadly, then leaned her head on his shoulder, wrapping her arms around his chest. "I won't think about it right now. I'm going to enjoy every precious minute we've got."

She took a moment to glance about the interior of the car. Wide, leather seats faced each other across an expanse of dark grey carpet. A small television was built into the textured leather wall on one side, along with a stereo receiver. Above it, a tiny bar held a row of crystal glasses engraved with the Cadillac logo. A phone hung on the opposite wall, beside a magazine rack. The green neck of a bottle poked out from an ice bucket at their feet.

"This is incredible," she breathed, then turned to him. "You remembered what I said that night, didn't you? About the limo?"

"I did."

She glanced down at her denim cutoffs and the lavender T-shirt that hugged her curves, silk-screened with the KICK logo in black and silver. "I feel terribly underdressed. If I'd known I was going to ride in a limousine tonight, I would have worn my electric-blue silk dress."

"You mean the one that's—"

"Open in the back, cut just off the shoulder, terribly chic," they sang out in unison. It had become a standing joke with them, and they laughed.

"Don't worry. For what we're about to do, you're dressed perfectly."

For the first time, she noticed he wasn't wearing his usual three-piece suit. Instead, he'd dressed casually, in a cream-col-

The Harrison Duet

ored polo shirt and blue jeans that fit like old friends—snug across the hips, and whitewashed at the seams and pocket edges. His running shoes looked well-worn, white fading into gray.

Her eyes narrowed curiously. "Where are we going?"

"You'll see. This night is for you." He squeezed her hand. "You're going to see all your fantasies come true."

"All my fantasies?" she repeated in amusement.

He nodded, grinning. "First, a stop at your favorite restaurant."

There were two or three elegant restaurants in the area that she was particularly fond of, but she didn't remember specifying a favorite, and they were underdressed for any of them. Since he refused to elaborate, she sank back into the seat with a resigned sigh and enjoyed the ride. A few minutes later, the limousine pulled up to a McDonald's and parked in front of the door.

"You've got to be kidding!" she squealed, nudging him in the ribs. "A limo to take us to McDonald's?"

He just smiled with delight.

The driver stepped to her side of the car, opened the door, and helped her out. Once inside, Kyle ordered five Big Macs, three large orders of fries, and a chocolate shake.

"Someone's joining us?" she asked.

"No, it's just the two of us. You did say these were your favorite?"

She nodded with helpless laughter. "I did."

"I don't want you to go hungry. Anything else?"

"No, thank you. This'll do just fine."

A pleasant-looking man with silvery hair stepped in through the door, accompanied by a woman of about the same age. They both looked over their shoulders. "Whose do you think it is?" the man whispered, gesturing toward the waiting limousine.

The woman searched the faces in the crowded room as they stepped behind Kyle and Desiree in line. "I don't know. I don't recognize anyone famous. Seems funny to see it here. Maybe—"

"Look no further." Kyle put his arm around Desiree and faced the couple with a charming smile. "No famous faces here tonight, folks, just a famous voice. This is Desiree Germain from KICK-102 FM."

Desiree felt her knees grow weak. Famous voice? She wanted to sink into the floor and disappear. But to her surprise, the man's eyes widened with recognition and apparent admiration.

"No kidding? You're Desiree?" The man clapped his hands together. "Well, what do you know. I listen to you all the time!"

"So do I," said the woman at his side, who was now beaming with excitement. "And so does our son. He especially loves your show."

Desiree's face lit up with a heartfelt smile. Instinctively, she held out her hand. "Thank you. It's so nice to meet you."

The man shook her hand with enthusiasm and introduced himself and his wife. "I'm honored to meet *you*. Really honored. Wait until Ron hears about this!" He grabbed a napkin from the dispenser on the counter and pulled a pen out of his pocket. "Would you autograph this for—for my son, please?"

"Sure."

She wrote "Life's a KICK at 102 FM" and signed her name. The couple were clearly thrilled. Several other people came forward and clamored for her autograph. It seemed as if she'd signed a dozen napkins and placemats when Kyle finally

The Harrison Duet

grabbed her arm and steered her out the door with their bags of food.

She leaned back against the seat, incredulous, as the limo pulled away. "I can't believe you told them who I was."

"Why? You're a celebrity. Don't tell me no one's asked for your autograph before."

"Only a few times. People don't usually recognize me by my voice. And I don't go around introducing myself so brazenly, the way you did."

"You should. It'd be great publicity."

Where had she heard that before? Barbara. The day the woman from some restaurant had called and asked her to emcee their opening party. Suddenly Desire wanted to do that kind of party, lots of parties, wanted to get out and meet the people who listened to her on the radio.

"I feel so fantastic when you're here," she cried happily. "You make me feel like anything is possible."

His eyes shone with tender admiration. "Only because it is."

The driver took them to the mile-wide, tree-shaded park where they'd ridden bicycles two weeks before. Kyle handed the McDonald's bags to Desiree. He pulled a bulky canvas bag out of the trunk, threw the strap over his shoulder, and grabbed the ice bucket. "We'll be back in a while," he told the driver. "I hope you brought a good book to read."

The driver chuckled and signaled goodbye with a courteous wave.

Kyle put his arm around Desiree and gave her a squeeze. "Follow me."

The sun hung low in the sky, bathing the lush green lawns on either side of the bike path in warm, golden light. They followed the path until it curved around a small lake, and climbed up a short hillside to a grassy knoll. He stopped

152

beside a picnic table and set down the canvas bag. A cement fire ring stood in a clearing a few yards away.

Kyle pulled out a red plaid blanket and shook it open. "I hope you like dining alfresco. This spot was crucial for phase two of my plan."

"Phase two?"

"You'll see."

"You *always* say that." Desiree helped him spread the blanket on the grass. "Well, if your Picnic in the Park is anything like your Day at the Beach, I'll *really* be impressed."

"Oh yeah?"

"You're a master of creativity when it comes to picnics. Not to mention other out-of-door...activities."

Laughing huskily, he put his arms around her and drew her close. She met the warm look in his eyes, and felt her throat constrict with an overpowering rush of affection.

"It's been a long two weeks, hasn't it?" he whispered.

"It seemed like two years." Her heart pounded as his lips nuzzled the softly curling hair at the side of her neck. She wanted to melt against him, to wrap her arms around his neck, to tell him how much he meant to her.

Kyle, I love you, she wanted to say. But was this the right time? Would he feel pressured to admit to the same depth of feeling, or think she expected some sort of commitment in return? Before she could speak, his mouth came to hers in a quick, urgent kiss, and he withdrew.

"Let's eat while it's still lukewarm," he said gruffly. He grabbed the bags of food and sat down on the blanket.

Desiree took a deep breath, dropped down beside him, and crossed her legs, managing a smile. "Right. Let's eat."

The sun had descended below the treetops and the sky had turned a pale dusky grey by the time they finished the

The Harrison Duet

milkshakes, consumed two hamburgers each, and ate most of the French fries. Several yards below them, a flock of ducks gathered at the water's edge, bobbing about expectantly.

"Let's throw them a hamburger bun," Kyle suggested.

Desiree plucked off the top bun from the remaining burger and scrambled down the incline. Kyle followed. They both ripped the bun into small pieces and tossed them into the water near the shore.

"Here, little quackers," he said.

The ducks made grateful noises as they darted toward the food. When they'd flung them the last piece, Desiree raised her palms. "Sorry. All gone." Disappointed, the ducks turned tail and glided away across the silent water.

Kyle took Desiree's hand in his and led her back up the slope. "Okay. Main course is finished. Leftovers dutifully disposed of. Now, for dessert."

Drawing out several small logs from the canvas bag, he arranged them in a pile inside the cement fire ring, on top of the paper trash from their dinner.

"Why a campfire?" she asked, crouching down beside him.

Casting her a mischievous grin, he lit the fire and fanned it to life with an empty styrofoam carton. All at once she realized what he must be up to, and she drew an astonished breath.

"S'mores?" she cried. "But how—"

"Phase two of Your Fantasies Come True." Kyle dug out several additional items from the canvas bag and placed each one in her arms with a flourish. "One bag of marshmallows. One box of honey graham crackers. Two extra large bars of chocolate. And two specially modified coat hangers."

She laughed her delight and would have hugged him if her arms hadn't been full. "How did you remember the ingredients?"

154

His eyes twinkled. "I didn't. But I have five sisters, remember? It seems a loyal Girl Scout never forgets how to make a S'more."

A refreshing summer breeze blew across the lake, cooling the evening air. They sat close together on the hard-packed earth, toasting handfuls of marshmallows to a golden brown over the glowing embers. She showed him how to squeeze the hot marshmallow and squares of chocolate between two graham crackers. When he pressed the crackers too hard, she leaned forward and licked the molten white goo that squeezed out the sides. They laughed, kissed, and passed the sweet confections back and forth until their hands were sticky and their faces were streaked with charcoal.

"Happy?" Kyle asked when they'd consumed as much as they could stand. Darkness was fast approaching now. The park was lit only by the last rays of sunlight and the glow of a few well-placed pole lamps. "Feel indecently indulged?"

"Yes," she sighed contentedly.

"Good." He brought her back to the blanket and pulled her down beside him. "It's time now to indulge one of my fantasies: sipping Perrier Jouet in the park at sunset with the girl of my dreams."

He withdrew a slender bottle from the ice bucket, then proceeded to open it. Delicate white flowers were hand painted on the dark green grass. Desiree knew an expensive bottle of champagne when she saw one. "Wow, this must be a special occasion."

"It is. It's the three week anniversary of the day we met." He retrieved a champagne glass from the bucket, filled it, and lifted it to her lips. She sipped.

"Mmmmm. Delicious."

The Harrison Duet

He brought the glass to his own lips and drank. Their eyes met and never wavered as they passed the glass back and forth, slowly finishing the tangy bubbling wine. Her heartbeat performed an erratic dance and she felt all at once enveloped in tenderness; it seemed as if her very soul would melt under the endearing affection she saw glowing in his eyes.

He set the glass aside, and murmuring her name, he collected her in his arms and sealed her mouth with his.

Warmth spread through her body like wildfire as she wrapped her arms around him, answering his kiss with all the fevered urgency in her heart. They sank down on the blanket and rolled to their sides, clinging together, mouth against mouth, tongue meeting tongue, her softness molding against his hard strength. His hands roamed down her back, over her buttocks, then up again to her shoulders as her hands tangled in his silky hair.

She swallowed his kisses like nectar, each kiss alternately filling her and increasing her thirst until she felt almost limp with desire. She lost pace with her breath, her blood spinning through veins that seemed delighted to swell and pump. Through the layers of their clothes she felt the heat of his body and of his desire, and that part of her which sought him throbbed in joyous response.

He left her mouth to scatter hot open kisses across her cheek, along her jaw, to the softness of her throat. His chest moved in rapid sync against hers, and she felt his breath, moist and fragrant, against her ear. When at last he spoke, his voice was deep and rusty, caressing in its warm intensity.

"Desiree, I love you."

Tears welled in her eyes. She wound her arms around his back and held him to her, wanting to heighten their contact, to prolong it for all eternity. "I love you, too," she whispered.

156

He rolled with her to his back and kissed her again, long and lovingly, his hands stroking her hair. "If you only knew how much I've longed to say those words aloud. I fell in love with you the night we met. The very first night."

"So did I," she murmured against his lips. "I've wanted to tell you for such a long time, but I was afraid—"

"Afraid of what?" He smoothed the hair back from her forehead. "That I didn't feel as strongly about you as you did about me?"

She nodded. A tear spilled from her eye to trickle down her cheek as she saw his answering nod, and she understood that he'd harbored the same fears.

"It seems we've been holding back our feelings to no purpose." He smiled warmly, tracing a fingertip across her lips. "But there's nothing to stop me from saying it now. I love you, Desiree. With all my heart. I love you."

A radiant smile curved her lips and she pressed her mouth against his in a soft kiss. "I love you," she whispered. "I love you. I love you. I love you!"

She punctuated each tender admission with a kiss at the corners of his lips, on his chin, his nose, his eyes, his forehead. She rested her cheek against his, slowly drew it across the scratchy pull of his day's growth of beard, then covered the roughened skin with small kisses.

The depth of her emotions coursed through her, filling her with such joy that she couldn't help laughing out loud. He hugged her to him, laughing in return. It felt so good to have him here, so wonderful to be in his arms, so right to be able to show—and voice—her love this way.

He rolled her to her back and cupped one of her hands in his. Bringing her fingers to his lips, he gazed down at her,

The Harrison Duet

his eyes a mirror of the love she knew must be shining within her own.

"I don't want to leave you, ever again," he said. "Not even for a day. I want to share the rest of my life with you, to have you by my side, with me always. Desiree, will you be my wife? Will you marry me?"

11

Ten seconds dragged by as Desiree lay still beneath him, her mind in a whirl of confusion. His proposal astonished, flattered, and thrilled her all at the same time. On the one hand, she wanted to jump to her feet and shout, *Of course I'll marry you!* But on the heels of this joyous possibility tread the painful wrench of reality, keeping her earthbound.

"I love you," she said finally, as she reached up to caress his cheek. "More than I'll ever love anyone. And I would love to be your wife. But how can we get married? Where would we live?"

"That's something we'll have to figure out. Would you consider moving to Seattle?"

Disappointment coursed through her. She could hardly believe he was asking her this. All the times they'd discussed this dreaded subject, hadn't he been listening? She rolled out from under him and sat up with a sigh. "Kyle, we've talked about this. You know how important my career is to me. I—"

"I know," he cut in, "and—"

"Wait, let me finish. Let me explain. I've wanted to be a deejay ever since my seventh birthday, when my grandpa gave me my first transistor radio. I used to lie awake at night, dreaming up the things I'd say and do on the air. My voice is my biggest asset. The personality I've created on radio is an important part of me. Radio is my *life*. I couldn't give it up."

159

The Harrison Duet

Kyle sat up and grasped both her hands earnestly in his. "Desiree, I respect your talent. I admire you. Don't you realize that? Your career means as much to me as it does to you. I'd *never* want you to give it up. Never."

"But I'd have to if I married you."

"Why? That's ridiculous. Why can't you have both marriage and a career? I know this is a lot to ask, since you're doing so well here. You have fans...boy do you have fans!" He grinned, and she knew he was thinking of the scene earlier in McDonald's. "But a talent like yours would be welcome anywhere. I'm sure you could find a job in Seattle. Any decent station would snap you up, especially after the rave reviews you've gotten lately in the newspaper."

"It's not that easy. Good jobs like mine are hard to find, especially for women. And I have definite goals for myself. Some day I'd like to do animation, voice-overs, commercials. Southern California's the best market for that."

He frowned. "Seattle might be a smaller market, but I'm sure you could find opportunities there, too. And in five years, maybe ten, who knows? You might even find yourself managing a station."

"That'd be great," she admitted. "I'd love to have that kind of control. But the basic problem *now* still remains: as a radio jock, no matter I'm working, there's no guarantee how long it will last. Even if we start out in the same city, at some point I'd have to move away."

"That's a bridge we'll cross if we come to it. It's no reason not to get married."

She chewed her lower lip pensively. Was he right? Had she been clinging to that same, old excuse far too long? Was it time to move forward, to take a risk, to believe in the possibility of a future together? Suddenly, she remembered what Dave had told her at the station earlier that day. "Kyle: I forgot to tell you. My station might be up for sale."

"Really? Why?"

"The owner, Adam Westler, bought the place as sort of a hobby a few years back. He made his money years ago in something else. Oil, I think. If he sells, there's no telling what will happen to me or anyone else at KICK. The new owner might not be so keen on female deejays. I could be out of a job in two seconds."

A grin spread across Kyle's face. "That's great! Then you'd have no reason to stay down here."

Desiree batted his arm playfully. "Hey, I'm talking about being fired. Whose side are you on?"

"Our side. I just want us to be together. I say, look for another job fast, before the station changes hands. You'll get a far better offer from another station if you have a good job behind you."

"I doubt it'll make any difference. Wages are tops here. There's no way any station in Seattle could come close to matching my salary."

"Who gives a damn about salary? I make more money than we will ever need. I'm talking about the *job*, the drive-time shift you want so badly."

"It'd be nothing short of a miracle if I was offered a drive-time shift in Seattle. I've never been there. I don't know anyone in the business."

"But I do."

"You do?"

He nodded. "I've done some heavy radio advertising for Sparkle Light in the past year." He laid her hand across his thigh and stroked it with gentle fingers. "I've been thinking about this for the past few weeks—I hope you don't mind. I know you would have done it on your own, but I took the liberty of making a few phone calls. I thought if I set something up, it would move things along that much faster."

Her eyebrows shot up. "And?"

"Ed Alder, the program director at KXTR in Seattle, is on the lookout for some new talent. He'd like to meet you. Do you have an audition tape?"

"Yes. It's about a year old, but still pretty good."

"Would you like me to deliver it to him? Do you want to fly up for an interview?"

Her heart beat faster. "I suppose I could—"

"Fantastic!" He drew her to her feet, squeezed her hands excitedly. "I'll give you the grand tour of Seattle. I'll even set up a dinner at my parents' house. You can meet my family. I've told them all about you. They're dying to meet you."

"Your family? Oh, no!" she laughed. "This is sounding more and more official by the minute."

"It *is* official." His arms encircled her waist and he kissed her soundly. "How soon can you get away? Can you fly back with me tomorrow?"

"Tomorrow?" She laughed, caught up in his enthusiasm. Even if she did find a job in Seattle now, how long would it be before she would have to move on? *Don't think about it,* she told herself. *Catch your moments of happiness while you can.* She coiled her arms around his neck, her heart turning over with love for him. "I have to work tomorrow. But I'm free for the weekend. I could take the evening flight. Can you set up an interview for Sunday?"

He hugged her fiercely. "You bet I can."

"Two dozen?" Desiree cried with delight as Kyle placed the enormous bouquet of red roses in her arms. The modern Seattle airport terminal still bustled with activity as she stepped off the plane at ten-thirty Friday evening.

"You shouldn't spoil me like this," she added. "A dozen roses the day after we met. Now two dozen at the airport. What's it going to be next time? *Three* dozen?"

"Definitely." His arms closed around her, sandwiching the flowers between them. "Every bride should carry three dozen red roses in her bridal bouquet."

She smiled against his lips. "Don't go jumping to conclusions, Mr. Harrison. I agreed to meet you for the weekend, but I *didn't* say I'd marry you."

"You will, my beautiful lady." His lips meshed with hers in a loving kiss. "You will."

Through the wide, plate-glass windows in the terminal, Desiree caught a glimpse of tall, dark pine trees silhouetted against the black sky. It was a refreshing change to see a city airport surrounded by pines instead of palms.

"I see you have a thing about Maseratis," she said a short time later, after Kyle had loaded her small bag in the trunk of his silver sports car and spun out onto the highway.

He nodded as he shifted the Maserati into high gear and zoomed around slower traffic. "The only way to drive. I've managed to get ahold of one of these beauties every time I've flown into L.A., but I'm not always so lucky. You should have seen the crate I got stuck with all week in Tulsa."

When he described the many problems he'd encountered with his rented sedan, from a door that wouldn't open, to windshield wipers that wouldn't shut off, he was so comical in his delivery and so good-natured about it all that Desiree's shoulders shook and her eyes watered with helpless laughter.

The Harrison Duet

A short drive took them to an elegant condominium complex in a lovely, wooded area on the outskirts of town. The Tudor-style brick-and-stucco buildings, enhanced with dark wood trim, seemed to sprout up from the depths of a dense pine forest.

"How beautiful," Desiree said as she stepped out of his garage and breathed in the heady scent of the surrounding pines. "You'd never know we're so close to the city."

"A few more minutes down the freeway, and you're really in the countryside. You'd love it in winter. You can reach deep snow in practically no time." He unlocked the heavy, oak front door and led her inside, flipping on light switches ahead of them.

Desiree took a step down into the spacious sunken living room. Her shoes sank into the luxurious, champagne-colored carpet as she looked around her with awe. Books of every size and description and a myriad of art objects filled floor-to-ceiling teak shelves on two sides of the room, along with an elaborate stereo system, speakers, and a large television. Colorful modem prints hung over the long, blue-grey sofa and Danish teak end tables. Track lighting illuminated the room from beams in the vaulted ceiling. There was a brick fireplace, a built-in wet bar, and a long, dark-blue tile counter that passed through into an immaculate, modem kitchen with gleaming wood cabinets.

"It's wonderful, Kyle."

He dropped her suitcase by the door, then caught her hand in his. "It is now that *you're* here. Come on. Let me show you the rest." In addition to the living room and kitchen, the condo boasted a study, a cheerfully decorated guest bedroom and bathroom, a large master suite, a laundry room, garage, and a small fenced yard.

164

"I love it," Desiree exclaimed as Kyle rested her suitcase on a low table in a corner of the master bedroom. "But I have a confession to make. When you mentioned your house in Seattle, I never imagined a condominium. Somehow I expected to find an enormous mansion on five acres, complete with a circular driveway and an army of servants."

"A man on his own doesn't need a big, fancy house to rattle around in. This complex was a far better investment."

"You own the whole complex?" she asked in surprise, and then laughed. "I should have guessed."

"After we're married, it'll be different. We'll build the biggest, most elaborate house that money can buy."

"We will?"

"Yes." He pulled her into his arms. His mouth traveled up her neck to nibble at the soft skin behind her ear. "We'll get an architect to design the place to complement all your beautiful old furniture." His breath was a warm, moist vapor against her ear as his fingers brushed the sides of her breasts, then slipped around to the buttons on the front of her blouse. "We'll get rid of my modern stuff if you want. Build a huge, formal dining room for your new table." He opened first one button, then another, punctuating the action with each word he spoke: "We'll have a music room. Game room. Two offices. Country kitchen. A giant master suite complete with sauna and Jacuzzi bathtub, built around an indoor garden." He pulled apart the soft fabric and reached around to unsnap her bra. Then, with one hand splayed across the small of her back, he reached around with the other to cup her breast in his hand. "And five additional bedrooms. No, six."

"Six?"

"One guest room, and one room for each kid."

She gasped, as much from the effect of his nimble fingers as from his startling declaration. "Five children?"

"Well, that's negotiable." He laughed, slid his arms around her bare midriff and hugged her tightly against him. "I enjoyed growing up in a big family, and always wanted one myself."

Suddenly he drew back slightly, his voice deeply serious. "You do want children, don't you?"

"Very much. I don't know about five, but two or three at least."

He smiled. "As many as you want. And we'll hire a nanny and a cook to help take care of them while we're working."

"Sounds perfect. Almost too perfect. I think I'd be afraid of a life filled with so much...perfection."

"We can do it, Desiree," he said softly. "Together, we can do anything."

They gazed into each other's eyes for a time, and she felt as if time had crystallized around them, sealing them in a sweet, safe vault, where happiness was guaranteed to those who loved and hoped and worked hard and dreamed the same dreams.

"I always wished I had a twin sister," she said at last. "My mother used to console me by saying I'd grow up and have twins of my own one day."

"In that case you're in luck. Twins run in my family." His eyes danced mischievously. "And I can't think of anything I'd enjoy more than making children with you."

"Oh, no. It's raining." Desiree looked out the bedroom window the next morning to find a light drizzle falling from a gloomy grey sky.

"A little rain won't stop us from sightseeing." Kyle opened his closet and pulled out a pair of jeans. "I've got plenty of umbrellas. And I'll make you a dollar bet it stops by noon."

She tossed a pair of shorts and a few summer blouses onto a nearby chair as she rummaged through her suitcase for something warmer. Thank goodness she'd decided to pack jeans and a long-sleeved shirt after all. She hadn't even thought of bringing a raincoat—it was still summer.

"You're willing to risk a whole *dollar?*" she said teasingly. "What faith."

"It's my father's favorite saying. Every time he makes a dollar bet on something, he wins."

"*Every* time?" Desiree sat down on the edge of the bed to put on her sandals, then changed her mind and pulled on socks and tennis shoes instead. "This I've got to see. For a dollar, you're on."

By ten, the sky had cleared to a brilliant, cloudless blue. "I told you," Kyle grinned as they hopped into his car and headed for the wharf.

"I'm a believer," she replied, laughing. "I can't wait to meet your father. He sounds like a real character."

A weekend didn't leave much time for sightseeing, especially with a family dinner to attend that night and an interview at KXTR the next afternoon, but Kyle seemed determined to squeeze in as many sights as possible in the time allowed.

"Seattle was the last stop for prospectors rushing north to the Klondike in the gold rush of 1898," he explained as they walked hand in hand through the shops at Pier 70, a nineteenth century wooden steamship pier. They climbed the steep pedestrian staircase to Pike Place Market, a noisy, colorful profusion of sidewalk stalls overflowing with country

The Harrison Duet

produce, flowers, and seafood, then walked back down to the waterfront on Alaskan Way.

While Kyle waited for their take-out lunch of shrimp and clams, Desiree ducked inside a shop and ordered a bright green T-shirt for Kyle stamped with the slogan, THIS SHIRT IS GREEN.

"I'll get you for this," he laughed when she presented him with the gift. He dragged her to the water's edge, threatened to dunk her in the harbor, then drew her close against his chest instead. "Take that," he said, kissing her. "And that. And that." Despite the public place, despite the steaming fries and seafood growing cold on a nearby bench, the romantic punishment continued for quite some time.

Desiree loved the city. She loved the blending of old and new, the rustic waterfront and charming curiosity shops against the backdrop of modern skyscrapers just blocks away. She loved the crisp, clean air and the tall, green pines sprouting here and there and the blue, blue sky, more vivid and clear than any sky she'd ever seen. She was fascinated by the native Indian and Eskimo crafts, the folklore and totem poles, the nearness to Alaska, and the woodsy, carefree atmosphere that seemed to pervade the area.

At a curio shop, she bought an Eskimo rock carving of a bear devouring a wiggling fish. "It's a symbol of strength and power," she explained as they made their way back to the car. "Perfect for your desk at the office. Which, by the way, is the sight I'd like to see next."

"Which office? The one at Harrison Engineering in Auburn? Standard Tool and Die in Tacoma? Sparkle Light in St. Louis? Or maybe you'd rather see—"

"Stop showing off! I want to see your main office, in downtown Seattle."

168

A few minutes drive along city streets brought them to the tall, high-rise building that housed Harrison Industries headquarters on its top floor.

"I've only got a handful of people here to help keep an eye on things," Kyle explained as he gave her a swift tour of the simple suite of offices. Like his condominium, the furnishings and decor were modern and tasteful, a cheerful splash of color against stark white walls. "The important part of this corporation are the individual companies themselves. They only consult me for an occasional problem or an important negotiation. Mainly, I sit up here and run interference."

"What a view," Desiree remarked breathlessly as he led her into his office, a large airy room with a solid wall of windows overlooking the downtown area and Elliot Bay beyond. She stopped beside his wide desk, which was ringed with framed photographs of numerous grinning babies, grade school children, and five stunning young women. "Who are *they?*" she asked, indicating the women's pictures with a nod of her head.

"The kids? My nieces and nephews. Or were you referring to all these gorgeous, sexy women?"

She cast him a shrewd look filled with mock suspicion. "Well? Who are they?"

"Jealous?" His arms came around from behind her and he pulled her back against him, adding in a low voice, "They're my sisters."

"I figured."

"So you see, you have nothing to worry about." His voice became husky as he nuzzled her neck. "But I'm going to have something to worry about if we don't get out of here in a hurry. Unless you want me to make love to you right here on the floor of my office."

The Harrison Duet

"We can't," she replied softly, reluctantly. "Your parents are expecting us for dinner at six."

"True. And we don't want to be—" To her surprise she felt his body stiffen suddenly. His arm flashed out and grabbed a memo slip beside his phone. "This must have come in after I left last night." He stepped aside, picked up the phone, and rapidly punched a series of numbers. "I'll just be a minute."

Desiree moved to the windows to drink in the view while he conducted his phone conversation.

"Rand?" she heard Kyle say behind her. "What time did you get in? How'd things go?"

The sun gleamed on the windows of the city buildings below, which stretched out toward a sparkling blue bay. *Wouldn't I love to have a view like this every day,* she thought, *instead of the bleak, beige walls of my studio.*

"What?" Kyle cried. "You gave up our entire negotiating position. We can't break even on the contract now."

Desiree glanced at Kyle in alarm. He was leaning against the desk, one hand gripping the phone to his ear, the other curled into a tight ball at his side.

"Don't give me that," he said. "You knew where to call me. And I was back in the office yesterday at noon. Dammit, you gave the thing away!" He barked out a few cutting observations and then slammed down the phone. "Come on, let's get out of here," he muttered in her direction, before wheeling toward the door.

Desiree followed, her stomach knotting with anxiety. What had happened? Kyle brushed off her questions and barely spoke or glanced at her as they rode down the elevator and drove back to his condo to change their clothes for dinner. When he'd unlocked the front door and ushered her inside, he finally told her what was wrong.

170

"Because I left Tulsa early to see you," he said, stalking across the living room and down the hall, "because I left the negotiations in the hands of a bungling idiot, Standard Tool and Die just lost over a hundred thousand dollars."

She gasped in dismay. "A hundred thousand dollars! Why?"

Kyle stopped in the doorway of his bedroom and faced her. "The client put the pressure on while I was gone. Rand panicked. He lowered the price and gave away every cent of profit on the contract."

"Oh, Kyle. I'm so sorry." She reached out to touch him with a sympathetic gesture, but he broke both hand and eye contact with a swift turn and a deprecating wave of his hand.

"It's not the money. It's the *principle* of the thing. Two hundred people will be busting their butts to meet a deadline, and for what? We won't make a dime. We don't need busy work. What a *waste.*" He strode furiously into the room. "If I'd stayed and finished the job myself...damn! Rand ought to know what he's doing by now. If you can't trust your—"

He stumbled, uttering a sharp curse as he bent down to pick up something from the floor. A white leather sandal. Her sandal. He whirled on her, holding the shoe aloft. "Don't you ever put anything away? You've been here less than twenty-four hours and already the place looks like a pigsty."

His icy glare sent a cold wave of trepidation down her spine. Her eyes darted around the nearly immaculate room for evidence of her misbehavior. Her suitcase and vanity bag stood open on a low table. A few items of her clothing lay on the bed and on a nearby chair. A glass of water sat on the nightstand. Her other sandal lay smack-dab in the middle of the floor. But that was it. Not perfectly in order; hardly a pigsty.

The Harrison Duet

Her temper flared at his unjust accusation. "I'm sorry, Kyle, if I'm not neat enough for you," she said, her voice clear and even. "In future, I'll try to—"

His muttered curse silenced her. She winced as he picked up the second sandal, gathered up her scattered clothing, and threw it all into the suitcase.

"We've got fifteen minutes to get dressed," he hurled at her over his shoulder as he banged open the bathroom door. "I'm going to take a shower. Join me if you want."

"No thank you," she returned.

"Suit yourself." He slammed the door.

Desiree sank down onto the bed, heart pounding in pain and fury. Could this really be the same bed where they made slow, luxurious love that very morning? Could this be the same man who'd held her so tenderly in his arms, whispered words of love, and pleaded with her to be his wife?

She knew his anger stemmed not from a misplaced shoe but from the news of his negotiation gone wrong. And that was what hurt the most. If he hadn't left Tulsa a day early to see her, he'd have finished the negotiations himself and, no doubt, would have gotten the client to give up every penny of that hundred thousand dollars, and more.

She'd made him feel guilty for breaking their weekend date, and he'd ignored his obligations to appease her. If anyone was to blame for his company's loss, it was she.

She'd told him a long-distance relationship would be fraught with problems. Still, she hadn't expected anything so serious to happen, so costly, or so soon. Already she'd become a major thorn in his side.

With a heavy sigh, she unbuttoned her blouse, then folded it and the other clothes Kyle had thrown into her suitcase.

Taking her outfit for the evening out of Kyle's closet, she sat back down on the bed and clutched the hangers to her chest.

What timing, she thought. A family dinner. She had to go; it would be rude to back out at this point. But Kyle was barely speaking to her. How on earth would she get through it? *Smile*, she told herself. Be charming. Ask all the right questions, tell a few jokes, have yourself a great time. Don't let them see that you're hurting.

And leave. Tomorrow. On the first plane.

12

"You said this was going to be a small family dinner."

"It is. Just a few close relatives."

They'd finished dressing with a minimum of conversation and driven to a quiet residential area on the north side of town. She'd tried to tell him again how sorry she was. Sorry about his company's loss; sorry it had soured things between them. His answer had been a silent shrug. What more could she say?

Kyle parked at the curb near a charming, two-story, red-brick house, and helped Desiree out of the car. She counted seven other vehicles crowding the curb and driveway.

"How many relatives is a few?"

"Count your blessings," Kyle said in a clipped tone as he headed briskly up the curving, red-brick walkway. "My oldest sister and her four kids moved to Des Moines last year."

Desiree tried to ignore the irritation rising in her chest and concentrated instead on the heady fragrance of the rose bushes blooming vibrantly on either side of the path. Neat hedges and colorful flower beds surrounded a verdant, green lawn, and she noticed a long wooden swing, similar to the one she had at home, hanging from the porch rafters. The front door stood open behind an aging screen door, and she could hear laughing voices and bustling activity inside.

174

She readjusted the delicate combs that pulled her hair back on either side of her face. They were handmade and covered with tiny seashells. It seemed hard to believe that Kyle had just bought them for her on their carefree expedition that afternoon. The fluted neckline of her silky, midnight-blue blouse was embroidered in the same color with flowers in a cut-away design, and she wore steel-grey slacks and matching grey pumps. She'd packed the outfit with such high hopes, wanting to make a good impression on Kyle's parents.

"I hope I look all right," she said. Not that it mattered.

Kyle stepped up onto the porch without a backward glance. "You look fine."

"How would you know?" Desiree scoffed. "You haven't looked at me once since you stepped out of the shower."

He turned and threw an arm across her shoulder, pulling her against him. His voice sounded low and harsh against her ear. "Let's try and be civil to each other tonight, shall we? Keep a leash on your temper until we get back home."

Keep a leash on *her* temper? She pressed her lips together to prevent the sarcastic retort that formed in her mind. She'd be damned if she'd let him see how deeply his anger affected her. It was her last night with Kyle, her last night in Seattle. She'd act like she was having a good time if it killed her.

At that moment a boy pressed his nose against the screen, stared out at them, then darted away. "Hey, Mom, Kyle's here with his girlfriend!" a young voice cried.

Before they could move, a petite, attractive brunette pushed open the screen door. Desiree recognized her from one of the pictures on Kyle's desk.

"Finally! We were starting to think you two had skipped town on us." The young woman stepped out and squeezed Desiree's hands warmly. "It's Desiree, right? I'm so glad to

The Harrison Duet

meet you. I'm Linda, Kyle's sister." Desiree couldn't help returning the woman's friendly smile. Linda turned and gave her brother a big hug. "It's about time you brought someone home to meet the family. Mom's in a positive tizzy. She's been cooking all day. Now come on in," she said to Desiree, taking her hand. "Everyone's dying to meet you."

Desiree took a deep breath as she walked inside, mentally preparing herself for an evening of difficult role-playing. She'd done her best to avoid crowds and promotional events during her radio career, and her childhood, spent in a big rambling house with only one brother and a pair of reclusive parents, had in no way prepared her for the hubbub of a big family gathering.

And a big family gathering it was. In quick succession she was introduced to four friendly, beautiful sisters, three brothers-in-law with hearty handshakes, more than half a dozen giggling and gurgling nieces and nephews, an elderly aunt, a bachelor uncle, two Siamese cats, and a bouncing golden retriever.

To her surprise, Desiree found herself responding almost immediately to their infectious enthusiasm. Everyone seemed delighted to meet her and strove to make her feel welcome. Soon she was laughing and returning spontaneous hugs and kisses, matching quip with quip, and bantering as freely as she did on the air.

"Pay close attention, now," teased Joanna, a beautiful redhead, after she and her identical twin had introduced themselves. "There'll be a quiz on names and birth dates after dinner."

"I'll never pass!" Desiree laughed.

A tall, blond man with a thick mustache, husband to one of the twins, gave Desiree a particularly enthusiastic welcoming

176

kiss on the cheek, then punched Kyle on the back. "Way to go, buddy," he said, winking.

For the first time since they'd arrived, Desiree caught Kyle's eye. A flicker of deep emotion crossed his face, something like admiration mingled with sincere regret. She felt a stirring within her and she smiled hesitantly, hopefully. He started to take a step toward her when a cheerful voice rang out above the party hum:

"There you are!" A rosy-cheeked wisp of a woman in a blue dress and plaid apron squeezed through the crowd and laid a hand on Desiree's shoulder. Her short, dark-brown hair was streaked with grey, and the laugh lines around her mouth and pale-blue eyes promised a sunny personality. "I'm Stephanie, Kyle's mother. I'm so delighted you could come."

Desiree knew at once that she would like her. As she thanked Stephanie for inviting her, Desiree's heart swelled with gratitude for the welcome she'd received, and regret that she may never see these lovely people again.

"I'm sorry the place is such a zoo," Stephanie said. "I warned the girls to at least leave a few of the kids at home, but they all insisted on coming."

"I'm glad," Desiree said. "In a family this size, it's better to just jump right in and meet everybody at once."

"Brave girl you've got here," Stephanie told Kyle. She encased Desiree in a hug, then tilted her lips up toward Kyle. He leaned down and gave his mother a warm hug and a kiss.

"You look beautiful tonight as always, Mom. Is that leg of lamb I smell?"

Stephanie Harrison looked first at her son and then at Desiree, a quiet smile on her lips. "What else would I make for my favorite son but his favorite meal?"

The Harrison Duet

He chuckled and gave his mother another affectionate squeeze. At the same time his eyes met and found Desiree's. She read there a silent, earnest apology and a plea for a truce— for forgiveness. Her heart turned over. More than anything, she realized, she'd love to be a part of this happy, exuberant family. She didn't know if it would ever happen, but just for tonight she wanted to pretend that it could. She wanted to rush into Kyle's arms, to tell him all was forgiven. She settled for an answering smile that spoke of her love and granted him unconditional amnesty.

He heaved a sigh of relief, wrapped an arm around Desiree and pulled her close to his side. When he lowered his head to whisper against her ear, his voice was rife with emotion. "If we slip down the hall to the back room for a few minutes, do you think anyone will notice?"

Before she could reply, a glass door slid open at the back of the living room. "Hey, why didn't someone tell me they were here?"

Desiree jumped, startled. If Kyle hadn't been standing next to her, she would have sworn the voice she'd heard was his. She turned around and caught her breath. The man crossing the room could only be Kyle's father. Except for the facial lines etched by time in this man's handsome face, and the silvery hair threaded thickly among the red and brown, the resemblance between the two was uncanny. He possessed Kyle's trim powerful build, the same brilliant green eyes, the same high cheekbones and slightly upturned nose. She felt as if she'd been granted a vision of how youthful and attractive Kyle would still appear in years to come.

"Well, well. Hello and welcome," he said, enfolding Desiree's hand in both of his. "I'm Dan, the old man of the house."

"Old man, nothing!" Desiree heard herself say. Laughter shouted out around her.

"I knew I was going to like her." Dan grinned. "Say, has anybody given you a tour of this place yet? No? Well then, come on."

She flashed Kyle an apologetic glance as she was led away. He hid a smile and telegraphed a return message of frustrated longing. A small crowd of youngsters tagged along behind as Dan showed Desiree around the house. She felt overwhelmed by the sense of warmth and love of family that seemed to radiate throughout.

Pictures of Kyle, his sisters, and the grandchildren hung everywhere, together with framed awards and countless childish but clearly cherished attempts at pottery, weaving, watercolor and finger painting. The children proudly pointed out their own particular works of art, and Desiree praised their efforts. Dan had an amusing anecdote for nearly all of the rooms, which were stuffed with odds and ends of furniture, some new, some old, as if he and his wife couldn't bear to throw anything out. The general clutter made her feel right at home. At least his parents aren't neat freaks, she thought with a smile.

"Soup's on!" Stephanie cried. Dan led her back to the dining room and rang a loud brass gong hanging beside the kitchen door. The children scrambled out to the back porch, where a picnic table had been set for them. An arm darted out from the general uproar, and to her relief and delight, Desiree found herself nestled in Kyle's arms, against his chest.

"I think there's something to be said for small families after all," he growled. "Whose idea was it to come here, anyway?"

She tipped her head back and smiled at the love she saw reflected in his eyes. "Yours," she said. "And it was one of your better ideas. I love your family."

The Harrison Duet

He kissed her, long and hard. Around them she heard good-natured hoots and catcalls.

"Hey, cut out the mushy stuff!" a voice cried.

"Save it for Christmas, under the mistletoe!"

They pulled apart, laughing.

Desiree took a seat next to Kyle at one end of the long dining-room table. Throughout the delicious meal, she was besieged with friendly questions about herself and her work. She heard countless Harrison family stories and shot back with a few tales of her own, which were met with uproarious and appreciative laughter.

"Kyle offered to buy us a big, new house after he started doing so well," Stephanie confided, leaning across the table toward Desiree. "And you know what I said? I said, thank you, but no thank you. I raised six children in this house. It was big enough then, and it's big enough now. And if you think I'm going to pack all those pictures and knickknacks and whatnots to move somewhere else, you've got another guess coming."

"Grandpa! Grandpa! Guess what?" A small girl in pigtails raced into the room and climbed onto her grandfather's lap. "I passed the Polliwog test at swim lessons and next week I'll be a Frog!"

"Wonderful, sweetheart." Daniel kissed the freckled cheek. "Keep up the good work. Maybe you'll make the high school swim team someday."

"High school, nothing," said the girl's father. "Someday she'll make the Olympic swim team."

Daniel slapped the tabletop. "Damn right! Excuse me, Stephanie. Say, who wants to make a dollar bet Tracy makes it to the Olympics?" Wallets flashed and several dollar bills were flung on the table amid general laughter and applause.

180

"You wait and see," Kyle told Desiree with a knowing wink. "She'll make it."

By the time the peach and apricot pies were brought out for dessert, Desiree felt as if she'd been a part of this fun-loving family for years. After coffee, adults and children alike spilled out onto the front driveway, where Kyle's father pulled out a box of fireworks left from the family Fourth of July party the week before. The children raced around the yard, drawing designs in the darkness with blazing sparklers. Everyone clapped in delight as screaming rockets sailed through the air and fire fountains gushed red, white, and blue up to the night sky. Caught up in the excitement of the celebration, Desiree waved sparklers and shouted her delight along with the rest of them.

All too soon, the evening came to an end. Dishes were done, goodbyes said, and families piled into individual cars for the drive home. "I hope we'll be seeing you again soon, and often," Stephanie said as she hugged Desiree goodbye on the front porch.

"You will, Mom," Kyle said, wrapping his arms around Desiree.

"Who wants to make a dollar bet we dance at their wedding before the year's over?" Daniel asked, a twinkle in his eye.

"It's a bet." Kyle whipped a dollar out of his pocket and shook his father's hand with gusto.

A warm glow started in the pit of Desiree's stomach and spread to the tips of her fingers and toes. *Every time my dad makes a dollar bet, he wins,* Kyle had said. If things worked out at the radio station tomorrow, if they offered her a job, maybe, just maybe...

"Have a good time?" Kyle asked a few minutes later, after they'd climbed into his car and were speeding down the highway.

"I had a great time. Your family's wonderful. Every one of them."

"Ah! But then you haven't met my cross-eyed Aunt Bernice from Boston, who lives in her attic, has twenty-seven cats, and paints moody abstracts of dancing flamingos in tutus."

"Sounds to me like she'd fit right in."

They both laughed. "Hey, woman, come here." He extended one arm across her shoulders, pulling her against him as he drove with his left hand. "I've been dying for a moment alone with you all night. I wanted to apologize for acting like a complete jerk this afternoon. I could kick myself for the things I said."

"It's all right, sweetheart. I know why you were angry. A hundred-thousand-dollar loss is no laughing matter. And it's my fault that—"

"No, it's not. None of it was your fault. Leaving Tulsa early was my own decision, and I had no right to take out my anger on you. Harrison Industries isn't going to collapse over one lousy contract. And Kyle Harrison won't collapse if a few shoes are strewn around his bedroom." He kissed the top of her head and massaged her neck beneath her silky mane of hair. "Do you forgive me?"

"I forgive you."

"I love you, my darling," he whispered against her hair.

"And I love you."

The moment they got back to Kyle's condo, they came together in a hot, frenzied coupling of mutual need and desire, both of them anxious to erase the tension between them and the memory of their earlier argument.

Later, inside his glass-enclosed shower stall of gleaming blue and white tile, Kyle's soapy hands traveled across Desiree's shoulders, over her firm, rounded breasts, and down the sleek incline of her waist. "Your skin is so silky soft, so smooth and sexy. I love the way you feel."

"I love the way *you* feel," she replied, running her fingers over his slippery, wet biceps. She grabbed the bar of scented soap and stood on tiptoe to wash Kyle's shoulders and lather the hair across his chest. Her massaging fingers followed the bubbles which slid down the V-shaped wedge of hair and then further down, past his navel.

"Be careful what you touch down there," he cautioned, taking a sharp breath, "unless you want to be dragged out of this shower and back to the bedroom before we get a chance to rinse off."

"You wouldn't." Her eyes flashed a teasing challenge as she pulled him against her. She rubbed the soft bar of soap across the small of his back, down his buttocks, to the back of his thighs. "Think of the trail of hot, soapy water we'd leave across that beautiful carpet all the way to the bed."

"Yes. Think of it." He grabbed her around the waist and reached for the shower door handle, but she wriggled out of his grasp and jumped back under the shower's warm spray.

"Stop!" She raised her fists in a fighter's stance and glared at him. Water ricocheted off her head and shoulders in a fine spray and soapy rivulets drifted down her breasts to her abdomen. "It's your fault I got all hot and sweaty, and I'm not leaving this shower until I'm finished."

He laughed, then took the bar of soap from her and built up a frothy lather in his hands. "All right. I concede. As long as I'm allowed the honors of finishing."

The Harrison Duet

He crouched down before her and began to soap her calves with long, loving strokes. She didn't protest. When his soapy fingers reached up to tantalize her thighs, and then, with gentle massaging motions, moved ever-closer to her womanhood, a small moan escaped her lips and she was obliged to grasp his shoulders for support. Sliding his arms around her waist, he kissed his way up over her stomach, finally pausing to sip the warm water streaming down the smooth, narrow valley between her breasts.

"You're one beautiful woman, Desiree." He ran his tongue around the lower perimeter of one breast, then up to flick back and forth across its taut pink crest.

Her fingers twined in his wet hair, pulling him still closer against her. "Do you have any idea...what that does to me?"

In answer, he straightened to his full height and pressed her mouth against his. She could feel his desire pinned between them like a shaft of steel. "The same thing it does to me, my love," he said thickly.

Taking a ragged breath, he leaned back against the shower wall, worshiping the length of her body with his eyes, reaffirming how much he loved every plane and hollow and curve. A flame kindled deep within her and her eyes brimmed over in response. Taking her firmly in his arms, he sat on the tile seat, pulling her down onto him.

"Kyle...?" she said, more with surprise than hesitation. She wrapped her arms around his neck as he held her suspended in his embrace, propped on the tile seat.

"You said," he intoned teasingly, "that you wouldn't leave until you were finished."

"That's right. I did."

"Well, then. Let's *finish*."

She nodded her assent. She was ready, more than ready, and she lowered herself onto him, sheathing him with her loving

184

warmth. He filled the space inside her which ached with need for him, filled her to her very soul.

His fingers dug into the firm flesh of her thighs as he held himself within her and sealed his mouth to hers. She could feel the tension building within him, a mirror of her own turbulent passion. Their tongues moved in an erotic mating dance, keeping pace with the movement of their bodies, which rapidly increased in force and intensity. Heat pulsed through her veins, a fire that couldn't be quenched by the water spraying against their fevered skin.

They rocked, bodies fused together, with a rhythm as ageless as the sea. And then, together, they hurtled off the edge of the earth.

Much later, they lay in bed facing each other, heads cushioned by the same pillow, arms and legs entwined in the darkness. His fingers toyed gently with damp strands of her hair.

"Marry me, Desiree," he said softly.

"I want to, Kyle," she whispered. "You know that. But even if I manage to get a job in Seattle, even if everything works out the way we want...can you really put up with someone like me forever? I'm not the neatest person in the world, and I don't know if I can change."

"I'll put up with you any way I can get you," he said, lovingly stroking the curve of her neck. "I was so proud to be with you tonight. My family adored you, just as I knew they would."

She snuggled up against him, resting her head on his shoulder as she sighed. "I wish you could meet my family. They'd love you, too. But my brother's in Denver now. My

The Harrison Duet

parents moved to Florida after they retired. I can't take any more time off, and to get any of them to come out west before Christmas would take an act of God."

"Or a wedding."

She looked up to meet his gaze through the darkness. The hunger she saw there caused her heart to pump wildly. "Or a wedding," she echoed softly.

13

"It's *definitely* going to rain." Kyle took a seat opposite Desiree at the small table next to the window. Despite foreboding weather, they'd spent the morning touring the Pacific Science Center, and decided to have lunch at the elegant, revolving restaurant atop the 605-foot Space Needle.

Desiree leaned close to the glass, admiring the panoramic view of the city and surrounding lakes, bays, and mountains, marred only by the gathering dark clouds that seemed to be closing in on them with astonishing speed. "It's breathtaking," she said. "I just wish the sun would stay out for more than five minutes at a time."

"We've still got at least an hour of sunshine," Kyle responded, with the certainty of a man who's lived in a rainy climate all his life. "And since the restaurant makes one full rotation every hour, you'll get to see the whole view by then."

Their spinach salads and fresh broiled salmon were scrumptious. They agreed to skip dessert, admitting that they'd both splurged far too often on sinfully fattening foods over the past few weeks.

Just as they emerged below from the high-speed elevator, the sky opened up. They raced back to the car, huddling together under Kyle's umbrella. Despite the overhead protection, huge drops splashed against Desiree's open-toed shoes and seeped through her nylons to drizzle down her legs.

187

The Harrison Duet

"Wow!" She slammed the car door and slumped against her seat. "When it rains here, it really rains."

"You ain't seen nothing yet. This storm is just getting started." Kyle pulled out from the curb, adding, "I like the rain. I like the sound of it on the roof, and the smell of it in the air."

"I don't mind the rain if I'm inside looking out." The windshield wipers were fighting a losing battle against the steadily increasing torrent. Desiree shook out the skirt of her burgundy dress, trying vainly to dry the dark, wet spots left by the rain. Glancing in the vanity mirror on the visor, she cringed at the wayward tendrils of hair around her face which had frizzed in the moist air. "Splashing through puddles on a rainy day can be fun. But I don't like to get soaked right before a job interview."

"Don't worry," Kyle said. "They expect you to be a little soggy around here. Everyone's used to it."

Everyone but me, Desiree thought.

A few minutes later, he parked in front of a tall, high-rise building in the center of town, then gave her directions to find the radio station. "Ed Alder and the receptionist came in especially for this appointment. They said the door would be unlocked. I'll wait for you down here." He kissed her. "Good luck, sweetheart."

"Thanks. And thanks again for setting this up."

She opened her umbrella against the downpour, then stepped out and hurried up the street to the building's wide, glass doors. A quick elevator ride brought her up to the top floor. Desiree caught her breath in astonishment when she stepped into the sleek, modem lobby with its plush, red carpeting and gleaming oak furniture. The KXTR logo and slogan, *Something EXTRA for Seattle,* were mounted in shiny,

188

gold, three-dimensional letters on a mirrored wall behind the receptionist's huge desk.

This makes KICK look like a hick station, she thought. Her cheeks flushed as she remembered the black vinyl benches, ancient linoleum, and nondescript decor of her own station's small lobby.

She introduced herself to the receptionist, who buzzed the program director on her phone.

"Mr. Alder will see you now," the young woman said to Desiree. "Please follow me."

She led her past a glass cabinet filled with trophies and awards, down a long hall hung with framed photographs of deejays, and stepped into a room which put the offices at KICK to shame. Textured wallpaper was printed in subtle beige with the logo pattern of the broadcasting company that owned the station. The desk, which dominated the room, was massive and modem. A bar was built into one corner. Leafy potted plants stood regally beside floor-to-ceiling windows, which offered a magnificent if rain-streaked view of the city below.

"Mr. Alder?" the receptionist said. "This is Desiree Germain."

A ruddy-faced, dark-haired man unfolded himself from a swivel chair and extended a large hand to her across the desk. "Miss Germain. It's a pleasure to meet you." His face broke into a wide grin, flashing large white teeth. He spoke with a pronounced Texas twang.

She returned his smile and his firm handshake. "I'm pleased to meet *you,* Mr. Alder. Thank you for seeing me on a Sunday. I know the station runs seven days a week, but I'm sure you don't usually come in over the weekend."

"No problem, no problem at all. I understand your time constraints. You've got a job to do." His long arm swept toward

The Harrison Duet

the leather chair facing his desk. "Please, have a seat." He sat back down and lit a cigarette with a gold lighter.

While she continued to admire the imposing office, he told her the history of the station. She'd done her homework; she knew quite a bit about the station already, but he cited facts about its ratings and advertising rates that further impressed her.

"They stole me away from a top Houston station last year," he said proudly, blowing out a puff of smoke, "and I'm doing my damnedest to make us the highest rated station in the Pacific Northwest." She filled him in with details of her background and experience that weren't listed on her resume. His cigarette had burned down to a stub when he offered to take her on a tour of the place.

The station was the epitome of modern sophistication. The newsroom and sales offices were sharp and clean. Production rooms were outfitted with the latest equipment, and the music library was immense and well-organized. He led her past two small, empty control rooms, then stopped at the third door where a familiar red beacon flashed just outside.

Desiree looked through the window beside the door into the glass-paneled room. A man sat at an enormous, state-of-the-art console, moving his hands animatedly as he spoke into the mike. His deep tones emanated from speakers overhead. She took an excited breath. The equipment was *gorgeous*. Nothing like the antiquated console she worked with at KICK. Her hands fairly itched to touch that board, to move those beautiful levers up and down.

Then her gaze fell on the binder that lay open on the counter before the deejay. In dismay, she said: "Do you work from a script?"

"We do," Mr. Alder replied. "Only way to control what goes on the air."

Desiree bit her lip as disappointment surged through her. The stations where she'd worked in the past had always allowed her to speak extemporaneously—to ad lib and joke as she pleased. She'd never worked from a script, and wasn't sure she would like it. It seemed to her that it would remove all the spontaneity and excitement from the job. *Oh, well,* she reminded herself, *you can get used to anything.*

"So what do you think?" Ed asked after they'd returned to his office and taken their former seats.

"Very nice," Desiree said sincerely. "You run a beautiful operation here."

"That we do. Now, let's get down to business. I'll be honest with you. We've only ever had one female deejay at KXTR, and she didn't work out too well. But Kyle Harrison's spent a lot of advertising dollars at this station, so I listened to the tape you sent. It was pretty good." She waited expectantly as he lit another cigarette, sat back in his chair, and took a drag. "You've got some experience. Your on-air personality is a real departure from what we've tried in the past. I can't be sure how you'll go over, and ratings, you know, are the name of the game. But I'm willing to take a chance on you. I'd like to offer you a position."

Desiree's heart leapt. Was it going to be that easy?

"I have to tell you up front, though," he went on, "there's no way we can match or even come close to the salary you're earning now." He named a figure that was almost insultingly low.

"Mr. Alder," she replied, frowning, "that's not much more than I earned in my first position seven years ago."

"I'm sorry, but that's the best we can do. I've heard rumors about a possible buyout at KICK. You might be out of a job soon. I'm offering you a position if you want it. And after talking to Kyle—if I'm reading my signals right—salary won't really be the deciding factor here, will it?"

Desiree felt her cheeks redden. Striving to remain polite, she asked, "Which shift would I have? Morning or afternoon?"

He took a drag on his cigarette. "We can use a voice like yours on nights."

"Nights?" If he'd slapped her in the face, she couldn't have been more stunned.

"Two A.M. to 6 A.M. Five days a week." His white teeth flashed again as he added magnanimously. "With weekends off. How's that sound to you?"

Desiree struggled to keep her voice calm. "Mr. Alder, I worked evenings and nights for seven years. I have the afternoon drive at KICK now. My show receives critical acclaim. When Arbitron comes out with the new ratings, we expect it to be one of the top shows in the area."

"Yes, little lady, but that's Anaheim. People are different down there next to Hol-ly-wood." He emphasized the three syllables of the word with mild derision. "Maybe it's common to hear the voice of a lovely woman like yourself on the afternoon drive. But let's be frank. You've got a bedroom voice, the kind men want to hear late at night."

Desiree felt the hot rush of color sweep from her cheeks to her forehead. *A bedroom voice?* She shot out of her chair, her heart pumping furiously. "Thank you for your offer," she said calmly. "I'll certainly consider it and let you know." Then, before he could open his mouth to speak, she grabbed her purse and stalked from the room.

"Will this rain ever let up?" Desiree peeled her damp, clinging dress over her head and threw it over the shower stall in Kyle's bathroom. In her haste to leave the station, she'd forgotten her umbrella and had been drenched by the downpour.

"It should be over in a couple of hours." Kyle tossed her a fluffy towel and she vigorously dried her wet hair. "I'm sorry I didn't warn you to bring a raincoat this weekend."

"I should have thought of it myself." She stripped off her wet underclothes, hung them up to dry, and ran the towel over her body. "I knew that it rains a lot in Seattle. I guess I was hoping for blue skies in summer."

"We do get blue skies—you had a glimpse of them yesterday—and they're stunning. It's the rain that makes everything so crisp, clean, and green. Don't you get tired of all that sunshine back home?"

"Never."

"It's always the same in southern California. No change of seasons. No—"

"I like it that way. It's beautiful. Warm. And predictable."

He followed her into the bedroom, watching as she put on a clean, dry bra and underwear and a pair of jeans.

His eyes glimmered. "Are you sure you want to get dressed?"

"Yes. I'm cold." She drew her long-sleeved, cotton top over her head.

"I can think of another way we can get warm."

He stepped toward her, but she raised a hand to stop him. "Not now, Kyle." At his look of disappointment, she added, "I'm sorry, but I'm not in the mood. I just had the worst interview of my life."

He sat down on the edge of the bed with a frown. "I know, and *I'm* sorry. You have every right to be upset. But it's only one station. There are others. I can call—"

"No. I'm not going through that kind of embarrassment again." She crossed to the window, where beating rain blurred

The Harrison Duet

the glass in thick rivulets, obscuring the distant pines. "Ed Alder made it clear that the only reason he bothered to listen to my tape or meet with me was because of his relationship with you. I want a job on my own merit, not as payment for your faithful advertising."

He winced at that, but said: "I don't blame you. I was just trying to help."

"I know. And I appreciate all the effort you went to on my behalf—I really do. But I won't work for someone who doesn't respect my talent. And I refuse to take another night shift."

He nodded slowly. "Try another station, then. This time, I'll stay out of it. But Desiree—even if the only thing available is a night shift, it won't last forever. In time, they'll see what they've got, and—"

"No. I might be stuck doing nights again for years. You can't imagine what havoc that kind of schedule plays with your life. I won't take a step backward. I paid my dues. I won't do it again."

"So where does that leave us?"

She dropped down beside him on the bed. "Kyle, I love you. But—"

"But what?"

"I want to stay in California."

He blew out a deep, disappointed sigh. "For how long?"

"I don't know." She lay sideways on the bed and absently traced the line of stitching in the blue quilted comforter with her index finger. "When you first suggested I look for a job in Seattle, I agreed to give it a try. I almost had myself convinced it would work. But I was wrong. And it's not just the rain, or the rude things Alder said about my voice. It's everything that Southern California has to offer— commercials, TV, film. It's all there. I have a following, a reputation in that market. I can't leave just because the station *might* be sold. I'd be crazy to give up what I've worked so hard for."

He dropped down beside her, his jaw tense, his eyes riveted to hers. "You'd be crazy to give up what we have."

"I agree," she returned softly. "I'm not talking about giving up our relationship."

"You're not?"

She smiled lovingly into his eyes, touched his cheek with her hand. "I want to marry you, Kyle. But I want to stay at KICK."

His forehead furrowed. "How do you propose we do that? Live in separate cities?"

"Yes."

He cursed and looked away.

"There's no guarantee we can ever live in the same place for long, so there's no reason why we have to start out that way."

He stood up and raked his hand through his hair. "What makes you so certain you'd have to move on, even if you did lose a job? Who says you couldn't find work at another station in the same area?"

"Because a deejay cast adrift is practically untouchable in the same market. Don't ask me why. It's the way the business works."

He cursed again, then strode across the room and braced his arms on the dresser top, his back to her. "So even if we get married, we can only look forward to seeing each other on weekends and vacations. Twice a month here, twice a month in Southern California—at best. Or maybe we can buy a house in the San Francisco Bay Area and meet half way."

"That could work."

The Harrison Duet

He whipped around to look at her. "Is that what you want?"

"*You're* the one who suggested we meet on weekends. You're the one who said a long-distance relationship could work. I'm just trying to make the best of it."

He shook his head bitterly. "That was before I tried it. I can see now why your marriage fell apart."

She stared at him. "What are you saying?"

"I'm saying...you were right. I don't think it *can* work. At least not for me. I've spent the past few weeks here in body, but not in spirit. And now my business is suffering."

She swallowed hard, knowing he was referring to the blown contract. Tears threatened and she fought hard to keep them at bay.

"I love you, Desiree. But I don't want to be torn, day after day, between you and my work. I want to be together, live in the same house, share the same bed. I want to spend mornings and evenings with you, make love to you every night, and wake up beside you every morning. I want to make a home together, raise children together. I want a full-time partner... for life."

She nodded, the sound of the rain beating against the windowpane matching the dull thudding of her heart. "I want those things, too," she said quietly. "And I wish more than anything that we could make it happen. But I don't see how it's possible for us."

14

Desiree shivered beneath her old sweatshirt as she trudged barefoot across the damp sand, avoiding scattered masses of dark, stringy seaweed. An early morning fog hung low over the Santa Barbara coastline, casting a dull, white glow across the bay. She'd walked this beach every morning for eight days now, trying to make some sense out of her life and her reason for being. Sam, her boss, had insisted she take the time off.

"You've been walking around here all week like a ghost," he'd growled. "Something's eating you up inside. One of these days you're gonna break. And I like you too much to sit around and wait for that to happen."

"I'm fine," Desiree had insisted. "Really, I—"

"The hell you are. Look, I'm giving you next week off." He'd waved away her protest with an impatient hand. "Go away somewhere. Relax. Don't tell me where you're going. And don't come back until you've solved your problem, whatever it is. Got it?"

Santa Barbara, the quiet, stately community just up the coast, seemed the ideal place to meditate in solitude. But now, on the Monday morning she was due back at work, she had yet to make peace with herself. She'd checked out of the hotel and knew she ought to get in her car and drive home. But she

The Harrison Duet

didn't feel ready. Her heart still ached and tears came to her eyes every time she recalled the Sunday afternoon two weeks ago when she left Seattle.

Kyle had begged her to spend the night, to wait and take her scheduled flight the next morning. But there had seemed no point in staying. Every extra moment she spent with him would only make the ultimate parting even harder to bear.

"I'm sorry," she'd said, throwing clothes into the open suitcase on Kyle's bed.

"Sorry? What good is it to be sorry? Stop packing, please." Kyle had laid a restraining hand on her arm, but she'd shrugged it off. "Don't walk out on me like this. Not now. It's pouring outside."

"It's better if I go now." She'd snapped her suitcase shut with a bitter thud. "We've said all we have to say. I'll call a cab."

"Don't be ridiculous." He'd grabbed the suitcase from her hand. "If you're so set on leaving, I'll drive you to the airport."

"Thank you."

They'd sat in tense silence as Kyle steered the Maserati over the wet streets, rain pelting the windshield. When they finally reached the airport, he'd carried her bag to the counter, waited while she changed her reservation, then walked her to the gate. The flight was just about to board. Desiree had fumbled miserably with the shoulder strap on her purse as she purposely avoided his gaze.

"Kyle, I want you to know how much I appreciate everything you've done for me," she'd said brokenly. "I've felt like a different person since we met. You've given me more confidence than I've ever had before. I'll always be grateful to you for that."

His low, muttered curse had forced her to raise her eyes to his. The pain contorting his face hurt her like a physical blow. She'd bit her lip against an onrush of tears.

198

"I'm so sorry," she finished, her voice barely a whisper.

He briefly grabbed her hand and squeezed it tightly. "So am I." Without another word, he spun on his heel and disappeared into the crowd.

The day after she returned home, a small box had arrived with a card from Kyle. "Desiree: I'll always love you," the card read. "Like the contents of this white box, we're a perfect matched pair. We belong together. There's got to be a way we can work things out. Please. Come back to me."

A wistful ache wrenched at her heart as she stared at the box. It was pink, not white. Inside, on a bed of pale pink velvet, rested a set of custom-crafted pierced earrings: two delicate golden songbirds, similar to the pendant she wore, with a sparkling diamond chip in each eye.

She'd burst into tears.

The earrings were still in the box, buried under the scarves in her bottom dresser drawer. Would she ever be able to bring herself to wear them?

The squawk of a seagull yanked her back to the present. Desiree blinked back fresh tears, curling her toes into the damp sand as she walked. She remembered another sea gull's cry on an idyllic afternoon with Kyle at Catalina. Years, not weeks, seemed to have passed since that wonderful day. The pain of loneliness and loss spread throughout her body until her insides felt like one immense, gaping chasm.

Try to remember what life was like before you met him, she told herself, as she trudged up the sand and across the parking lot to her car. Did you feel happy? Energetic? Did you look forward to each new day? *Yes!* You were lonely, but you'd learned to accept it. *And you'll learn to accept it again.*

The Harrison Duet

She opened the car door, cleaned off her feet, and got in. Turning the key to auxiliary power, she flipped on the car radio.

"Hope you're having a great morning out there, Santa Barbara," said a cheerful masculine radio voice. "I sure am. On the way in this morning—"

She tuned out the voice, crossing her arms on the steering wheel as she wearily lowered her head. Radio. That's where the excitement was. The drama, the thrill, the power she wielded within the confines of her small control room. She'd always loved it. It had been her whole life. Why, then, didn't she care anymore? Where had the magic gone?

"And now for some Streisand," said the radio voice. A pause. And then sweet, familiar notes rent the air. Desiree's head flew up and she stared at the radio as if it possessed satanic powers. "Songbird." Of all the songs to play...

She leaned her head back against the seat and closed her eyes. She knew every note, every word. The lyrics wove through her mind and body, reaching down to her soul. The songbird's sweet music brings others joy, the words said. Her song sets people free. Yet no one knows the songbird. She's sad and alone...and lonely. Who will sing for her?

Desiree's chest constricted with an ache of longing and emptiness. *I'm nothing more than a voice coming out of a box*, she realized with sudden, agonizing clarity. I make others happy. *But no one sings for me.*

You fool, a voice cried within her. *He* loves you. He's the music in your soul, the one who can set you free. Everything will work out if only you're together. Nothing else matters. *Nothing.*

She gripped the steering wheel with fierce determination. How could she have been so blind? How could she have

200

imagined she could live without him? She loved him. She needed him. Her work meant nothing if she couldn't have him.

Desiree turned on the ignition and stamped on the gas pedal. The engine roared to life. She sped out of the parking lot, down the street, and pulled to a screeching halt in front of the first phone booth she could find.

I only hope I'm not too late, she thought desperately as she jumped out of the car and raced to the phone booth. She dipped into her purse, grabbed her address book, and searched for Kyle's office number with trembling fingers.

I'll find a job in Seattle, take whatever I can get, she decided. Who cares what shift it is? Who cares what I'm leaving behind? At least we'll be together.

She drummed her fingernails against the booth's glass door as she waited for the operator to put through the credit card call. She'd do her best, she reasoned, make a name for herself, and in no time she'd be on top again. If she lost her job some day and couldn't find another one...to hell with it! She'd do something else.

She didn't know what else she would do, couldn't think that far ahead. She only knew that she loved Kyle and wanted to spend the rest of her life with him, her professional future be damned.

"Harrison Industries," an efficient female voice said finally on the other end of the line.

"Kyle Harrison, please." Her voice sounded unnaturally high and shrill in her ears.

"I'm sorry, Mr. Harrison is out of town. Would you care to leave a message?"

Out of town? Where was he? In Tulsa again? "Well, I...this is Desiree Germain, and—"

"Oh, yes, Miss Germain," the woman replied cordially, as if they were old friends. "How may I help you?"

"I have to talk to him. It's very important. Can you tell me where I can reach him?"

"Certainly. He's in Southern California."

Southern California? Desiree gave a little gasp of surprise and delight. "Where's he staying? Can you give me the name and number of his hotel?" She scribbled down the information on the back of an envelope in her purse, said a hurried goodbye, and hung up.

The hotel was in Anaheim. What was he doing there? she wondered. Did he come down to see her? What would he do when he found her gone?

She called the hotel and asked for his room. She let the phone ring a good twenty times before she slammed down the receiver and glanced at her watch. Nine-fifteen. Damn. Where could he be?

She jumped back into her car and roared off. Thank God she'd missed the morning rush-hour traffic. She could be home in two hours, if she sped all the way and didn't pass any highway patrolmen. He might have stopped at the station and found out she'd be back to work today. If so, was there a chance he'd be waiting for her outside her house? Please, please, wait for me my darling, she prayed silently. I'm coming back to you.

The drive seemed interminable. The car shot past long stretches of dry, arid landscape, sped through the San Fernando Valley, over the mountainous Sepulveda Pass, and past the L.A. airport, on toward Orange County. At last she turned onto her street, her heart pounding like a locomotive, her eyes searching for another rented Maserati.

The driveway and curb stood empty.

Maybe he came in a taxi, she thought frantically. Maybe he used his key and is waiting inside. She pulled to a halt, raced up to the front door, unlocked it, and called his name. The house was hot and musty, as empty as the day she left it.

"Where are you, Kyle Harrison?" she shouted. Her voice echoed in the stillness.

She called the hotel again. No answer. She called his office in Seattle. "Sorry to bother you again, but I can't seem to reach Mr. Harrison at his hotel. Do you have any idea where else he might be?"

"He left word we could reach him at the station this morning. KICK. He—"

"Oh! Of course! Thank you." Desiree hung up, elated. Since she wasn't home, of course he'd wait for her at the station! She peeled off her clothes and took a fast, hot shower. Forty-five minutes later, she pulled into the parking lot behind the station, dressed in a denim skirt and blue cotton blouse. She pushed open the double glass doors, disappointment surging through her when she saw the deserted lobby. Only Barbara was in the room, speaking rapidly into the phone behind the reception counter.

"Yes, sir. Fine. I will." Barbara caught Desiree's eye and gestured emphatically for her to wait. "I'll put it in the mail today. Thank you for calling." She disconnected the line and stood up. "Des! At last! You're back." Her eyes gleamed with some indefinable emotion. "How was your vacation?"

"Therapeutic. Listen, has anyone been by here to see—"

"Des, big things have been happening around here while you were gone," Barbara cut in. "Westler's been in meetings all week. And guess what? He sold the station."

"Sold it? When?"

The Harrison Duet

"They finalized everything yesterday. Westler took off, but the new guy is here. He said he wants to talk with you as soon as you get in."

"Talk with me?" Desiree asked, stunned. "Why?"

"You'd better hurry. He's been waiting for over an hour." She shooed Desiree off toward the door that led into the station. "Go. He's in Westler's old office."

Frowning, Desiree opened the door and hurried down the hall. What was he going to do? Fire her? If so, she didn't care. She intended to leave anyway.

The door to Westler's office stood open. She stepped over the threshold, then stopped, frozen. The man behind the desk looked up from a stack of papers, his handsome face grim, unreadable, his green eyes wary.

"Hello, Desiree," Kyle said quietly.

Her mouth flew open, but no words came out. What was he doing, sitting behind Westler's desk? Was this some kind of a joke? Then suddenly, all the jumbled pieces of information she'd learned this morning fell into place in her mind like a reassembled jigsaw puzzle. She gasped in astonishment. "*You bought the radio station?*"

"Close the door, will you please?"

She complied mechanically. He gestured toward the chair facing his desk. "Have a seat."

Desiree dropped stiffly into the chair, her mind whirling, alternately accepting and rejecting what she'd just heard. Kyle's eyes seemed to search hers for a sign, an indication of her feelings. But she was so taken aback she could only return his stare blankly.

He frowned, then turned his attention back to the papers in his hands. He made a few notations, then set them aside. "I hope you enjoyed your vacation?" The cold, brittle edge to his voice cut the air like a knife.

"It was...fine."

"Good." He lifted several sheets from a folder at his left and extended them to her across the desk. She didn't look at them, her eyes still focused on the hard lines of his cheeks and jaw. "It'll take a few weeks before the sale is final," he said. "But in the meantime, you'll be glad to know your future at KICK is secure. You can take over as general manager, or keep your spot on the air, or both—whatever you like. I've had papers drawn up to make you a partner in the firm. You'll want to get an attorney to look them over, but what it boils down to is a fifty-percent share after five years if the company shows a consistent profit."

If she felt astonishment before, now she was completely stunned. "Fifty percent share?"

His brief smile ended before it reached his eyes. "Yes. You won't have to worry about job security now. Of course you'll have a few more responsibilities, but nothing you can't handle."

Tears burned behind her eyes. How could he have thought she'd want the *station*? My God, the idea had never even entered her mind. She didn't even want her job anymore. She wanted *him!* If only she could fly into his arms, make him understand. She wanted to admit how wrong she'd been, to tell him she loved him and wanted, more than life itself, to marry him. But he was acting so cold, calculating, and impersonal. Had his anger killed his feelings for her? If so, why had he done all this?

"I don't know what to say." She swallowed over the lump in her throat. "I never expected you to buy the station. I don't deserve such generosity. Really. I—"

"It wasn't generosity." He stood up abruptly. His eyes impaled hers across the desk. "I had the funds available. I've

The Harrison Duet

been looking for an alternate investment for the past month. At the moment, this station breaks even at best. But you show outstanding devotion to your work. I'm convinced that, under my direction, with the incentive of partnership, you can turn this place into a real money-maker."

She gasped at his harsh words. He still thought the only thing she cared about was her job. He'd never forgive her for walking out on him, for choosing her career over him.

"I...see," she strangled out. "Well...I'm sure you'll—" Her voice broke as a sob burst from her throat. Tears streamed down her cheeks. One hand flew up to cover her eyes and she turned blindly, found the door handle, and yanked it open.

"Dammit!" Kyle crossed the floor with urgent strides and slammed the door shut. "Are you going to walk out on me again?"

She shook her head, his face a blur through a sea of tears. "I don't want to walk out on you, Kyle. But I can't stand it when you look at me that way, as if...you hate me."

"*Hate* you? Don't you know by now how much I love you?" Unfamiliar tears shone in his eyes. "I'll always love you, Desiree. Good God, what more can I do to prove it to you?"

She sobbed with relief as she threw her arms around him. "Oh, Kyle. I love you, too."

His arms instantly tightened around her as she went on:

"I've been so stupid. Can I say now what I've been wanting to shout to the world all day? My career doesn't mean anything to me if I can't have you. Do you still want to marry me? Please say you do. Because I will. I tried to call you this morning in Seattle to tell you, and then at your hotel when—"

"Say that again," he demanded as his hands cradled the back of her head, tilting her face up to his. His eyes began

206

to twinkle in a familiar way and her heart lurched with new-found hope.

"I tried to call you—" she began distractedly.

"No, no. The first part."

"I said...I love you. If you still want me, I'll marry you."

"I accept." Their eyes met, each asking the other for forgiveness and receiving it. Then his lips came down on hers in an impassioned kiss. She molded herself against him, returning his kiss with unrestrained fervor, trying to pour into him all the love she'd been saving, harboring, resisting.

"Has it been as hard for you as it has been for me these past weeks?" he whispered.

"Yes. I've never been so lonely, so miserable. When you sent the earrings...they're beautiful, Kyle. I wanted to call, to thank you. But I couldn't. I knew if I heard your voice again, I could never bring myself to say goodbye."

"I longed for you. I reached for you in the night, but you weren't there. When you didn't call after I sent the earrings, I gave up hope. I knew, then, you were lost to me forever. I thought I'd go out of my mind." He shuddered and hugged her more tightly against him. "I bought the station not only to secure your job, but so I'd have an excuse to see you every now and then."

She lifted teasing eyes to his. "Rather drastic measures to take, don't you think, Mr. Harrison? Thank goodness you don't have any stockholders. What if the place doesn't turn a profit?"

His mouth tilted up in the lopsided grin she'd come to love so well. "Oh, it will. With you at the helm, I'm sure we'll be the top rated station in Orange County in no time."

She hesitated. "Kyle. Wait. What you've done, it's incredible—I don't know what to say. But I can't stay here. Not if you're in Seattle." He started to protest, but she raised a finger to his lips. "I love my work, but I love you more. I want to live where you are. I'll move to Seattle, and if I don't find a job or if the job doesn't last, I don't care. I'll—"

He cut off her words by covering her mouth with his. His kiss was long and sweet, communicating his love far more expressively than words. When he drew back, his eyes danced down at her. "You don't have to move to Seattle, my darling."

"Why not?"

"Because I'll be moving down here to be with you."

"What? How can you? That's impossible. Harrison Industries is—"

"Moving to Orange County," he finished. "I own a radio station here, don't I?" He lifted her hand to his lips and planted a warm kiss on her palm. "I could have looked into buying a station in Seattle, but I saw how important it was to you to stay in Southern California. So I took a good look at my own needs and interests. Hell, I've only got a suite of offices up there. I can operate anywhere, as long as I'm near an airport. It'll take a few months to complete the move, and I'll have to do a bit more traveling than before, but I'll be here most of the time. My secretary's not speaking to me, but—" He grinned. "At least my wife will be. On a daily basis."

She tried to assimilate the impact of his words. "But... your whole family is in Seattle. You've lived there all your life."

"High time for a change. And we'll see my family on vacations, the same as yours."

"When did you decide all this?" she asked, dazed. "Why didn't you tell me before?"

"I didn't contact Westler about the possibility until a week ago. By then, you were out of town and no one knew where to find you. He had another offer, so I was forced to make a quick decision. I went ahead, hoping you'd approve. Do you?"

"Do I?" She hugged him, her heart so filled with joy she felt it might burst. "Do I ever!"

His chuckle vibrated against her chest as he lowered his face to hers. "Are you sure you won't mind spending every day of the rest of your life with me, Mrs. Harrison?"

"Even that won't be long enough, my love," she whispered before his lips claimed hers once more.

"After those thundershowers this morning, who'd expect such a gorgeous afternoon?"

Desiree smiled into the microphone. She ran her hands lovingly over the gleaming, state-of- the-art console, which Kyle had ordered the day he took possession of the station. "We've got clear blue skies all across Orange County to welcome the first day of spring. And you've got Desiree on KICK, Anaheim."

She started a commercial break, then sat back and scribbled a To Do List for herself, one of the many efficient habits she'd picked up from Kyle in the eight months they'd been married.

1. Call travel agent. Kyle's birthday was next month, and she'd planned a surprise vacation to Tahiti. His coworkers knew all about it. She couldn't wait to see the expression on his face when she picked him up at the office and whisked him off to the airport.

2. Go over financial statement. The station had received its highest ratings ever in Arbitron's latest book, and they'd been able to raise their advertising rates accordingly. She'd hired an assistant manager to help with her duties, but conferred with

The Harrison Duet

Kyle on all major business decisions. And of course she'd kept her spot on the air. It was a hectic schedule, but the daily challenge and excitement thrilled her, and she was proud of her accomplishments.

3. Choose paint colors. Their new house in the hills above Newport Beach was well underway. In a few months they'd be able to move in. She couldn't stop a grin as she thought about the exciting news she planned to tell him tonight at dinner. *A different color scheme for each bedroom,* she added to her list. All six of them...

The promo ended and she switched on the mike, then flicked the lever for traffic. "It's time now to check on the traffic situation. Let's talk to our man in the skies. How are you doing up there, Dave? Are the wet streets causing motorists any problems today?"

"No major accidents, Desiree." The unexpectedly deep, resonant voice caught her off-guard and sent a paroxysm of delight spiraling through her. She hadn't heard his voice over the air since the day they met! Would he ever tire of finding ways to surprise her?

"I see we've got Killer Kyle filling in for Deadly Dave Dawson today," she said. "What happened? Did Dave take a rain check?"

"You've got it. Thought I'd step in and take this bird up for a spin." Kyle went ahead with the traffic report, speaking smoothly, expertly, like a seasoned radio professional, giving no clue to his true identity or his lack of experience at this particular job.

"Thanks, Kyle. I hope we'll be hearing more from you," she said when he was through, unable to disguise the pride and admiration she felt for her remarkable, fun-loving husband. "Before you sign off, though, I've got a news flash that might interest you. It just came in, hot over the wire."

"I'm all ears."

"Inside sources predict there's going to be a new little deejay at KICK in about…oh, seven months or so." Desiree bit her lip to keep it from trembling in the silence which followed.

Finally, with a slight break in his softened, deep voice, Kyle said: "Let me be the first to congratulate you…and your husband. I'm sure he must be absolutely *delighted* with the news." He let out a sudden exultant whoop of glee. "I've always said, what this station needs is some fresh young talent! Who wants to make a dollar bet it's twins?"

And as all the phone lines in her control booth began to flash, their joy and laughter vibrated over the airwaves.

propositions

BOOK TWO

THE HARRISON DUET

ACKNOWLEDGMENTS

Heartfelt thanks to Eric Fütterer and Paula Fisher Thompson for their many hours of invaluable help and consultation as I researched this novel.

And with all my heart I dedicate this book to Bill, my husband, soul mate, and kindred spirit, whose love, faith, and encouragement have helped me to achieve so many dreams.

AUTHOR'S FOREWORD

Dear Reader,

I am pleased to share with you this newly edited edition of my second novel, previously published under the title *The Sky's The Limit*.

Book two in *The Harrison Duet* series, **Propositions** focuses on the beautiful and talented Kelli Ann Harrison, sister of Kyle Harrison, the hero in *Songbird*. A fiercely independent artist, Kelli is about to receive some unexpected propositions from a man who is every bit her intellectual and creative equal, and to experience a love so deep, immediate, and profound, it forces her to rethink her future and the very meaning of romance.

I wrote this book in 1986. This gently edited version better reflects my current sensibilities as a novelist, but the story is unchanged—and it holds a very special place in my heart. The hero and heroine both work in advertising, a field in which I was involved many years ago and really enjoyed. In reading the novel today, I couldn't help but smile fondly at the technical aspects of the graphics and design business at the time, which have since radically changed. In some ways, reading the book is like stepping back in time, to an era before computers

The Harrison Duet

and cell phones took over the world and changed the way we do everything.

The basics of the creative process, however, remain the same, and so do the joys we experience in a new relationship, on the road to falling in love.

In looking over all the books I've written since this one, I notice that an immediate attraction between lovers and a whirlwind courtship is a recurring theme. There's a reason for this. From my great-grandparents to my parents to my own relationship with my husband, my family has many examples of couples who met, fell in love, and married within a matter of weeks or months—all marriages which have stood the test of time and have been very happy. I was delighted to give this same family history to Kelli.

Love at first sight may be rare, but I know from personal experience that it's possible. As one of my characters says in this novel: *When you know, you know.*

Happy reading!

Syrie James

1

The slot machine whirred. Three bright streaks of red, blue, and orange whizzed past. Kelli took a sharp breath and held it, watching as the first cylinder dropped into place with a clang: an orange on the top row, a plum in the center, cherries below. Three chances to win.

A split second later came another clang; another plum in the center. The third cylinder continued its mad spin. Could it be? Another plum? Three plums and she'd win—

With a final clang, a cluster of red cherries popped into the slot next to the plums. The slot machine froze into metallic stillness.

Kelli sighed. No wonder they called it a one-armed bandit. In five seconds she'd lost three quarters—a third of tomorrow's lunch money.

Oh well, she thought with a small shrug. Fortunes like mine come and go. She didn't drive all the way from Seattle to South Lake Tahoe to gamble, anyway. She came to watch over her brother's vacation home in its last three weeks of construction and to get in some skiing—a few days of glorious downhill on some of Lake Tahoe's finest slopes. And of course there was the job interview in San Francisco.

Kelli slid up onto the stool next to the slot machine and straightened the calf-length skirt of her white silk evening

The Harrison Duet

dress. Last summer, she thought with amusement, if someone had told her she'd be sitting in a casino lobby on a Friday night in early December, waiting for a man she barely knew—a man who might be her next employer—to escort her to an exclusive party on the hotel's top floor, she wouldn't have believed it.

If she hadn't acted so impulsively, hadn't let her temper get the best of her, she'd still be working away at the ad agency in Seattle. But in the past year she'd experienced a rash of compulsions to do the boldest, most brazen things. Like the time she accepted her brother Kyle's dare and took over the controls of his twin-engine Bonanza over Puget Sound. Crazy! And the morning, six months ago, when she asked Wayne to pack up his things and move out, then told her boss of four years to go fly a kite and stormed out the office door without a backward glance. Madness! Her actions had shocked everyone—including herself.

It was only later, in the ensuing weeks on her own, that she'd come to understand her motivation. For twenty-eight years she'd allowed well-meaning parents and sisters and then a domineering boyfriend to influence her every move. Afraid of losing her job, she'd kept silent while higher-ups stole her best design work and claimed it as their own. All the while her resentment had simmered, until finally she'd blown her stack.

Life, she'd come to realize—like the ad slogan she'd helped to create—life is *not* a spectator sport. Never again would she calmly sit back, letting people manipulate and take advantage of her. She was going to be in the driver's seat from now on.

She hadn't wasted any time getting her new life in order. Out from under Wayne's judgmental eye, she felt more capable, more attractive. She had a slender figure, a face that men seemed to notice, and wavy, shoulder-length, reddish-gold hair that her hairdresser envied. The world was over-flowing with limitless, exciting possibilities, and she was going to enjoy every minute of it.

She had immediately indulged herself in all the things Wayne would have disapproved of. She bought clothes that were beautiful, not practical, ate take-out Chinese food five nights in a row, and went to see movies *she* liked—all comedies and romances without a single too-macho hero or blast of machine-gun fire. She'd felt terrific, like a new woman, like a caged sparrow at last set free.

She decided not to work for another agency and tried free-lance advertising instead. Within a few months she'd built up a small but steady clientele and was enjoying herself immensely. She loved being her own boss, reporting to no one, allowing her creative energies to have free reign.

The only problem was money. Business was undependable—too busy one week and quiet the next. When Bob Dawson called from San Francisco, he caught her in a weak moment. She'd just gone over her bank statement, and had been forced to admit that her earnings barely covered her living expenses and her savings would be gone in another month.

Bob had seen her design work on a recent, award-winning campaign, and had tracked her down. He'd been so profuse with his compliments that when he asked her to come down for an interview, she couldn't say no. She had to be at Lake Tahoe for three weeks anyway, to watch over her brother's house, so she agreed to stop off in the city to meet him on the way.

Remembering her meeting two days before in Bob's office made her frown.

"Your artwork and design show remarkable versatility," Bob had said, bracing tense fingers on the immaculate expanse

The Harrison Duet

of desktop between them. "I've been looking for someone like you to take over when our creative director leaves next month. We've got an exciting campaign coming up for Cassera's Hotel and Casino, one of our largest accounts, and I'd like you to work on it."

She'd been amazed by the generous salary he offered—even more amazed when he invited her to the party tonight to meet Ted Lazar, the casino's general manager. It was an excellent professional opportunity, the dream position she'd been working toward for six long years. She hadn't liked Bob at first, but he'd turned out to be polite and charming. She ought to have accepted the job in a flash. Instead, she'd told him she needed time to think it over.

Why was she hesitating?

People in jeans and ski jackets streamed in through the double glass doors at the casino's nearby side entrance, bringing in laughter, a blast of cold air, and a flurry of snowflakes. Kelli checked her watch again. Nine o'clock.

Bob was an hour late. What could be keeping him? What if he never showed up?

This is ridiculous, Kelli decided. Go on up to the party and let him join you.

She slid off the stool and hurried past the slot-machine area, around the corner to the hotel elevators. A bell announced the impending arrival of the closest elevator and she stopped in front of it. The doors hissed open and she took a purposeful step forward. At the same instant a man propelled himself out, and they collided with an impact that sent Kelli staggering backward. She uttered a startled cry just as hands grabbed her arms to steady her, and she found herself eye to eye with the lapel of a charcoal-grey suit.

"Excuse me," said a deep voice.

He took a step sideways, away from the elevator and the other departing passengers. She looked up, still numb with surprise, into a face that was handsome even though its dark brows were drawn together in a distracted scowl. He looked a few years older than she was; thirty, maybe thirty-two. He had a straight nose, a determined set to his jaw, a wide mouth that was pressed together in a tight line. His short, wavy hair gleamed almost black beneath the overhead lights.

The survey took only a fraction of an instant. He stood just inches away, still gripping her arms with his head tilted down to hers, so that despite his height, she couldn't help but stare directly into his eyes. They were a rich, vibrant blue, like the Tahoe sky, surrounded by thick, dark lashes; quick, intelligent eyes, which at this moment sparked with irritation. Despite this—for some inexplicable reason—she felt a sudden, wild fluttering inside her—a feeling of momentous, impending change.

"Fate," she thought, and realized, too late, that she'd said it out loud.

He released her arms. His scowl vanished and his eyes lit with interest and a surprising warmth. "What?"

She cleared her throat. "Nothing."

"I thought you said fate."

"No, I said...late."

"Late?"

"I'm...late," she said. "For a very important...date."

His lips twitched with amusement. "Curiouser and curiouser."

She realized she'd babbled a line straight out of *Alice's Adventures in Wonderland,* and he'd responded in kind. She blushed. "I'm sorry I rammed into you. I shouldn't have been in such a hurry."

The Harrison Duet

"My fault." He waved away her apology. "I wasn't in the world's best mood, or I would have watched where—" In a single, rapid glance he took in her formal attire, and a speculative gleam came into his eyes. "You wouldn't by any chance be going to the party upstairs, would you? The one on the top floor?"

"Well—yes, I am."

"And you're on the list? They're expecting you?"

"I think so."

He rubbed his chin thoughtfully for a moment. "Listen, would you..." He checked his watch and a perturbed look flitted across his face. "I know this is an imposition, but...can I ask you a favor? I'm supposed to meet someone at that party, but it looks like he forgot to leave my name at the door. No one gets in if they're not on the list, and they've got Attila the Hun guarding the door. I've come up all the way from San Francisco and I'll be damned if I'm going to leave now."

"So, you want me to...what?" Kelli asked, a spark of excitement surging through her. "Smuggle you in? Pretend you're my date?"

He nodded, his eyes searching her face. "Would you?"

"I don't know. Who are you supposed to meet?"

"Ted Lazar."

"The casino general manager?" she asked. He nodded. The very man Bob wanted her to meet tonight. "What's it about?" she asked.

"Business." He waved his hand impatiently. "It's too complicated to go into. But the timing on this thing is critical, and it's getting late. I want to get in there before Ted decides to take off."

Kelli wondered how much of his story was true. *Business*, he'd said. How vague was *that*? But she saw no threat in his anxious, blue gaze. Instinct told her she could trust him. And the element of intrigue...well, intrigued her.

The elevator touched down again and a handful of people in party dress spewed out. "Well?" he asked, gesturing toward the waiting lift.

Life is not a spectator sport, Kelli thought. This was the most interesting, attractive man she'd met in years. A smile lit her face. "Sure," she said. "Why not?" And she stepped lightly into the empty elevator in front of him.

He punched the button for the top floor. "I can't tell you how much I appreciate this." They began to ascend, and he leaned against the side wall and smiled at her for the first time. He looked even more handsome when he smiled. Disarmingly so.

"What's your name?"

"Kelli Ann Harrison."

"Kelli Ann. Beautiful name. It suits you."

She held on to the side rail, her heart beating oddly as his eyes held hers for a long moment. "Thanks. And you are?"

"Grant Pembroke."

She was going to say "Pleased to meet you," but decided that sounded trite, so she settled for a simple "Hi."

He said hi back, his gaze never leaving her face. Bemused by his intense study, she dragged her eyes away from his, focusing instead on the way his short, black hair curled slightly above the collar of his blue shirt. Expensive-looking shirt. Gorgeous hair. Conservative cut. Probably a desk job. No, something more adventuresome than that. "Are you with the CIA?" she asked.

His eyes widened. "The CIA?"

"Well, you know, all this cloak-and-dagger stuff. Very suspicious."

The Harrison Duet

He laughed. It was a low-pitched, pleasant laugh, and she liked the way it sounded in the enclosed space. "This is hardly cloak-and-dagger. More like block and tackle."

She wanted to ask him more, but the elevator slowed and jerked to a halt. Another bevy of party-goers waited in the hotel hallway as they squeezed out. Grant led the way down the ribbon of red-and-black patterned carpet to a small table where a stocky guard in the hotel uniform sat reading a magazine. Kelli could hear the hum of laughter and conversation through the closed door beside him marked Presidential Suite.

"My date finally got here," Grant said, and told the guard Kelli's name. "Check and see if Lazar put her on the list instead of me."

The doorman picked up a sheaf of papers from the table and made a slow, meticulous check mark beside her name.

"This man is with you?" he asked, frowning.

Kelli smiled and nodded. With a shrug, he hauled himself out of his chair and opened the door. Grant's hand dropped from her shoulder to the small of her back and he accompanied her inside, where a crowd of people in elegant evening dress milled against a backdrop of soft music and drifting cigarette smoke.

Christmas was still three weeks away, but red and green tinsel garlands were strung across a wall of brocade curtains, along with a banner that read Happy Birthday in large, red letters. Tantalizing, spicy aromas wafted toward her from an elaborate hors d'oeuvres table in the center of the room.

Grant drew her away from the door and leaned close to her ear. "Thanks," he whispered.

His breath was a sweet, moist vapor against skin that seared with unexpected heat.

"You're welcome," she said softly.

226

He straightened and inclined his head to search through the crowd. His hand still at her back, he said distractedly, "Will you be free later? Because if you are, this won't take long. Would you like to meet back here in say, about an hour?"

Kelli was seized by an impulse to accept, to say as a matter of fact, I'm free for the evening, and I'd love to meet you anywhere, anytime. But reason intervened. Bob *had* invited her, and he'd show up any minute. "I'm sorry. I can't. I'm meeting someone."

Grant turned back to face her, his blue eyes dimmed with apparent regret. "Anyone important?"

"Possibly my boss."

"*Possibly* your boss?"

"He offered me a position with his company. I haven't accepted it yet."

"I see." He ran a hand through his dark hair and shook his head with a worried frown. "Still, is this going to get you in trouble? Letting me in the way you did? The doorman's sure to tell him—"

"Don't worry about it. I'll come up with some excuse."

"I don't know. I'd hate to see—"

"I'll be fine. Honest."

He sighed. "Well, then, so be it." He paused for a couple of heartbeats, looking into her eyes. "Goodbye, Kelli Ann Harrison." He held out his hand.

She placed her hand in his. As she returned his firm handshake, unsteady pulses began to thump in strange places in her body.

"Thanks again," he said.

She had to blink twice to watch him as he turned and wove his way through the crowd. It wasn't until he'd disap-

The Harrison Duet

peared from sight that she let out the breath she'd been holding in a long, wistful sigh.

Well. So much for a brush with destiny—the proverbial chance encounter with a mysterious stranger. She had acted spontaneously, lived a bit dangerously, then duty called and *poof!* She was right back where she started. Normal, everyday existence.

She caught herself. What was wrong with *normal?* Things were shaping up very nicely in her life at the moment, thank you very much. She relished her independence. She wasn't looking for another entangling relationship; she'd barely recovered from the last one. It was just as well that Grant had walked away.

Kelli wandered idly through the room for several minutes, observing the party-goers, mulling over a few possible explanations to give Bob. A tuxedoed waiter offered her a glass of champagne—one of her favorite beverages—but she declined, wanting to keep her head clear for the meeting to come. Instead, she crossed to the circular buffet table, where a tiered silver centerpiece spilled over with fresh fruit of every color and description. An attractive arrangement of trays below was filled with plump prawns, stuffed mushrooms, puff pastries, and marinated chicken wings. The mingling aromas made her mouth water.

She was about to reach for a plate when a laugh caught her attention. Her eyes shot toward a wide doorway into an adjoining room, where she saw Grant shaking hands with a rotund man in a dark-blue suit. Lazar? she wondered hopefully. A giddy sense of elation swept over her, as if she'd just helped perpetrate an undercover scheme of vast magnitude and importance. He couldn't have done it without me, she thought—and then realized she didn't know what *it* was. Was

Syrie James

that fair? Couldn't he at least have told her what business he was in?

She slipped across the room, through the open doorway. She squeezed between a knot of people and stopped behind a leafy potted palm as tall as the door. I'll just listen long enough to find out why he's here, she promised herself, parting the fronds slightly and peering through at Grant's back a feet away.

"Don't be too hard on him, Ted," Grant was saying. *Ted. So it was Ted Lazar.* "He was just doing his job."

"Job, shmob. I'm gonna give him hell." Ted was a head shorter than Grant, about the same height as herself, a paternal type with a fringe of white hair and a congenial yet commanding air. "Stupid of me to forget, it's been a hectic day, but he shouldn't have turned you away without looking for me."

"Don't worry about it," Grant said. "I managed to get in." Kelli liked the way his tapered grey suit jacket fit smoothly across the wide expanse of his shoulders and the slope of his back. "I know you're on a tight deadline so I didn't want to waste any time. I've had my eye on Cassera's for years, Ted. We're the people you're looking for. We can do a hell of a job for you."

"Not so fast, Grant." Ted's laugh was low and gravelly. "I didn't promise anything. I just said we'd talk."

"If you're not happy with the people handling you now, I'd think you'd want to do more than just talk."

"Maybe." Ted lifted a cigar to his lips and inhaled deeply, then squinted puffy eyes and blew out a slow column of smoke. "When you called this morning, I agreed to meet you because I've seen your work. Damned good. One of the best ad agencies in San Francisco, I'm told, even if you're not one of the biggest. And your list of clients is impressive."

The Harrison Duet

Kelli let the palm fronds flip back into place and froze, her heart pounding in sudden comprehension. Grant Pembroke owned an advertising agency. He was here to try to steal the casino account from Bob Dawson!

"Kelli! There you are." A hand touched Kelli's shoulder and she jumped, repressing a startled scream. "I've been looking all over for you," Bob said.

He wore a black suit and striped shirt that looked positively dapper, and his thick shock of silvery-blond hair was carefully combed, not a hair out of place.

"Sorry I'm so late," he continued. "I got tied up at the office and couldn't get away. Then traffic was horrendous—it took me five hours to get here." He elbowed his way back into the main suite, pulling her with him. "The guard told me you came in with someone. Why didn't you tell me you wanted to bring a friend?"

"I...ran into him unexpectedly," Kellie said. *That was certainly true, wasn't it?* "He only stayed a few minutes."

"Where did he go? You shouldn't have brought him up here. He wasn't cleared." Bob grabbed two champagne glasses from a passing tray and handed one to Kelli. He raised his glass. "To my newest and most attractive creative director. Cheers." He took a long drink.

I haven't accepted the job yet, Kelli wanted to tell him, staring dubiously at her glass. Champagne was for celebrations. Weddings. Christenings. Bon-voyage parties. Romantic evenings for two. Somehow she didn't feel like celebrating tonight.

"What do you think about all this?" Bob indicated the crowded room with a nod of his head. "Did you take a look around downstairs? Ever work on an account this size?" He took another drink. "Wait till you meet Lazar. He's a sweetheart of a guy. Let's go find him and introduce you."

Syrie James

Kelli tensed with anxiety. "No, wait." Grant would no doubt be talking to Ted Lazar for a while. What would Bob say if he discovered *she'd* admitted one of his *competitors* to the party? Somehow she had to keep them apart. "Before I meet him I should know everything that's going on with the account," she said, trying to stall for time. "You told me yesterday there's a big campaign coming up?"

Bob nodded. *"Big* is an understatement. The board decided they're tired of the old logo and the look we've been using on all the collateral materials. They want a brand-new print image for the hotel and casino, everything revamped. And a new campaign to go with it."

Kelli took a surprised breath. Everything revamped. A hotel and casino this large would use a ton of collateral materials—brochures, menus, coupons, stationery, rate cards—not to mention a whole new ad campaign.

"The account's kept us pretty busy for six years," Bob said, "but we're talking big bucks now."

Kelli felt a rush of excitement. She'd never worked on a project of such magnitude. Dawson Advertising must not be on retainer, or Grant wouldn't be here trying to steal the account away. "Is anyone else bidding on this?"

"Just one agency, a small fish out of Reno. Routine stuff, to make sure our prices stay in line. Nothing to worry about."

So, he didn't know about Grant. "Why nothing to worry about?"

"They don't have a chance in hell of coming up with a workable campaign," Bob said with a self-indulgent smirk. "I took a little trip to Reno a few weeks ago. I've got three of the guy's top people working for me now—his head account exec, copy chief, and art director. Wasn't hard to spirit them away. Even dedicated souls will move on if you offer them the

231

The Harrison Duet

right price." His chuckle stopped when he saw the expression on her face. "Don't look so shocked. Everyone does it. It's a cutthroat business. You don't stay on top by sitting back and twiddling your thumbs. You've got to nip trouble in the bud before it starts."

Bob drained his glass. "Take today, for instance. This hot shot from San Francisco tried to move in on my territory. When Ted told me he called—Ted likes to keep me on my toes, it's a power trip he plays—hell, this account's been mine for six years. I'm not going to waste my time on a proposal of this size while he puts it out to bid to every Tom, Dick, and Harry that comes along. And I'm sure as hell not going to let Pembroke Advertising steal it away."

Kelli's pulse quickened. "What did you do?"

"Just told Ted a few things I 'heard' about Pembroke." Bob chuckled. "Spread a few rumors."

"What did you say?" Kelli asked, her stomach knotting.

"Who cares, as long as it works? Fifty bucks says Ted won't give Grant Pembroke the time of day now."

Kelli felt sick. She'd been uncomfortable in Bob's office the day before, and now she knew why. This man's business tactics turned sleaze into a new art form. How could she even have considered working for him? How could she have considered working for *anyone*?

I may not make much money free-lancing, she thought, but at least I have my integrity. She'd only agreed to the interview in a moment of financial despair. Now she realized she'd never wanted the job in the first place. When she got back to Seattle she'd build up her business, make a go of it somehow. And she'd never—no, *never*—work for anyone else again.

A weight seemed to lift from her shoulders with this decision, and her gaze slanted back into the adjoining room.

She spotted Grant, still talking to Ted Lazar. Did Grant know Bob was bad-mouthing him behind his back? Someone ought to tell him. She wondered if Ted believed the rumors about Grant, whether they might ruin Grant's chances to bid on the account.

It would serve Bob right if Grant stole the account out from under his nose, she thought.

"Bob," she said, taking his arm and leading him deeper into the crowd, away from the palm plant shielding Grant, "I wonder if you'd excuse me for a minute." She glanced meaningfully toward the front door and he nodded in understanding.

"The ladies' lounge is just down the hall," he said, pointing. "Look for me around here when you're through."

"I will." When he'd gone, Kelli made her way back through the crowd into the other room, her heart racing with anticipation. She stopped behind the palm plant again, listening.

"I appreciate you coming up here," Ted said. "The thing is, I don't want to waste your time on this if we're not right for each other. And there's so much going on. I'm supposed to propose a toast to the birthday boy in half an hour. Why don't you call me next week? Give me a few days to check some things out before I give you any details."

"Check what out? Ted, I'll need to get started on this as soon as possible. Let's go down to your office, where it's quiet. Five minutes, that's all I ask."

Ted sighed. "Grant, let me be frank with you. I've heard nothing but praise for the work you do. But quality isn't the only thing I'm looking for. I need performance, someone who can meet my schedule, who's easy to work with. And since I talked to you last, I've heard a few things I don't like. Things that say you don't fit the bill."

The Harrison Duet

"I don't fit the—what are you talking about? Who've you been talking to?"

"I heard you're temperamental," Ted said. "Stubborn. No one wants to work for you. You like to run the whole show. And worse yet, I hear you're slow. You take forever to finish a job."

"That's absurd. I probably have less staff turnover than any agency in the city. We meet our deadlines, Ted, and then some. Ask any one of my clients. I'll give you a list. You can call them tomorrow."

Kelli fumed inwardly. Bob Dawson's nasty rumors were working far too well. She had to do something to help.

Something…

"I'll make a few calls tomorrow," Ted said. "Maybe I'll talk to someone who'll change my mind. But right now I don't want to spend any more—"

"Excuse me," Kelli said, brushing past the palm plant to stand at Grant's side. Out of the corner of her eye, she could see him stiffen in surprise. "Don't believe everything you've heard about Grant's temperament," she said, fixing Lazar with a dazzling smile. "He's not really as difficult to work with as you'd imagine. Honestly, he's a pussycat at heart. And as for the company being slow…ridiculous. Ten minutes in your office and I'll prove otherwise."

Lazar's bushy brows lifted in fatherly admiration. "Is that right? And who are you, little lady?"

Kelli grinned at Grant, who was staring at her in wide-eyed astonishment, then turned back to Lazar and extended her hand. "I'm Kelli Ann Harrison, Creative Director for Pembroke Advertising."

2

"Creative director?" Ted Lazar beamed and shook Kelli's hand with a hearty grip. His tanned, leathery face and kind, dark eyes reminded her of her feisty grandfather, and she liked him at once. "Grant, why didn't you introduce this lovely lady before? Where've you been hiding her?"

"I just arrived," Kelli said. "In fact, Grant wasn't even sure I'd be here tonight." She heard a small choke from Grant beside her, but plunged on. "But as long as I am, I thought, why not stop by and put in my two cents' worth?" She smiled brightly.

"Glad you did." Ted waved his cigar from Kelli to Grant and back again. "How long have you two been working together?"

"Not long," Grant said sharply.

Kelli dared a glance at Grant. His direct gaze seemed to pierce through her. The initial astonishment was gone, replaced by wary incomprehension and a silent, deadly serious warning. She could only guess how all this would appear to him. He didn't know what she did for a living, didn't know she was only doing this to help win the account. But there was no way to explain. She'd gone this far; she couldn't back out now.

"I may be new with the company," Kelli told Ted, "but I can tell you this: any rumors you've heard about Grant's temperament

235

The Harrison Duet

are just that. Rumors. In all the time I've been with Grant, I've never heard him raise his voice to an employee or make an unreasonable demand of anyone." And that, she thought, is the truth.

An even more puzzled look flashed across the deep blue of Grant's eyes. He opened his mouth to speak, then shut it again.

"Well, well, well. This puts a different light on things." The tip of Ted's cigar glowed as he inhaled deeply, then blew out a slow column of smoke. "Grant, if I'd known you had a charming associate who thinks so highly of you—" He shrugged. "I guess I can spare a few minutes in my office, as long as you're both here. Come with me."

"Hold on a minute, Ted," Grant said, but apparently Ted didn't hear. Ted took Kelli's arm and led her away, through the crowd and out a nearby side door, commenting that the champagne hadn't been cold enough and anyway the line for the cocktail show would be starting soon downstairs and people would be leaving in droves. Over her shoulder, Kelli saw Grant just a step or two behind.

"In here," Ted said, unlocking a wide door at the end of the hall and ushering them inside. The large corner office was carpeted in deep, vivid blue and furnished in polished oak. Paneled walls were hung with oil paintings depicting Lake Tahoe's Mount Tallac in different seasons. There was a wet bar, an assortment of bonsai pine trees, and a row of what looked like antique slot machines. But the most astonishing feature of the room was the view.

Kelli felt herself drawn to the solid wall of plate-glass windows across the back of the room. Stars twinkled in the inky darkness like finely cut diamonds, and the three-quarter moon cast a midnight-blue sheen on the waters of Lake Tahoe stretching out endlessly some fifteen stories below.

"Beautiful," Kelli said.

"You should see it by day." Ted moved around his desk, which was wider than a door and covered with a collection of bronze and glass figurines in athletic poses: snow skiing, golfing, sailing, waterskiing. From a credenza behind he picked up a stack of art boards covered in heavy blue paper. "Miss Harrison—it is Miss, isn't it?"

"Yes. But please, call me Kelli."

Ted sat down in his large armchair, indicating the two leather chairs opposite the desk. "Take a seat. I don't have much time." He slid the stack of boards across a clear space of desk to rest in front of Kelli. "Kelli, I'd like your opinion on this. It's a presentation our agency put together for us some weeks ago, for a series of—"

"We'd both be delighted to take a look at what you've got," Grant cut in tersely, leaning a hand on the desk, "but if you want an off-the-cuff analysis you'll have to get it from me."

"I'm familiar with your work, Pembroke." Ted motioned politely for Grant to move out of the way. "I want to hear what Kelli has to say."

"No!" Grant shook his head. "Look, Ted, Kelli doesn't—"

"What are you afraid of, Grant?" Ted glared at him. "Maybe those rumors are true, after all. Don't you have any faith in your employees? Do you always have to run the whole show? Let the woman talk."

Grant pushed off the desk and threw up his hands in resignation. "Oh, the hell with it." He shoved his hands in his pockets and crossed to the far side of the room, shaking his head, the tension coiled in his shoulders and limbs almost tangible.

Kelli sensed how much was at stake here and felt a stab of guilt, followed by panic. What if this whole thing backfired?

The Harrison Duet

What if Ted didn't like what she had to say? She'd only intended to help get Grant in the door and have him take over from there. Apparently Ted had other ideas. Just do it, she told herself. Follow your instincts. It'll be all right.

She pulled a chair up to the desk and sat down. Lifting the heavy paper and inner tissue covering the first art board, she studied it with a practiced eye. It was a colorful, felt-tip pen layout for a magazine-size ad. Showgirls in brief costumes and spectacular headdresses were encircled by a collage of caricatures of recognizable stars. The headline, in a swash of red script, stretched across the top in two lines: *Catch A Show. Cassera's Tahoe!* Small lines indicated where additional copy would go below. After a moment she moved the board aside and glanced at two similar layouts for *TV Guide* ads, and color comps for a brochure and a menu.

"What do you think?" Lazar asked.

Kelli's palms began to perspire. She couldn't be overly critical. She knew Dawson Advertising had prepared the comps, and they hadn't handled this account for six years for nothing. The ads were well composed, highly professional. But layout was subjective, and these comps were not her style.

"About concept or composition?" she asked.

"Both."

She leaned forward in her chair and took a deep breath. "Composition first. Let's take this ad. There are some good ideas here, but the layout is too busy."

"Busy?" Lazar asked.

"There's too much going on. The collage of stars takes away from your primary focus—the showgirls. I'd recommend using fewer spot illustrations or dropping them altogether, for a clean, sharp look."

Lazar slapped the desktop with his palm. "Exactly what I said!"

238

Syrie James

"And I'd use a different typeface for the headline. Kabel Ultra or maybe Avant Garde Extra Bold. This script is too hard to read."

Across the room, Kelli saw Grant's hands come out of his pockets. His lips parted in consternation. She flashed him a proud, sprightly grin. *Who are you?* he'd probably ask in wonder when this was all over. *How on earth did you pull that off?*

"Do you have any scratch paper?" Kelli asked. "I'll show you what I mean."

"Sure." Ted found a blank notepad in his drawer and handed it to Kelli with a pencil.

Sitting back in her chair, propping the notepad on her knee, she quickly sketched out the ad as she saw it, a quick but detailed illustration with a bold headline across the top.

"That's much better," Ted agreed when she was finished. "How did you do that so fast?"

Kelli smiled modestly. "If you think I draw fast, you should see the rest of the staff. Believe me, meeting a client's deadline is never a problem." A little white lie couldn't hurt. With any luck, it might be true.

What was Grant thinking? Why didn't he say anything? She wanted to turn and see his face, but didn't dare. Instead, she answered Ted's questions about possible ideas for a new logo, commented on the color scheme of the brochure, and made a few suggestions for reworking the menu layout. Ted listened with rapt attention, pursing his lips and nodding in agreement.

Grant crossed the room and picked up the sketch she'd drawn. His eyes widened as he studied it. Darting an amazed glance in her direction, he set it aside and went through the art boards one by one.

"Good ideas, Kelli," Ted said when she'd finished her critique.

The Harrison Duet

"Yes." Grant leaned casually back against the desk, watching her. "Very good ideas." His thigh, lean and hard beneath his gray wool slacks, was just three inches from where her forearm rested on the desk edge. She could almost feel the dynamic energy his body radiated, and the heat of his gaze was like a magnet, drawing her eyes up to his. But when she looked up, instead of the admiration or appreciation or even grudging acceptance she'd expected to match his words, she met only calm, intense scrutiny with a hint of still-vital anger. Why? she wondered, alarmed. Couldn't he see that she'd meant only to help him?

"Now tell me," Ted said, "what you think of the overall concept for the ads. Based on what you know about the casino industry, do you think this would be an effective campaign?"

Kelli's mouth went dry. Bob had said they wanted a new look and a new media campaign, but he hadn't given her any details.

She didn't know a thing about the casino business.

Grant glanced at her, then tossed the boards onto the desk and faced Ted. "I think it's a mistake," he said bluntly. "Why place so much emphasis on your shows? I realize entertainment is a big selling factor, but it's such a small part of what you have to offer here in Tahoe." Grant went on to suggest that the new campaign emphasize the natural environment at Lake Tahoe, or try an approach that played up the fun-and-games aspect of gambling.

Ted leaned back in his chair, slanting his eyes at Grant, then chuckled. "Have you been talking to one of our VPs out there, Pembroke?"

"No," Grant said in surprise. "Why?"

Ted stood up. "Never mind. I like your style, Grant. And I like your associate. She's as talented as she is pretty, and with a

240

drawing arm that fast and accurate, I'd say you've found yourself a gold mine." He ripped a clean sheet off the notepad and scribbled a point-by-point listing, then handed it to Grant. "I'd like to see what you can cook up together. This is what we're looking for." He checked his calendar. "I'm going to be out of town tomorrow, but let's meet back here on Sunday for a tour and final details. Can you get a presentation to me, complete with pricing, in two weeks?"

"Two weeks?" Grant was clearly stunned. He studied Ted's list. "This is a lot to ask for, Ted, with only a two-week turn around."

"I understand. But we're up against a time limit here. Dawson Advertising's putting together a comprehensive presentation by that date, and you'll have to do the same if you want to compete."

After a brief pause, Grant said, "Okay. We'll do it. I'll give you a quote for the presentation work on Sunday, before we go ahead."

"A quote?" Ted let out a small laugh and shook his head. "Sorry if you misunderstood, but this is purely on spec, Grant. We don't pay unless you get the job."

"We don't work on spec." The two men faced each other across the desk. "You pay Dawson for every stroke of his artists' pens, don't you?"

"Yes, but that's—"

"We don't work for free, Ted. We're not that hungry. If you want to see our presentation, you pay for it."

Ted began to protest, then sighed. "All right, just make sure you stay in the ballpark. And you better make this worth my while, Grant."

Only the briefest upward twinge of Grant's lips hinted at his delight in their victory. "I will."

The Harrison Duet

"Great." Ted stood up, circled the table, and shook first Grant's hand, then Kelli's. Grant took Ted aside, pulled out his pocket calendar, and set up a meeting time.

Kelli stood idly by, listening but not included, and felt a sudden, ridiculous sense of loss and betrayal. She'd acted completely on impulse; she'd wanted to give Grant a chance to bid on the account, and she'd achieved that. He could move on without her now, make some excuse to Ted as to why she wasn't working for him anymore. She hadn't expected him to actually hire her. Had she?

"Let's get back to the party," Ted said. But when they reached the door leading to the presidential suite, Kelli thought of Bob, who was probably still inside, looking for her. She didn't want to run into him now.

"I'm sorry, but I have to go," she said, and thanked Ted once again for the meeting.

"I have to leave too," Grant said, much to her surprise. He gave Ted a parting handshake, and when Ted had disappeared inside, Grant strode down the empty hall in silence beside her until they reached the elevator. He pushed the call button, leaned against the wall by the doors, and looked at her. Equal measures of curiosity and controlled anger seemed to vie for dominance in his level blue gaze.

"Okay, lady, let's have it," he said calmly. "What's your game?"

She looked at him blankly. "Game?"

"I suppose you expect me to be grateful for all this. I got what I came for. I should pat you on the back because you helped make it happen." He shook his head, frowning. "That was quite a performance you gave in there. A real knockout. I may be pleased with the way things turned out, but I'm no fool. I don't appreciate being jerked around, and your methods leave a bad taste in my mouth."

242

Kelli took a step back, stunned into silence. Whatever reaction she'd anticipated from Grant, it wasn't this.

"You said you were meeting your boss at the party, or was it *possibly* your boss," he went on. "I saw you talking with Bob Dawson. Either you're working for *him*, or you're working for *yourself*. Which is it?"

"I'm not working for anyone," she replied.

"Come on." He laughed lightly. "I know how Bob operates. He's about as scrupulous as a four-handed pick-pocket. The minute you barged in and introduced yourself to Ted, I smelled a rat. At first I thought you were going to be charming but demonstrate a shocking lack of expertise. Ted would then question my judgment in hiring you and I could kiss the account goodbye. But then you came out with that speech about layout and logos and typefaces...you had the man eating out of your hand. I guessed then that I must have the scenario all wrong. You were there to wrap Ted around your little finger, to make yourself so indispensable to the account that I'd hire you on in an instant."

Hot waves of both anger and despair surged through her at this unflattering interpretation of her actions. "You don't understand. I wish I could have explained earlier, but there wasn't time."

"There's time now. I've got all night. I'm sure I'd find your story fascinating." He glanced up at the elevator indicator, which seemed to be stuck on the fifth floor. He pushed the call button again. "What I want to know is, are you in it for yourself? Are you so desperate for a job that you concocted this little scheme to force me into hiring you? Or are you the Trojan horse, well prepped by Dawson and sent to infiltrate my ranks?"

"Bob Dawson doesn't know anything about this. He offered me a job, but then I saw you were having problems

The Harrison Duet

with Ted and I just wanted to help. I can see now that it was a mistake. Believe me, the last thing I'd ever do is work for you!"

The doors to the presidential suite burst open. Party hum and laughter filled the hall. Bob Dawson stalked out, followed by two other chattering couples who headed for the elevator. Bob caught sight of Kelli and Grant and walked slowly toward them, his lips turning up into an icy grin.

"What do you know?" Bob stopped in front of Kelli and shook his head. "He told me, but I didn't believe it. Kelli, I have to admit, I'm a little disappointed in you. I thought you'd enjoy working for us, especially on this account. But obviously that's not in the cards."

Kelli had no idea what to say, so she clutched her handbag and took a step back, lowering her eyes. The elevator arrived with a ding and she hurried inside, behind the other two couples.

"My hat's off to you, Pembroke," Bob said. "You stole away my new creative director before day one on the job. Good show. I hope she sticks around for you longer than she did for me."

Grant glanced over his shoulder at Kelli and the closing elevator doors in alarm. "Count on it, Bob," he said. He lunged for the doors, caught them just in time, and stepped in.

Two women were wedged between them in elevator tightness, yet Kelli felt Grant's eyes boring steadily into her as they were whisked downstairs. Had he changed his tune? Was he going to apologize? Or would he demand an explanation? She saw no reason to give it to him. When they'd been deposited in the lobby, she swept past him and headed straight for the coat-check counter.

"Kelli, wait."

244

She had long legs and was a fast walker, despite her high heels, but he matched her stride easily.

"You were on the level, weren't you?"

"Forget it."

"I'm not going to forget it. If you had a job with Dawson, why'd you abandon ship to help me?"

"It doesn't matter."

"It does matter." His hand closed over her arm and he stopped, pulling her to an abrupt halt beside a busy roulette table. Voices buzzed around her and she could hear a distant ringing bell, a shout, the accompanying clatter of coins. "We need to talk."

The gentle pressure of his fingers sent hot shivers up her arm, and she realized it was the only time he'd touched her other than their brief handshake earlier that evening. Come on, Kelli, she reproached herself. The man accuses you of professional conspiracy and you turn to jelly at his touch? "We don't need to talk," she said firmly.

"Yes we do. I owe you an apology, and you owe me an explanation. Come on, I'm buying you a drink."

"You are *not* buying me a drink. I have nothing to say to you. And I'm *not* thirsty." Which was untrue. She'd barely tasted the champagne at the party and was dying for something cold and frothy. But she wasn't about to let him bully her into going anywhere.

He released her arm with a frustrated gesture. "Kelli...the Cassera's account means a great deal to me and to my company. I saw you talking to Dawson at the party and I suspected the worst. I'm sorry. I'm grateful for what you did, even if I did come off like a complete jerk back there."

She fought back a smile. "You did."

"At least we agree on something." He laughed softly. "Look, can we forget the past ten minutes and start fresh? Can we go somewhere and talk? Please?"

In his eyes she saw the same vulnerability, the same warmhearted plea that had made her agree to help him in to the party in the first place. She couldn't doubt his sincerity. Something inside her—like the whirring roulette wheel beside her—went *zing* and spun and turned over. She gave in to her smile.

"Where," she said, "did you have in mind?"

"So when I found out the way Bob takes care of his competition, I knew I could never work for him."

"I don't blame you. I've known that guy for seven years. This isn't the first time he's tried to stab me in the back." Grant sat next to her at a small corner booth in a lounge off the casino floor, and they'd just ordered drinks.

"I figured you ought to know," Kelli said. "And when I overheard Ted, that was the last straw. I thought if I could somehow convince him the rumors weren't true...I guess it was pretty reckless of me—"

"It was damn reckless. And totally crazy." Grant grinned. "And I'd probably have done the same thing in your shoes."

"You would?"

"I would."

She laughed. "I'm lucky it didn't backfire. I wasn't really thinking ahead or considering the consequences."

"Sometimes spontaneous actions are the best kind. If you think too hard about doing something you can usually talk yourself out of it."

He seemed about to say more, when the waitress arrived with their drinks. Kelli accepted her piña colada gratefully and took a sip of the refreshing coconutty froth.

"Where do you live?" Grant asked. "Here in Tahoe?"

"No. Seattle." Her brother Kyle, she explained, was building a vacation house at Glenbrook Bay, a sleepy little cove about eleven miles up the road. She'd agreed to stay there for the next three weeks to supervise the details during the final phase of construction. "What about you? Your agency's in San Francisco?"

He nodded. He'd been in business for himself for the past eight years, he told her. He'd had his eye on the casinos, but most of them had in-house agencies or were tied up with long-term contracts. "This morning, when I heard Cassera's was out to bid, I saw my chance. Ted agreed to meet me at the party and I dashed up here."

"Hardly a *dash*," Kelli said, knowing that San Francisco was a three-hour drive from Tahoe under the best conditions.

"True. I didn't get out of the office until five, and then I hit traffic. I was afraid I'd be too late, miss Ted entirely. And I would have, if not for you."

He lifted his Scotch in a salute and took a sip. Leaning back, he stretched one arm across the top of the seat and smiled at her. She smiled back. She liked the charged directness of his eyes. They approved of her looks, made her feel feminine, attractive, admired. His complexion was fair, smooth looking, touchable. His shoulders were broad and his arms, beneath the suit jacket, had a look of strength to them. She remembered the rest of his body was slim, trim, gracefully put together.

"That long, huh?"

With an embarrassed flush, Kelli realized she'd missed something he said. What was she doing, thinking about his body? "I'm sorry?"

The Harrison Duet

"I asked how long you've been in advertising?"

"Oh! Six years."

"Have you always been able to draw that fast?"

Matter-of-factly, she said, "Yes. When I was a kid, I won the Quick Draw Contest at the county fair three years in a row."

"The Quick Draw Contest? That's a new one. I take it that's with a pencil, not a revolver?"

She laughed. "Yes."

"What happened after three years?"

"I stopped competing."

"Decided to give the other kids a chance, huh?" He raised his eyebrows, smiling. "Well, you sure impressed the heck out of Ted back there. Not only fast, but damned good."

"Thank you."

"So what happened after the county fair? Did you study art in college?"

She nodded, brushing back a lock of her reddish-gold hair. "For the past four years I've been working as the art director for T & M in Seattle."

"Thompson and McGuire? I know them. Top-notch firm. You must have worked on the Great Pacific Bank campaign. The one that won the art direction award?"

"You saw it?" she asked, delighted.

"Who could miss it? Imaginative logo, the way the people's profiles blended into the trees. And the colors were both subtle and eye-catching..." He paused, apparently catching something in her expression. "Was that your design?"

"Yes."

He whistled. "Hot stuff, lady. I'm impressed." He sat forward, his eyes alive with interest. "What else have you done?"

She mentioned a few national campaigns she'd worked on, including a popular color ad for a cruise line that he'd seen and admired. It had showed a leggy young woman in a bikini, relaxing on deck in the hot sun, her tropical drink and festive sombrero lying beside her lounge chair. The headline had read *Bake Sale.*

"I wished I'd done it," Grant said. "Who came up with that great headline?"

"I did."

His eyebrows lifted. "A woman of many talents. You do award-winning design and write copy, too?"

"Sometimes. I like coming up with the whole concept, but I didn't often get the opportunity."

He regarded her for a moment. "Why'd you leave T & M?"

"I decided to try it on my own." She'd been free-lancing for the past couple of months, she explained, when they announced the Advertising Association awards. "The next day Bob Dawson called and asked me to come down for an interview. I had to be in Tahoe anyway for a few weeks, and San Francisco wasn't too far out of the way, so I decided, why not?"

"Why not, indeed. I'll say one thing for Dawson. He's a shrewd businessman. He finds the best, most talented people in this industry and he goes after them."

Kelli flushed at his praise. In the ensuing silence he lifted his glass, took a drink. Her gaze dropped to his hands. She couldn't help noticing what long, well-shaped fingers he had. The backs of his hands and wrists, visible beyond the cuffs of his shirt, were lightly dusted with dark, soft-looking hairs. Incredibly masculine. To distract her thoughts, she plucked the paper umbrella out of the pineapple wedge adorning her glass and twirled it between her fingers.

"You deserved that award," Grant said. "The design was sensational."

The Harrison Duet

"Oh, it was no big deal, really," Kelli said with attempted nonchalance. "The idea came to me in a flash one night while I was taking a bath."

He choked on his drink. Her cheeks grew hot. Did she actually say that?

"Is that where you get all your ideas?" he asked.

She tried to swallow. "A lot of the good ones."

"I'll have to remember that." Grant's lips twitched with amusement.

"What about you?" she asked, in a desperate effort to change the subject. "What have you done that I'd recognize?"

"I guess my favorite over the past year was the Shop N Go chain-store commercials. I had a lot of fun with those."

"You mean those hilarious TV and radio spots with all the little kids?"

"I don't know if I'd call them hilarious—"

"They were! I loved them."

He shrugged. "No big deal. The idea came to me in a flash one night while I was—"

"Oh, stop." She resisted an impulse to punch him playfully on the arm. "You wrote them, then?"

"Wrote them, produced them. I have a top-notch staff, but I like to play my hand on the big projects. Copywriting is my strong suit. That, and rough creative direction."

He went on to name a few of his clients and recent campaigns his agency had worked on, but Kelli unconsciously tuned out his words, her attention drifting instead to the soft gleam of the overhead lights against his dark hair, the long eyelashes that veiled his eyes, the way his mouth moved as he spoke. His lips were perfectly formed, sensuous. It'd be a wonderful mouth for—

"Are you thinking what I'm thinking?"

250

Kelli blinked, becoming aware that he was gazing at her with disarming intensity. "What?"

"I think you are. I think you know we'd make one hell of a team." His voice was low and deep and seemed to vibrate through her. "Kelli, come work for me."

3

Kelli stared at Grant across the table, trying to rein in her wandering thoughts. *Come work for me. We'd make one hell of a team*, he'd said. She realized she had a completely different sort of team in mind.

"I just picked up three new accounts that are as big and important as Cassera's," Grant went on. "My staff is up to their ears. On my way up here tonight I realized if I *did* get the chance to bid on this thing, I was going to have to hire some new help. When Ted named his deadline, I knew I was in trouble. I've only got two weeks to put this proposal together. I don't usually make a job offer without seeing an artist's portfolio, but I've seen your work. I can use another creative director. Ted already thinks you're working for me, so why not keep it that way?"

After all that had happened that evening, Kelli certainly hadn't expected a job offer from Grant Pembroke. But he was a fascinating man: charming, talented, obviously intelligent. He was respected in the business. She couldn't deny her attraction to him. And it might be exciting to live and work in San Francisco...

No, she thought, with sudden determination. She'd already decided *not* to take a job with another agency. She wanted to prove to herself that she could be a success on her own. If Bob and Grant were both so anxious to hire her, she must have more potential than she realized. She ought to stick to her guns.

"I'm flattered by the offer," she said slowly. "But to tell you the truth, I'm committed to my own free-lance business in Seattle."

"Then why did you accept a job with Dawson?"

"I didn't accept the job; I told you, I was just considering it."

"Considering it strongly enough to show up here tonight."

"Yes," she admitted, "but only because my financial situation's been tight. I've thought more about it this evening. I'm hoping, since I won the art-direction award, that my business will pick up when I get back home."

"I'm sure it will." He frowned. "Okay. How about free-lancing for me, then? Join my staff just until this job's done. I need the help, and your input would be valuable on this proposal. You can drive down to the city tomorrow, look my place over. If you like what you see, you can start on Monday."

Kelli hesitated. It was a tempting proposition. She'd love to work free-lance on this job for the casino. She could use the money, and it would look terrific in her portfolio. But...there was her promise to her brother to consider. Reluctantly, she said, "I wish I could. But I can't."

"Why not?"

"I'm committed to staying here at Tahoe for at least another three weeks, until my brother's house is finished."

He stared at her. "Three weeks?"

She nodded, trying not to let her disappointment get the best of her. "Kyle's had a lot of problems since they started construction, because he couldn't be here very often to keep an eye on things. Walls and doorways and windows in the wrong

The Harrison Duet

places, they built the stairs and fireplaces wrong—you name it. The contractor wasn't doing his job and didn't keep to the schedule—the house was supposed to be finished two months ago—and now he took off on vacation, leaving nobody in charge. Kyle is furious. He wants to bring his family up for Christmas, and I agreed to oversee the last phase of the work, to see that it gets done in time."

"Wow. How'd he rope you into coming all the way down from Seattle to do that?"

"He didn't rope me into it. He asked. He lives in Newport Beach, and is a very successful businessman. He didn't have time to come out here right now. I did. I was glad to help." She shrugged, adding lightly, "Then, of course, there was the bribe."

"Bribe?"

"Free and unlimited use of the house, in perpetuity, anytime I want."

"Ah! I'm beginning to understand your motivation." He smiled. "Still, he might be able to find someone else to fill in as contractor. If he knew you had a—"

"There's no time to find someone else, and he's not going to trust this to a stranger. I made a promise, Grant. I wish there was some other way—" she sighed "—but there isn't."

Grant fell silent. After a moment he leaned back with a shrug. "Well, I guess that's that. It was worth a shot." He checked his watch. "I'd better hit the road. I have to get back to the city tonight. Let me walk you to your car."

She slid out of the booth and accompanied him across the casino floor to retrieve their coats, feeling let down and mildly dejected. It occurred to her with sudden clarity that if she didn't work for Grant on this job, she might never see him again. That eventuality didn't seem to bother him, however. In fact, as they

254

crossed the immense back parking lot, she felt certain she saw a speculative gleam in his eyes. She remembered that same look from the moment they met, in front of the elevators. What was he thinking?

She had to hurry to keep up with him. Her cheeks stung from the crisp night air by the time they reached her car.

"*That's* your car?" Grant asked, his eyes widening with apparent amusement when he caught sight of the old, boxy-looking sedan with its fading paint job in British racing green.

"It is," Kelli said proudly, opening her door. They didn't sell or service Rovers anymore in the U.S. and most people thought it odd that she owned one.

"This is uncanny." He leaned down to look inside. "I've never—"

"I searched long and hard to find this car. It's the best model Rover ever made, and this one's in tip-top condition." For some reason she felt compelled to defend it. "I just had the seats recovered. Better than new." She would have covered them in real leather, if she could have afforded it, but the soft beige vinyl was a good imitation.

He stood and met her gaze, seeming to choose his words carefully. "It's very nice. Really."

She tossed her purse onto the front seat and waited, realizing she didn't want to talk about her car, but didn't want to say goodbye, either.

He stood nearby in silence, watching her, his lips pressed together in a regretful frown. He lifted his hand as if to touch her cheek, then seemed to think better of it and extended it to her to shake. "Kelli...you're a terrific lady. Thanks again for your help tonight—for winning Ted over. It was an experience I won't forget."

The knot of disappointment she'd felt as they crossed the parking lot intensified, surging hot and sharp through her chest. Was he really going to just say goodbye? Just like that? Had she only imagined the glimmer in his eyes each time their gazes had touched? She thought of offering him her phone number, then realized she didn't know the new number back at the house.

What about her phone number back in Seattle? Wasn't he even going to ask for that?

No, she reprimanded herself sternly. She shouldn't be thinking of him that way. After her breakup with Wayne, she'd promised herself to stay free and independent for a while, to avoid any relationships with a man until she'd proven she could make a success of her life on her own. And she hadn't proven it yet. Far from it.

She shook his hand. "Goodbye."

Before letting her hand go, he gave it a firm squeeze. "Good night, Kelli," he said softly. "I hope we'll meet again sometime."

He smiled and then walked away.

Kelli opened her eyes to bright sunlight. She rolled over inside her sleeping bag and picked up her watch from the plywood floor beside her, peering at it through sleep-blurred eyes.

Almost ten-thirty. Damn! Saturday, the first day no workmen were due to arrive, and she'd overslept. No point in going skiing now. By the time she got there, half the day would be gone, and the slopes would be crowded with weekend skiers.

It was no wonder she'd slept so late. The night had passed miserably. It wasn't only the eerie, creaking sounds of the empty house that had kept sleep at bay, but thoughts of Grant—his smile, the look in his eyes, and the feel of his hand pressing firmly against hers both times he'd said goodbye. She wished, now, she hadn't been so definite in her refusal to work free-lance with him on the casino campaign.

Couldn't they have come up with some kind of compromise? What if he'd met her here for a few brainstorming sessions? Another artist, back at his agency, could have drawn up the presentation. No, she realized, that would never work. Another artist couldn't accurately interpret her ideas. She'd seen enough of that in her last job. The finished product never came out the way she'd envisioned.

She sighed. It obviously wasn't meant to be.

Kelli crawled out of the sleeping bag, shivering when her bare feet touched the cold floor. She quickly pulled on a pair of jeans, a woolly red pullover, and heavy socks, then stepped into her comfortable after-ski boots.

She looked about the large, freshly paneled master bedroom, empty except for her suitcase, sleeping bag, pillows, blankets, air mattress, and the toolbox she'd brought in from the car to attach wall plates over the electrical outlets. She'd made sure the rooms upstairs were nearly finished before she moved in, so she'd at least have *some* space to herself that was away from the workmen and free of sawdust.

This room, despite its size, was especially cozy with a rock fireplace, a sliding glass door on one side that led to a second-floor balcony, and an enormous bay window and window seat with a view of the sparkling lake below.

The Harrison Duet

Kelli freshened up at the double sink in the master bathroom, grimacing at the layer of dirt and dust covering the counter, mirror, and tile floor. All the fixtures, including the shower and soaking bathtub with its expanse of surrounding tile, were newly installed and just as dirty.

She'd clean today, she decided. A nice hot bath would be great to sink into tonight, when shadows crept around the house and not even the central heating could keep away the lonely chill. She'd scrub the tub, the whole bathroom, to a brilliant sheen. She'd done the kitchen the afternoon before, using up all the cleaning supplies and every single rag she'd had the foresight to bring from home. But a quick trip to the Laundromat in town and a stop at the supermarket, and she'd be set for another day's work.

After a hasty breakfast, she gathered up the bundle of laundry, hopped into her car, and headed south to the town of Stateline, so named because it crossed the Nevada-California border. The sky was overcast with the promise of snow. Dense pines stretched up the mountainside on her left as she drove. On the opposite side of the winding highway she caught glimpses of the lake through the trees.

Soon she rounded a bend and the row of modern hotels and casinos came into view. People in colorful ski hats and jackets strolled down the sidewalk on both sides, wandering from one casino to another. She passed the state line, into California. The casinos immediately stopped, as if divided by a giant hand, and the business district began. The casual, small-town atmosphere set against the wintry countryside reminded her of Seattle, and she felt right at home.

By one o'clock she'd finished her errands and was loading her groceries into the trunk. A light snow silently drifted from the sky, melting as it hit the pavement. She felt refreshed, invigorated as she breathed in the crisp air.

She climbed into her car and turned the key in the ignition. It sputtered a bit, then died. Cold, she thought. She tried again. This time it started with its usual ease, although the engine idled erratically. Frowning, she pulled across the supermarket parking lot and turned onto the highway. The engine speed began to waver dangerously from high to low and back again. Oh no, she thought. She'd only heard that sound once before, when—

The engine died.

She cursed out loud, yanked the wheel to the right, and steered awkwardly to the curb. With experience born of years of practice, she surveyed the situation under the hood, flipped a valve, got back in the car and tried to start it again. Nothing happened.

She heaved a frustrated sigh. If only she had her tools and somebody to help her, she could probably get it started. Stupid, she thought. You know better than to go anywhere without your tools.

"Need a hand, lady?"

The familiar, deep voice made her start in surprise. Grant was looking in at her with concern through the open door. Kelli's heart leaped in delight. Unable to stop her grin, she climbed out and stood beside him in the busy street. "What are you doing here? I thought you went back to San Francisco last night."

"I did. I came back. I was going to take pictures of the casino, and then—" he paused "—I saw your car, and knew it had to be you."

He looked more handsome than she thought permissible. His jeans, as old, worn, and form-fitting as her own, emphasized the masculine strength of his long legs. His blue ski jacket was unzipped, revealing a matching cashmere sweater. Snow touched lightly on the dark waves of his hair, and his cheeks were rosy from the chill air. Looking at him, her heart beat as erratically as the recent idling of her car.

"What happened?" he asked, nodding towards the open hood.

"It's the automatic enrichment device. You can't predict when it will give out. If only it had warmed up, I could have turned on the bypass. As it is—you wouldn't happen to have a toolbox handy, would you?"

Five minutes later, Grant was sitting behind her wheel, waiting to turn the ignition, while Kelli was buried elbow deep in the engine of her car. It seemed he always carried a toolbox in the trunk of his Mercedes. He'd offered to do the dirty work, but she'd insisted he didn't understand her car the way she did.

"Okay," she cried, leaning over the engine and lifting the air filter with grease-stained fingers. "Start her up."

The engine roared to life. She reassembled the air cleaner and wiped her hands on a rag.

"I'll be all right now. Thanks." She brushed snow from her sweater and hair. "Once the engine's warmed up for a while, it'll get me home."

"You don't know that. It might go out on you again."

"I doubt it. I'll need to get a new part eventually, but it'll be fine for a while."

"I don't trust it. I'm going to follow you home."

"You don't have to do that."

"I want to." He paused, then added, "I admit: I have an ulterior motive. I'd love to see the house your brother is building."

She shrugged in resignation, laughing. How could she say no? He *had* rescued her from the roadside, after all. "Okay. Sure. Let's go."

Syrie James

She climbed behind her wheel and took off. The Mercedes followed close behind as she sped down the highway toward Glenbrook. A few miles out of Cave Rock, the sprinkling of snow stopped and sun shone through parting clouds. She turned left on a narrow side road, winding down and around the wooded hillside until she spotted the white flag marker tied to a tree trunk, where she made a sharp right. The driveway, recently paved, was more like a narrow road, sloping downward through a dense growth of tall pines and leveling out at the last moment in front of the garage.

They got out of their cars at the same time. "This is some house," Grant said, clearly impressed.

"It *is*, isn't it?"

The new redwood siding gleamed beneath the afternoon sun. Rows of huge windows stretched across both floors, reaching clear up to the majestic peaked roof. Redwood railings edged a second-floor decking that spanned the width of the house and continued around on one side. The scent of pine hung heavy in the air, and birds twittered in the clusters of tall trees around them. Just twenty yards away, she could hear the soft ebb and flow of the lake lapping against the shore.

"It's not exactly a haven of comfort yet," she said, opening her trunk and taking out one of the grocery bags. "It's still a work in progress. There isn't a stick of furniture, and I'm afraid I can't offer you anything to drink—but you're welcome to come in anyway."

"Thanks." With a wide smile, he took off his ski jacket, slammed his car door, and retrieved the other bag and her bundle of laundry. She unlocked the carved oak front door and they issued inside. The house smelled of dust and newly-cut wood. Fortunately Kelli had left the thermostat turned up,

The Harrison Duet

and the temperature was warm and pleasant after the chilly air outside.

"The kitchen's this way," Kelli explained. When they'd both set down their grocery bags, she led him into the nearby living room.

"Welcome," she said with a grand sweep of her arm, "to my brother's humble vacation retreat."

He whistled, and she laughed in delight. She loved almost everything about the new house, even in its unfinished state, but felt a renewed sense of awe each time she entered this huge, open room. Filtered sunlight shone in through two dirt-streaked sliding glass doors and through windows high in the vaulted ceiling, illuminating the freshly paneled knotty pine walls and the bare, plywood floor. A table saw stood against one wall, and long strips of wood molding and assorted boxes of hardware lay in scattered piles, but Grant stepped around them, his footsteps echoing in the silent, empty room.

"Incredible," he said. Matching stained glass windows, as tall and narrow as florists' boxes, were inset on either side of a massive granite fireplace. He stopped to study the intricate depiction of a robin surrounded by flowers in colorful shades of smooth, opaque glass. "These are exquisite."

"Songbirds. My sister-in-law's favorite symbol. Kyle had them custom-made to surprise her. Terribly decadent, wouldn't you say? But Kyle's always doing things like that."

Grant looked at her. "He must love his wife very much."

Something in his gaze made her stomach flutter. Her next words stuck in her throat. "He...does."

Grant offered to help her put the groceries away, and they worked together in the spacious kitchen with its shiny, new appliances.

262

"Sorry, no cabinet doors." Kelli stashed food in the refrigerator as she gestured toward the oak cabinets lining the walls. "They don't arrive until next week."

"Ah! But you lied." Grant picked up a jar of instant coffee from the countertop. "You said you didn't have anything to drink."

She laughed. "I only bought that as a last resort, because there's no coffee maker. I'd be embarrassed to serve it to you."

"I can see that you're roughing it here. I can adapt."

"Are you serious? Would you like a cup?"

"I'd love one."

Although she felt a little ridiculous serving instant coffee to a guest, she put on a pot to boil and glanced back at him. She liked his smile. It came so easily. When he'd spoken of her brother's love for his wife, Grant had sounded sincerely moved, almost wistful. Was he a romantic at heart, as she was? How different that would be from most of the men she'd known.

How different, especially, from Wayne.

If she wasn't careful, she realized, she could easily fall for someone like Grant. *No entangling relationships*, she reminded herself. Not now. Not so soon after the last one. Even her sisters told her she needed to take a break, to be on her own for a while.

"So, you're the acting contractor now?" he asked. "You must have experience in house construction?"

"No. But I took a few classes in architectural drafting in college, so I can read a blueprint, and Kyle left a detailed list of instructions. I'm supposed to make sure the subcontractors come out on schedule and do what they're supposed to do, and that everything is delivered and installed as ordered."

"Your brother is lucky to have you on the job."

"I guess, but I don't mind helping out. He's a great guy." She stacked soup cans in an open cupboard. "Ever since he became a father last year, he's been cutting down on his business trips and spending more time at home. My sister-in-law's a deejay and she can't spare much time away from the radio station. A week over the holidays—that's all the time they've got this year, and this is sort of my Christmas present to them. Besides, I have a special interest in this house."

"A special interest?" He leaned on the counter barely an inch away from her. "You mean besides free and unlimited use of the house, in perpetuity?"

His nearness distracted her and set her heart racing. "Yes."

"What kind of special interest?" he prompted.

"I helped with the initial design."

"You design houses, too?" he asked in surprise.

"No." He was standing so close she became aware of the mild, woodsy scent of his aftershave. "But when Kyle told me he wanted a house on the lake, I envisioned the place in my mind. I had to put it on paper. So I did a few interior and exterior watercolors for him, and then I sketched out a rough floor plan. He liked it so much he told the architect to build it, just the way I'd drawn it."

"You never cease to amaze me, Kelli," he said softly. "This house is beautiful."

Grant's blue eyes caught hers and held, with a gleam so intense it seemed he had touched her. Taking a deep breath to steady herself, she stepped back and smiled brightly. "Would you like to see the rest of it?"

Kelli made the coffee in disposable cups which they took with them. After showing him the nearly-finished rooms on the lower floor, they headed upstairs. When they reached the master bedroom suite where she was camping out, he said, "Hey, you really *are* living here."

"Kyle offered to put me up at a hotel, but I told him there was no point in spending the money. Especially since he wanted me to be here all day to admit and oversee the workmen, who have a nasty habit of starting at dawn. They're finished in this room, at least—except for paint and carpet."

"It can't be very comfortable, though, without any furniture. Are you really sleeping on the floor?"

She shrugged. "I'm fine with the floor. I was a Girl Scout. Growing up, nearly every summer I spent a month at camp, sleeping in a tent or outdoors, sometimes on ground as hard as a rock. In comparison—with this fancy, double air mattress my brother ordered for me—this is the Ritz."

"Where do you eat?"

"At the kitchen counter. Or on the—"

"—floor," he finished with her. They shared a grin.

"Or at one of the casinos," she added. "Weekday breakfast special: bacon, eggs, and hotcakes, ninety-nine cents. You can't beat it."

"Unless you drop five bucks in the slot machines on your way out."

"Five bucks? Never. My limit is two."

"Big spender."

"Sometimes I risk more. If the mood grabs me."

His gaze met hers. "I noticed," he said softly.

She supposed he was thinking about the way she'd agreed to help him into the party the night before, and the way she'd barged in on his conversation with Ted Lazar. But his expression seemed to indicate he was thinking of something else, too; something in the future, something far more intimate.

Her insides fluttered wildly and she moved to the bay window, standing with her back to him. Outside, beyond a narrow strip of white beach, sunlight danced on the rippling water. Puffy white clouds gathered low in the clear blue sky over distant, snow-capped Mount Tallac.

"I haven't always been so impulsive," she said, straining to keep her voice light.

"No? What were you like before?" he asked from behind.

"Kind of…shy and retiring."

"That's hard to believe." His hands closed over her shoulders. The unexpected touch sent a spark of electricity racing through her. "You seem anything but shy and retiring."

With a slight pressure he turned her around to face him, and she gazed up into his captivating eyes, which didn't attempt to disguise his attraction to her. Her pulse pounded. He didn't intend to kiss her…did he? Did she want him to?

"I promised myself, once," he said, his voice husky, "that I'd never mix business with pleasure. I can see, in your case, that's not going to be easy to do."

She glanced away, confused, willing her heart to resume its natural cadence. Why was he talking about business, when she was thinking about pleasure?

He released her and took a step back. "Kelli, I've been doing some thinking. I have a proposition for you."

"A proposition?"

"If you can't come to San Francisco and work free-lance for me, how about if I come up here and work with you?"

It was the last thing she'd expected him to say. "What do you mean? Do you want to hold a brainstorming session, like I suggested last night?"

"I'm talking about putting together the whole creative part of the presentation here—just you and me."

"Just you and me?" she repeated, astonished.

"If I'm going to bid on the Cassera's job, I need someone like you. You can't leave Tahoe. Which only leaves me this option. I think it could work. A good chunk of this proposal is the quote. I can turn that over to my staff, while we concentrate on the creative end. Ted wants the campaign to focus on two things: gambling and the environment. Working up here would have a lot of advantages. The casino's here for research and sudden inspiration if we need it. And all this natural beauty's bound to generate some great creativity."

Kelli hardly knew to say. "Where would we work?"

"I was going to suggest that we work at Cassera's—I'll get a hotel suite there. You could oversee everything with the construction crew every morning before you come out. But—"

She shook her head. "I should be here as much as I can. The details in these last weeks are too important. Deliveries are made and questions can come up at any hour. If the workers put in the wrong sink or paint a room the wrong color, it can cause extensive delays and get really expensive."

"I figured you'd say that. So let's go to Plan B. Let's work here."

Now she was truly flabbergasted. "You want to work *here?* In this unfinished house?"

"Why not?" He nodded toward the bay window. "This room's perfect to work in. Great natural lighting."

"Grant—this is crazy."

"It's not crazy. It's thinking outside the box. I told you last night: my creative people are overloaded and I don't want to pull them off the jobs they're working on. I expected Ted to

267

The Harrison Duet

give me more time on this—I was hoping for a month. When he named his deadline—honestly, I didn't know how on earth I'd be able to pull it off. But I saw the kind of work you can do. If we put our heads together, we ought to be able to come up with a package that sizzles in a couple of weeks. I'll pay you top Bay Area wages as a free-lance consultant." He named a fee. "Plus a thousand-dollar bonus if we win the account."

She took a sharp breath. She only charged her clients in Seattle half the rate he'd offered—and work was intermittent. Two weeks at that hourly rate would be a small fortune. She could afford to buy new equipment, maybe even rent a small office when she got back home.

"It's an intriguing proposition, I admit," she said slowly. "But can you really be away from your agency for two weeks?"

"It's no different than if I took a vacation. I can keep tabs on everything as long as I'm near a phone." He nodded towards the new phone that was already plugged in and waiting in a corner. "If a problem comes up, I can go back to the city any time. After we work up the rough creative, you can do the comps on your own."

His plans were tumbling out so fast it made her dizzy. "But I don't have any equipment here. I'd need a drafting table, lights, art supplies—"

"I'll bring up everything we need in the company van tomorrow."

Kelli sat down on the window seat, trying to think. Something wasn't right about this. He made it sound so easy. Too easy. Glancing at the bare plywood floor, she said, "Wait, Grant. You're forgetting something. We can't work here. A pack of carpenters are coming on Monday. All that sawdust and hammering—they make a racket like you can't believe."

"You said they're finished upstairs, right?"

268

"Yes, but—the painters come after that. Upstairs *and* down. Then the hardwood floors and carpet go in. Have you ever heard anyone put in a hardwood floor quietly? We couldn't get any work done here if we tried."

"Noise doesn't bother me. If it gets to you, though, we can always take a break. Do some research to spark the creative juices. Are you any good at blackjack?"

"Grant!" She stood up. "You're not listening. There will be interruptions—"

"Par for the course. I'm pulled in at least six different directions on any given day."

"We'll be in the way. Whatever equipment you bring up would have to be moved when they lay the carpet in here."

"When's that?"

"A week from Wednesday." Two days before the proposal was due.

"By then we'll be done."

"How can you be so sure?"

"We only need a couple of days of research. A day or two of brainstorming. Three days to whip up the collateral materials and a few more to come up with the ads. Ten days. Eleven, max." He crossed to stand in front of her, leaning one hand on the wall as he smiled down at her. "We ought to have at least two days to spare. And just think," he said, raising his eyebrows above teasing eyes, "what we could do with a little free time."

She turned away, cheeks warming at his unspoken thoughts. What was he implying? Why was he going to so much trouble to work with her? There must be plenty of artists in San Francisco who'd jump at the chance to work on this presentation. She sensed he was attracted to her, but that couldn't be the only reason. He clearly had faith in her

The Harrison Duet

abilities; he wouldn't risk such a vital account on someone whose work he didn't trust.

Uncertainly, she said, "I'd like to do it, Grant, but I have to check with my brother first. He might not be thrilled about me turning his master bedroom into an advertising studio before he's even had a chance to move in."

"It's all right. He's agreed to the whole thing."

She stared at him. "What? How could he?"

"I called him this morning."

"You *called my brother?*" She was dumbfounded. "How on earth did you—"

"You told me his name and where he lives. Directory assistance did the rest. I didn't want to put you in the position of having to say yes or no for him, so I decided to check with him first."

It took a moment to sink in. "But...if you already talked to Kyle...he must have given you the phone number here. You could have called me to—"

"I didn't want to bring this up on the phone, Kelli. I wanted to see the place first, make sure it was feasible before I proposed it, and then talk in person."

"So you're saying you were on your way up to the house today, to talk to me, when—"

"—when I saw your car at the side of the road. Yes."

Irritation prickled through her. "You conveniently forgot to mention that. You said you were here to take pictures of the casino."

"I was."

"You made me think we met by chance, that I led you here of my own free will."

"You did."

"I did not! You insisted on following."

Syrie James

"I said I'd love to see the house, and you agreed," he said quietly.

"That's like lying by omission." Kelli glared at him. He must have thought of this last night, before he said goodbye— that explained the little gleam she'd noticed in his eyes. He'd gotten Kyle's permission without even consulting her. Today, while he was bantering with her in the kitchen, he was actually sizing the place up to see if he wanted to work here with her. And he'd never said a word.

The situation was all too familiar. Memories she'd tried to bury came flooding back; memories of another man who'd planned every single thing in her life and made all her decisions without ever asking her. "I found us a new apartment today," Wayne had said, and was surprised when she wanted to see it before signing the lease. *Didn't want to get you involved in all that paperwork, honey. It's taken care of. We move in next week...*

Kelli headed for the door. "Your plan is a little too neat for me, Grant. I've had about as much of domineering, overbearing men as I can take. Thanks, but no thanks."

"Domineering?" Grant asked, coming after her. "Overbearing? *Moi?*"

"Yes! And don't get condescending on me." She stamped down the stairs and turned in the entryway to face him, her chest tight with fury. "My last boyfriend was exactly like you. A Mr. My-Way-or-the-Highway. So was my boss. I finally got out from under their thumbs, and I'm not about to put up with that again. I don't like having my life and my work prearranged for me. I don't like people stepping in and taking over. I like to have some say in what I do. I like to be asked."

"Seems to me," Grant said, his own temper rising, "you don't have any scruples about stepping in and interfering in

The Harrison Duet

other people's lives. You didn't lose a minute's sleep over the stunt you pulled on me with Ted Lazar, did you? All for a good cause, right? If you can dish it out, you've got to learn to take it."

Kelli felt a stab of guilt and fell silent.

"You seemed interested in the work last night," he continued fervently. "The only thing stopping you, I thought, was your obligation here. I arranged this with your brother ahead of time to make things easier for you—not to exercise some kind of power trip."

"Then why didn't you tell me about it sooner?"

"I was going to tell you as soon as we got here. But I got... distracted." His eyes caught and held hers.

She hesitated, reading the unspoken message in his gaze, unable to deny how much his presence distracted *her*.

"If you'll simmer down and think about this," he added, "it's not just for my benefit. It's a good opportunity for you, a showcase for your talent."

It was true. She'd worked hard over the past six months to start her own business, be her own boss, and she was fed up with other people calling the shots—but the job for Cassera's *was* a terrific opportunity. Only a prominent agency could secure a client of that magnitude. She needed the work and needed the money. How could she turn it down?

She felt Grant's eyes on her, watching her closely, as if sensing her change in mood. She tried to imagine what it would be like to work with him. The presentation for the casino would be an exciting challenge. It would be fun to toss ideas back and forth with Grant; she could envision the creative energy that might flow between them. He was a writer, a leader, a project coordinator; she was an artist. They might indeed make a good team.

She took a deep, wavering breath. "Okay. I'll do it."

"Great." He grinned, his eyes a brilliant blue in the sunlit hallway as he stuck out his hand.

It was the third time they'd shaken hands, she realized—and just as before, the warmth of his firm grip sent a tingle dancing up her arm.

"Welcome aboard," he added. "I'll reserve a room at the hotel and be back here with the equipment some time tomorrow morning. We'll unload, set up, and then head down to the casino for my two o'clock meeting with Ted Lazar."

A few minutes later they said goodbye and Kelli shut the front door, her mind spinning. It had all happened so fast. She needed to call Kyle right away, to confirm his approval. But if everything Grant said was true, it ought to be clear sailing.

It was only after she heard Grant's car drive away that a new problem came to mind—one that, she realized, could easily turn the weeks to come into a disaster.

How could she work side by side with Grant for two solid weeks, locked up alone in this house? A high-voltage charge seemed to flow between them. At times, she'd barely been able to concentrate on their conversation. How would she be able to concentrate on her work?

4

The decor at Cassera's Tahoe Hotel and Casino had an Alpine flair that Kelli found fresh and inviting. Sunday afternoon she toured the facility with Grant and Ted, saw the back offices and inner sanctums that the average guest was never allowed to see, and met staff from all parts of the business. She enjoyed herself immensely.

Ted complained that the hotel lobby was too bland and needed sprucing up, but when he showed them the rotating bar in the center of the casino, which was modeled after a German beer garden, he beamed with pride. There were three restaurants: gourmet French, an immense buffet that changed the nationality of its cuisine each night of the week, and the Swiss Chalet coffee shop that served everything from bacon and eggs to cheese fondue.

"Our showroom has never been a money-maker," Ted explained when he'd brought them upstairs to his private dining room for an early dinner. "The big-name talent is getting more expensive all the time. We've only kept it this long because it draws crowds to the gaming tables. We'll still have a few small showrooms going, but we've decided to do away with the dinner show starting this spring."

Kelli remembered how, at their first meeting, Grant suggested they'd be better off steering away from so much

274

emphasis on their shows, and she saw now why Ted had been so impressed.

"Dawson's given us enough ads promoting the buffet special to last another six years, so you don't need to cover that angle," Ted explained. "What I want is a couple of different campaigns, one that concentrates on sports and the great outdoors, and one that highlights the fun of gambling. Dawson's been avoiding ads that play up gambling because they're so hard to do."

Kelli nodded, remembering that it was illegal to advertise gambling in California. "Can we show people at the tables? Or rolling the dice?"

"You have to be careful how you do it," Grant answered. "The lower the profile, the better."

"That's right," Ted agreed. "We can't promise anyone they'll win. We can allude to it in a subtle way, just so long as we don't come straight out and talk about it."

Some trick, Kelli thought, replacing her monogrammed coffee cup in its saucer with a click. Here was a challenge she'd never encountered before. How did you advertise something if you couldn't even mention it?

When they returned to Ted's office and reviewed the requirements for the final presentation, Kelli was struck for the first time by the sheer volume of the workload. They wanted a new logo—something completely different and original, according to Ted—to emphasize their Alpine theme. Two layouts in color for a stationery package to go with it. Pencil comprehensives with a fresh, new look for their collateral materials, all to work around the new logo. Rough comps for a media campaign with two themes and five or six different creative approaches. No TV and radio; just newspaper, magazines, billboards. Complete copy for a couple of them, and pricing for all of that.

The Harrison Duet

She bit her lower lip, thinking: *what a tall order.* An exciting order, but a tall one nevertheless. Grant's staff would do the quote, but the creative was up to the two of them. And everything was due before Ted's board-of-directors meeting a week from Friday, less than two weeks away.

"No problem," Grant said.

Kelli glanced at him, marveling at his self-composure. How could he be so confident they'd finish in time? Grant handed Ted a neatly typed form with his quote for their presentation, and Ted sucked in his breath, shook his head slowly and muttered something, then stood up and stuck out his hand.

"Okay, Grant. Let's do it." When he'd shaken Kelli's hand, he said, "I think we're all set. The only place I haven't really shown you is the casino floor, but I'm out of time today." He picked up his phone. "Let me see if—"

"Relax, Ted," Grant said. "We don't need a tour guide. I've been playing blackjack here since I was seventeen."

Ted chuckled and clapped Grant on the back as he walked them to the door. "You're lucky we never checked your ID."

The moment they stepped out of the elevator, Kelli felt the air of nighttime excitement in the crowded casino. Slot machines whirred and jangled, mingling with the murmur of laughter and voices. The blackjack tables were busy, and people clustered around the roulette and craps tables.

"Have you spent much time in a casino?" Grant asked.

Kelli shook her head. "This is my first trip to Tahoe. Friday night was the one and only time I'd ever set foot in a casino, and all I had a chance to play were the slot machines."

"Let's take a look around, then." Grant told her to keep in mind that the campaign proposal had to concentrate on the fun, capture the excitement of the place in words and in pictures. "We've got to lure people here who might be just a little bit nervous about gambling."

Like me, Kelli thought. "Have you really been gambling here since you were seventeen?"

"Yep. My parents brought us up here every summer ever since I can remember, and we'd snow ski three or four times a year, too. I started sneaking in here when I was—oh, about twelve, I guess. I watched and listened and learned. They don't usually bother you when you're underage as long as you don't try to play."

"And now? Do you play a lot?"

"No. Not a lot. It takes too long to earn a dollar. There's no fun in watching it slip through your fingers. But once in a while, if you know what you're doing and limit the amount you're going to spend, you can have a great time."

She stopped beside a silver-dollar slot machine as big as a refrigerator, called Fun Fred. A hard hat topped the huge, animated head that housed the money slot and giant cylinders, and the side lever was fashioned like a construction worker's arm. "This guy," she said, "needs a new name."

"You don't like Fun Fred?"

She shook her head. "On Friday I dropped five dollars into that twelve-inch grin of his. It wasn't fun at all. He ate them all."

"Well, there goes my idea for one of the newspapers ads. I was going to show a beautiful woman pulling Fred's handle with the headline—" he painted an imaginary banner through the air with one hand "—For a good time, call Fred."

They laughed together.

"I'll talk to the casino manager," Grant said, "see if he can rename the guy Hungry Harry."

"Or Benny the Bandit."

"Cute. In all the years I've been here, I've only seen one person win on that infernal machine. Five hundred dollars. It

The Harrison Duet

was something. The ringing bell, all those coins spilling out. Almost enough to turn me into a slots player."

"Almost? You mean you never play the slots?"

"Never. They have the worst odds of any game in the house."

"Why? Are they preset to pay off only a certain percentage?"

"Exactly. Which is why Ted wants Cassera's known as *the* place to play slots. Anyway, they're too monotonous for me. If I'm going to play, I want a game that requires some concentration, a little skill." With one hand at her elbow he propelled her forward to the gaming tables. "Come on. I'll explain how a few of the games work."

For the next half hour, Grant went over the basic concepts of keno, roulette, and baccarat, explaining the denominations for the colored chips. At the craps table, half a dozen players lined the sides, all eyes intent on a gray-haired man in an aloha shirt who shook a pair of dice in cupped hands, murmuring over and over to himself under his breath.

Kelli stopped to watch. The table was long and narrow with high, padded sides, white lines dividing a field of green felt into an array of numbered sections.

"Do you want to play?" Grant asked beside her.

Kelli shook her head. "This looks complicated. I wouldn't have the faintest idea what I was doing."

"Neither do most of the people around here. I'll explain as you go."

"No. I'd lose all my money in two seconds."

"I thought you liked the idea of living dangerously," Grant teased.

"I do. Sometimes." She'd promised herself to overcome her cautious nature, to participate in life, not stand on the sidelines while it marched by—but what little money she'd brought had to last for at least two more weeks, until Grant paid her for her part in the project. "Right now, I'd rather watch."

"Come on six," the man cried, throwing the dice. The small crowd groaned. The dealer—blond, cool, and businesslike in a black skirt, white blouse, and black bow tie—gathered the chips from the table with a hooked stick. "Any craps?" she called out. "Any craps?"

A thin, snowy-haired woman slid up onto the stool next to Kelli and pulled a stack of blue chips from her purse.

"Place all bets," said the dealer. "Any craps? Hard ways? Come? Don't come?"

"That's why I play this game," said the old woman, winking mischievously. "I love it when they talk dirty."

Grant grinned and leaned on the side of the table next to Kelli. "I've got our headline," he said in a low voice. "Cassera's: Crappiest Game in Town."

Kelli joined in his laughter, and when his arm brushed hers, the brief touch sent that familiar, warm glow spreading through her. Aloha Shirt rolled again and apparently won. Kelli cheered along with the rest of the crowd.

"Would you like to roll the dice?" the dealer asked Kelli after the man had gathered his chips and left.

Kelli shook her head. "No, thank you."

Grant reached into his pocket, pulled out three twenty-dollar bills, and tossed them on the table. "Yes, she would."

Alarmed, Kelli said, "I can't gamble with your money."

"Yes, you can."

"I can't," she insisted.

"Then we'll say it's company funds. All part of the job. Think of it as research."

She shook her head, but it was too late. The dealer placed a stack of chips in front of her. Grant took her hand with gentle

The Harrison Duet

firmness and turned it over, placing the dice in her palm. "The odds are better here than almost any other game, as long as you avoid the propositions."

"Propositions? What does that mean?"

"See that area in the center of the craps layout, where the high payouts are printed? The Horn bet, the One Roll bets, and so on? Those are the proposition bets, and they're some of the worst bets in the game. All of them have a very high house edge. I never play them. Just play the Pass/Don't Pass Line."

In confusion, she watched him put a five-dollar chip in an area marked Pass, and then the dealer was telling her to go ahead and shoot.

"Make sure the dice hit the back wall," Grant said, standing close beside her, "or it's not legal."

Kelli's heart began to pound, as much from Grant's nearness as from her nervous anticipation about the game. She still had no idea what she was doing. Pretend it's a Frisbee, she thought, shaking the dice and tossing them hard. They bounced against the side and shot back, finally coming to a stop at the center of the table.

"Nice arm," Grant commented.

"Three," said the dealer, instantly clearing most of the chips off the table.

"What happened?" Kelli asked.

Grant's response was low and deep against her ear. "You lost."

"Just like that?"

"Just like that."

She shook her head. "Wow. Now *this* is what I call fun."

He laughed softly. "Don't be a sore loser. Try it again."

"You *like* to lose money?"

"On the Pass Line," Grant said calmly, "you only lose if you roll two, three, or twelve on the first roll. You win on seven or eleven. Put out another bet."

She hesitated a moment, then put a three-dollar bet on the Pass Line.

"Twelve," said the dealer after Kelli rolled. "House wins." She cleared off the table.

"I have an idea." Kelli turned to Grant with a bright smile. "After we're through here, why don't we go back to the house and burn a handful of twenty-dollar bills in the fireplace? Wouldn't that be fun?"

Grant shot her a disparaging look. "Just stick to the Pass Line. It's bound to pay off sooner or later."

"Okay, fine. But this time, I'm only going to bet a dollar. In my family, whenever you make a dollar bet, you win."

Kelli threw a seven. "I won!" she cried with delight. All around her were bright colors, gleaming lights, smiling people, murmuring voices, clatters and clinks and bells. She felt a vibrant rush of excitement, wanted to embrace it all. Why hadn't she had the nerve to try this before?

Grant grinned. "See? I told you it'd pay off if you stuck with it."

Kelli's exhilaration dissipated, however, as she watched the dealer pay off the other players in tall stacks, then match her single-dollar chip on the table. When you bet small, you win small, she realized. No fun in that.

The old woman next to her placed a one-inch stack of five-dollar chips on the Pass Line. "I just won this at black-jack," she said, patting Kelli on the arm, "so don't disappoint me, honey."

"I'll try not to." With sudden conviction Kelli shoved out her remaining chips, fifty-three dollars in all.

The Harrison Duet

Grant's grin faded as she picked up the dice. "You're betting the whole thing?"

"Sure," she said loftily.

"I wouldn't," he cautioned.

"Why not? Who said I ought to live dangerously?"

Grant began to protest again, but she threw the dice.

"Ten," said the dealer. "Your point."

Uncertain what that meant, Kelli turned to Grant. He shook his head, laughing silently. "Okay, hot shot. Keep shooting. You're looking for another ten. If you roll your point before you roll a seven, you win even money."

"And if I roll a seven first?"

"You lose."

Perspiration beaded Kelli's neck and brow. A glance the length of the table showed several bets riding. If she rolled a seven, she wouldn't be the only one losing money. Concentrate, she told herself. *Clear your mind. Visualize only a ten.* She threw the dice, again and again.

"Come on, ten!" someone called out.

"Give me that ten!"

She leaned forward and flung the dice one more time with a dramatic sweep of her arm.

The crowd groaned. A three and a four. She'd lost. She watched the dealer clear the table, feeling hollow inside with disappointment and embarrassment. Fifty-three dollars! Why had she bet so much?

Kelli managed a brief smile and thanked the dealer before moving away from the table.

"Hey, don't worry about it," Grant said, seeing her forlorn expression. "It's all part of the game. Let's try something where we really have a chance."

"Such as?" she asked skeptically.

"Blackjack." He stopped at a nearby table and gestured toward an open stool.

She frowned dejectedly. She knew how to play blackjack, used to beat her brother and sisters all the time for sticks of gum. But this time it was for real. "I've lost enough for today. I'd rather go, if you don't mind."

"Come on. We'll win back everything you lost."

"Some other time, Grant. We should really leave. If we're going to be holed up in that house for two weeks, I've got grocery shopping to do, and the stores are about to close."

He shrugged. "Okay. But we're coming back before the week is out. I'm going to make sure you win back every penny you lost."

"Why did you tell me not to bet so much?" she asked as they drove back in Grant's van. "How did you know I'd lose?"

"I didn't know. But craps is all luck. Betting a few dollars is one thing, but you were so hesitant to bet in the beginning, I didn't want you to feel guilty if you lost."

She sighed. "I guess I just got caught up in the excitement of it. It was so much fun when I won."

"That's the whole point. That's why I wanted you to play. Remember the excitement, how it felt to win. Because somehow—without making any promises—we've got to bottle and sell that to the public."

Next morning, Kelli awoke to the sound of a car pulling into the driveway. She rubbed her eyes, at first not certain where she was. A pile of cardboard boxes came into view. She sat up with a start, remembering she'd moved her makeshift bed to a far corner of the master bedroom the day before when

The Harrison Duet

they'd unloaded Grant's van, before driving out to the casino. In the light of early morning, she surveyed with renewed amazement the temporary studio that took up nearly half the room.

Two drafting tables with attached, adjustable-arm lamps now faced the bay window. Between them, a taboret—a storage unit the size of a two-drawer file cabinet—held a lazy Susan filled with graphics tools, everything from Exacto knives and burnishers to a complete set of Rapidograph pens. A portable opaque projector for enlarging and reducing images sat atop a folding table, next to a waxer, a box of assorted felt-tip pens, and a stack of typographer's books. Scattered packing boxes held crescent board, pads of tracing paper, and other supplies. He'd even brought an electric typewriter, typing table, and two swivel chairs.

She could see why Grant had earned a reputation for being thorough. He said he'd bring up the equipment they'd need, but she hadn't expected a setup anywhere near so elaborate on such short notice.

A knock sounded at the door. A glance at her watch told her it was only six-thirty. Damn those workmen, anyway. Why did they have to start so early?

She scrambled out of her sleeping bag, gooseflesh covering her skin as she pulled jeans and a white turtleneck sweater over her skintight long johns. She finger-combed her hair and, in her stocking feet, hurried down the stairs, careful to side-step the piles of discarded nails, pieces of drywall, and other debris scattered about.

It was just as cold downstairs as up, and she stopped to adjust the thermostat before throwing open the door.

"Hi," Grant said.

Kelli blinked in surprise. Silhouetted by the soft early light, Grant's shoulders seemed even broader, his waist beneath his

284

black sweater even trimmer, his legs incredibly long. She wondered if his hair, so dark and shining, was as soft as it looked. His face glowed as if morning air were a tonic, and he was so very, very handsome. His features reminded her of a statue she'd once seen of a Roman warrior. He had the same masculine cut to his jaw, the same perfectly straight nose, the same beautifully formed lips, as if chiseled out of stone by a master.

The night before, after they'd returned from the casino, he'd taken her hand in his and had given it a warm squeeze as they stood at the door.

"Good night, Kelli Ann," he'd said quietly, before turning to walk down the drive. From the darkness, his voice had come back to her again, soft and deep, like a caress. "Pleasant dreams."

She'd watched the gleam of his taillights disappear, had stood with the door open to the cold night air for quite some time before it had occurred to her to close it. The tingling she'd felt from the gentle pressure of his hand on hers had lingered in her mind throughout the night.

How easy, she thought, staring at him now, it would be to fall for this man.

Be honest, Kelli. You're already halfway there.

She scolded herself to stop thinking of him that way. She didn't want to get involved with anyone right now, and even if she did, it couldn't be with Grant. They had to work together. Their relationship had to be professional—nothing more.

"You were expecting someone else, maybe?" he asked, when she continued to stare at him. He sounded breezy and self-assured—the opposite of the way she felt.

She laughed self-consciously and let him in, closed the door. "I expected to see three men wearing dirty jeans and carrying toolboxes. I didn't think you'd be here so early."

The Harrison Duet

"I told you I'd be back with breakfast in the morning."

For the first time, she noticed he was carrying a paper bag and a small tray with two ceramic mugs covered with foil. "This isn't morning. This is predawn. My stomach doesn't wake up for another three hours yet."

"Oh. Sorry. I'm an early riser by habit. If you want to go back to sleep, I can come back in a couple of hours."

"That's okay." The tantalizing aroma of strong coffee filled the room. "I can forgive you when you bring coffee that smells like this." Unable to resist, she took one of the mugs from his tray, uncovered it, and breathed in deeply, letting the steamy rich scent fill her senses. "Mmm. Take-out coffee never smelled so good. Where did you find it?"

"At a great little coffee shop near the hotel. Best coffee in the town, freshly brewed. They don't do take-out, though. I had to promise on bended knee to return the tray and mugs."

"Well, please tell them how much I appreciate the loan. And thank you for going to the trouble."

"You're welcome, ma'am. I aim to please."

"How's the hotel? Comfortable, I hope?"

"It's nice. The bed's too short, but I'll live."

"At least you *have* a bed, which is more than I've got."

His eyes twinkled devilishly and he leaned closer. "Should I make the obvious rejoinder?"

She realized at once what that would be: *You're welcome to join me in mine.* Her cheeks grew warm. "Let's not go there." She quickly turned toward the staircase, bringing her coffee with her. "I'd better go get...freshened up. You're welcome to come upstairs in the meantime."

A few minutes later she found Grant sitting astride a stool at one of the drafting tables, paging through a book of color photographs of the Lake Tahoe area. He motioned toward the paper bag on the table. "Help yourself."

Inside she found two egg and cheese sandwiches on toasted bagels. *Food, the best kind of distraction. Yay!* "This looks great. Thanks." She wasted no time taking a bite.

"I thought you weren't hungry this early," he commented, still bent over his book and clearly amused.

"My appetite suddenly returned." Chewing, she went over to stand behind him. He'd taped a brochure and letterhead to the table and had circled the existing Cassera's logo. "Where do you want to start? With the new logo?"

"Yes. Let's work up two or three ideas and see how they look with the collateral materials. If we can figure out the size and colors for all the pieces today, I can call my office tomorrow and have them start working up printing prices."

They ate the sandwiches and sipped coffee as they discussed possible directions for the new logo. Just as Kelli was about to sit down and sketch out an idea, the doorbell rang.

"Morning," said the man at the front door when she ran down to answer it. He had a ruddy face and very little hair, and wore a baggy jumpsuit beneath his heavy jacket. "I'm John McClellan, the painter. You Mrs. Harrison?"

"Miss Harrison. We spoke on the phone. I thought you were coming the day after tomorrow?"

He squinted at his clipboard. "Yeah, but I figured I'd better stop by and give the place another look-see, so I know how much paint to order."

"Okay." Kelli admitted him inside. "Take a look around. If you need me, I'll be upstairs."

He tramped down the hall, scribbling notes. She was just about to head upstairs when the doorbell rang again. It was the carpenters. They entered and shrugged out of their jackets.

The Harrison Duet

"You're here bright and early today, Larry," Kelli said, glad now that Grant had arrived as early as he did to wake her up.

"Thought we'd better get moving," replied Larry, the oldest of the three, a tall man in a stained work shirt and faded jeans. "Weather report says snow the end of the week. We want to be done and out of here long before that."

Kelli frowned as she hurried back up the stairs. If it snowed, she'd have to get a plow out there right away to clear the driveway, or the next batch of workmen wouldn't be able to reach the house.

In the master bedroom—which she now thought of as the "studio"—Grant was still standing at the drafting table, tapping a pencil against the open page of a book of typefaces. At his feet were scattered a few crumpled wads of paper.

"Good. You're back just in time," he remarked. "How about if we try this typeface for the logo, worked in with a graphic that alludes to the setting here—the lake, the snow, the pines—a clean, fresh look. I tried a few approaches. Nothing's worked so far."

Kelli sat down and glanced through the book on Tahoe, seeking inspiration. After a while, she said: "Oh! I think I see it. Let me show you."

She grabbed a fresh sheet of tracing paper. Working fast and furiously, she put on paper the image she saw clearly in her mind: a pine tree, sharply defined, blending into the "C" in Cassera's Tahoe. When she was finished, she sat back, not at all satisfied, then lifted her eyes to Grant's. He was leaning one elbow on his table, chin on his hand, staring at her with open admiration.

"It's not really any good," she said honestly.

"No. But it's not that bad, either. What's amazing is how fast you drew it."

288

"I can't take credit for my speed. It's not something I've worked hard to develop. It's just...there."

"Take credit for it anyway, Kelli Ann. It's an extraordinary talent. And I'm beginning to think it'll come in very handy on this proposal."

"*If* we hit on the right ideas."

"We will." Grant picked up his pencil and leaned over her drawing. "Why don't you try this?" He brought the length of his body up against her back and began to sketch.

Kelli had to stifle a sharp breath. Her entire body seemed sensitized by the contact, and her pulse raced. *Very inconvenient*, she thought—this dramatic, sexually charged response to his simplest touch.

"Excuse me." The painter poked his head in the open doorway, startling Kelli so much she jumped sideways off her stool. "It says here Mr. Harrison wants standard white everywhere there's no paneling, and I'm to leave the choice of paint color up to you. Can I borrow you for a minute to take a look at these paint charts?"

"Sure," Kelli said, both sorry and relieved at the interruption.

The painter swore and held up a hand. "Hold on, I've got me the wrong ones. Let me run out to my truck. I'll be back in a jiffy."

"It's really hopping around here this morning," Grant said after the painter left the room. "Do they always keep you this busy?"

"No," Kelli began, "this is—"

"Miss Harrison?" Larry strode in, his tool belt jingling at his waist. "We got us a problem. Can you come down for a minute?"

Grant sighed in frustration. Kelli shrugged apologetically and escaped to the kitchen. Larry gestured toward a large hallway

The Harrison Duet

closet just off the kitchen, intended for the washer and dryer. He opened a blueprint. "I've got the doors for this closet out in my truck," he said without preamble, "but the print calls for—"

"Well, there you are, ma'am," interrupted the painter, panting with exertion as he entered the room. "I just went upstairs looking for you."

From the living room behind them, there began a loud hammering. Then the ear-splitting screech of a table saw rent the air.

The painter leaned closer. "I've got two different paint companies here," he shouted, opening two brochures and spreading them out on the counter, "both top quality. Which color white do you want?"

Kelli glanced at the brochures. Each paint company offered fifteen different shades of white. "I need to look these over in natural light," she said, taking the brochures and moving to the window, where she stared at the small, colored squares.

Navajo White. Cloud White. White White. Eggshell. Ivory. Alabaster. Swiss Coffee. Which one would look the most neutral? The hammering on the other side of the wall increased in intensity, seeming to echo through the floor-boards. *Bam, bam, bam!* With each blow Kelli found herself blinking involuntarily.

Someone nudged her. It was one of the younger carpenters. What was his name? He wore a red sweatshirt, and was opening a blueprint. "Sorry to interrupt, but this calls for three shelves in that built-in bookcase in the dining room," he said loudly. "Do you want the shelves permanent or adjustable?"

"I...don't know," Kelli said. She was about to study the print, when Larry reached over her shoulder and covered the

290

blueprint with his own. To her relief the sawing and hammering stopped at the same instant.

"Hold off on the shelves a minute," Larry said. "I need a decision on these closet doors. The print calls for louvered doors. Don't know if somebody made a mistake, but the doors I've got with me are solid. If I have to take them back and order new doors I need to know now."

"Just a minute," Kelli said, trying desperately to keep her cool. "Let me take things one at a—"

"Excuse me, ma'am?" The painter moved closer, nervously scratching his head. "I realize you're busy, but these gentlemen'll be here for a while, and I've got an appointment in Carson City this morning. If you could just take a quick look at those paint chips, I'd appreciate it."

"Take a number, buddy," Grant said. He stood behind her, his back against the opposite counter, his arms crossed as if he'd been watching and listening for some time.

Larry snatched the print from Kelli and turned to Grant. "Do you know anything about these doors?"

"How long will it take to order louvered ones?" Grant asked.

"A couple of weeks."

"Order them." Grant gently lifted the paint brochure out of Kelli's hands and glanced it over. "Eggshell," he told the painter.

"Good choice." The painter scribbled on his clipboard.

"Wait a minute," Kelli said. "I didn't—"

"Sign here," the painter said, extending the clipboard to her, "and I'll be out of your hair."

Stubbornly, Kelli grabbed the paint brochure and turned her back on the two men. Eggshell *was* a nice, neutral shade, she had to admit. A good compromise between white and

The Harrison Duet

off-white. Probably the same one she would have chosen. But still...

"I'll sign," Grant said.

"You can't—" Kelli began, wheeling around, but the painter was already grinning appreciatively and handing Grant his card. He said he'd be back on Wednesday and hurried out.

Grant took Red Shirt aside, issued a few instructions, and consulted again with Larry. The table saw started up again, rising in volume right along with Kelli's temper.

How dare Grant start handing out orders, as if he owned the place? How dare he sign that form? She wasn't some little, fainthearted maiden in distress. To her further indignation, he took her by the arm and propelled her out of the room and up the stairs. When they reached the studio and shut the door, blocking out much of the noise, she whirled on him furiously.

"What do you think you were doing down there?"

"Helping you."

"I don't need your help. This isn't your house, Grant. The men report to me. I was handling the situation just fine."

"I saw how fine you were doing. The minute that saw started you went into a catatonic trance."

"I did not."

"You would have been down there all day at the rate you were going."

"I would not have taken all day! I just needed a few minutes to think. I want to make sure I'm making decisions Kyle would approve of. I have a responsibility to keep this house on schedule, and to do it right."

"I know that. But you have a responsibility to keep *our* work on schedule too."

"I told you it wasn't going to be easy, working here."

292

"It *can* be easy, if you'll just let it." He shook his head with rising frustration. "My entire reputation is at stake on this presentation. If you spend too much time worrying over every little detail on this house, we'll never get finished. Hell, we'll never even get started!"

"Details are important. I'm sorry if I don't make decisions fast enough for you, Grant. And I didn't appreciate you taking over the reins like that."

"I was just trying to speed things up." He heaved an exasperated sigh and sat down at his stool. After a moment he added carefully, "Look, Kelli, we've got a lot of work to do. Can we bury our weapons for the rest of the day? Call a truce? We'll get a lot more done if we're not at war."

Fuming, Kelli took her place at the drafting table without another word. Bury her weapons, indeed. It wasn't as if she was being unreasonable. He hadn't even said he was sorry. How could she ever have imagined she was attracted to this man?

But as they plunged into their work, there was so much to do, and so many creative problems to solve, that her niggling irritation over the way Grant had usurped her authority with the workmen was soon forgotten. He was quick and highly inventive. Despite their poor start, they soon began operating as partners, with the give and take and constructive criticism that made for a successful creative session.

The carpenters continued their labors without interrupting them further, and a brief check reassured Kelli that they were moving forward according to plan. By the end of the day, she and Grant had thumbnails for most of the collateral materials—small-scale layouts she'd have to work up into full-size comps—and they had agreed on two possible color schemes. They also had three new logos sketched out, all variations on Kelli's mountain idea.

The Harrison Duet

They didn't like any of them.

"I know what the problem is," Grant said. "It's the Alpine theme. Let's dump it. Tell Ted it's time for a completely new look. A logo that's really different."

"Good idea. Get rid of the pine trees. How about palm trees?" she kidded.

"Palm trees," Grant mused, trying to look deeply serious. "Yes, I think palm trees are good."

"We center the name between the sun and the surf. Add a grass hut. A few sweet-and-sour spareribs."

"I love it. They can redo the interior of the casino to match. Indoor waterfalls. Barmaids in leis and sarongs. The possibilities are endless. And as for the ad campaign..." He drew something on his sketch pad, then turned it toward her: a cartoon of a grinning pineapple on snow skis, wearing a lei and grass shirt, and shaking a pair of dice. Above it, the headline: *Hula for Moola.*

She couldn't help laughing. "That's pretty good. I thought you said you didn't do illustrations."

"I said it wasn't my specialty." He tossed the sketch pad aside and looked at her. "We made a lot of progress today. More than I expected."

"It did go pretty well," she agreed. "All things considered."

He mused a moment, then turned to her with a contrite smile. "I admit, I probably overstepped my bounds this morning with the workmen. The house is your territory. I had no right to charge in there and take over."

Her lips curved into a wry grin. "Is that an apology?"

"It is."

"Apology accepted."

He stood up, took her hand in his, and kissed it. The soft touch zinged up her arm, sending her heart into a skid. "How about having dinner with me?"

The invitation caught her off guard. She'd managed to get through a day with Grant on a purely platonic, professional level—but was it wise to spend the evening with him as well? Before she could protest, he'd leaned a hand on her drafting table, bent down, and was staring directly into her eyes.

"You've got to eat, Kelli. And I just happen to know this little Italian place with food you've got to taste to believe."

She laughed. "Italian?" Her favorite.

He grinned. "I'll go to my hotel and change. Be back for you in about an hour?"

5

"I found this place a couple of years ago," Grant said. "Now I come up here every time I'm in the area."

"How often is that?" Kelli asked.

"Every chance I get."

The restaurant was warm and cheerful inside, with a fire crackling in the nearby hearth, red-and-white-checked cloths on the tables, and clusters of grapes entwined in trellises overhead. When they arrived, the waiter greeted Grant like an old friend and led them immediately to a secluded booth.

"They make the world's best veal Marsala," Grant said, touching his fingers to his lips. "Just like Mama used to make."

Kelli laughed and sipped her cocktail. "Are you saying that literally? Was your mother a good cook?"

"The best. Her grandmother was from Italy, and a real tyrant, from what I'm told. They say I got my temper from her, and my stubborn streak from my father's side of the family."

"Are they Italian, too?"

"No. Welsh."

Of course, Kelli thought. Welsh. That explained Grant's dark good looks, the black hair, and the blue, blue eyes. And it explained, too, his strength of character, his determination to succeed, and the stormy side of his personality she'd seen

296

surface on occasion; inherited from ancestors who'd had to fight hard every day for survival.

"My great-grandfather came from a little fishing town on the southwest tip of Wales. He emigrated to America when he was fifteen."

"Our ancestors had a lot in common," she said. "My grandfather came over when he was twelve. From Ireland."

"An Irish lassie. So that's where you got your devastating wit and fiery hair."

She laughed again. "And fiery temper. You wanted to add that, didn't you?"

His eyes twinkled. "Those are your words, not mine."

"But you thought it."

"I thought it." He finished his drink and smiled at her across the table. "I was also thinking how much alike we are. Have you noticed how much we have in common? Both creative types. Same gutsy approach to life. A lot of the same tastes and interests."

"Maybe we're too much alike. Maybe that's why—as you put it—we were at war this morning."

Grant shook his head. "You can't be too much alike. That's a fallacy. An old wives' tale." His voice had dropped a decibel or two, and as he studied her, some new emotion flared brightly across the blue of his eyes.

She looked away, the expression on his face causing her heart to pump in an odd rhythm. You're not out on a date, she reminded herself. Grant is temporarily your boss. *This is just a business dinner.*

The waiter rescued her from further distracting thoughts by arriving with antipasto salads for each of them. Being served without ordering was a new experience for Kelli. She looked at Grant in surprise.

The Harrison Duet

"No menus?"

"Veal Marsala isn't on the menu. I had to call ahead of time to order it. I couldn't let you leave Tahoe without trying it. And what's an Italian meal without antipasto salad and minestrone soup?"

She forced a smile and said nothing. It was nice of him to arrange all this in advance for her enjoyment, but she was also a bit annoyed. He was keeping the upper hand again, not allowing her any say in what they did. What if she didn't like veal, or his choice of soup or salad? She might have preferred something else on the menu.

The waiter smoothly withdrew the cork from a bottle of wine. Kelli saw it was a Cabernet Sauvignon. She opened her mouth to protest, then thought better of it. Once Grant had approved his sample taste, the waiter moved to fill Kelli's glass.

"None for me, thank you."

"You don't drink wine?" Grant asked.

"Not red wine. I'm allergic to it."

"Allergic?"

She nodded. "It's too high in...something in the grapes' skins, that gives the wine its color. I love *white* wine. And I adore champagne. But..." She shrugged apologetically.

"You should have said something."

"You didn't ask."

He fell silent, blushing slightly. "You're right. I should have asked. Let me order you something else. How about a white Zinfandel? Chenin Blanc?"

"No, please, don't bother. I couldn't drink a whole bottle. I'm fine."

He frowned. She could see he wasn't pleased with himself. "Not allergic to veal, I hope?"

"No."

He blew out a relieved breath.

The salad and soup were truly excellent. When their dinner arrived—veal smothered in a sauce of mushrooms, wine, and onions—Kelli inhaled its rich aroma, took a bite, and pronounced it delicious.

"Batting 500, anyway." Grant sipped his wine, looking at her thoughtfully. "I'm sorry about the wine. And for ordering ahead of time."

"It's okay."

"No, it's not. I should have checked with you first." He sighed. "I'm beginning to think I've been my own boss for too long. I'm used to handing out directives, making instant decisions without consulting anyone. That's the only way a business can operate sometimes. When something matters to me, my instinct is to plan it out, make arrangements in advance, so things will run more smoothly." He laughed softly, in self-reproach. "But I can see the instinct doesn't work *quite* so well away from the office. Lately, even my brother and sister have been telling me to lay off."

"Lay off what?"

"I have this tendency to jump in whenever either of them has a problem, to try to fix things, make things easier for them. When Glen lost his job last month, I set up three job interviews for him. He was really annoyed, told me to mind my own business." Grant shrugged. "They used to turn to me for help and advice all the time, but now—"

"*Turn* to you for advice? Are you sure? Or were you handing it out unsolicited?"

He looked at her in surprise. "I don't know. Maybe I was. There's five years between me and Glen, and my sister's two years younger than he is. I've been through so many things, when I see them about to make some of the same mistakes

The Harrison Duet

I've made, I can't help—" He paused. "Did I really say that? I sounded exactly like my father."

"And my father, too." Kelli laughed. "And my four sisters."

"Counting your brother, six kids?" His eyes widened and he whistled. "Wow, that's some family."

She nodded. "I'm the youngest. When I was born, I think they all got together and decided, hey, this scrawny kid is never going to make it without our help. So they took me under their collective wings. Every time I turned around they were telling me how to dress, how to talk, what to eat, what classes to take, where to go, who to go out with. I didn't like it, but I went along with it because I looked up to them. Finally, I realized I wasn't living my own life. I was pleasing everyone but myself."

"So you said, forget this. From now on, I'm my own boss. Is that why you quit your job at T & M?"

"Yes. I loved it there at first. I had a lot of creative freedom, did some of my best work. But then they brought in a new creative director. He was incredibly insecure. Always looking over my shoulder, telling me how to do my designs, afraid I'd come up with something better than he did. When I managed to sneak through ideas of my own that met with approval, he took credit for them himself."

"No wonder you quit. The guy was an idiot. A wealth of talent at his fingertips and he was afraid to use it. Sounds to me like you've been surrounded by pushy people all your life."

"I have. But I have only myself to blame. I let them push me around. I just hope I learned from it, so I can keep it from happening again."

"The other day, you compared me to your last boyfriend, said he was—what did you call him?"

"It's a name my brother came up with, actually. Mr. My-Way-or-the-Highway. Kyle didn't like Wayne. Wayne had definite opinions on everything, and the way he saw it, he was always right."

"I take it he rarely asked anyone's opinion or took advice?"

"Rarely? Try never. When I look back on the time I was with him, I feel like I just disappeared. But he didn't act that way out of malice. He was a wonderful man in so many other ways. He just believed that he knew what was best for me. He had this way of joking about it. He'd say 'Babe, when I want your opinion, I'll give it to you.' After a while, I didn't find it very funny any more."

"No wonder you were so reluctant to work with me when I showed up here with the whole thing sewn up. And no wonder you bit my head off this morning over that mess with the workmen. I'm surprised you didn't get up and leave tonight when the waiter brought the wine."

"I'm glad you finally understand."

He leaned forward on the table. "*I'm* glad you explained all this. I'll do my best to watch it from now on. I won't plan anything or do anything that affects the two of us without consulting you first. Okay?"

Kelli held back a smile. "I have a feeling that's easier said than done."

"Maybe. But I'm going to give it a try." He paused. "And I'm going to ask you for something in return."

"Oh?"

"There's something I want you to do. Even if you're not particularly wild about the idea, will you agree to try it once, for my sake?"

She looked at him. "I assume this *something* is strictly business-related?"

His lips twitched as he considered the question. "Yes. In a manner of speaking."

There's a hidden motive here, she thought. But what? Cautiously, she said: "Okay. To quote you: I'll give it a try."

"Good." He sat back. "What do you say we head down to the casino now and play blackjack?"

The dealer's name tag read *Sean*. He grinned at Kelli as he shuffled the cards and presented them to her.

"Cut?"

Kelli smiled back, trying not to be nervous as she divided the deck in half. Grant had refreshed her memory on the rules of the game as they drove down.

"Why don't *you* play?" she'd asked when they arrived, but Grant insisted she take the open spot on the stool. He wanted her to win back the money she'd lost the first day, he said, and he wanted her to do it herself. He was just there to help if she needed it.

There were three other players. The heavyset man sitting on the stool next to her was named George. She placed two dollars, the table's minimum bet, inside the small, white circle in front of her. Sean dealt. Grant moved up behind her, resting one hand on the padded edge of the table beside her. Although their bodies weren't touching, she felt the heat radiating off of him and from his cheek so close to her own. Her pulse moved into high gear.

"Grant," she whispered sternly, hoping he'd take the hint and move away. He didn't budge.

"Relax," he whispered, his breath warm against her ear. "This is strictly research. You want to win, don't you?"

She guessed his hidden motive now. This wasn't just research. He didn't just want her to experience the thrill of gambling, or win back her money. He felt the unspoken chemistry flowing between them as strongly as she did. He'd stayed friendly but businesslike when they were alone together, but she sensed that he'd wanted to touch her, to be close to her—and this public place where she couldn't put up a fight without making a scene was the perfect setting.

She took a deep breath and picked up her cards, struggling to will away her awareness of him as a man. *As if that were humanly possible.*

Her hand totaled thirteen. She saw the dealer's up card: a two.

"Stand," Grant said in a low voice.

She looked aside at him. "Stand? On a thirteen?" He nodded silently.

She needed twenty-one to win. She'd never stood on anything as low as thirteen. She flicked her cards against the felt tabletop to indicate a hit.

The dealer turned up a nine. Disappointed, Kelli laid down her cards. "Bust."

The dealer also went bust. Two of the other players collected their winnings. Kelli felt a prickle of disappointment. If she'd stood pat, as Grant had insisted, she would have won, too. But there was no way Grant could have known the dealer would go bust—was there?

She played another hand and won. On the third hand, Grant murmured another direction against her ear. It seemed less sensible than the first.

"I know you're trying to help, but I'd rather play it my way," she said firmly.

She lost.

"You're one stubborn lady," Grant said. "I'm offering free advice. You ought to take it."

The Harrison Duet

"I told you, I like to make my own decisions. I know how to play."

"Can't you trust me, for once? You promised, if I asked you to do something, you'd try it. I'm asking now. Follow my advice."

She sighed. "All right. But just this once."

On the next deal she held two sevens. The dealer's up card was a king. A tricky hand to play. She looked at Grant.

"Hit," he said. She asked for a hit. She reached nineteen, and the dealer went bust. Kelli grinned.

"Now don't get cocky," she said, "just because you were right this once."

But she soon noticed that Grant's eyes were fixed in concentration on every card that was played, and it occurred to her he was using a system. She had no idea how a system worked, but as his advice continued to work, her excitement grew.

Grant moved up even closer behind her now, until the warm strength of his body rested against her back. "You're doing great," he whispered softly, his lips against her hair.

His nearness distracted her and disturbed her senses, sending shivers dancing through her. She kept on playing, hardly aware of what she was doing, relying completely on Grant's directions.

Grant encouraged her to up her bet. When an hour had passed, she'd won more than twice as many hands as she'd lost, and had stacks of chips in front of her.

"You've brought me good luck, pretty lady," one of the other players said, gathering up his winnings. "I'm gonna quit now while I'm ahead."

"How much have we won?" Kelli asked.

Grant made a quick mental calculation. "About three hundred dollars."

304

She had no idea it was so much. "Shouldn't we quit now, too?"

"Not quite yet."

" Hit? " the dealer asked.

Kelli's eyes darted to the table. She hadn't even realized he'd dealt. A fifty-dollar bet stood inside her circle. When had she put it there? It was too late to take it back. Heart pumping with alarm, she picked up her hand. She had an ace and a ten. Blackjack!

Both thrilled and relieved, she reached out to collect her winnings. Grant stopped her hand. "We'll let it ride."

She stared at him. Let it ride? A hundred and twenty-five dollars? She was about to protest, but Grant silenced her with a look.

"Trust me," he said. "This time, it's double or nothing."

George, who'd been about to leave, sat back down on his stool. "I've got to see this."

Kelli's stomach felt queasy. She picked up her cards. *Over a hundred dollars.* It was crazy to bet so much on one hand. Then she caught her breath. A king and a queen! Twenty points; almost a blackjack.

"Stand," she said. The dealer had a six and an ace; soft seventeen. He had to take a hit. Kelli's heart began to pound. She watched him turn up an eight. The ace could count for one, so he now had a total of fifteen.

The dealer paused a split second before turning over his next card. Kelli wondered where all the air in the room had gone. Grant squeezed her arm, and she felt a bond of camaraderie pass between them in that moment of tense excitement, of shared danger.

The dealer turned over his card. A jack. He'd gone bust.

"We won!" Kelli stood up and threw her arms around Grant's neck, laughing in delight.

305

The Harrison Duet

Grant responded immediately, capturing her around the waist and grinning. "I told you we would. It doesn't hurt to let someone else take the lead once in a while, does it?"

Looking up at his lips just inches away, Kelli's face flushed with sudden color at her spontaneous hug and she started to pull away. He wouldn't allow it.

"Nothing like it, is there?" he said softly.

"No," she whispered, unsure if he meant the act of winning or the feel of her embrace. "There isn't."

Kelli felt high as a kite. She could walk on water. She could float on air. Altogether they'd won more than five hundred dollars. The thrill was so great she felt as if they'd won the Irish sweepstakes.

"I couldn't believe it," she said later, as they drove back to the house, "when I saw that fifty-dollar bet. Did I really put it out there?"

"No. I did."

"I thought so." She slapped his thigh. "That was sneaky."

"Somebody had to place the bet. You didn't seem to be paying much attention to the game for a while there."

How could I, she thought silently, with you standing so close behind me? She said: "I was paying attention. Enough to know you were using some kind of system. What do you do? Count cards?"

"It's a bit more complicated than that."

"Explain it to me."

He spent the rest of the drive going over the theory he'd learned from a book and had practiced over the years. There was a whole series of rules, but it basically involved keeping a count of the cards that had been played, and keeping in mind the ratio of face cards to non-face cards that were left in the deck. He raised or lowered his bet according to the odds.

306

"Does it always work?" she asked.

"No. It can work spectacularly, as you saw tonight. But when it fails, it fails dismally."

"And you told me to trust you! What if we'd lost that last bet?"

"We would have lost," he said simply. "But I knew the deck was heavy on face cards at that point. The odds were well weighted in our favor. It was worth the risk."

"Maybe," she said. "I wonder if I'll ever have the nerve to bet that high again."

It was nearly midnight when they reached the house. He walked her to the front door and followed her in, shutting the door behind him against the cold.

"Thank you for coming tonight," he said. "It was fun."

"It was. I'm glad I came. And thank you for dinner. It was delicious."

"Have you forgiven me yet for ordering ahead of time?"

"I have."

Their eyes met in a warm smile. He didn't say anything for a while, just stood a few feet away, watching her, his eyes brimming with affection. She found her mind straying to the way his body had felt, pressed against hers, as she'd struggled to keep her mind on the game. Wanting to brush away such thoughts and fill the silence, she cleared her throat and said: "Well. It's late. I have to get some sleep. The guy I'm working with thinks 6:30 A.M. is a fine time to start."

"Slave driver. I'll have to talk to him."

"Please do. Tell him I was up late doing research. Ask him if we can start at a more civilized hour tomorrow. Like maybe seven-thirty?"

"I'll see what I can do."

"Well...good night." It seemed ridiculous to shake his hand yet again, so she kept her arms at her sides.

The Harrison Duet

"What?" he asked in mock chagrin. "You're not going to invite me to stay for a cognac and a fireside chat on your couch?"

"No cognac. No fire. No couch."

"We'll have to make do without, then." His arms glided around her so naturally it seemed as if she were made to fit within them. Her tiny, surprised intake of breath was lost as, suddenly, his lips were on hers. He kissed her softly, slowly, a feather-light touch that aroused her instantly. She knew she should tell him to stop, but she couldn't. Beneath her skin, she was quivering. Heat spread through her. She could barely think.

She gave in, let her mind go, forgetting everything but him, his delicious scent and taste, the way his body felt against hers. Her hands went up around his neck and she closed her eyes. One hand caressed the strength of his broad shoulders, the other tangled in his hair. It felt soft and silky, just as she imagined it would.

Her body melted against his, her breasts swelling with desire. His mouth moved so slowly, tenderly over hers. If he took as much time, she thought, with the rest of her body as he did with his kisses, he'd make a wonderful lover.

A wonderful lover.

Those three words invaded her thought processes, and her mind slowly began to clear. What was she doing? How could she allow herself to respond to him like this? She ended the kiss and gently pushed out of his arms, her heart beating wildly.

"Kelli—" he began, his voice deep and rough.

"Please. Just give me a minute." She took a few shaky steps toward the living room and stopped to look out the windows, trying to still her rapid breathing, waiting for the wave of desire to fade. The inky silhouettes of the pine branches outside framed a brilliant crystal moon in a midnight sky. Below, a glowing moonlit path crossed the surface of the lake, fading to darkness just before it reached the shore. A sight for lovers, she thought, smiling grimly at the irony. *But we aren't lovers. We can't be.*

"Grant, we can't do this," she said at last. She heard him move closer.

"Do what? Kiss?"

"We can't get...involved. You said yourself, it's not a good idea to mix business with pleasure."

"I said I *used* to think that. Since I met you, I've changed my mind. I think you know I've been attracted to you from the start."

She turned to face him, struggling to maintain her resolve, hoping he couldn't see that she felt exactly the same way. "And I think we'll do far better work if we stay just friends."

"Friends?" He shook his head. "I disagree."

"Haven't you seen what happens in office romances? The two people are so caught up in each other that their work suffers. They don't concentrate on the job. Worse than that, if anything goes wrong between them, it creates tension like you can't believe. It disrupts the entire working environment."

"We're not working in an office, Kelli. It's just the two of us. Nothing we do can affect anyone else."

"No, but it will affect *us*. There's no way to avoid it. As you pointed out yesterday, there's a lot at stake here. This account is too big important. We've got less than two weeks to do a major presentation. A relationship between us will only get in the way."

His eyes locked with hers, rife with emotion as they stood in the dimly lit hallway. He sighed heavily. "You're probably right."

The Harrison Duet

He stepped closer, reached up to gently touch her cheek with his fingertips. "I have to admit, it's not going to be easy, given the way I feel about you. But I guess we can be professional about this, and keep our hands off each other until the job's finished."

Until the job's finished.

What then? she wondered. The pleasant bantering they'd shared over the past few days swept through her mind...the joy she felt in his company, the pleasure of talking with him over dinner, the magnetic attraction that sizzled between them, the melting effect of his embrace. Even now, the light touch of his fingers against her skin was rearranging her breathing patterns.

A few days ago she'd been certain she didn't want to get involved with anyone for a long, long time. Now that she'd met Grant, she wasn't quite so sure.

Then she remembered the part of his personality that clashed strongly with hers: his instinct to hand out directives, to make arrangements in advance, unasked. Tonight, he'd resolved to consult her in future before making decisions— but she doubted he could alter a part of himself that was so deeply ingrained.

Why did she always seem to fall for men who were so overbearing and dictatorial? Wayne had always promised to change, but he never did. If she let herself get involved with Grant, Kelli realized, she'd be stepping right back into the same, self-destructive pattern; she'd simply disappear.

"Grant," she said, flashing him a protective smile, "please don't take this the wrong way, but... I don't expect this... relationship...to turn into anything else down the road." She forced herself to continue, feeling her resolve slipping even as she uttered the words aloud. "I need time to explore life on my own for a while. I don't want to get involved with anyone."

310

For a second he seemed to reject what she was saying; then disappointment took over his face. He jerked his hand back, his lips tightening as he struggled to compose his features into a mask of calm, polite indifference. "Oh. Okay. I get it."

He opened the front door. "I'll see you in the morning at eight. I hope that's a civilized enough hour for you." And then he was gone.

It was a good thing, Kelli thought the next day, that they'd done most of their creative planning the day before, because now Grant barely spoke a word to her. While she worked steadily on pencil comps for menus and brochures, he spent a good part of the day on the phone, giving his production manager details so he could get prices from printers.

The little talking they did was strictly related to the project at hand. Grant was pleasant and businesslike; he still approved of her work in general; but it seemed to Kelli that he was more critical today, and his comments were less constructive.

"I don't like it," he said late that afternoon, when she presented him with a new logo idea.

"What's wrong with it?"

"The typeface is too ornate. I want something sharper, something clean and bold."

"Is there anything you like about the concept?"

"No."

She worked up three more designs, all different. He studied them with narrowed eyes. "I like the mountain in this one, and the typeface over here. Try doing one that combines the two."

The Harrison Duet

"I think they work fine the way they are," she said defensively. "Let's show them to Ted and see what he thinks."

"I'm not going to show Ted ten different logos. It'll take his board a year to make a choice. We'll come up with one that we like, maybe a runner-up, and that's it."

"But there's no way this combination will work. It's a waste of—"

"Try it," he said curtly.

She sighed in frustration. "You're just making me do this because of last night. You want to get back at me for—"

"This has nothing to do with last night."

"Doesn't it? Then why have you been in such a bad mood all day? Acting so distant and standoffish?"

"I thought that's the way you wanted it."

"You know it's not. I said I didn't want to get personally involved. I just want a professional, working relationship."

"Well, this is the working relationship you got. Take it or leave it."

Holding her temper in check, Kelli sat back down at her table. Clearly, he was taking her resolve as a rejection. Why couldn't he understand how she felt? She'd tried to explain it to him. Why did he have to be so picky? Why did he think his ideas were best?

Just keep going, she told herself. Stay composed. Be competent. This job will look great on your resume. When it's finished, you'll be back to working for yourself, with all the creative freedom you want.

When she completed the new drawing according to Grant's directive, she sat back and studied it. It was a graphic representation of a rugged, snowy mountain-top, with the name *Cassera's Tahoe* superimposed across the bottom in bold, outline-style letters. To her surprise, it wasn't bad. In fact, she had to admit, it was far better than the originals she'd done on her own. The more she looked at it, the more she liked it.

"Hey," Grant said, looking over her shoulder. "Great job. That's what I'm looking for. The shape is really interesting—it'll lend itself to all the different pieces—and it's easily recognizable, easy to read." A grin spread across his face for the first time that day. "Everything about it is just right. That's *it.*"

She was hugely pleased, felt the tension in the air recede. Since the result was due to their combined efforts, she reasoned that she owed him an apology. "You were right. I shouldn't have objected when you told me to try it this way. I'm sorry."

He sat on the stool next to her and picked up a pencil, rolled it between his fingers. "Kelli," he said at length, "I'm the one who should be apologizing. I didn't want to hear what you told me last night, and I've been acting like a teenager with a bruised ego all day. I'm sorry. Is there a chance we can forget what happened, and get back to square one?"

"I'll forget it if you will," she said with relief, wanting more than anything to restore peace between them.

He didn't reply, only smiled. After a while he got up, opened the studio door, and listened to the silence. "Carpenters gone?"

"They finished a couple of hours ago. The painters start tomorrow."

"If there's one thing I can't stand, it's the smell of wet paint." He slowly crossed the room, musing. "What do you say we get out of here tomorrow, and do something fun?"

"Really? You think we can afford to take a day off?"

"I think we've *earned* a day off. We've put in two long days, and got an outstanding amount of work done. My people are busy on the quote, and we've got plenty of time left."

"Here. Twist my arm."

The Harrison Duet

He laughed. "What would you like to do?"

"You're asking me? You're the Tahoe expert."

"True. And if you were anybody else I'd walk out this door, plan the whole thing myself, and spring it on you in the morning. But I took notes at the dinner table the other night. You tell me what *you* want. Anything goes."

"Anything?"

"Anything."

"Let me think." She was about to suggest they go skiing, when her gaze drifted to the lake view beyond the bay window. "How about a boat ride on the lake?" she said impulsively.

His eyebrows lifted. "A boat ride? In December?"

"I've cruised the Seattle harbor and I've sailed bays and lakes all across Washington State, but I've never been out on Lake Tahoe. It's so beautiful. I'd love to go out on the water, see the view of the shoreline from the middle of the lake. I guess it'd be pretty cold out there—"

"Freezing."

"And they probably don't rent boats this time of year—"

"They don't."

"But you said *anything goes.* So. If I could really do anything I wanted...I'd love to go boating."

He chuckled to himself. "Just for the fun of it, what kind of boat did you have in mind?"

"A powerboat. Something fast."

She saw the familiar gleam in his eyes that meant he was plotting something. He slapped his hand against the table and grinned. "If a boat ride is what the lady wants, a boat ride is what the lady gets. I'll be here tomorrow about ten. Dress warm."

"Should I pack a picnic lunch?"

Syrie James

"I'll take care of it." He stopped halfway to the door. "Maybe I should ask…is there anything else you're allergic to?"

"Peanut butter."

"Then rest easy tonight. I won't serve PBJs."

6

Kelli leaned on the railing above the private dock, admiring the craft below, water lapping quietly against its white hull. She'd never ridden in a powerboat quite so big or so sporty and luxurious. It was huge—at least twenty-eight feet long, she guessed. Navy and red stripes raced its length at deck level, and waist-high metal railings skirted the top of the V-shaped bow.

Most boats were in storage this time of year, Grant had explained during the short drive to Logan Shoal. Lucky for her, an old friend of his family was on the sheriffs' posse, and kept his personal inboard/outboard ready to go all year long. It had a radar wing, tilted up and backward like an enormous handle over the rear of the cockpit. The name *Lassie* was proudly painted across the stern.

"I really appreciate this," she heard Grant say. He came out of the nearby boathouse with a man of about her father's age. She went to meet them by the steps, where Grant introduced them.

"Thanks so much for letting us use the boat, Mr. Anderson," Kelli said.

The lines in his tanned face deepened as he broke into a wide smile. "I can't stand formality when I'm shaking the hand of a beautiful woman. Please, call me John."

316

Syrie James

"John, then." Kelli smiled with pleasure at the compliment.

"On second thought, maybe I'll take this lady out on the lake myself," John replied with a wink.

"Don't even think about it, John," Grant growled.

"My, my. Possessive, aren't we?" John laughed. "Don't worry. It takes a younger man than me to go out on the lake for pleasure this time of year. Too cold for my bones. At least you picked a good day for it. Clear sky. Not much wind." He slapped Grant on the back. "I don't lend my craft out to many people, but I never could say no to Grant. I think by now he handles a boat better than I do. Care to guess how long I've known this young whipper-snapper?" he asked Kelli.

"Since long before he had so much snap in his whip, I'll bet," Kelli said, laughing. No wonder Grant hadn't been bemused when she asked to go for a boat ride in the dead of winter. He was an experienced sailor. And he had connections. She was struck with the realization of how much she had to learn about him—and the fact that, with each passing day, she was discovering more and more interests they had in common.

The two men hopped onto the deck and Grant reached out a hand to Kelli, helping her climb on board. The cockpit, high atop the boat behind a tilted windshield, took up the back third of the boat and was fitted with padded benches. The instrument panel held as many dials and gauges as a small aircraft.

While Grant stowed a picnic hamper in the quarters below deck, John opened a storage locker and handed her the flotation cushions that substituted for life vests.

"Grant's family's been coming up here since he was, oh, about three, maybe four. We used to rent them our guest

The Harrison Duet

house down the road. What a little daredevil he was, scaring his mother half to death, jumping in and out of my boat. And then when he grew up—" John shook his head with a loud chuckle "—every girl within fifteen miles was dying to go out on the lake with him. He kept begging me to let him drive, so I had to teach him the ropes."

"So you've lent Grant this boat before to take girls out on the lake?" It was totally irrational, but Kelli felt a spark of jealousy.

"Not this boat. I just got *Lassie* a couple of years ago. But before that—you know these hot-blooded young guys." John's lips twitched as he looked at her. "Ever since he was in high school, he used to bring up a different girl every month in summer."

Before Kelli could respond to that, Grant reappeared on deck. "What am I missing?"

Kelli shot him a sweet smile, but her eyes were scurrilous. "John was just telling me about your dark and sordid past. About what a *hot-blooded* young guy you were."

"John, are you spreading lies?" Grant said.

John laughed. "Wipe that scowl off your face, young lady. Can't you take a little teasing from a jealous old man? Take my word for it, you've got yourself a great fellow here. This man's the salt of the earth. If I could have had a son, he's the one I'd choose." He clapped an affectionate hand on Grant's shoulder, then jumped back onto the dock and knelt to loosen the tie line. "Now you two have yourselves a good time. I'm not on call today, so you can keep her out as long as you want."

Grant stood at the helm and waved to John. Kelli sank into the curving bench across from the helm and crossed her arms, glancing at Grant with feigned indignation. "What a relief to find out I'm spending the day with an *experienced* man of the sea. A different girl every month in summer, huh?"

Grant looked surprised beneath his grin. "Is that what he told you?" He cupped his hands over his mouth and shouted, "Thanks a lot, John. Ought to know I can always count on a buddy like you."

"Anytime." John chuckled expansively as he waved from the dock.

"Is it true?" Kelli asked.

"Do I detect a note of jealousy in your voice?"

"No! I just like to have an idea of who I'm dealing with here."

"It's not true." Grant adjusted two levers on the instrument panel and glanced her way, his eyes deeply serious. "I only brought a different girl every *other* month."

Stifling a laugh, Kelli bent forward menacingly. Grant held up an arm to ward off her blow as he turned over the ignition, his laughter joining hers, the sound disappearing beneath the engine's roar. He guided the boat out of the stone breakwater to the choppier water of the lake, where he relaxed against the wide helm seat, one hand on the controls, the other at the wheel.

"I thought we'd head north, around the lake," Grant said. "Let you see how big it really is. That is, if you're still speaking to me."

She let her wry smile answer in confirmation. Kelli zipped up her ski jacket against the chilly air, and as they moved past the dense thicket of pines along the shoreline she sat back, hands in her pockets, her face tilted up toward the sun. The loud hum of the engine kept their conversation to a minimum. After a while they spotted her brother's house, almost hidden by the trees. Along the northern shore they passed

The Harrison Duet

Mount Rose, a majestic peak beyond snow-covered pines. At Crystal Bay, Grant cut the engine and they drifted in delicious silence for a while.

She saw another boat cutting across the water, far in the distance, but otherwise they were alone. The lake stretched endlessly around them in gleaming sapphire-blue splendor, and the sky above matched its brilliant hue.

"Let me know if you get too cold and want to go back," Grant said.

Kelli shook her head. "We can stay all day if you want. I love it out here."

He grinned, obviously pleased that she was enjoying herself. "So do I. I wish I had more time to go boating. I'd buy one of these for myself and dock it at San Francisco Bay."

"Why don't you have time?"

"I practically live at the agency. This is the first time I've been away in two years. Even though we've been working up till now, it's been like a vacation for me."

"You ought to get away more often. You have to make time for the things you love. Hasn't the place been running just fine while you've been gone?"

"As a matter of fact, it has. My staff keeps things moving." He leaned back and stretched out his legs, clasping his hands behind his head. "Our presentation's moving along at a steady clip, too. Once we finish those comps for the collaterals, we can start on the media campaign. Have you given it any thought?"

Kelli shook her head. "Not yet." They talked about the ads for a time, repeating the competition's catchy slogans, and going over a few possible concepts they might try. When the sun was high in the sky, Grant said they'd talked enough about business and it was time to start thinking about finding a place for lunch.

320

"We validated our trip. We can now say we were out on business with a clear conscience. Where would you like to throw anchor for lunch?"

"I read about a famous bay that's supposed to be really beautiful, I forget what it's called."

"Emerald Bay?"

"That's it! Can we go there?"

"We can. But it's at the opposite end of the lake."

"Is that too far?"

"It depends on how hungry you are."

"How fast does this thing go?"

"I usually keep it at thirty or forty knots. It planes at forty-five."

"Let's go to Emerald Bay. And let's plane it."

Grant's eyebrows rose. "Anything the lady wants." He moved the throttle slowly forward. Kelli watched the shoreline recede as the boat picked up speed. Soon the trees blended into a dark-green blur stretching up to the snow-covered mountains above. The boat beat against the cresting water before them, vibrating powerfully with the engine's hum.

She stood up, bracing herself against the windshield for support, squinting against the cold slap of wind that roared in her ears and blew her hair out behind her like a flag. And then, suddenly, the boat stilled, skimming across the water as if they'd left a runway and had truly taken off into the air. *Wonderful*, she thought exultantly, drinking in the clean taste and smell of the crisp, fresh air. *Magnificent!*

Cheeks glowing, she ducked behind the protective windshield and sat down again. They broke into laughter at the same moment, lost in the pure joy of movement, sight, and sound. When he'd slowed the pace to a safer speed, Grant slid to the far side of the double-width helm seat and gestured toward the waiting space. "Want to drive?"

The Harrison Duet

Kelli's lips parted in astonishment. She'd never driven a boat before. Her first impulse was to say no. But then she saw the challenge in his eyes, which brought to mind a similar challenge she'd accepted not too long ago, to briefly take over the controls of her brother's small plane over Puget Sound. *That* had been thrilling.

"Sure," Kelli replied, her pulse quickening with excitement as she moved behind the wheel. "Just tell me what to do."

He showed her how to move the throttle to change the speed, and pointed out Mount Tallac, a lofty white peak far in the distance. "That's our guide. Keep it at eleven o'clock, and we'll end up at the mouth of the bay."

It proved easier to pilot the boat than she'd expected, and her anxiety soon vanished in the thrill of the ride.

When they reached the other side of the lake, with Grant's direction she found the narrow opening in the trees that led to a lovely, oval-shaped bay. A small island was nestled in its protective shelter, and around them, tree-covered cliffs rose up sharply from a narrow strip of rocky beach.

"A poet couldn't do justice to this view," Kelli enthused.

Grant reached across her to cut the engine. "This is probably the most photographed spot in the whole area."

She watched him climb, swift and surefooted, to the bow of the boat to drop anchor. With his dark hair blowing in the breeze, his jeans clinging to his long, lean legs, and the blue ski jacket that fit snugly across his shoulders, he was the epitome of masculinity: Tall. Handsome. And utterly desirable.

She gave her head a shake. *Wrong. He's your boss on this project. You work for him. And, as you so clearly stated the other night, that's as far as this is going to go.*

When Grant returned, she pointed to a turreted stone castle on the nearby shore and asked, "Does anyone live there?"

"No. That's Vikingsholm Mansion, a replica of a ninth-century Norse fortress built by an heiress in 1928. The property is now part of the Emerald Bay State Park. I'll have to take you there when the tours start again this summer."

She let out a regretful sigh. "I'd love to see it. But this summer—hopefully—I'll be knee-deep in work back in Seattle. I don't know if I'll have time to come down."

"You ought to get away more often," he said softly. "You have to make time for the things you love." The gleam in his eyes and the way he'd echoed her earlier words disconcerted her. She felt a shiver dance down her spine and knew it wasn't from the chilly air. She tried to look at something neutral—the instrument panel in front of him or the back of the seat—but her stare kept drifting back to the dark sheen of his hair, the way sunlight reflected on his smooth-shaven cheek, the inviting curve of his lips.

She stood up abruptly. "You wouldn't believe how hungry I am. How about if I bring up the lunch?"

Grant told her she'd find a box lunch in the refrigerator, and Kelli pushed through the narrow folding door to the cabin. It was warmer below deck, and its cozy sophistication delighted her at once. Floor space was limited, but there was plenty of headroom. On one side was a compact dinette booth upholstered in blue velveteen. The galley opposite boasted a gleaming stainless-steel sink and stove below teak cabinetry. At the bow of the boat was a luxurious double berth, and when she turned she found a matching berth at the stern. The dinette probably opened into a bed, too. Cozy, she thought again. Enough sleeping space for six.

Sleeping space. The thought made her heart race, and to prevent any distracting images from coming to mind, she quickly opened the tiny refrigerator. Its contents made her start in surprise. Stuffed in one corner was a cardboard box with a deli label and two stemmed glasses. Around it, the shelves were piled high with more than a dozen bottles of wine. What were they all for?

She pulled one out: Sauvignon Blanc. She pulled out another: Chenin Blanc, from one of her favorite Napa vineyards. There were three different Chardonnays. A Gewurztraminer. Riesling. Zinfandel. All from different wineries, and every one of them white. There were also two bottles of very fine champagne—Krug and Dom Pérignon.

Her heart warmed at Grant's thoughtfulness. She put the cardboard box into the picnic basket he'd brought, added the bottle of Chenin Blanc, the Dom Pérignon, and the glasses, and brought it all up on deck.

"You really know how to spoil a girl," she said, giving Grant a grateful smile as she set the basket on the cockpit floor.

He smiled back. "You said white. And you said you adored champagne. I didn't know what kind you liked best. Did I hit the mark with any of them?"

"The bull's-eye." She handed him the bottles and the corkscrew. "I've been known to kill for a glass of either of these."

He laughed. "So have I. Shall we start with the Chenin Blanc?" At her nod, he expertly opened the bottle and filled the glasses. "Here's to..." He paused, seeming to change his mind about what he was going to say, before finishing: "...a winning presentation for Cassera's."

"Tell me," Kelli said, "about all the girls you used to take out on John's boat."

Lunch had been scrumptious—cold, fried chicken, fresh fruit, potato chips, French rolls with butter, and moist, chewy brownies for dessert. They'd been deep in conversation when a freezing wind had come up, so they'd escaped to the warmth of the cabin below, where they now relaxed side by side at the dinette table, sipping delicious champagne.

"You really want to hear about the girls I've dated?"

"I'm intrigued by a man who—as you so blithely stated—has had a new girlfriend every other month."

Grant laughed and shook his head. "You know I was pulling your leg. So was John. I believe he's a bit envious that I brought you out here today. I told him that we're working together—that this is just a business arrangement. He seemed inclined to think otherwise." Grant sipped his champagne, catching her gaze, his expression suggesting that his hopes were more in line with those of his friend.

Kelli blushed under Grant's scrutiny, unable to deny that—despite her resolve the other night—she'd been harboring similar thoughts about him which were anything but businesslike. "You're avoiding my question," she blurted out.

"Am I?"

"Yes."

"Just because we're working together, it doesn't mean we can only talk business. It's good for colleagues to share aspects of their personal lives, in order get to know each other better."

"Okay." His voice seemed to lower an octave. He set down his glass, slid one arm behind her along back of the dinette seat, and turned to face her. "My dating history. I'm not seeing anyone now, if you were wondering about that. I haven't been in a relationship for quite some time. I've dated a number of

The Harrison Duet

women, but nowhere near as many as John would like you to believe. Everyone plays the field. Don't you?"

"I...no."

"No?"

"I can only handle one relationship at a time. The men I went out with—it was always a steady thing. Either it ended after one date or it lasted for years."

When had he moved so close? Grant's thigh, hard and lean beneath his jeans, now pressed against hers, trapping her between his body and the wall of the boat.

"The ones that lasted for years...were there many?" he asked quietly.

"Just two."

"I take it the second, long-lasting relationship was Wayne?"

She nodded. The frankly admiring look in his blue eyes caused her pulse to pound. "When we broke up a few months ago, I promised myself I would stay solo for a while. Not get involved with anyone until—"

"Until what?"

His face was just inches from hers, his lips so close...so incredibly close. Her nerve endings started a frenzied rain dance and her fingers began to tremble, prompting her to set her champagne glass down on the table. "Until I'd found out if I could survive on my own, answer to no one, become my own person."

"You are definitely your own person, Kelli Ann Harrison." Grant's fingers closed over hers. "Every day I discover something new and even more remarkable about you. You're a beautiful, strong, ambitious, talented woman. Any goal you set for yourself, anything you want to achieve, you'll do it. You've got what it takes."

"Thank you," she said, her voice little more than a whisper. "I hope that's true."

His hand slipped into her silky hair, and then he bent his head and brushed her cheek with a brief, soft kiss, as gentle as the touch of a butterfly's wings. "Believe me," he said, "it *is* true."

Kelli gripped the table edge to steady herself against the tremor that ran through her at his touch. He drew back slightly, a silent question in his eyes as they held hers for a long, heart-stopping moment.

She'd said she didn't want this. She'd tried to resist. But she saw in his expression such heartfelt tenderness that it stripped away her defenses. She didn't want to think, only wanted to feel.

Her eyes must have mirrored both her yearning and her change of resolve, because his arms suddenly tightened about her with confidence and his lips came down on hers in a deep, clinging kiss, kissing her as she'd dreamed of being kissed by him—open-mouthed, drinking her in. He tasted of champagne, and his delicious scent filled her, surrounded her. His hands caressed her back, pressing the softness of her sweater against her sensitized flesh. When the kiss was over she gazed up at him, her vision desire-misted, and she saw open affection in his eyes.

He now pressed fiery kisses across her cheeks, nose, and throat. Her eyes closed in rapt absorption as he moved aside the soft cowl neckline of her sweater to expose her neck. She breathed in long, deep waves, enjoying the moment; and after what seemed to her a pleasurable eternity, his lips once more reached her waiting mouth.

There was no need to speak; they were communicating their feelings and thoughts now through touch, through silent gesture. Their lips met and parted and met again, liquid, searching. Her fingers combed through his soft, windblown

The Harrison Duet

hair and she drew him closer still. Her breath came faster as his lips and tongue found her most sensitive spot at the side of her throat and his hand slipped beneath her sweater, brushing the side of her breast. The feeling she had of wanting him to touch the tips of her breasts was so strong that her head fell back and she let out a small, yearning sound.

"Ah, Kelli," he murmured, his voice throaty and sensual, and she felt his strong arms around her back, drawing her forward, up, and out of the booth; and then he was lifting her, settling her gently onto expansive softness. She was hazily aware that he'd brought her to the bed, and she felt light and dreamy, waiting heedlessly for what was to come.

She felt a sensation of movement beneath her, of the world gently rocking, and wondered at it. Then he was beside her and she forgot everything as he tugged at the hem of her sweater, pulling it up and over her head. In seconds he'd removed her bra. She gasped when his hands touched her bare flesh, massaging the undersides of her breasts. His mouth moved slowly over her collarbone and down, and then he was kissing her breasts, his tongue warm and wet, working her nipples to tight arousal. She moaned unconsciously, tiny, violent explosions echoing through her body.

He moved above her, melding his mouth to hers once more as he covered her body with his. His lips and legs pressed her into the soft mattress, infusing her with his warmth. She was vaguely aware of an increase in the movement beneath her, a rhythmic rolling, back and forth—what did it mean? His hand covered her breast again, molding it with palm and fingertips. She was spinning, lost in the pleasure of his hands and mouth. It felt so right to be in his arms, to have him touching her this way. She wanted to feel his flesh against hers, wanted him to make love to her, wanted him as she'd never wanted anyone before.

Suddenly the world jerked sharply, heaving them to one side. His weight hurtled against her and she clung to him, eyes widening in surprise, her mind still reeling on some distant plane. Then the boat tilted back again and they rolled with it. He hugged her tightly and spoke softly in her ear.

"It's all right, Kelli. We're anchored down. We're not going anywhere."

She tried to control her breathing and the pounding of her heart. "Is it a storm?" she whispered.

He shook his head. Softly, with affection, he touched his nose to hers. "It's just a wave. The wind."

"How do you know?"

"There was hardly a cloud in the sky today."

Anxiety filled her. They were so far from shore. "Don't you think we should check?"

He raised himself above her with a sigh. "If it will make you feel better, I'll go and check." He rolled out of the bed and moved to the cabin door. The loss of contact with his body sent a chill running through her. She rolled to her side, all at once uncomfortably aware of her nakedness as the boat continued its gentle rocking.

"Just a strong wind," Grant said, dropping back into the cabin. "We've got a few whitecaps, but nothing to worry about." He slid back onto the bed and stretched out beside her. "Now where were we?" Tenderly his arms gathered her up and he lowered his mouth to hers.

Her heart hammered in her chest and she tried desperately to let her mind drift back to where it had been only moments ago. But now, for some reason she kept hearing his voice saying *Everyone plays the field. Don't you?*

The Harrison Duet

She'd never made love to a man she wasn't in love with. She'd known Grant less than a week. In that short time, she'd come to—how should she put it?—to like him intensely. She deeply enjoyed his company. She felt very close to him after all the hours they'd spent together. She'd felt a magnetic, physical attraction to him from the moment they met. That's what had brought them together now. But that wasn't love—was it?

She'd felt certain, after his kiss the other night, that any further physical contact would lead to this very dilemma, and now she saw she'd been right.

How could she face him tomorrow, the next day, the next week, working together in the close confines of the house, knowing she'd had casual sex with him? What would he think of her? What would she think of herself?

He felt her tension, sensed the difference in her response, and he pulled back, searching her face. "What's wrong?"

"I..." she began, but couldn't put her feelings into words. She felt his eyes on her face and couldn't look up, her cheeks flushing with guilt and confusion.

He sat up. Taking a deep, steadying breath, he gathered her sweater and bra from a corner and handed them to her. He swiftly moved off the bed, grabbed his jacket and went to the door. "Come up when you're dressed," he said, and to her relief there was no trace of anger in his voice. "We'll head back."

A few minutes later she climbed up on deck. It seemed ironic that the sky was still such a bright blue, the distant pines and snowy mountains still breathtaking in their magnificence, when inside she felt as if she'd withered up and died.

Grant sat at an angle across the helm seats, legs stretched in front of him, his hands in the pockets of his jacket. The wind blew briskly through his hair and whipped her own hair

330

about her face, but otherwise it was silent. She sat opposite him and made herself look at him, but his gaze was focused downward, avoiding hers.

"I'm sorry," she said.

"It's all right. Don't worry about it."

"I've never done that before." Her face grew hot. "Gotten so close and then stopped, I mean. I just—"

"You don't have to explain, Kelli." He lifted his eyes to hers. She saw no accusation there, only self-reproach and frustration. "You made it clear the other night how you wanted things to stand between us, and you repeated those feelings today. I overstepped my bounds, that's all."

"No, it wasn't your fault." Tears stung behind her eyes. She wanted to say, *I wanted it just as much as you did,* but the words wouldn't come.

"It was." Grant toyed with the keys in his hand. "I just want you to know, I didn't bring you out here for this—as a pretext to make love to you. I promised myself last night I'd play it by your rules, that I could think of you as no more than a friend, a business partner. I see now that I was lying to myself. You must have known—there's no way I can hide it—from the moment we first bumped into each other in front of that elevator, I've been crazy about you. And today...I couldn't help myself. I just got carried away." He let out a deep sigh and faced her again. "I'm sorry. It won't happen again."

The ride back to the dock seemed interminable. Grant barely said a word. Kelli told herself she'd done the right thing. She ought to be relieved they hadn't made love, instead of feeling this irrational disappointment that ached, hollow, inside her. *Don't think about it. Don't think.*

They returned the boat, got into Grant's van, and drove back to the house. When he pulled into the driveway and

The Harrison Duet

stilled the motor, he sat back, tapping his fingers on the steering wheel. She was trying not to imagine what the next few days were going to be like, how she should act, when Grant spoke.

"I'm going back to the city tomorrow morning."

"Tomorrow?" Her eyes darted up to his, but the dismay that rang in her voice embarrassed her and she looked away.

"Yes. I've been gone long enough. I have meetings with clients on Friday. I was going to have to go back late tomorrow in any case."

She knew why he was leaving early. After what had happened, he felt just as uncomfortable as she did. "When will you be back?" she asked quietly.

"Saturday, if everything's going smoothly at the agency. You don't need me here for a few days, anyway. We've got the logo design, you just need to work up a tight comp. All the thumbnails are done for the collaterals, so you can do the full-size comps on your own. That ought to take you another two or three days at least. When I get back, we'll get started on the media campaign. We'll have almost a week left, plenty of time."

She nodded, afraid to speak because her throat had suddenly, inexplicably constricted and she felt the hot threat of tears.

He looked at her, hands still on the wheel. "Will you be all right while I'm gone?" She nodded. "You'll call if you have any questions?" She nodded again. "Good," he said. There was a silence. "So. Do you have your key?"

She realized he was signaling for her to go. She fumbled for her purse and threw open the door. "Have a good trip. See you Saturday," she said. But her lips wouldn't smile.

"See ya." He turned on the ignition, backed up, and drove away.

332

7

Kelli's eyelids grew heavy. The drawing blurred. She sat up, arching her neck and back, and checked her watch under the glare of the lamp above her drafting table: 3:00 A.M., Friday. She'd been working since nine the previous morning, with only short breaks for food and fresh air. No wonder waves of sleep were lapping at her. No wonder her entire body ached.

Pushing herself up from the drafting table, she switched off the overhead lamp and made her way to the bathroom. The painters had finished that morning and fortunately the smell of paint was beginning to dissipate. She got ready for bed, then opened the bedroom window a crack. A rush of cold air surged in, and she breathed deeply. She was about to move away when a soft, whispering sound made her pause and look outside. Through the darkness the pine branches looked thicker and heavier than before, and tiny specks seemed to be drifting softly through the air.

Snow! A light fall of beautiful, delicate flakes. She'd been working so hard, she hadn't even noticed it start.

Fresh powder on the mountain, she thought, with a small burst of excitement. She hadn't scheduled any workmen for the next day, since she wanted to give the paint a few days to dry before the carpet was laid. She was almost done with the

The Harrison Duet

work Grant had left for her. At last she could get out for a day and go skiing.

Grant. Shivering, she slipped into her sleeping bag and pulled her blankets over her, then curled into a ball and hugged one of her pillows to her chest, waiting for her body heat to generate warmth. She tried to lull herself back to sleep with images of the next day's activity—a glorious day out on the mountain—but she kept seeing Grant's face before her, lined with hurt and self-reproach. She kept hearing him say, *I'm sorry. I couldn't help myself. It won't happen again.*

Grant. She wondered how many times she'd whispered his name in the day and a half since he'd been gone. The first night she'd tossed and turned, her mind tormenting her with memories of his kisses, of the way his hands and lips had felt on her body, of the desire he'd awakened within her when he held her in his arms. At last, near dawn, she'd fallen into a heavy sleep, only to awaken, hot and highly aroused, from a dream that had moved rapidly from romantic to erotic, and had featured Grant as the lead.

Today she'd worked frantically to make the hours pass more quickly, but it hadn't helped to banish thoughts of Grant or to ease the pang of loneliness and longing she felt each time she looked up and saw the empty drafting table beside her. She missed him—and not just his embraces. She missed his company—their teasing banter, their meaningful conversations, his smile, his ready laugh, his keen interest in her and everything she said.

How could she feel such attachment to someone she'd known only a week? Kelli realized now that the day on the boat, when they were about to make love, the attraction *hadn't* been merely physical—at least, not on her part.

I shouldn't be surprised, she thought. Relationship experts and cautionary friends often insisted that it took months,

334

sometimes years, of sharing and caring before a person could truly say they were in love with someone—but her own family history had taught her otherwise. Ever since she was a child, she'd been told by her parents and grandparents—whose relationships she had as living proof—that it was entirely possible to fall in love overnight, and for that love to last a lifetime.

She hadn't really believed that something so magical would ever happen to *her*. But she couldn't deny it any longer: the magnetic pull she'd felt when she and Grant first met had grown into something far deeper and richer in a very short time. With a certainty that filled her with equal measures of joy and confusion, Kelli admitted that she was falling in love with him—that she might be *in love* with him already.

What was she supposed to do with all these newfound feelings? Could she tell him? No—not yet—it was much too soon.

The timing, she knew, was all wrong. She'd meant it when she said she wanted to stay single for a while, to prove that she could be happy and make it on her own. How was she supposed to do that, if she got involved with Grant? It still worried her that he had such a forceful personality. At times, the two of them were like gasoline and flame; all it took was a spark to ignite their tempers. They were too much alike, and something told her they'd always be fighting each other to retain control. But none of that seemed important any more.

She had no idea where this would lead, or what the future might hold for them. It might be a very short-lived affair. But he clearly had feelings for her. He wanted to be lovers *now*. Admittedly, so did she. She'd been afraid that a romantic liaison would hamper their working relationship, but she saw now that by denying them the chance to express their feelings for each other, she'd only put up a barrier between them that would become more difficult to cross with each passing day.

Who knows, she thought; maybe an affair would actually be good for us. He'll be my muse, and I can be his. Hopefully, we'll bring out the best in each other.

Her heart pounded with excitement as she thought of the days ahead. She'd have to let him know that she'd changed her mind, that she *did* want him. But when? How? He was due back the day after tomorrow.

I'll tell him soon, she decided. Somehow she'd know when the time was right.

"Are you kidding me?" Kelli scooped up a fistful of snow, formed it into a ball, and threw it against a nearby pine in frustration. "I don't believe this!"

The sky was still a threatening gray, but the snow had stopped falling at nine A.M., so she'd cleared her car windows and strapped her skis to the roof rack. A four-inch layer of snow covered the long, sloping driveway that led to the main road, but it was still navigable as long as she put chains on her tires. After an hour of struggling, she'd finally managed to attach them.

But just as she'd climbed behind the wheel, the engine had died. The situation under the hood told a familiar story: it was the automatic enrichment device again. She had hoped the earlier repair would last her another few weeks at least.

If she had four sets of hands, she could get it working again, but she knew it would just be another Band-Aid. What she needed was a new part—and she'd never find one in Tahoe. She'd be lucky if she found one anywhere in the state. There were no Rover dealers in America anymore. Unless a specialty shop happened to have the part in stock, she'd have to order it directly from England, and that would take weeks, maybe months to get.

"It's not fair!" Scooping up another snowball, she turned and threw it down the driveway with all her might.

"Hey!" She saw him at the same moment that she heard his deep shout. He came to an abrupt halt about twenty feet away, one arm raised to protect his face. "Are you through, or should I start arming myself?"

"Grant!" Her heart gave a little leap of delight and she ran to meet him.

"Who did you think I was? The county building inspector? A bill collector?"

"Neither. I didn't even see you."

"A likely story." He brushed the splatter of snow from his red parka and quickened his pace in her direction, his boots making deep footprints in the soft snow. Beneath his open jacket she saw that he wore the familiar jeans that accentuated the lean, muscular strength of his thighs and calves.

She stopped close to him, curbing an almost desperate need to throw her arms around his neck and hug him. She'd been worried, after what happened on the boat the last time they were together, that he'd feel awkward and uncomfortable around her. To her relief, she saw no trace of discomfort in his gaze. If anything, she detected warmth in his eyes as he looked at her, a mirror of the joy she felt at seeing him— although his smile was reserved, as though he was holding himself in check.

"I thought you had meetings with clients today," she said. "You weren't coming back until tomorrow."

"I heard on the news that you had snow up here. I was afraid you might be snowed in."

The Harrison Duet

"You missed your meetings just to make sure I was all right?"

"I did. Shameful, isn't it? I shirked my responsibility and sent someone else. I had images of you stuck out here alone with an impassable driveway, and six-foot drifts piled up against your door. So I loaded my van with enough food and supplies to last for a month's siege, and beat it up here. I figured I'd hire a sleigh and a team of huskies if I had to pack it all in."

She laughed. "It would have been a daring rescue. I'm sorry I missed it." This proof of his feelings for her was both flattering and thrilling. She grinned shyly. "You know, you could have called."

"I did. Your phone's out of order."

"It is?" she said in surprise. "It *has* been quiet, but I wasn't expecting any calls. And I never used the phone."

"The snow probably weighed down and broke the line. It happens every winter around here. It can take days to fix."

"Well, thank you for coming." She wanted to tell him how lonely it had been without him, how much she'd missed him. *Not yet. Not yet.* "Where'd you park?"

"At the side of the road. They were just clearing it when I got here, so I didn't bother to put on chains. I couldn't risk that snowy driveway of yours, though." He took in her outfit—royal blue bib ski overalls with a white sweater. "Were you going skiing?"

"I *hoped* to. I need a break. I'm almost finished with the comps for the collaterals. Only two left."

"Are you serious? You must have worked all night!"

"Actually, I did."

"Then you *definitely* deserve a break." He glanced at her car. "What's wrong? Did it die again?"

338

She nodded. "Same old problem. The A.E.D."

"Then you're in luck. I brought a new part with me."

"What? An A.E.D.? For this model Rover?"

"Yep."

"You're kidding." Kelli stared at him. "How on earth did you get it?"

"I looked in the right place. I didn't want you stranded here." He moved past her and slammed down her hood. "We can install it tomorrow."

"That was so thoughtful, Grant. Thank you so much! But I still don't see how you—"

"Heavenly Valley has a foot of new snow," he interrupted, unhooking her skis from her roof. "I've got my ski equipment in the van. Let's unload the food I brought, I'll glance over the work you did, and then what do you say we go hit the slopes?"

She could see why it was called Heavenly Valley. Standing at the top of the mountain, surrounded by puffy white clouds in a bright-blue sky, with the warm sun beating down on her face, Kelli felt as if she truly had reached the heavens.

Miles below, past the long expanse of frosty white mountainside, beyond the snow and pine-covered valley, the lake spread itself out like a shimmering mirror, echoing the blue of the sky. Even from this height, the lake seemed enormous, curving toward them in a giant arc and then disappearing around a bend in both directions. The opposite bank appeared only as a hazy mass of white and green, like a distant, massive island.

She grasped her ski poles with gloved hands and leaned forward, stretching her legs and arching her back, catlike, to

The Harrison Duet

counter the effect of the long ride up the mountain on two separate chair lifts.

Grant kick-stopped at her side. "Nice view."

"It's beautiful!" Kelli said, taking a deep breath of the crisp, sparkling air.

"I wasn't talking about the lake." His eyes twinkled as he admired Kelli's slim form.

She blushed, both flattered and embarrassed. Her close-fitting jacket of vivid royal blue was inset with white V-shaped panels to match her sweater and overalls. She'd tucked her hair into a knit ski hat, but reddish-gold wisps had come loose and blew about her face.

"I can see why you love it here so much," she said.

Grant stamped his skis, shaking off a thin layer of snow. "We can take Ridge Run first, if you want." With his pole he pointed out a gentle slope along the top edge of the mountain. "It's the easiest, and you can see the lake all the way down."

He'd asked, on the way up on the chair lift, how well she skied. In fact, she'd been skiing since she was three years old, but some attempt at modesty—or maybe it was a mischievous instinct—had made her shrug and say simply, "I've hit the slopes a few times."

Grant shoved off and slipped past her. "Just take it easy," he called out over his shoulder. "I'll wait for you at the first bend."

Smiling to herself, Kelli followed him down the long, curving trail, enjoying the feel of the smooth, freshly packed snow beneath her skis and the crisp wind against her face. It was Friday, and the slopes weren't overly crowded.

Against the backdrop of pure white, Grant's red bib ski pants and parka stood out like a beacon. He moved with expertise and precision, his skis perfectly parallel, slowing almost

340

imperceptibly before each turn and then picking up speed again in a fluid, graceful motion. An expert, Kelli thought. Why hadn't she thought to ask how long *he'd* been skiing?

He stopped at the side cresting the next ridge, hands resting on his ski poles, looking up at her. She could almost feel the heat of his gaze as she finished the slope with quick, even turns and slid to a stop, her skis just inches from his.

"You ski like a pro," he said.

She tried to hide a smile, but couldn't. "So do you."

He laughed, shaking his head in disbelief. "Here I've been taking it easy, and you could go down this thing backward with a blindfold. What were you sandbagging for?"

"I wanted to surprise you."

"It worked." He grinned as two other skiers zoomed past them. "But it's the nicest surprise I've had all day."

The morning passed in a rush of shared laughter and vibrant energy. At lunchtime they huddled over hot coffee and sizzling hamburgers in the noisy, steamy cafeteria, then attacked the slopes again, delighting in their matched abilities. When the clouds gathered, graying the sky, and the wind turned cold, they agreed to take just one more run before tackling the lower slopes that led to the parking lot.

"I'll race you," she said, pointing to a sign classifying a nearby slope as most difficult. "Last one to reach the line at Waterfall Chair has to cook dinner."

"A serious challenge. Don't you have to throw down a gauntlet?"

She pulled off a glove and tossed it at his feet. "Will that do?"

"Admirably." He bent to pick up the glove and handed it back. "You ready?"

The Harrison Duet

She nodded. They pushed off. Kelli sped down the mountain, snow flying, her breathing increasing with her rate of speed. The slope was so steep it was nearly deserted, and she was glad. It was not going to be easy to beat him, she saw, when they were three-quarters of the way down. Grant was still keeping pace with her, now a few feet ahead, then behind. She zoomed around a high mogul and forged to the front in a burst of speed. Moments later she heard a victorious cry as he sailed past her through open air, then landed smoothly a good dozen feet beyond.

He jumped the mogul I avoided, she thought. She should have tried it. But then, to her horror, she saw him waver on his skis, lose his balance, and fall. He rolled over himself in a tangle of snow, skis, and poles, finally sliding to a halt at the far side of the hill beneath a tall tree.

"Grant!" Kelli screamed. Her chest tightened with fear as she sped down the slope to his side. His skis had disengaged and come to a stop in the snow a few feet above. He lay limply on his back, his eyes closed, his hat gone, snow in his hair. Awkwardly, still wearing her skis, she knelt down in the soft, unpacked snow and leaned over his prostrate form. Half-choked with fear, she reached out to touch his cheek.

He grabbed her, pulling her down on top of him, knocking the breath out of her in the impact against his chest.

"You...cheater!" she gasped. She tried to squirm out of his arms but failed. She lay across his chest, gulping great breaths of air, her legs twisted behind at a crazy angle, her face close to his. He grinned up at her, infuriatingly pleased with himself. Annoyance replaced fear and then both dissipated in a shaky laugh. *Thank God you're all right*, she thought. She said: "That was a rotten thing to do."

"What? Taking advantage of a perfectly good ski jump to gain some ground? Or nearly killing myself?"

"You know what I meant. Playing possum."

"Simple revenge. You sandbagged. I played possum."

"I thought you were hurt!" she said with a good-natured glare. "You owe me an apology. I was terrified."

"Were you?"

"Yes!"

"Then I *am* sorry." His voice was suddenly quiet. He brushed a stray lock of curling hair from her forehead. Her pulse quickened, and, lying on his chest, their faces nearly touching, she imagined she could feel his heart pounding through the layers of their clothing.

She wanted his kiss so much she trembled, but she could see from the hesitation in his eyes that he was holding himself back. Afraid to say aloud how she felt, she tried to tell him with her eyes. Then she lowered her mouth to press against his.

She heard his sharp intake of breath, and then his arms tightened around her and he met her kiss with unrestrained passion. A tight knot loosened within her and desire flowed through her. Her hands slipped around his neck, wet with snow. She knew they were meant to kiss each other like this, meant to be in each other's arms.

"Grant," she whispered, and was about to say, *I want you so much. I was wrong before.* But just then a spray of snow hit the back of her neck and she jerked up with a start.

The icy coldness slid down inside the collar of her jacket and sweater. She shuddered and cried out, quickly shaking out the snow, wanting to shout something obscene at the skier who'd sent the offending blast and who now swooshed past them. Instead, she caught Grant's eyes, and they both burst out laughing.

He sat up, took off her hat, and freed it of snow. He ran his fingers through her tangled hair, smoothing it, then replaced her hat on her head. Hesitantly she turned toward him, wondering if he'd read the message in her eyes. But the intensity of the previous moment had gone.

"Ah," he said, shaking snow out of his hair, "the joys of the great outdoors."

"No respect. Absolutely no respect."

He stood and flexed his legs. "Well, they still work."

She sidestepped up the hill, retrieved his skis and poles, and brought them to him.

"Thanks," he said. "I guess you're going to ask for a rematch."

"No way. I've had enough racing for one day. It's late, anyway, and I don't like the look of those clouds. Let's go home."

"You've talked me into it. Only one problem. How will we know who's supposed to cook dinner?"

"Easy. You've been disqualified on two counts. One: unauthorized use of ski jump. Two: failure to finish the race. You lose."

He was still putting on his skis. "But you didn't finish the race either."

With a grin, she shoved off and headed down the mountain. "I will now."

"I won a contest on the back of a cereal box."

"You're joking."

"I'm serious," Grant said. "That's what got me interested in advertising."

They sat over dinner in the living room at a folding table covered with a white cloth, china, silverware, and glowing candles that he'd brought from home. A fire blazed and crackled in the hearth beside them, casting waves of light and shadow across Grant's face. In the hushed room, Kelli felt the same tense excitement she'd felt all day on the slopes.

When they'd returned to the house, she'd offered Grant the use of the shower downstairs. After her own shower and a change of clothes, she'd found him in the kitchen, whistling as he chopped vegetables for salad, while the microwave defrosted a container of his own homemade spaghetti sauce. He was dressed in a cashmere sweater and jeans, his hair glistening-wet and clean. The urge to slip up behind him and wrap her arms around his waist had been so strong she'd had to turn away and steady herself against the counter.

Looking at him now, across the table by candlelight, she felt the same warm rush of desire. She wondered what he was thinking and feeling, and what might happen between them later that night. He said he'd checked into a motel that morning. She wanted him to spend the night here, with her. But after everything she'd said and done, how and when should she let him know that she'd changed her mind?

"The cereal's advertising mascot was a tiger," Grant was saying, "and he needed a name. I entered the contest and won."

Kelli willed her heartbeat to slow down as she twirled her last bite of spaghetti around her fork. "You named a tiger on a nationally advertised product? Pretty good. What did you call him?"

"Grrrrr-egory."

She laughed. "That's great! How old were you?"

"Nine."

The Harrison Duet

"Nine! A child prodigy. Your parents must have been proud. What did you win?"

"A free trip for two to Madison Avenue, New York, to tour the ad agency that handled the account. I tell you, I was impressed. Plush, plush, plush. They treated me like visiting royalty. I was suckered in on the spot."

"And you vowed at that moment to have your own ad agency someday."

"Something like that." Grant grinned.

He stood up and together they cleared the table. Standing side by side at the sink, they washed the dishes by hand.

"What about you?" he asked. "What got you interested in this crazy business?"

"I just like to draw and paint. I always have. My mom enrolled me in art lessons when I was in fifth grade, and before long it became my passion. When I realized that a person could actually earn a living as an artist, I was over the moon. It's a good thing it worked out, because my back-up profession—at least the one I imagined in childhood—was to be a chef."

"A chef?"

She nodded, smiling. "I thought cooking would be glamorous. As it turns out, I'm hopeless in the kitchen."

"No kidding? Someone as creative as you?" He dried his hands on a towel and leaned on the counter. His hand rested just inches from hers. She wanted to touch it.

"I could never make a spaghetti sauce like yours—it was delicious. My mind is always somewhere else. I forget ingredients, I leave it on the stove or in the oven too long, something gets burned...I guess I don't have the patience to cook. All that effort, and the food disappears in an instant. At least when I do a painting or a sketch, I have something lasting to show for my efforts."

"I enjoy cooking. I find it relaxing. After the pressures and decisions at the office all day, breaking my neck to solve conflicts and please clients, it's a treat to come home and whip up something to suit just my own taste."

"I'm glad you feel that way. At least one person in this relationship ought to be good at—" She broke off, heat rising to her face.

His eyes met hers, and she saw a tangle of emotions there—surprise, puzzlement, desire, doubt. He started to speak, then stopped himself.

Kelli groped for words. *Say something. Tell him how you feel. Tell him you were wrong before, that you want him.* The words didn't come.

His lips tightened and he moved to the kitchen window. "Damn," he said. "It's snowing again."

Disappointment surged through her. She took a shaky breath. "I thought it wasn't supposed to snow until tomorrow."

"So said the weatherman."

"He probably used that blackjack system of yours to make his prediction. When it works, it can be spectacular, but when it fails..."

He didn't smile. Why were they standing here talking about the weather? Her heart beat like a drum. In the quiet room she was aware of his presence with such force that her skin felt his touch even though he was half a dozen feet away.

"I guess I'd better get going."

She tried to hide her dismay. "Already?"

"If I wait too long I'll have to put chains on."

"Oh."

He went to the window again. "I was going to say—you might think about getting out of here yourself, so you don't get snowed in. But it still looks pretty light out there."

The Harrison Duet

"Like last night," she offered.

He nodded, hands in his pockets.

The tension was so thick in the air, it crackled.

She took a deep breath, forcing the words out. "You could...stay here if you like. I wouldn't mind. I know there aren't any beds, but I have a sleeping bag and lots of blankets."

A long silence fell. He lowered his gaze. She blushed furiously, desperately embarrassed, unable to look at him. Did it mean he was no longer interested?

After a moment he said quietly, "I don't think so. But thanks." She heard him move to the kitchen door. "And thanks for the skiing today. It was terrific."

"Yes. It was." She stared at the floor, her pulse beating wildly, her eyes burning.

"Well, good night."

"Good night."

She heard the front door close with a final, agonizing click. The tears she'd been holding back sprang into her eyes, then flooded her cheeks. Sobbing, she snapped off the kitchen light and stumbled up the stairs in the darkness, clutching the rail.

She stubbed her toe on the top step and cried out, flicked on the hall light, splashing a diffused glow across the floor of the master bedroom. In spite of the studio equipment filling one side, the room had never seemed so huge or so empty until that moment. In the corner where she slept, wiping her tears, Kelli dropped to her knees on the blankets that lay across her sleeping bag, taking a deep, choking breath.

A footstep sounded on the stairs. Her mind spun with confusion and she turned, rising shakily to her feet. Grant stood in the open doorway, his eyes finding hers across the softly lit room. She tried to find her voice, but couldn't. Hesi-

348

tation warred with desire within her, and even halfway across the room she saw the same turmoil reflected in his gaze.

"The snow is coming down harder than I thought," he said. "I don't think you should—"

"Grant." Tears welled once more in her eyes. Barely above a whisper, she said, "Please. Stay with me tonight. I want you to."

As if her words had released him, he was suddenly beside her, his arms catching her up, enfolding her in his embrace. And then his lips were covering her face with kisses, and finally, urgently, melding with her own lips.

With gratitude, pleasure, and relief, her hands wrapped around his waist, holding him close, the way she'd longed to hold him all day. She buried her face in the softness of his sweater, then pressed kisses across the whisker- roughened skin on his neck and cheeks. His mouth came to hers again, and then, gazes locked, they undressed each other, taking their time because they knew, now, that nothing would stop them.

The room should have felt cold but she was warm, flushed. They touched the skin they bared with wonder and delight, as if discovering a treasure that was theirs and theirs alone. His smile was radiant as he looked at her slender body, his eyes telling her he found her beautiful. He smoothed his hands across her skin, felt the softness of her breasts, the curve at her waist. She touched trembling fingers to his chest, through the dark curling hairs, where she felt his heart beating wildly against her palm.

Gently, her hand in his, he pulled her down beside him atop the blankets, cold at first touch and then warm as her body molded to the heat of his. He gathered her into his arms, her softness curving against the lean, hard muscles of his arms and stomach and legs. Her hands glided down the length of his back, over his firm buttocks and back up again, delighting in the smoothness of his skin. He covered her neck and shoulders with soft kisses, every touch setting her flesh tingling, and she felt his arousal, which added fuel to the flames that already raged within her.

"Kelli..." His hands moved slowly across her body, gently molding her breasts and their sensitive peaks. His lips followed where his hands had been, and he took into his mouth first one nipple and then the other, until they grew erect beneath his tongue.

She wanted to hurry, hurry, an urgency building within her at each touch of his hands and lips. She moaned when his fingers traveled the length of her body, then found the warm, pliant flesh that ached for his touch. Her body was on fire, everywhere, wanting him, needing him to fill the void he'd created.

He moved on top of her, and driven by the passion they'd both held back for so long, he thrust into her, joining her body with his own. She moved against him, pulling him closer still, his flesh hot against hers.

With each thrusting rhythm he took her higher, soaring until she shuddered on the very brink of ecstasy. It's never been like this, she thought, and then she let herself go, releasing her mind to the bright light of sensation; and it seemed they were one being, a perfect melding of souls, nothing left but feeling and the joy of discovery they saw in each other's eyes.

A patch of light spilled across the floor, bathing their bodies in its reflected glow. Kelli's arms were wrapped around the smoothness of Grant's back, wanting to prolong the peaceful feeling of sharing with him, the sensation of naked flesh against naked flesh as they lay clasped together.

"I wonder," Grant whispered in her ear, "what this'll do to your theory."

"What theory?"

"The one that says we'll do far better work if we just stay friends."

She laughed softly. "Well, I had trouble concentrating before. It can't be any worse now."

He raised himself up on one elbow, looking at her. "You had trouble concentrating?"

She nodded.

"I thought I was the only one. You'd be sitting there, sketching away, deep in thought, so beautiful, so close...and yet so far away. I couldn't keep my eyes off you. I wanted so badly to touch you, to take you in my arms, but I knew once I'd done that, there'd be no stopping."

"I felt the same way," she whispered.

"I can see us now. We won't be able to work five minutes without a break."

"But the work we get done in that five minutes will be brilliant. Inspired."

"No doubt." His fingertips trailed across her shoulder, slid down to cup her breast. All at once she shivered, aware she was covered with gooseflesh.

"Grant," she whispered. "I think my toes are numb."

"So is my backside." He grinned and kissed her. "What do you suggest we do about it?"

"We could open up the sleeping bag and crawl under the blankets."

"An excellent idea."

The Harrison Duet

A few minutes later, snuggled under the blankets and wrapped in each others arms, he murmured, "Good advance planning."

"What?"

"Bringing two pillows."

"I always sleep with two pillows."

"Why?"

"One for my head. One to hug."

"You hug your pillow?"

"Every night."

"What for?"

"I don't know. I guess I feel more...secure, if I've got something to hug."

He rolled back on top of her, eyes shining in the moonlight. "Tonight," he whispered, "you'll have all the security you need."

To Kelli, the night passed as if in a dream. In Grant's loving embrace, she felt truly, completely alive for the first time in her life. He brought her to a peak of brilliant awareness, a joyful surrendering, a pleasure unlike any she'd ever imagined. Afterwards they talked, getting to know each other more fully as they shared their personal histories and revealed intimate details of their lives.

Intermittently she slept, tender visions filling her dreams, from which she'd rise through heavy, swirling darkness to find Grant's hands and mouth gently loving her into wakefulness, waiting until she was wet with desire, and then, almost without moving, he was inside her, making them one.

At dawn, Kelli awoke in Grant's arms, their legs entwined, her cheek warm against his chest. She felt his heartbeat, heard the soft brush of the wind and the tap, tap of pine branches

352

Syrie James

against the house. Lifting her head, she squinted against the soft morning light. Beyond the window it was a blur of white.

Grant stirred and opened his eyes. "Morning, beautiful."

"Morning yourself. I think we have ourselves a blizzard."

8

"A blizzard?" He rose from their makeshift bed and went to the window, unheedful of his nakedness.

"Wow. It's a beauty of one. Damn, it's freezing out here." Quickly, he grabbed both their sweaters from where they lay on the floor and slipped back under the blankets, shivering. Pulling his sweater over his head, he encouraged her to do the same. "About a foot and a half of new snow out there and still falling hard," he said when they were snuggled once more in each other's arms.

"Does this mean," Kelli asked lazily and without regret, "we're going to be snowed in?"

"Not going to be. Already are. Unless you want to hike out, we're not going anywhere today."

"What a shame." Their eyes met and they shared a low, contented laugh.

"It's a good thing," Grant said, his lips moving against hers, "that I left my suitcase here when I showered and changed last night, or you'd be stuck here with no phone and a man with no clothes."

"That's right," Kelli murmured. "I forgot the phone was out. But believe me, I wouldn't have minded about the clothes."

"It's also a good thing," he went on, "that I brought extra food with me. Because I just realized I'm starving."

354

"You can't be starving. It's too early to be starving."

"I am. What do you say we get up, go downstairs, and whip up something?"

"You'd leave this nice, warm bed and brave sub-zero temperatures to forage for food?"

"Well—" Grant's hand moved beneath her sweater "—I could probably be persuaded to do otherwise."

With a sultry smile she rolled on top of him, moved her hands along his body, and brought her lips to his in a leisurely kiss.

"Still want to get up?" she whispered, gently rocking her feminine core against that part of him which instantly grew hard beneath her.

Bright desire glowed in eyes that had never seemed so blue. "I'm as up," he said breathlessly, "as I'll ever get."

When they woke later that morning, the storm was still raging—a heavy, powdery snowfall driven by freezing-cold winds.

"You are about to learn how to make perfect scrambled eggs." Dressed in his warmest clothes, Grant stood at the kitchen counter, whipping eggs and milk together in a bowl. "Here, you grate the cheese."

"Cheese? When I put cheese in scrambled eggs, it sticks to the pan."

"It doesn't if you do it right."

Kelli dutifully grated the cheese, watching as he coated the pan with melted butter, then poured in the egg mixture when the butter was bubbling hot. When a fine layer of egg was cooked at the bottom, he added a few spices and stirred. At the last minute he added the cheese.

The Harrison Duet

"Voila." He served the eggs onto plates heaped with fresh fruit and toast. "Eggs: fluffy. Cheese: melted. Pan: clean."

Kelli applauded, then bowed before him with admiration. "*Wunderbar, Herr Pembroke. Merveilleux, monsieur.* Sorry, I don't know how to say it in Italian. It is, without a doubt, the ideal Alpine breakfast. We'll call it *Oeufs a l'Alpine,* and suggest they include it on the menu at the Swiss Chalet."

Laughing, he grabbed her with one arm, pulling her to him. "You," he said, kissing her softly, "are my ideal Alpine breakfast. And I don't know what it is, but I seem to have developed an insatiable appetite."

They may be snowed in, they decided later, but there was no reason why they couldn't work. They spent the afternoon in the studio, finishing the last of the comps for the collateral materials and going over the basics of what they needed for the media campaign. With the bundle of wood Grant had brought in earlier they built a fire in the living-room hearth and relaxed that evening, wrapped in blankets, sipping hot chocolate.

"The simple life has its merits," Kelli admitted, as they ate delicious, foil-wrapped fish and potatoes they'd baked on charred embers at the side of the fire.

Afterward, Grant filled the oversize bathtub with hot water and they eased into its soothing depths.

"I've always had this fantasy," Kelli said, "of sharing a romantic, candlelit bubble bath with my lover while sipping champagne."

"Wait here just a minute." Grant left the bath, wrapped himself in a towel, and returned a few minutes later with several candles, a bottle of champagne, and two stemmed glasses. "No bubble bath," he apologized, propping the lit candles in makeshift foil holders on the tile ledge above them, "but you've got candlelight, champagne, and your lover. Will three out of four do?"

Kelli laughed with delight. "Thank you. It's perfect. Absolutely perfect."

He opened the bottle of champagne, poured two glasses, and handed her one. Turning off the overhead lights, he slid back into the tub. The candles' combined flames cast a soft glow on their faces which faded into darkness around them. They touched their glasses gently together, then sipped the bubbly, sparkling wine.

Eyes locked with hers, Grant said in a dramatic, lowered tone: "Come quickly, I am tasting stars."

Kelli smiled, puzzled. "What?"

"That's what Dom Perignon famously exclaimed to his companions after his first taste of champagne."

"Oh...I love that. It's just right—the ideal description of this delicious champagne."

"And it brings to mind yet another way," he said gruffly, setting both of their glasses aside, "to come quickly...and taste stars." Eyes gleaming, he pulled her naked, willing, slippery body close to his.

"What do you say we forget the ad campaign?" Grant said when the storm continued the next day. "Let's spend the rest of the week camped out here in front of the fire."

Kelli laughed. "You'd never forgive yourself if we did that."

"You're probably right." They'd moved their makeshift bed in front of the master bedroom's fireplace the night before, and had slept in front of its cozy warmth. He now sat on the floor behind her, his long legs stretched out on either side of her, his arms wrapped around her waist, as they both stared into the mesmerizing flames. "It's tempting, though. I never realized it could be so much fun to be snowed in."

The Harrison Duet

"It *has* been fun." Kelli leaned her head back against his shoulder and sighed. "But we'd better get going. The storm could stop any time, and we still have to meet our deadline. If we put our heads together—"

"Put our heads together? That sounds promising." He cupped her chin gently and tilted her mouth up to his. His kiss was slow and sweet, and she felt the stirrings of renewed desire, the desire that never seemed to diminish no matter how many times they made love. *I've never wanted anyone this way before*, she thought, wanting to let go of time and reason, to melt back against him. But then she remembered the reason they were there in the first place, and she broke the kiss and took a deep breath.

"Grant, if we keep this up, we'll never get any work done."

"That depends on what you mean by *work*."

"This is *your* campaign. The account you were so hot to trot for a week ago. Remember?"

"I remember." He sighed, adjusting her within his arms until she was resting comfortably against his chest. "Okay. Let's try word association again."

She nodded and closed her eyes, remembering that they needed a series of ads that emphasized gambling, and a series with an Alpine theme—at least five or six different headlines in all. "I'll give you a word. You say the first thing that comes to mind. Ready?"

"Ready."

"Casino," she said.

"Gamble."

"Gamble."

"Frolic."

She tilted her head back and looked at him. "Gamble, frolic?"

"Gambol." He spelled it out loud.

358

She swatted his thigh playfully and repeated the word. A thought occurred to her and she said facetiously: "I've got it. We aren't allowed to say *gamble*—so we show a couple cavorting in the snow, and the same couple having fun at the craps table. *Gambol at Cassera's Tahoe.*"

He groaned.

"I knew you'd like it. You have such good taste."

"And you taste so good." His arms tightened around her and she felt his lips against her neck.

"Let's get serious now."

"Serious. Right. Go."

"Jackpot," she said.

"Win."

"Money."

"Pay."

"Game."

"Play."

"Pay, play..." Kelli mused. "I know! How about: *It pays to play... at Cassera's.*"

"Good."

She brightened. "You really think so?"

"I do. Harry's Club might frown if we used it, though. It's been their slogan for the past ten years."

"Oh." Kelli laughed. "No wonder it sounded so familiar." She closed her eyes again, leaned back against him. "Okay, let's start over. Blackjack."

"Deal."

"Cards."

"Hand."

"Poker."

"Bet."

"Chips."

"Eat."

She swatted his thigh again. "Stay on subject. Excitement."

"Sex."

"You're not concentrating!"

"I *am* concentrating." His hands slid up to cover her breasts. "Believe me, I'm concentrating."

The wonderful things his lips were doing to the side of her neck sent tingling sensations racing across the surface of her skin. "R—roulette."

"Wheel."

"Spin."

"Win." He laughed softly, his breath warming her cheek. "I've got it. We show a naked couple in one of the hotel rooms, a roulette wheel, and a roll of money. *Cassera's Tahoe. Sin. Spin. Win.*"

She couldn't help but join in his laughter. "Ted will love it. Guaranteed."

"He has good taste, too." Grant turned her until she was facing him, his lips moving tenderly across her face.

"Grant," she whispered. "Stop. I can't think—"

"Neither can I," he murmured. "So let's stop trying." He kissed her mouth—a long, deep kiss—and this time she couldn't fight the desire that rose to meet his. She wrapped her arms around his neck, forgetting everything but Grant and the moment and the joy and wonder of being in his arms.

On the third day after the storm began, with the deadline for the presentation looming nearer, they decided they'd better get down to some serious work. They spent long hours tossing ideas back and forth, trying to come up with the catchy angles they needed for the campaign.

"This is it," Grant said, pacing slowly across the studio floor. "We're going to wrap this thing right now. Clear your mind. Think: *Alpine.* Tell me the first thing you see."

"Julie Andrews."

"Julie Andrews?"

"In her nun's habit, standing in a meadow filled with wild-flowers, singing her heart out to the sky."

"That's great." Grant raised his eyes and hands to the ceiling as if asking for divine assistance. "We build an advertising campaign for a gambling establishment around a singing nun."

"You *said* to say the first thing that came to mind."

"I think we'd better try another approach."

They tried another approach, and then another, for several more hours. Nothing sparked an idea worth pursuing.

"This is ridiculous." Grant tossed his pencil onto the table and sighed in frustration. "We're not getting anywhere."

Kelli sat down at her drafting table and leaned her chin on her hand dejectedly. "We could use a few of those brilliant copywriters of yours about now."

"I think you're right." He went to the window and looked out. Snow whirled in a white frenzy. The wind howled. Pine branches brushed against the roof. "But even if the weather report's right and the storm ends tomorrow, it'll be another day or two at least before they clear the roads. No one can get in, and we can't get out." He sighed again. "If I could just get a few of my people on the line, I'd drag them off their other projects for a few hours, have them start hashing out some ideas for us. But without a phone—"

Kelli felt guilty suddenly, knowing it was because of her that he was stuck here, cut off from the world, unable to keep tabs on the work at his office, unable even to make any decent progress on their own work. "I'm sorry this is going so slowly."

"It's not your fault."

"When I work by myself, I usually come up with a list of ideas in just a few hours."

"So do I."

"Then why are we coming up empty-handed? It was such a breeze, doing the logo and the other comps, but when it comes to the ads... You thought we'd make such a great team, and it hasn't worked out that way at all."

"We do make a great team," he said softly.

Her blood stirred as she met his gaze, recognizing that I-want-you look in his eyes. "I didn't mean *that* kind of team," she said, although in truth she'd been thinking about him precisely that way since the night they first met.

Grant came up behind her, wrapping his arms around her waist. "Kelli, I think you were right about us—about what might happen if we got too involved. We got all that work done in the first few days because we were just business associates. We were attracted to each other, but we'd hardly touched. We hadn't made love. But now—if we had a chaperone to keep us apart, we'd probably have come up with seventeen brilliant ideas by now."

"Are you sorry, then, that we...got involved?" she whispered.

He scooped one arm beneath her legs and lifted her off the stool. "No, ma'am," he said emphatically. And then his mouth found hers.

"It's like a fairyland!" Kelli cried the next morning, looking outside the window. She could hardly wait to go outside.

The landscape was covered with a soft, deep blanket of sparkling white. The sun shone in a blue sky and snow frosted the pine branches like whipped cream.

Her exhilaration in the beauty of the landscape faded when she saw the worried expression on Grant's face. He was staring at the immense, curving mound of fresh snow beside the garage that had once been her car, and the long, winding driveway leading up to the road, now buried beneath four feet of new snow.

His van was parked at the far end of the drive, but even if they hiked to it and dug it out, it couldn't go anywhere until the road crew cleared the roads.

"Only three days left after today," Grant mused, frustrated, "and we've drawn a big fat zero on this campaign. We've got to try—somehow—to get out of here."

Only three more days. Kelli nodded, realizing with a sudden pang of regret that their special time alone together was about to end. It had been a wonderful few days, the best of her life. But when the presentation was finished—*if* they ever finished it—would that be it for them? They had never discussed the future. Grant had never hinted that he wanted or expected anything more than this brief affair, and she'd made it clear that she wanted to live life solo, on her own terms, for the foreseeable future.

That *was* what she wanted... right? Uncertain, she heaved a deep sigh and turned from the window.

They agreed to trek up to the other two houses within walking distance to see if anyone had a phone that worked. After dressing warmly, they plowed through the deep snow in their after-ski boots—an exhausting effort. When they reached the second house they were red-faced and out of breath. They found it deserted and locked up just as tight as the first.

The Harrison Duet

"So much for that." Grant shrugged in resignation. "At least the road crew works quickly in this area. They ought to be up here by tomorrow."

When the road was clear, he said, he'd get his van out, stop by a garage, and have them send a plow to clear the driveway down to the house. Meanwhile, there was nothing else they could do. They might as well sit tight and wait.

Grant's idea of sitting tight and waiting, however, had nothing to do with sitting. "As long as we're out here," he said when they reached her Rover, "let's do something useful. Let's clear the snow off this thing."

"Shouldn't we go back in and get to work?" Kelli asked in surprise. She was dying to play in the snow, but they'd put in a few more hours in the studio the evening before, and to their disappointment, had gotten nowhere. "We're so short on time."

"I know. But if our creativity's dried up, it's because we've been cooped up inside too long. A few hours off will do us both good."

With the shovel he'd brought, they dug out her car. Next, Grant suggested they install the new part he'd brought for her engine.

"Are you sure you know how?" he asked when she insisted on doing the simple job herself.

She cast him a sidelong glance. "Do I know how? Do bees have knees? Just watch me."

He stood at her side like a surgeon's assistant, watching her with a sharp eye as he handed her tools. "I'm impressed," he said when she was done. "You did that like a pro."

"It was no big deal. Someday, if you want, I'd be happy to teach you a thing or two about cars."

364

He opened his mouth to say something, then apparently changed his mind. "Wouldn't that be nice," he said, smothering a grin.

"You Mercedes owners are all alike. Stuck up." She grabbed a handful of snow and threw it at him, narrowly missing him when he ducked down behind the car. A second later a snowball came flying over the hood, splattering against her arm.

"Hey!" Kelli ducked down. "This means war!"

They exchanged snowballs, laughing and shouting, until their hats lay yards away and both their jackets and hair were laced with the powdery snow.

"Uncle!" Grant called, beckoning her to follow him up to the hillside above the house. "I have this urge to do something totally frivolous. Let's build a snowman."

Kelli grinned. "Are you sure you know how?"

"Do I know how?" Grant said, mimicking her tone. "Do bees have knees?"

Grant, it seemed, was a champion snowman builder. They created a big, round fellow on the hillside in front of the house, using tiny pinecones for eyes and nose and a small, curved stick for his smile. Grant added his ski hat and gloves, and when Kelli pointed out that it was chauvinistic to just build men out of snow, he insisted on building a snow woman, complete with hourglass figure and a spray of long green pine needles for hair.

Grant retrieved Kelli's ski hat and adjusted it just so on the snow woman's head. "This couple is missing something."

Kelli pursed her lips, studying their handiwork as she might study a painting. "You're right." She turned to Grant and their gazes touched. "They look—" she began, and in unison they finished "—lonely."

The Harrison Duet

Without another word, Grant knelt down and began forming a smaller heap of snow at the snow woman's side. Kelli joined in, laughing. Her fingers were starting to feel numb inside her gloves when, some time later, two snow children with matching pine-needle hair smiled back at them from the hillside. At the snow people's feet reclined a snow dog with a lopsided muzzle and long floppy ears.

"Now *that's* what I call one happy family," Grant said.

By now the snow had begun to melt on the pines, and icicles danced from the branches like sparkling lights on a Christmas tree. Kelli breathed deeply of the cold, fresh air, letting go a sigh of the purest pleasure and contentment she'd ever known. She felt lucky to be alive, lucky to be here, lucky to be sharing this beautiful day with Grant. She didn't want it ever to end.

"Gotcha!" The shout came from behind. Suddenly she was down in the soft snow, rolled onto her back with Grant on top of her. Her shriek was cut off abruptly by his possessive kiss. "Kelli," he said huskily, "you and I..." He hesitated, and his lips tightened in a regretful frown. "You and I ought to get back to work."

"I know." She wondered what he'd been about to say. She ought to feel cold, lying on her back in Grant's arms, surrounded by powdery snow, but she didn't. Even through the layers of their heavy clothing, the heat of his body seemed to warm hers.

"We'll go in and make a fire," he said. "We'll talk this thing through. Sooner or later the ideas have to start flowing again."

"Right."

"In fact I have an idea. It's not worked out yet, but I keep seeing it in the back of my mind. There's—" He paused, brushed his lips against her temple. "Did I ever tell you that you have beautiful eyes?"

"Yes," she whispered, smiling now.

"And a beautiful nose?"

"Yes."

"And a beautiful mouth?" Their eyes met for a long, silent moment, and she knew hers shone with the same open affection she saw in his. He kissed her softly. "Now what was it that I was saying?"

"Something about an idea you had."

"No, before that."

"You were telling me how much work we're going to get done when we get back inside."

"Ah, yes. Why is it, when we're together, I always lose my train of thought?"

"Because," Kelli said with an impish grin, "you've developed a one-track mind."

"You're right. And the train's been on that same track since the night we met."

Kelli opened her eyes. In the dim light, she noticed the empty space and untouched pillow beside her, and heaved a deep sigh. Grant still hadn't come to bed.

She'd stayed up with him until well after midnight, reading and rereading their research books and the casino's existing brochures, going over their stacks of rejected ideas and sketches, and looking once more through Kelli's comps for the collateral materials. They'd each come up with a few passable ideas for ads and had sketched them out. Nothing too bad, but nothing to get excited about, either. Finally, exhausted, she'd told him she had to go to bed.

The Harrison Duet

"You go ahead," he'd said. "I'm going to keep at it for a while."

Kelli sat up now and looked across the studio. Grant sat at the table next to a single lamp, his head bent, his forehead furrowed in concentration. He held a pen poised over a notepad scribbled with writing. His dark hair was tousled, his cheeks were darkened by a day's growth of beard, and even from across the room she could see his eyes were bloodshot with weariness. She felt the same dynamic pull she always felt when she looked at him, yet at the same time felt a dart of anguish at the frustration she saw in his face.

"I'm sorry if I woke you," he said, not looking up.

"You didn't. Why are you still up? You must be exhausted."

"I'm fine."

"The work will still be there in the morning."

"It *is* morning," he said tightly.

She got up, wrapping herself in a blanket as she went to him. "I meant later in the morning. It's three-thirty, Grant. You have to get some sleep."

"I couldn't sleep. Not now."

"Could we ask Ted for an extension? Because we were snowed in?"

"No way. He's heard rumors, remember—that my agency's slow, that we don't meet our deadlines? How will it look if we don't bring this in on time?"

"Not good." Sighing, she began to massage the muscles that pulled his neck and shoulders taut.

To her dismay, he tensed beneath her hands and said, "Don't."

She jerked back as if she'd just touched a hot brand. "I'm sorry. I just wanted to—"

368

"Don't apologize," he said abruptly. "Just go back to bed. It's my problem. There's no reason why we should both lose sleep over this."

"Since when did it become *your* problem?" She was both hurt and irritated. "I thought we were in this together."

"Together we've come up with a big fat zero."

She'd said the same thing the day before, but now, he said the words with such disgust that they stung. "Okay, fine. I'll work here, and you work there. We'll see how we do on our own."

He didn't reply. Rubbing sleep from her eyes, she grabbed a pencil and paper, turned on the lamp over her drafting table, and climbed up onto her stool. For the next hour, she tried to follow her usual procedure for coming up with a slogan: list key words and features of the product or place. Hit on the key benefit to the target audience. Try for a pun, an alliteration, or a clever turn of phrase. But the silent tension in the room was deafening, and she couldn't think.

Outside, she could hear the rustle of the wind in the trees and the lapping of water against the icy shore. The sounds reminded her of the day they'd gone out in the boat on the lake. *The lake.* She closed her eyes, remembering the vast, peaceful blueness that stretched out toward the distant mountains, remembering the beauty of the trees and the puffy clouds in a brilliant, sapphire sky.

That's it, she thought. *It was in front of our noses all the time.*

"Grant." Her voice seemed to echo in the enforced stillness of the room. He looked up at her. "I think we've been forgetting something. In all the hours we've been going over this, we've talked about gambling and skiing and mountains

The Harrison Duet

and God knows what else, but we haven't once talked about Tahoe's biggest draw."

"You mean the lake." When she nodded he said, "I was just thinking about that."

Funny, that they should both realize it at the same time. "Most of the ads run in this area, and the lake is our most identifiable landmark."

"*And* the primary reason a lot of people come here—not just to gamble." Grant chewed on the end of his pencil. "If we could use the lake as a primary focus, come up with a theme that ties it in with Cassera's—"

"Isn't Cassera's the biggest high rise in Stateline?" she asked.

"Yes."

"Which makes it another identifiable landmark?"

"Yes. To the people who know Tahoe."

"Okay, so why don't we take a sensational photograph that highlights both?"

He leaned forward in his chair, making a frame with his hands. "Pine trees in the foreground. In the center, distant, we see Cassera's poking out above the trees."

"Behind it, the lake stretching out in all its glory, and beyond, snow-covered mountains and lots of sky."

He stood up, rubbed his chin thoughtfully as he paced the room. "I can see it. It's just the look I wanted. We put in Cassera's new logo where you can't miss it, and a big bold headline—" He stopped, palms up, searching. "We need a slogan that contrasts with the beauty of the scene. Back to the gambling idea. Give me some gambling slang and see if one fits."

"Go for broke."

"Double or nothing."

Ideas flew back and forth.

370

Syrie James

Grant kept shaking his head. "It's got to fit with the lake, or mountains, or sky. Let me think." He strode the length of the room and back, muttering to himself. Pacing back and forth. Like a caged tiger, she thought.

"What if——" He went back to his table and wrote something, still standing, then crossed it out. Kelli scribbled out a few ideas of her own. Nothing was quite right.

"Damn!" Grant crumpled up the sheet he'd been writing on and threw it into the trash. "Where the hell are those snowplows? How much longer are we going to be stuck here? This is such a waste of time."

Tired and irritable, Kelli leaned both elbows on her drafting table and massaged her temple. "I hate wasting time too, Grant. I haven't had any workmen here in almost a week. The house is way behind schedule. It'll never be finished on time."

"The house isn't the only thing that won't be finished on time," he snapped. "Two days to go and we haven't even come up with one decent idea."

She let out a long breath. "I'm sorry things haven't worked out the way you'd planned. But if you'll recall, this setup wasn't my idea. You proposed it."

"Don't you think I know that?" He whirled on her. "I took a gamble, coming up here. Put all my eggs in one basket. But I figured if things didn't go well, I could call an emergency creative session with my staff and pull the thing off. What I didn't count on was the storm, being snowed in here while the clock kept ticking. I didn't count on wasting five days in a creative washout. And I didn't count on——" His eyes darted to meet hers, and then he flung himself away again. "I should have known better than to come back here after I left. I should have called things off long before the storm, put my people on double overtime. We would have finished this whole thing a week ago."

371

The Harrison Duet

Called things off before the storm? Kelli thought in dismay. Canceled out all those wondrous, loving days they'd shared? Didn't she mean a thing to him?

Obviously not. The campaign was the only thing that mattered. Hurt and despair rose in her chest and she burst out, "Fine! Cancel them out if you want. Pretend they never happened. I'm sorry if I didn't perform to your expectations, but I'm sure if you just hike up to the highway and catch a ride to San Francisco, that hotshot staff of yours will come up with seventeen smashing slogans in no time. When it comes to talent, I can see *they've* got the corner on the market. The sky's the limit. So why don't you just go get a flashlight and—"

"What? Hold on. What did you say?"

"I said go get a flashlight." When had she started to cry? Kelli moved to the door, wiping tears from her cheeks. "There's one in the kitchen. You're in a hurry, aren't you? No time to lose. The clock keeps ticking. So get out of here, before—"

"Wait, would you shut up a minute?" He crossed the room and grabbed her by the shoulders. "You just said it, Kelli. The perfect slogan. Exactly what we've been looking for!"

372

9

It took her a moment, her mind working backward over what she'd just said, and then she understood.

The Sky's the Limit.

The image formed in her mind, the bold headline set in a huge field of sky above Cassera's, above the lake.

It was catchy. It was memorable. It had visual impact. It would work. "I like it."

"So do I."

They both started talking at once, jotting down the gist of the balance of the copy, outlining a few other ads that would have a different look but use the same slogan. She forgot their prior argument, felt an adrenaline surge, and saw the rising excitement in his eyes as new ideas came to their minds simultaneously. Gesticulating with enthusiasm, they interrupted each other, sentence fragments darting back and forth, thoughts started by one and finished by the other.

They came up with a whole series of ads to go with the first one, centered on a skiing theme—snow skiing for winter, waterskiing for summer.

A shot of Cassera's with the snow-covered slopes of Heavenly Valley behind it: *Cassera's Tahoe: Skiing Is Believing.*

The Harrison Duet

A collage of photos of the mountains and lake with a snow skier and a water-skier: *See. Ski.*

To highlight Cassera's restaurants—a place to relax after a day on the slopes—a young couple in love, sitting at a table in the cafe, light sparkling on stemmed glasses of champagne, forks crossed as they share steaming bites of cheese fondue: *Apres-ski.*

Their success seemed to open a dam of pent-up creativity, and all at once a flood of new, even more exciting ideas came spilling out—so fast they could hardly keep up with them. The second theme they'd been struggling with all week fell into place. The campaign focused on gambling. Each ad highlighted a different game or group of games in the casino, and the headlines they came up with didn't just click, they sang.

A close-up of a winning blackjack hand: *Feel Twenty-one Again.*

A view of the casino's dance floor, spliced in with a hand shooting craps: *Rock 'N' Roll.*

A slot machine hitting a jackpot, pouring out so much money it had burst into flame: *Hot Slots.*

A roulette wheel combined with a baccarat dealer in action: *Wheel and Deal.*

At the end of a few heated hours and two pots of coffee, they had a stack of rough thumbnail sketches. Kelli felt punch-drunk. She sank into the chair by the window and closed her eyes. "What time is it? What day is it? Do we have enough ideas yet? Can we quit now?"

"Yes, we can quit." Grant's voice was infused with exhaustion, yet it held a jubilant note that made her heart feel as light as her head. She heard him collapse into the other chair. "And in answer to the rest of your questions, it's 6:30 A.M., it's Wednesday, and we have enough ideas now to last three seasons. Maybe a couple of years."

"Good. Because my mind just filed a complaint. It shut down for the winter. Went into hibernation. Kaput. History."

He chuckled softly. "I knew we'd make a good team from the moment I met you. I *knew* it."

She was about to agree, when their argument slipped back into her mind. *I didn't count on wasting five days in a creative washout. I should have called things off long before the storm.* The hurt and anger she'd felt came back in a rush and she took a long, deep breath, waiting for it to subside. "I guess we do make a good team, Grant," she said quietly. "But only when we're both hot, steaming mad."

There was a moment of silence, and then she heard him get up from his chair and cross to her side. She felt his hand on her arm and she opened her eyes. "I'm sorry about what happened before." He was kneeling beside her, and she could see how tired he was, yet hope and regret mingled in his direct gaze. "I'm sorry for the things I said. I didn't mean any of it. I'm exhausted, and I haven't slept. I was so frustrated " He lifted her hand to his lips and kissed it. "You're a very talented woman, Kelli. I should have been thanking you for everything you've done on this project, not ranting and raving about what wasn't finished. But I want you to know...what I feel for you is a lot more than gratitude."

The warmth in his eyes, the touch of his lips and hand, worked their way into her heart. "Is it?" she asked, all at once breathless with hope. Would he tell her he loved her? Could she reveal, now, how she felt about him?

"Yes. Coming up here, leaving the company for days at a time so I could work with you—it's so out of character for me I could hardly believe I was doing it. At first I told myself it was just business. You have extraordinary talent, and I wanted you on this job. That was true, but it wasn't the only reason I came up here. It took me a while to admit it to myself, but—"

He stood, pulling her into his embrace. "Once I'd met you, I couldn't get you out of my mind. You'd refused the job I offered. You were only going to be here for a few weeks. I had to do something, and fast. I know I was unforgivably pushy. I backed you into a corner to get you to work with me. But I had to do it. I couldn't take the chance you'd say no."

"I'm glad you did it," she admitted. "I wouldn't trade these past weeks for anything."

"Neither would I." He cradled her head against his shoulder and held her for a long, silent moment. "You're a very special lady, Kelli, and you mean a lot to me."

You mean a lot to me. She squeezed her eyes shut, her heart heavy, knowing now that she could never tell him she loved him. *Maybe it's better this way,* she decided, wishing she didn't suddenly feel like crying. *When we're finished here, when we say goodbye, there won't be any binding ties. No promises to break. He can go his way, and I can go mine.*

"I wish," he said, his head drooping with fatigue, "I could take you downstairs and make love to you right now, but I'm so tired, the minute you put me in a horizontal position I'll fall asleep."

She took a deep breath, steeling herself. "Why don't you go catch a few hours, then? I'll start working on these comps."

"I don't have time for sleep. We may have concepts for all the ads, but I still have to write rough copy for a couple of them, and you're going to need help on these comps if we're going to finish by Friday morning."

"Help? I don't need help. We've got two days, Grant. If I start now, I can have them finished in time."

He looked at her in surprise, then chuckled softly, shaking his head. "That's right. I forgot for a minute that I'm working with Seattle's Quick Draw Champion, two years running."

"Three." She batted him on the arm. "And don't make fun of me. Now go lie down and go to sleep before you collapse."

"Aren't you tired, too? You said your brain was on the fritz. You only got a few hours' sleep."

"I'm fine. To tell you the truth, I'm itching to get started."

"Okay." He moved across the room toward their sleeping area, adding: "But if you hear anything that sounds like a snowplow, please wake me up. I've been out of touch with my office far too long. I need to get to a telephone today, even if we have to hike out of here."

Kelli sat down to work with renewed energy, breezed through a pencil comp for one of the ads, and started on another. The early-morning sun filled the room with golden light when, a few hours later, she heard the shower running and Grant's cheerful whistling. She'd been so engrossed in her work, she hadn't even noticed him get up. After a while he appeared from the bathroom, freshly shaven, dressed in jeans and a sweater.

"How's it going?" he asked.

She gestured for him to take a look at the *Apres-ski* ad she was sketching. He came up behind her, rested both hands on the edge of the drafting table and leaned his cheek against hers. "I like," he said.

He smelled wonderful, of shampoo and soap and the cologne that she loved. "I'm glad," she said as he began kissing her neck. "I wasn't sure if you'd want such a close-up of the two people, but I thought it was a little sexier, with—"

The Harrison Duet

"I wasn't," he whispered, "talking about the ad."

"Oh."

"What you've drawn is very, very good." His hands left the table to capture her breasts. "But what I really like is *you*. The way you feel. I missed you. It's no fun sleeping alone, with you halfway across the room. I think—" He stopped, listening.

A sound caught at the edge of her awareness. A distant roaring, like the whirr of the electric saws. No, no like the sound of heavy machinery. The sound of...

Their eyes met at the same moment. "Snowplows!"

By the time they reached the road, the plow had passed by, heaping a ton of snow on top of Grant's van at the roadside.

"Come on," Grant said much, much later, when they'd finally cleared the van and cleaned the windshield. "We have to get to a phone."

They climbed into the van and headed south to Stateline, where they stopped at the first gas station they came to. "You might want to give your brother a call," Grant suggested, parking in front of the phone booth. "And get ahold of the phone company to fix your line. I'll see if I can get this guy to clear your driveway."

Kelli called the phone company first, and they assured her if they couldn't fix the problem from their office they'd send someone out on Friday. So many phones out of order, they said, they couldn't possibly get there sooner. Next, she placed the call to her brother's office. She was put through immediately.

"Kelli!" Kyle cried with relief. "Where are you? Are you all right?"

"I'm fine. I thought you might be worried, so—"

"I've been frantic. They said the airport and roads were closed, and I couldn't get through to you. I hoped you'd got-

378

ten out before the storm, but I've been calling every hotel and motel in Stateline and you weren't registered at any of them. I called Grant's office Monday, and they told me he was up at Tahoe. Is he with you?"

"Yes. We didn't realize it was going to be such a blizzard until it was too late. We've been snowed in at the house all this time."

"All this time?"

"They just cleared the road a few minutes ago."

"My God, I'm sorry. If I'd thought..."

"Don't be sorry. We ended up...making good use of the time," she said, a teasing note in her voice.

There was a pause, and then he laughed. "Well, what do you know. My little sister Kelli. I never would have guessed."

She noticed Grant standing over her shoulder, waiting anxiously to use the phone. "I have to go, Kyle. Grant needs to call his office. Everything's been going fine on the house. Now that the storm's over I can make up for lost time. I'll call you again in a few days and give you a more detailed update." They said goodbye and she hung up. "Next."

"Thanks." Grant placed a credit-card call, and while he waited for it to go through he said, "The guy's going to follow us back and clear your driveway. He gave me some line about being too busy but I offered to double his rate and he—" Grant turned back to the phone. "Hi, Charlene. It's Grant."

Kelli lifted her face to the warm sunshine—such a treat after so many days of freezing cold. Traffic whizzed by on the highway and the gas station was crowded, but the pines were laden with snow and she heard Christmas music from someone's car radio drifting on the breeze. She'd almost forgotten that Christmas was coming, less than two weeks away.

The Harrison Duet

She'd have the comps done by tomorrow. The presentation was due the next day. If she scheduled workmen like crazy she might be able to have the floors and carpet laid and furniture delivered before Kyle and his family got here. Everything was going to be all right.

"Carl! How goes it?" she heard Grant say. And then: "Heard what?"

His sudden change of tone made Kelli turn. His shoulders were tense, his forehead lined with anxiety. "Which account?" he asked curtly. There was a pause, and then he cursed under his breath. "That should have been finished three days ago. Where's Andy?" Grant's mouth opened in surprise. "What do you mean, he left? Where did he go?" Practically spitting out the word, he said, "Dawson!"

Kelli froze in alarm. She remembered Grant mentioning Andy, his creative director. While he was gone, Grant had given Andy complete control of creative, under Carl, the executive vice-president. Andy was a talented guy, Grant had said. The best. He'd been with him for five years. And now he'd quit? To work for Bob Dawson?

"So. Bob's been up to his old tricks again. Terrific. Any more good news or is that it?" Grant listened for a long moment. At first his face registered surprise, then frustration, then barely repressed anger. "After all I went through to land that account...this is ridiculous. Another few days wouldn't kill them, if Dawson wasn't shooting off his mouth. Look, tell them to hold tight. See if you can stall them. We'll get the thing to them tomorrow...I don't know how, Carl. I'll figure something out. How many are there?...Nothing's impossible. To hell with Andy. Tell Jim to get on the phone, find another illustrator... Okay, okay. Set up a meeting, then, for this afternoon. I'll placate them somehow, get us some extra time." He checked his watch. It was just past nine. "It'll take me three hours to get there, maybe more, and I'll need time to change, go over a few things. Make it as late as possible. Four-thirty." Hanging up, he cursed again, more loudly this time. Signaling for the snowplow driver to follow, he headed straight for the van, frowning furiously.

Kelli hurried after him and got in. He gunned the engine and she sat back, her heart thumping in alarm, waiting for him to explain. Finally, when they were halfway back to the house, he heaved a deep sigh and looked at her, his hands gripping the wheel.

"One of our brand-new accounts is threatening to pull out if we don't deliver a job *today*. The Harrington Company. Real-estate developers. We're doing a brochure for them, really slick. Everything was going fine. Now it seems Bob Dawson's been spreading his rumors about us again, saying we're slow as molasses and don't meet our deadlines. Only this time he got smart and made sure it came true." Grant let out a short, sarcastic laugh.

"Andy was in charge of the Harrington job," he continued. "He obviously knew well in advance that he was leaving to work for Dawson, because he let it slide. My people put in an all- nighter to finish the paste-up, but Andy farmed out the illustrations and what came back this morning is pure garbage. My senior art director's out with the flu, Andy's gone— they're my only two illustrators. The client wants the whole job or nothing, and they want it by the end of the day or they're pulling out."

"Oh, Grant...I'm so sorry."

"It's not your fault," he snapped. "It's mine. It was my decision to come up here. You, as you so clearly pointed out this morning, tried to talk me out of it." His words stung,

The Harrison Duet

and she fell silent. After a moment his features softened and he reached across, gave her leg a gentle squeeze. "I'm sorry. I shouldn't be lashing out at you. It's Andy I'm mad at, and Dawson, and the entire Harrington Company. I was looking forward to finishing the Cassera's job with you, now that we're finally on course again, and now I have to go back to the city."

"Can I help somehow? Can I come with you? I could do the illustrations you need, and—"

"No. You stay right here. Finish those comps. Let's at least get one job delivered on time. I'll have one of my writers do the copy and I'll be back here bright and early for the meeting Friday morning."

"But...what if you don't like the way I do them? If you don't come back until Friday there won't be time to make any changes before the meeting."

He gave her a reassuring smile. "I'll like them. I know your work. I trust you. Besides, you can't leave, remember? Your house is behind schedule. Once this guy clears the driveway you can get your carpet layers and hardwood floor installers and God knows who else to finish the place, and make your brother one happy man."

His tone was lightly sarcastic, but she knew he didn't mean to be cutting. He had good reason to be in a foul mood, and in fact he was right. She *did* have to finish the job for Cassera's, and her place was here, finishing the house as she'd promised. But the thought of Grant leaving under these circumstances made her feel miserable. No need to make an issue out of it, she decided. He felt bad enough already.

She swallowed hard. "I'm going to miss you."

382

"I'll miss you too, babe." He reached out to gently caress her shoulder as he drove. "The next few days aren't going to be any picnic."

Kelli tucked her pencil behind her ear and leaned forward on the drafting table, resting her head on her hands.

Barely an hour since Grant left. Sixty-five minutes. The snowplow had just finished clearing the driveway, and the house was so silent she thought she'd go out of her mind. When Grant had stood at the roadside and kissed her goodbye, it was all she could do to keep from crying. She'd wanted so badly to go with him, to help, but he'd insisted she could help him best by staying put and finishing the job for Cassera's.

Not knowing what else to do, she'd gone straight to her drafting table to finish the *Apres-ski* comp. But she couldn't get Grant and his problems out of her mind. Despite his reassurances, she felt the mess was her fault, at least partly. She felt certain, if he'd been in San Francisco the past week where he belonged, his creative director wouldn't have flown the coop. Grant would have seen it coming and no doubt persuaded him to stay. It was too late to get Andy back, but she couldn't bear the thought of Grant losing an account because of her as well.

She *had* to do something. She sat up, thinking. Grant needed an illustrator. He was meeting the client today at four-thirty. She had Grant's card, knew the address of his agency, and she had a map of the city. If she left now, she could be there by two, two-thirty at the latest. If there weren't too many illustrations, if they weren't too complicated, she might be

The Harrison Duet

able to finish them that afternoon and he could deliver them. Grant had told her to stay put, but he couldn't refuse her help once she was there. He'd meet his deadline, and the client would be satisfied.

But what about the house? The driveway was clear. After a six-day hiatus she could finally make some calls, arrange to have workmen here tomorrow. No, she decided. The house could wait; Grant's client couldn't.

She didn't hesitate. In fifteen minutes she'd showered and dressed in the only businesslike outfit she had—the gray wool skirt and silk blouse she'd worn to the meeting with Ted at Cassera's. Throwing a few things into a suitcase, she gathered up the thumbnail sketches for the rest of the comps. She'd work her fingers off tomorrow, finish them at Grant's agency. She put everything in her car and left.

Her watch read a quarter to two when the freeway signs began to read Berkeley, and she glimpsed the distant Bay Bridge. She took in an excited breath, forgetting her mission for the moment. She'd been here only a couple of weeks before for the interview with Bob Dawson, but then she'd been in a hurry to get to Tahoe and it had taken her so long to find her way through the city's confusing, congested streets, she'd had to leave without even a glimpse of the famous wharf. Now, knowing she'd be able to stay for at least a day or two, she let herself be caught up in the spell of the bay and the city before her.

The bridge seemed to fly across the water, linking the East Bay cities with the hills of San Francisco on the other side. A mass of skyscrapers clustered next to the shore, and on either side, brightly colored rectangular houses clung to the slopes like stair steps. The bay sparkled, dotted with boats and hovering sea gulls, even bigger than Lake Tahoe and with a different kind of beauty and excitement, as if it had a sense of its own importance, felt the pulse of a city alive and in love with itself.

The scene struck a chord in her memory. Suddenly she was eleven years old again, on holiday, holding her father's hand, watching the fishing boats at the wharf, laughing with her brother and sisters as they tore into a loaf of sourdough bread, smelling the fish and the salt in the air. It was seventeen years ago, yet she remembered as if it were yesterday. She felt an insane urge to forget the work, forget the problems Grant was facing, and spend the rest of the day sight-seeing. The idea made her laugh out loud. If everything went according to plan, she'd get Grant out of this jam this afternoon, finish the Cassera's job tomorrow, and have enough time left over for a night on the town.

She was crossing the Bay Bridge when another thought struck her. What was Grant's staff going to think of her, barging in like this? Grant must have told them who he was working with at Tahoe. You didn't stay snowed in with a woman for nearly a week without raising a few eyebrows.

Wouldn't it be obvious to everyone exactly what the two of them had been up to? No way would that help her credibility. How could she expect anyone to respect her?

Don't worry, she told herself. Grant can't have left for the meeting yet. He'll smooth things over. Still, the temptation to turn back was so strong she had to grit her teeth and grip the wheel. *He needs you, Kelli. You're almost there. Go through with it.*

It took her a while to find the place, holding the map in one hand, the steering wheel in the other, fighting through congestion on the busy streets, missing turns, passing one-way streets that always seemed to go the wrong way, taking

The Harrison Duet

streets that ended in dead ends. Finally she turned onto Union Street, and with a relieved sigh saw she was in the right block.

Near the San Francisco marina, in an older section of town, the street was lined with restored buildings in variety of architectural styles, housing little bakeries, delis, restaurants, clothing stores, and other small businesses. She liked the area at once. It had character. She recognized Grant's agency from a vivid description he'd given her one evening, and she smiled in delight. The Victorian house, three stories tall, was freshly painted in a rich cream color, with delicate gingerbread trim in a dark forest green—just as lovely as she'd pictured.

She found a small parking lot at the back, but saw with alarm that the space marked *Pembroke* was empty. It was only two-fifteen. Where was Grant? She couldn't go ahead with her plan if he wasn't there to approve it. Could she?

Unsure what to do, Kelli walked around to the front and pushed open the heavy, oak door. Inside she stopped, taken aback for a moment by the beauty of the place.

The lobby was huge, dominated by a wide oak staircase with a matching banister. It was furnished in dark oak and decorated in a French country theme—forest green and ivory, with burgundy accents. Plants were everywhere, their brilliant foliage spilling from hanging containers and strategically placed wicker baskets, and the high bay windows filled the room with light. A sofa, antique tables, and chairs were grouped in a cozy comer, and the walls were hung with row upon row of framed awards the agency had won.

It was warm and inviting, yet at the same time sophisticated and highly professional looking. Nothing like the offices of Thompson & McGuire, where she'd worked before—a cold, modem place of glass and steel. And a far cry from her own "office" at home—a drafting table set up in a corner of her living room.

"May I help you?"

Kelli started, remembering why she was here. A lovely, impeccably dressed woman rose to her feet behind the receptionist's desk. Her nameplate read Charlene Wong.

Hesitantly, Kelli went forward. Before she could say anything, a stocky man with a neatly trimmed red beard came hurrying down the stairs, carrying a huge cardboard folder that Kelli guessed held artwork.

"Char!" He handed the receptionist the folder. "Pace Printing is sending a messenger to pick this up in the next half hour. And I need to talk to Grant. Do you know where he is?"

Charlene smiled at Kelli, said she'd be with her in just a moment, and turned back to the man. Kelli stood to one side, listening with growing apprehension. Grant, it seemed, had just left to meet a client at a restaurant, and after that was heading straight for a meeting at The Harrington Company at four-thirty. Carl, the vice-president, was with him, along with someone named Marc, no doubt an account executive.

"Can you call and leave a message for him at the restaurant?" the bearded man asked.

Charlene shrugged helplessly. "Sorry, Jim. He didn't tell me where he was going. I could call the client and ask."

"Do that."

Charlene apologized again to Kelli for making her wait, and made a quick call. She hung up, shaking her head. "They don't know which restaurant either."

"Damn," Jim said. "No way to reach him until four-thirty. I don't know what to tell this guy."

"Who? What's wrong?" Charlene asked.

The Harrison Duet

"It's the job for The Harrington Company. I got ahold of the illustrator that Grant asked for, but he isn't available until Monday, and I have to commit now or never for his price and Monday because he's got another offer. I don't know if Grant wants to wait that long."

Kelli's heart began to hammer with nervous excitement. She was an illustrator. She was here, now, and she'd do the work for free. She'd hoped to have Grant give her the go-ahead, but he wasn't available—and time was running out. She was about to introduce herself when Jim swore and shook his head in disgust.

"If it wasn't for that stupid broad in Tahoe, we wouldn't be in this mess in the first place. Grant wouldn't have let Andy farm out those illustrations. If he'd been here instead of—"

Charlene's eyes slid to Kelli and back again. "Jim," she warned sternly.

He swore again. "Now I'm stuck trying to pick up the pieces."

Kelli took a step back, her cheeks burning. She'd been afraid these people wouldn't think much of her, but this was even worse. They were blaming her for what had happened. She understood why; she'd blamed herself. But how could she introduce herself now? If Jim's indiscreet remarks mortified her, he'd feel even worse if he knew who she was.

Jim turned and looked at her for the first time. His frown disappeared. He held up a hand apologetically. "Sorry to leave you standing there like that. A few problems, nothing beyond our control. Charlene, take over." He backed away.

"No, wait, it's...it's you I've come to see," Kelli said, making a quick decision. "You're Jim, the—" she paused, fishing.

"Production supervisor," he said with a nod.

388

Syrie James

"Right." She smiled, trying to ignore the loud drum of her heart. "Grant Pembroke just told me you need an illustrator, pronto. So I came right over. I'm ready to work."

His eyes brightened in surprise. "An hour ago Grant was on my back to find someone. Where'd he run into you?"

"In...an elevator," she replied.

"Well, terrific! You just made my day. Come on up."

She followed him up the stairs thinking: you did it, Kelli, and you didn't have to tell a single lie.

"Grant wanted to deliver this today but I told him there's no way," Jim said. "If you can finish by tomorrow, though—"

"How many illustrations do you need?"

"Four. Two spots and two full-page. It's for a new condo complex."

"Where is The Harrington Company? How long would it take to get there from here?"

"About fifteen minutes."

Kelli checked her watch. That gave her a little less than two hours. "If I finish this by four-fifteen, can you find someone to deliver it to the meeting?"

Jim stopped at the doorway to the art department, a large sunny room where Kelli saw three artists bent over their drafting tables. "Lady," he said, with a skeptical lift of his brows, "if you finish this by four-fifteen, I'll deliver it myself. Right after I eat my hat."

10

Traffic crawled. Kelli tried to be patient, drumming her fingers on the steering wheel, checking her watch again and again. Four-thirty-five. Four-forty. "How much farther?" she asked.

Jim, sitting beside her in her car, shrugged his wide shoulders. "Couple of miles. But at this rate, it might take half an hour."

"I could get there faster by walking."

"Not in those heels, you wouldn't."

Kelli remembered the high-heeled pumps she was wearing and sighed. Jim was right. Inching forward through the San Francisco rush-hour traffic, she'd passed streets that soared up hills and seemed to disappear at the top. Even if she knew where she was going, the streets were too steep here to move anywhere fast on foot.

"I still can't believe you finished those drawings," Jim said, running his fingers through his thick, red hair. "Never saw anyone work so fast." He glanced aside at her with a grin. "Here I'd been harboring all these nasty thoughts about you, how you tricked my brilliant, rational boss into this absurd working arrangement—Lord, I thought you must have been some kind of witch—and then you turn out to be a bona fide *artiste*. One of the best I've ever seen." He chuckled. "And

390

Syrie James

don't think that's not a compliment, because I've seen a lot of artists."

"Thank you." Kelli smiled to herself. Jim hadn't thought to ask her name until she was halfway done with the last illustration. By then, the three other artists in the department had crowded around to watch her in awe, and when she introduced herself and extended her hand he'd just stared at her, speechless, his face turning the same color as his beard and hair.

Later, after she'd finished with ten minutes to spare, he'd apologized for his rude remarks in the lobby, and she'd admitted that Grant hadn't really sent her. She'd come on her own, and hoped Grant wouldn't mind. Jim had laughed, then, and reassured her it was all right.

It did seem to be all right, except that she'd gotten stuck making the delivery. She'd hoped to stay in the background of all this, but most of Grant's employees took public transportation, and the few with cars were either up to their ears in work or out on a call.

They would have made it to the meeting just before it started if traffic had moved. Now they were almost a half-hour late, and Kelli was getting nervous, wondering if this was such a good idea after all. No doubt Grant was explaining to the client at this very moment why the art wouldn't be ready until Monday. Would it make him look like an idiot if she showed up with the art at the door?

At last, the traffic opened up. In a few minutes they reached the building that housed The Harrington Company and left her car in a nearby parking structure. Once inside the office, Jim gave his name and asked the receptionist to call Grant out of the meeting. Kelli stood a distance behind him, waiting and worrying. In what seemed less than a minute

391

The Harrison Duet

Grant appeared around a corner. It had been a while since she'd seen him in anything but casual clothes, and she felt a magnetic jolt at how attractive, masculine, and professional he looked in his three-piece suit. He didn't appear to see her at first, walking straight up to Jim with a questioning look on his face.

"Jim. What's up?"

"Got a little package here your client might be interested in," Jim said. "It's finished. Thanks to your...artist friend."

"My artist friend?" Grant stared at him, confused, as he took the oversize art briefcase from him.

Jim nodded, glancing over his shoulder at Kelli with a grin as he stepped aside.

Grant's eyes flashed to hers. Please, don't be angry, Kelli prayed. Her heart pounding, she watched a succession of emotions cross his face: surprise. Dawning understanding. And then, to her relief, a hint of an incredulous smile.

Slowly, his eyes still locked with hers, he took one of the art boards out of the briefcase. He lifted the cover sheet, glanced at it briefly, and replaced it, his smile growing wider. In a few quick strides he was at her side, his eyes glowing as he looked down at her.

"Looks like I've just spent half an hour buttering up somebody for nothing."

Her heart soared. She had to bite her lip to keep from grinning.

"Thank you," he said softly.

No response seemed adequate. She ached to touch him, but she couldn't, not here in this lobby in full view of Jim and the client's receptionist, so she only smiled with her eyes, telling him *I did it for you.*

"Why don't you join us in the meeting?" he asked.

392

She shook her head quickly, finding her voice. "No! No. I wouldn't even have come, but no one else had a car."

"I'm glad you came." He turned back to Jim and thanked him. "I know it's quitting time, but can you hang around a few minutes until the meeting's over?"

"Sure, boss."

Grant smiled at Kelli again and gestured toward a couch in the lobby. "Sit. I'll try to make this brief."

He reappeared about twenty minutes later, laughing and shaking hands with a group of very happy-looking businessmen, who congratulated Grant on the excellent artwork and told him how pleased they were to be working together. Kelli felt a surge of excitement and relief that it had all worked out, and was even more thrilled when Grant introduced her to both his clients and his associates as the illustrator who'd come through for him.

Grant arranged for Carl to drive Jim and Marc back to the office in the company car. When she was back in her own parked car, with Grant behind the wheel—she'd decided he knew the area best so she handed him the keys—he sat for a long moment, watching her, a heart-stirring combination of gratitude and affection in his face.

"Come here," he growled finally, as he pulled her across the front seat into his arms. "You've been known to pull some crazy stunts, but that was by far the craziest. And the sweetest."

She wrapped her arms around his neck and looked up at him, eyes shining. "I was so afraid you'd be angry."

"Angry? Why? Because you went out of your way to help me save an account?"

"No. Because I acted on impulse. I rushed in without your approval."

"I told you once, sometimes impulsive actions are best. If you think and worry too much about some things, you can

The Harrison Duet

miss your only chance to act." He kissed her again. "I'd like to know how you pulled this off. When did you leave Tahoe? Five minutes after I did?"

"Sixty-five minutes. I had to wait for the guy to finish clearing the driveway."

"That's right."

She told him how she'd found his agency, even the details about her run-in with Jim.

"I'm sorry you had to hear all that," Grant said, frowning. "I thought a lot of Jim up until now, but if—"

"Please, don't chastise him. He thinks the world of you, Grant. And we're friends now. I think I managed to win his respect."

"*That* doesn't surprise me. I wish I could have seen his face when you whipped up those illustrations in nothing flat." With a teasing smile he added, "I suppose you finished the whole batch of comps for Cassera's in the sixty-five minutes before you left? Or maybe you sketched with one hand while you were driving down here?"

"No." She laughed. "I thought I'd do them tomorrow at your office, if that's okay with you. Then we can follow each other back to Tahoe Friday morning."

"A good plan." He smiled. "You know, it would have been a lot easier if I'd just let you come with me in the first place."

"You're right. It would have."

"What's next on the agenda? Dinner? At the wharf?"

"Sounds good to me."

He looked lovingly into her eyes. "Kelli," he said, his voice husky, "I'm glad you're here with me."

His arms tightened around her, and this time his kiss was long and deep. When their lips parted they were both out of breath. "How about we forget dinner and go to my place?" he said. "For once, I'd like to make love to you in a real, live *bed.*"

They tumbled into Grant's big, brass bed the moment they reached his house, and made love slowly, luxuriously—a union so sweet and gentle and satisfying, Kelli felt her senses had been spoiled for anything else. Then they slept deeply, exhausted from the long, eventful day and the previous night without sleep.

Sometime in the middle of the night Kelli awakened to Grant's kisses on her neck as his arms drew her into his embrace.

"Speaking of kids," he whispered against her ear, "what do you think of them?"

The question brought her from sleep to groggy wakefulness with a small laugh. "I love kids," Kelli said, happily nestling within his arms.

"So do I. Did I ever tell you I used to baby-sit?"

"Baby-sit?" she said sleepily.

She loved these late-night conversations that had been occurring in between slumber and lovemaking ever since they'd first slept together. They'd talked about everything, covering a wide range of subjects from childhood to the present, and everything she'd learned about him only whetted her appetite to learn more. "When did you baby-sit?"

"Ever since I can remember. I was the oldest, so I stood in for my parents a lot. When I was twelve, I started babysitting for a family down the street. Two girls and a boy." He sounded nostalgic. "I loved being with those kids; talking to them, lis-

The Harrison Duet

tening to them, playing with them, reading to them. At times they'd say the most surprising—and enlightening—things."

Kelli rearranged herself so that she could glance at him across the pillows. The room was partially illuminated by moonlight through the blinds, and she was touched by the affection she saw in his face. She could just see him, someday, with two dark-haired, blue-eyed sons, getting down on the floor, tinkering with their toys, helping them with their homework, teaching them to appreciate Mozart and Monet and explaining about the rotation of the earth. "You'll make a wonderful father someday."

"And you'll make a wonderful mother." He kissed her. "When you have kids—how many do you want?"

"Two."

"Is that all? I'd like four. Two of each. I figured you would, too, coming from a big family."

"A big family was great fun for us kids—but it was so hard on my parents. They never had time for themselves. I can't remember them ever taking a vacation alone together until after I graduated from college." She rolled to her back and let out a sigh. "My oldest sister has this long-standing joke, saying my folks should have stopped after two kids. They always protest, insisting they couldn't give any of us up, but she's probably right."

Grant raised himself on one elbow, a twinkle in his eyes. "I, for one, am glad your parents didn't stop after just two kids." His arms wound around her and then he was kissing her shoulder, her throat, her cheek, until their mouths met, opening to each other. As his hands slowly, tenderly explored her body, she slid her hands along the warm hollows and hard, defined muscles of his shoulders, back, and buttocks.

"Beautiful," she whispered.

"You are," he said, his voice low and rough.

He kissed her breasts, his lips moving slowly against the softness of her skin. When they joined together, the sharing of the past weeks became the sharing of their bodies, gentle loving giving way to rising peaks of passion that brought them higher and higher until they stopped, hovering weightless on the edge of pure feeling, and then fell into blinding brightness, an echoing descent as brilliant and thunderous as an electrical storm.

Afterward they lay spent in each other's arms, legs entwined, gazing at each other with small, wondering smiles.

"I don't think I realized how much I was missing in life until I met you," Grant said. Softly, tenderly, he added with heartfelt urgency: "I love you, Kelli."

She felt a surge of joy spread through her. She hadn't expected him to say the words, and she was thrilled to be able to respond in kind from her heart. "I love you, too."

He sought and found her hand, squeezing it affectionately as he brought it up between them. "It's incredible, isn't it—what's happened between us?"

"Yes," she breathed.

"I never thought it was possible to fall in love like this—so deeply, and so fast."

"Neither did I." Her smile widened. "I guess I should have, though."

"Should have? Why?"

"Whirlwind romances seem to be a common theme in my family. My brother and his wife fell in love at first sight and were engaged a month later. My grandparents got married four months after they met. My parents got engaged two weeks after they met—"

"Two weeks!"

She nodded. "And they were married four weeks later."

The Harrison Duet

"Wow. That's fast."

"The amazing thing is, all the marriages have stood the test of time, and have been very happy. My dad says when he met my mom, that was it; on their first date, he knew he was going to marry her. My mother always says: *When you know, you know.*"

"I like that." He brought her hand to his lips and kissed it. "It sounds like we're in good company. What do you think? Is it a sign?"

"A sign?"

"Should we get married?"

Her eyes met his across the pillow. Her heart pounded. "Are you serious?" Was he really talking about marriage in the same breath as their first admission of love? But then, she was the one who'd brought it up, by mentioning her family history.

"Do you remember what you said the day we met," he asked, his voice low and deep, "when you bumped into me outside that elevator?"

Kelli cast her thoughts back to that memorable night. "I hope I said...excuse me?"

"No, that's what *I* said. You said: *fate.*"

She gave a little gasp. "You're right. I did...I remember now. I suddenly felt as if my entire life was about to change."

"That's how I feel now. Kelli: I never really thought of marriage as a viable option for me. I figured I'd probably stay single all my life. But that's because I'd never met anyone I could imagine sharing my life with. Since I met you, I've been thinking very differently. We have so much in common, I feel like we're kindred spirits."

"So do I," she replied with a smile.

He caressed her cheek with his hand, his eyes filled with emotion. "Could you imagine being happy, married to me?"

"I think I could," she returned softly. "But this has all happened so fast...I think we both need a little time, just to make sure it's real and lasting."

"I agree." He kissed her deeply, his hand gently kneading her breast, the combined caress causing sparks to spiral throughout her body. Then he moved on top of her, his hard arousal proving that he was ready to make love yet again. "But it's a subject," he whispered against her lips, "that will definitely come under consideration."

"I always knew you were an artist at heart," Kelli said.

Having gotten only the barest glimpse of Grant's house the night before, she asked for a tour the next morning before breakfast.

His home was beautiful, built in the California ranch style with rounded arches in the open doorways and plaster walls and ceilings. It was sunny, cozy, and immaculate, and she found he shared her eye for color and attention to detail, and had similar taste in decor and furnishings.

When she came upon a series of watercolor landscapes hanging in the hall—lovely desert, mountain, and ocean scenes—she stopped in surprise. Every one of them was signed with his name. "Why didn't you tell me you painted? These are wonderful."

He shrugged. "Nothing special. I did those years ago. I haven't painted since college."

"Why not? You're really good."

"Not good enough. Not half as good as you." She started to protest but he scooped her into his arms and silenced her with a kiss. "Besides, I'm too slow. What you could paint in

The Harrison Duet

an hour would take me half a day." The kissing went on several minutes longer before the tour guide reluctantly agreed to proceed.

"I don't believe this," Kelli said moments later, noticing a framed print hanging in the living room. "I have the same one at home."

They both laughed with amazement when she opened his kitchen cabinet to set the table for breakfast and discovered they had the exact same set of stoneware dishes.

"We have the same taste in so many things, it's uncanny," Kelli commented. "I think we agree on everything except cars."

He turned from the stove where he was flipping pancakes onto plates, and looked at her. He seemed to be smothering a little grin as he said: "I told you: we're kindred spirits."

She studied a stoneware casserole dish and tea-pot in the cabinet. "You have the last two serving pieces I'm missing. If I moved in, we'd have sixteen of everything, and a perfect matched set." Her cheeks grew warm as soon as she spoke the words. She hadn't meant to imply that they should live together.

She felt Grant's hands slip around her waist from behind. "If you moved in, huh?" His lips were warm and tantalizing against her neck, his breath a moist vapor against her ear. "That's a great idea. I'd love to have you move in with me, Kelli. It would be the perfect way to find out if we're supposed to get married."

In his embrace, she began to melt like jelly. "Do you really think so?"

"I do."

"But...my work is in Seattle."

"It doesn't have to be. Come work for me."

400

"Grant..." She couldn't concentrate when he held her this way. Breaking free of his embrace, she spun to face him.

"The night we met, I made a proposition: I offered you a job as creative director. At the time, I figured I could use two people in that position. Since Andy left, the spot's wide open. I'll have to fill it soon." He caught both of her hands and drew her close again. "Kelli: will you take the job? I don't want anyone else but you."

Flattered but uncertain, she tried to organize her thoughts as she gazed up at him. "I have to admit," she said slowly, "from the minute I turned down your original offer, I wondered if I'd made the right decision."

"Did you?" He seemed pleased.

"Yes. I think I'd enjoy working for you. Your office is lovely. It would be exciting to live in San Francisco. But—"

"But?"

"But...there's a lot to consider, Grant. I've only known you for two weeks—and this would mean changing my entire life. I worked hard to build up my own business. I don't know if I'm ready to give it up yet."

"Why? Are you still determined to work freelance so you can prove yourself in some way? Because believe me: you have nothing to prove. You're one of the most talented artists I've ever met. Any agency would be lucky to have you."

"Thank you. But it's not just about proving myself. I get a lot of satisfaction from knowing that the clients are mine—all mine—and the creative decisions I make won't be overruled by upper management."

"Upper management? Meaning me."

"I didn't mean..." She broke off, suddenly self-conscious. Upper management *was* Grant.

"I understand how you feel, Kelli. I wouldn't want to work for anyone else if I didn't have to, either. But you and me—has

The Harrison Duet

it really been like that? All this time, I never felt as if you were working *for* me. It was more like we were a team."

"I felt the same way...most of the time."

"Most of the time?"

She nodded.

Grant sighed. "Okay, I admit: I'm not perfect. But I have only the greatest respect for you and your work. And I'm trying."

"Wouldn't our relationship pose a problem at your office?"

"Lots of married couples work together."

"But we're not married yet. If I move down here to work for you, and things don't work out between us the way we hope...I'd be out of a job and have to start all over."

"There is that risk," he admitted, "but I don't see that happening." He wrapped his arms around her, heartfelt affection shining in his blue eyes. "I love you, Kelli. The past two weeks have been the best of my life. I think we'd be good for each other. I want you here with me—not in Seattle. I realize this is a big decision for you. If you need time to think it through, you've got it."

"How much time?"

"However long you need. One hour. Two."

Her laugh was cut off by the warm pressure of his mouth. After a long moment, he asked against her lips: "If you do take the job...will you move in with me?"

She closed her eyes, molding her softness against his strength, thinking how perfectly they fit together, how good it could be between them. She loved him. She wanted him. But—family history or no—was it wise to live with a man she'd known for such a short time? And if she took the job—was it wise to live with—or marry—a man she worked for? "Let me take one thing at a time," she

402

said finally. "Let me decide about the job first, and then about...us."

Grant's office opened at nine. He took her on a complete tour that morning and introduced her to his large staff. It was an impressive setup, complete with a state-of-the-art audiovisual room that resembled a small theater. Everyone, from public relations and media placement to the clerical staff, seemed to have heard about the way Kelli had rescued The Harrington Company account, and they greeted her warmly.

The morning sped by, passing quickly into afternoon. Kelli was set up at the same drafting table where she'd done the illustrations the day before. Grant was so busy he only had a chance to stop in once, but she enjoyed working in the sunny, cheerful art department, joining in the bantering that went on back and forth across the room, and laughing with the staff over deli sandwiches on their lunch break. Even with people from different departments rushing in and out, small erupting crises, and the usual complaints, Kelli found it a pleasant place to work.

At one o'clock, when she'd finished the comps for Cassera's, Jim poked his head in the doorway.

"How's it going?" he asked.

"Great. In fact, I'm all done."

"That's terrific. Now you can join us."

"Join you where?"

"A bunch of us put in so much overtime the past week, Grant gave us the rest of the day off. We're going over to Golden Gate Park to catch the exhibit on Chinese art. Want to come?"

The Harrison Duet

Julie, the art director who was sitting beside Kelli, added: "I heard they've got some incredible murals. If you're only here for a few days, you ought to see them."

Kelli had never been to Golden Gate Park. The exhibit sounded tempting, and going out with the group would be fun. But having seen so little of Grant today, she decided she'd rather be here when he was through. Shaking her head regretfully, she explained why she couldn't go.

"Okay. Maybe next time. Catch ya later. Come on, Jules." With a wave, the two of them left.

Kelli was cleaning up her work area when an idea popped into her mind. *Murals*, Julie had said. She remembered something Ted Lazar had mentioned at their meeting: *I'd like to spruce up the hotel lobby if I could, but so far no one's come up with anything.* She had a sudden vision: a mural for the lobby's back wall. But not just any mural; a highly specialized mural...

She got out the materials she needed and started to work. It would take four separate paintings to show the full effect. An hour later the first watercolor was completed. It was an exciting concept, and she couldn't wait to show it to Grant. She was about to begin on the second painting when Grant's voice resonated from the doorway.

"Kelli." He gestured with his head for her to get up and come with him. He strode purposefully down the hall, and the moment they were inside his office he shut the door, wrapped her in his embrace, and kissed her deeply.

"It's torture," he murmured, "walking past that doorway and seeing you in there, knowing I can't just walk in and take you in my arms the way I did up at Tahoe."

She melted against him. "It's been tough on me, too. I kept hoping you'd come by. What have you been up to?"

"Meetings with clients. Putting out fires. The usual." He rocked her slowly back and forth in his arms. "Forget your freelance business, Kelli. Forget this place—there are too many people around. Let's open up a two-man shop. Correction. One-man one-woman shop."

She laughed. "Is that yet another new proposition, Mr. Pembroke?"

"It's a subject," he smiled, repeating his statement from earlier that morning, "that should definitely come under consideration." His lips found hers again. "How are you doing on the comps?"

"Done."

"Done? You are truly amazing."

"I'm working on something else now to surprise you."

"Oh? Well, finish it fast. Because I plan to knock off early tonight. I want to take you out on the town. Have you seen the view from Coit Tower? Been to Ghirardelli Square after dark? Ridden the glass elevator to the top of the Fairmont? Had dinner at the Blue Fox?"

She shook her head no to each question. "I was only here once, for a few days. Seventeen years ago."

He whistled. "Then you haven't really seen San Francisco. Pier 39 didn't even exist back then. We'll do it right. Tonight. Okay?"

She nodded happily. "I'd love to."

A buzzing sound interrupted them. Grant swore under his breath and picked up his phone. "Yes?" He heaved a sigh and shrugged at her apologetically. "Okay, put him on."

Grant leaned back against his desk, his tone changing to warm cordiality as he greeted the person on the other end of the line. After a short conversation, he said he'd be there at two-thirty, and bring Carl and Marc with him. When he hung up, he put his arms around Kelli again and hugged her.

The Harrison Duet

"I'm sorry, but I have to go. Another fire to put out. I'll try to be back by four, so we can get to Coit Tower before dark." He kissed her again, lingering a long moment before pulling back. "Remember where we left off, okay?" he said, touching a finger to her lips.

"I will."

He walked her back to the art department and stopped at her drafting table. "What's this?" he said, looking down in surprise at the watercolor she'd been working on.

"It's an idea I had for Cassera's lobby. A fifty-foot mural, to go with their European and Alpine theme."

"A mural?"

"Yes." She reminded him of Ted's comment about the bare walls. The panorama she'd painted showed cities and towns below the snowy Alps, with flags of the seven countries whose borders they crossed. "What makes this special is the lighting system I had in mind. It changes with the time of day. And here's how it would look." The painting showed the scene at sunrise, awash with an amber glow. "I want to do three more paintings: one at midday with a bright-blue sky, one at sunset, and a midnight sky filled with stars. We could use a black light that makes the mountains glow in the dark, and mount tiny lights in the—" She saw his dubious expression and broke off. "You don't like it?"

"Kelli, it's a nice idea, but a mural in the hotel lobby—it's not even our territory. Why waste your time on it?"

Crestfallen, she said, "It may not be our territory now, but if we win the account, it *could* be. I thought Ted might like it, and that every little bit of creative thinking would help."

"It's creative all right." He frowned and headed for the door. "But we've got a new logo, racks of collateral materials, and two ad campaigns. That's a lot to lay on a client all at once. Let's not confuse the issue by crossing over into interior design. Let's just present what we've got tomorrow and leave it at that. Okay?"

"Excuse me." A half hour had passed, and a worried Charlene was standing in the doorway, looking from one artist to the other, as if unsure whom to address.

Kelli had been working on the second watercolor for the Alpine scene. She was disappointed by Grant's reaction, but she liked the idea too much to throw it away. She had nothing else to do, and figured if they won the account, Grant could present the idea to Ted at some later date.

"What's the matter, Charlene?" Kelli asked.

"I've got Pace Printers on the line. They have a problem, but everyone who handles this is gone for the day. It's Marc's account, but he's with Grant, and they're somewhere in transit."

"Don't look at me," said Doug, the production artist sitting at the table next to Kelli. "I don't get involved in that stuff."

"I'll take it." Kelli picked up the line at a nearby desk. Grant had offered her a job here, after all. The least she could do was help out in crisis. "This is Kelli Harrison. I'm filling in for the creative director. What's the problem?" The printer explained that he had invitations on the press for one of their clients, a travel agency, and a question came up so he was holding up the printing. Could she come down and take a look at it? The print shop was just two blocks down the street, within walking distance. Sure, Kelli said. When she hung up, Doug frowned at her and shook his head.

"Grant only lets Dave and Jim approve press runs."

The Harrison Duet

"But Dave's sick, and Jim isn't here," Kelli said. "They can't hold the presses forever."

Kelli was glad to get outside, and smiled to herself as she walked through the busy neighborhood to the print shop. The sky was blue, the air was crisp, and the quaint shops she passed beckoned her to come inside. The print shop itself looked small from the outside, but opened into a large, spotlessly clean back room where presses roared at a fever pitch.

"We followed the artwork exactly," the printer explained, leading her to one of the presses at the back. "But we think you should have asked for a lighter screen." He picked up a sheet off the printed stack next to the press and Kelli studied it. The invitations had been designed to resemble a passport, with the travel agency's logo screened as a background pattern under the copy. A nice design, Kelli thought, although the background was a little heavy, making the copy a bit hard to read.

"See the problem?" he asked.

She nodded. "What's the deadline on these?"

"They're due at the mailing house tomorrow morning. Got to get out on time, I was told, since they're invites to some important bash."

"If we take these off the press, how long would it take to make plates with a new screen?"

"A couple of hours. The thing is, we shut down in an hour, and this stock's got to dry overnight before it can be folded. If I run this through now, we can have it folded and stapled and out first thing in the morning. If I take it off, I can't print until tomorrow, and we have to wait another day before I fold it."

Kelli studied the printed sheet one more time. The invitations looked beautiful. The text was readable, even if the art wasn't as perfectly designed as she might have wished. The deadline was more important, she decided, than absolute per-

Syrie James

fection. "Roll the presses," she told the printer, and to her satisfaction he grinned in delight.

She hurried back to the office, daydreaming about her upcoming night on the town with Grant. She was back at her drafting table working on her watercolor a while later when she heard a commotion going on downstairs. Going to the head of the stairs, she looked down and saw Grant arguing with Marc.

"You don't waste your time getting a client excited about something he can't have," Grant said, fuming. "If the guy wants radio, give him radio. There's no way his budget will stretch to TV. He'd be wasting a bundle just on the storyboards and we'd have to scrap the project in the end."

"I'm sorry," Marc said defensively, "I just thought—"

"I don't care what you thought. That's the last time I want to see that happen. The *last.*"

Letting out a sharp breath, Grant hurried up the stairs with Marc behind him. Grant passed Kelli at the top landing, then stopped, as if just noticing her. "Kelli," he said abruptly, "what's this I hear about the invitations for Dreyfus Travel? You went down to Pace and did a press check?"

His blue eyes flashed warily as if she were a stranger, an interloper, someone not to be trusted. "Yes," she said, taken aback momentarily, having expected a far different reception from him. "They called, and there was no one else to—"

"What'd you tell them?" Marc asked.

"I told them go ahead. The—"

"Did you bring samples?" Grant interrupted. "Let me see one."

She followed them into the art department and handed them each a printed sheet. To her dismay Grant let out a low curse. "You approved *this?*"

The Harrison Duet

"I did," Kelli replied, terrified that she'd made some horrible blunder.

"It's too hard to read, Kelli. The client will never go for this."

She tried to defend her decision, explaining about the deadline, but Grant kept shaking his head in disgust.

"I don't think it's so bad," Marc put in. "I promised they'd be mailed out by tomorrow. If she hadn't approved it we would have lost a whole day. And it wasn't Pace's fault that—"

"If Pace was worth their salt," Grant insisted, "when they recognized the issue, they would have offered to make new negs and plates, and worked overtime to run the thing tonight. If I'd been there, if Jim had been there, we would have insisted on that and made it happen." He turned to Kelli. "You may not have the same standards with your free-lance business, but we have a reputation to maintain here. We'll be lucky if the client doesn't refuse to pay for this job."

Kelli's cheeks burned. "I'm sorry." She was determined to maintain some level of dignity in front of Marc and the other artists in the room, who were all staring at her. "I was only trying to help."

"That kind of help I don't need." Grant turned and noticed the second watercolor she'd been working on. "What are you doing? I told you not to waste your time on this!"

"I know, but I decided—"

"*You* decided?" he said tightly. "You don't make the decisions around here, Kelli. You don't work here yet."

She stared at him in disbelief. Could this be the same man who'd held her in his arms only a few hours before, told her how much he loved her, and how much he admired her work? It was fine when she helped him out of the jam with The Harrington Company. There, she was just following instructions, drawing illustrations to order. But the first time she made a

Syrie James

decision on her own, and dabbled with a creative idea without his input, he couldn't handle it.

"You're right, Grant," she said, facing him defiantly in the silent room. "I don't work here yet. And I never will."

11

Kelli pulled into the parking lot at Cassera's Hotel and Casino the next morning and killed her car's engine. Nothing could erase the anguish she'd felt ever since the previous afternoon when she'd stormed out of Grant's office, ignoring his calls for her to wait, calmly stating that she'd see him in Tahoe for the presentation.

It was over between them; there was no doubt in her mind about that. It wasn't because Grant had humiliated her in front of his staff; she knew he'd arrived in a fit of temper after his argument with Marc, and his anger had snowballed. She could forgive him for that. But it didn't change the ultimate problem.

Her decision on the printing had been sound, even if he didn't agree. Her idea for the mural was innovative, but he hadn't been able to accept it. No matter how many times Grant claimed he'd allow her the freedom to be creative, to make her own decisions, in truth he needed to be the boss, doing things his own way. Even though she loved him, she couldn't work with him on those terms, certainly couldn't consider spending her life with him on those terms. She'd already suffered through one disastrous relationship with a controlling man, and she wouldn't—*couldn't* go through that again.

412

At ten sharp, she entered Ted Lazar's office. Grant jumped up from his chair next to the huge desk and took her hand with a warm greeting. He looked exhausted, yet his eyes told her how sorry he was. Kelli pasted on a brittle smile, struggling to remind herself not to think, not to feel. She had to end this now. The minute the meeting was over, she'd walk away.

Grant sat beside her, presenting the materials they'd conceived to the small assembled group of executives and board members, explaining their ideas for the collateral materials and the ads. During the entire meeting, she was acutely conscious of his nearness, the deep timbre of his voice, and the silent, private messages of apology he directed at her every time he turned her way. It was all she could do to maintain her composure, to make the appropriate responses when Ted asked her a question, to play the role of Grant's knowledgeable associate, when all she wanted to do was run from the room and cry.

"One more thing," Grant told the group, just when she was certain they were finished and she could make her escape. He pulled out another stack of covered art boards from his leather case. "Kelli came up with a unique and imaginative interior design suggestion. Although it doesn't fall within the scope of this work, I present it to you as a sideline, something you might think about for the future."

She looked at him in astonishment as he uncovered four watercolors depicting the Alpine mural and explained her concept to Ted in detail. *Four Watercolors.* She'd only finished one, and had barely begun the second. But there they were: all four scenes. She immediately recognized the artist's technique on the last three paintings. It matched the style of the landscapes she'd seen hanging in the hall of Grant's house.

The Harrison Duet

Sometime between the afternoon before and that morning, he'd painted them himself.

She remembered his words—"I'm too slow. What you could paint in an hour would take me half a day"—and her heart twisted at the thought of the effort this must have cost him. No wonder he looked so exhausted. Touched by his peacemaking gesture, she felt her resolve slipping.

But with a pang of profound regret, she realized—no matter how lovely the thought behind it—it still didn't change anything. The basic problem was still there. Sooner or later— and no doubt on a regular basis—Grant's need to control would take over again, driving a wedge between them, creating hostility, and ruining everything.

Ted and most of the board responded with enthusiasm to the mural idea. When the meeting ended and everyone shook hands, Ted said they'd make their decision by the end of the week and let them know.

As Kelli stepped into the empty elevator with Grant, images of the night they'd met in that very same elevator were all too vivid in her mind. When the doors closed she said quietly, "You didn't have to do that. Finish the watercolors, I mean. But thank you. It was a very nice gesture."

"I didn't mean it to be a gesture. I did it because you were right. It's a terrific idea. I should have let you follow through on it in the first place. I wish I had. But for some reason—I don't know, maybe the way you kept solving problems at my company without asking me—maybe, somehow, I felt that my authority was being threatened. I know that's ridiculous, but—" He reached out for her hand, but she shrank back, and the resulting hurt on his face made her ache inside. Yet she knew better than to let him touch her. All it would take was a tender touch, a softly uttered phrase, and she'd be putty

414

in his hands. If she let him take her in his arms, she'd be lost all over again.

"Can we go somewhere and talk?" Grant asked.

"I'd rather not."

"Kelli, we need to talk this through. I'm sorry for what happened yesterday—so incredibly sorry. I lost my temper. But I didn't mean—"

"It isn't just yesterday," she replied. The elevator stopped and he followed her into the lobby. "Yesterday opened my eyes, that's all. You said it once—and you were right. We're too much alike. We're both creative types, and we clash."

"That's not true. We were a team for two weeks, Kelli; a *team.* Not separate, opposing forces. We came up with our best ideas when we worked together. We were brilliant."

"Yes, we were. But after the creative session ended, suddenly you had to be the one running things, the one in charge. There's no way you'll ever be satisfied with anything I create or any decision I make on my own. You'll always have an idea you like better. *Always.* You need to be in the driver's seat, Grant."

"No I don't. I—"

"Yes, you do." She swallowed hard against threatening tears. "And let's be honest: so do I. Two chiefs can't rule the same tribe." Backing away, she added brokenly, "It was wonderful while it lasted, Grant—truly wonderful. But it's better if we don't see each other again."

He covered the distance between them in two strides and stopped before her, grabbing hold of her arms. "Kelli, you don't mean that. I love you. You said you love me."

"I do. But—"

"Then don't give up on me—on us. Give us another chance. What we have, it's so rare. You can't just walk away from it. We can work this out."

"No we can't." A tear trickled down Kelli's cheek. "I've been through it before, Grant. Let's end this now, please, before it gets any harder to say goodbye."

He stared at her for a long, silent moment. His face infused first with sadness, then with anger. A muscle twitched in his jaw, and all the light seemed to drain from his blue eyes. "Fine," he said stonily, dropping his hands from her arms. "Have it your way." Then he turned, strode across the casino floor, and vanished into the crowd.

Kelli stared into the flames in the hearth, trying to think about the Christmas week to come. Eventually, she promised herself, her time with Grant would be no more than a distant memory: two loving weeks, a sharing between two people that wasn't meant to last. She'd forget the pain sooner or later. She *would*.

If only she could forget now.

Over the past week, she had turned Kyle's Tahoe retreat into a beehive of activity. She'd had snow cleared away from around the house and the back porch and had all the windows washed. Carpet and hardwood floors had been laid in record time, bathroom accessories had been installed, and then, on Kyle's instructions, truckloads of furniture, bedding, kitchen supplies, and other household necessities had been delivered, all brand-new and labeled according to room. Kelli had overseen the placement of everything, unpacked many of the boxes, and gone shopping to buy a few odds and ends she'd thought would make the house even more comfortable.

Now, absently fingering the texture of the new cotton sofa in the living room, Kelli felt fresh tears brim in her eyes.

She may have stayed busy every day for the past week, but the nights had stretched long and lonely. The house with its gleaming floors, lush carpet, and new furnishings seemed strange and unfamiliar. Thank God Kyle and his family were due to arrive any minute. Once surrounded by their love, laughter, and warmth, Kelli was certain she'd feel good again.

There was the sound of a car in the drive, and then the honk of a horn. Jumping up, Kelli dried her eyes and ran to the door.

It was dark, well past dinnertime, but in the warm glow from the porch light she could see a shiny silver station wagon parked next to her Rover in front of the garage. Kyle got out first and she raced down the steps, flew into her brother's arms.

"Am I glad to see you! " she cried as he encased her in a hug. "How was the drive?"

"Long," he said with a laugh. "Next time I think we'll fly."

She affectionately brushed a wave of his short, reddish-brown hair off his forehead, thinking, with a fresh stab of loneliness, how much like Grant he was. Not as tall, but equally as handsome, with the same rugged strength in his arms and shoulders, the same well-proportioned physique, the same bright sparkle in his green eyes.

"Kelli." Kyle eyed her with concern. "Is something wrong?"

"No," she lied. "Everything's fine." Brightly, to distract him, she added, "You got a new car!"

"Shows how long since *you've* been down south. We've had this wagon almost a year. A few months of dragging baby paraphernalia around in the Maserati, and we'd had it."

"Hey, do I get a hug or is this reunion reserved for siblings?" asked a familiar, husky, feminine voice.

Kelli turned and joined in Desiree's friendly laugh as they hugged each other. Her sister-in-law's curly, honey-brown hair reached to just below her shoulders, and she had beautiful amber eyes. "Did you get shorter, or have I grown since I saw you last?" Kelli teased, borrowing the line her father used every time Kyle's petite wife came to visit.

"Oh, stop!" Desiree smiled. A loud wail came from inside the car, and she threw open the back door. "Didn't mean to ignore *you*, sweetie. Come see your Aunt Kelli." Desiree fiddled with the child's car seat and brought out a squirming baby in blue overalls.

"Hi, sweetheart." Kelli took the tiny girl into her arms. "Did you have a nice trip?" The infant stared at her solemnly, her pale, sweet face surrounded by wisps of soft, strawberry-blond hair. It had been months since her parents had brought her to Seattle for a visit, and Kelli couldn't believe how much she'd grown. Hugging her, she said, "Denise, I missed you."

"That's Darnelle," Desiree corrected.

"I did it again!" Kelli smiled and kissed the baby's chubby cheek. "Someday I'll learn to tell you two apart."

Kyle walked around the car carrying his other twin daughter, moving her small arm in a wave. "Say hi, Denise," he intoned against her ear. The toddler broke into a silent, toothy grin.

"They turned fourteen months old last week," Desiree explained. "Wait until you see how well they're walking now."

The pride in Kyle's and Desiree's faces, and the love they radiated, brought fresh moisture to Kelli's eyes. Everything, she thought, seemed to make her cry these days.

"I'm so glad you're all here." She blinked rapidly, hoping they wouldn't notice her tears as she held Darnelle close, trying to concentrate on the happiness of the moment. But somehow, the happiness seemed shallow and incomplete.

Syrie James

They spent the evening combing through the house, Kelli sharing anecdotes about the work that had been done. As she'd expected, Kyle, the perfectionist, made a list of things that needed to be finished or fixed, but overall, he and Desiree were delighted with the results.

"Thank you *so* much," they both said over and over, hugging her.

"If you ever get tired of advertising, you can start a whole new profession as a contractor," Kyle insisted. "Or an interior designer. You did a terrific job, and I'll always be grateful."

They appreciated all the unpacking Kelli had done on their behalf, and promised to reimburse her for everything she'd bought for the place.

When they reached the garage, where she'd moved Grant's graphics furniture and supplies the day the carpet was laid, Kyle reacted with surprise. "I figured Grant would have cleared all this stuff out by now."

"I haven't heard from him in a while," she said quickly. "I thought I'd ship it back to his agency next week."

Kyle looked at her curiously. She had told him earlier that the advertising project went well. "Why haven't you heard from him? What happened between you two?"

"Nothing. We were just business partners for a couple of weeks, that's all. He's probably been too busy to—"

"Just business partners?" he said skeptically. "That's not the impression I got when you called after the storm. I recall a distinct...lilt to your voice. A sort of ringing happiness. And something about making good use of the time."

To her frustration, Kelli felt herself blush. "Well, we did become sort of...close for while. But it didn't work out. I..." She took a deep breath, warning herself not to start crying again. "To tell you the truth, I'd rather not talk about it."

419

The Harrison Duet

Kyle nodded, frowning, and didn't bring up the subject again.

The next afternoon, they all piled into the station wagon and went out to buy a Christmas tree. While the girls played inside a portable playpen filled with toys, Kelli helped Kyle set up the fragrant, nine-foot pine in the living room.

"Why did you pack all that stuff?" Kyle asked Desiree, when she started unloading a cardboard box of Christmas tree ornaments. "I brought *my* box. Isn't it my turn to decorate the tree?"

Desiree made a face. "I couldn't stand another tree like last year's. Once was enough."

"Now hold on a minute," Kyle said. "I thought we had a deal. Every other year we—"

"Kyle," Kelli interrupted in disbelief, "you didn't force your family to live through an entire Christmas with that boring silver tree of yours, did you?"

"See?" Desiree exclaimed, as she unwrapped a delicate Mrs. Claus figurine. "I'm not the only one who thinks it's boring."

"Every single year, the tree at his condo looked exactly the same." Kelli grimaced. "Nothing but silver ornaments and silver tinsel. Very modern. Very monotone."

"And very cold," Desiree agreed. "A great tree for an appliance store. No imagination at all."

"At least it doesn't look like a hodgepodge, which is the only way to describe your tree." Kyle turned to Kelli, shaking his head in disbelief. "She's been saving ornaments since the day she was born—everything from old socks to candy canes—and she insists on hanging every single one on the tree."

"My ornaments are beautiful," Desiree argued. "Look!"

420

Kelli looked. The coffee table was strewn with lovely, colorful ornaments made out of wood, straw, porcelain, glass, and crystal. There was also an assortment of old, discolored glass balls and faded ornaments that seemed to have broken or missing parts.

Desiree stood up, holding a tiny Christmas stocking made of faded red and green fabric. "This is not an old sock, Kyle. It's an ornament my great-grandmother made. It has a lot of sentimental value." To Kelli, she added, "I've tried to explain this to my husband half a dozen times, but if something's not brand new, he thinks it should be thrown away."

"I do not," Kyle protested.

"You do!"

One of the twins let out a loud wail, which her sister quickly echoed.

"I'm not going to stand here and let you hang all that junk on the tree again," Kyle said, picking up one of their daughters and soothing her. "It's too much."

Desiree threw up her hands. "Talk to him, will you, Kelli? He's impossible." She picked up the other twin and rocked her in her arms.

Kelli opened her mouth to speak, then shut it again. She didn't want to be caught in the middle of a domestic squabble. "I think what you should do," she said finally, "is compromise."

"Compromise?" Kyle repeated.

"Yes." She told Kyle his silver ornaments would look great if he interspersed some of them with some of Desiree's, and suggested that Desiree use only her nicest ones, rotating in a few of the others every year. "They're beautiful, but you can't appreciate any of them if the tree's crammed too full."

The Harrison Duet

Desiree pursed her lips. "I guess you're right." She put Denise back in the playpen and slid her arms around Kyle's waist. "What do you say, sweetheart? Shall we compromise?"

Kyle's lips twitched, then spread into a grin. "Who could say no in the face of such wisdom?"

Later, when the tree was finished, they all stood back in admiration.

"It's gorgeous," Desiree said, glowing. "The prettiest tree we've ever had."

Kyle took his wife into his arms and kissed her. "Mmm. I think compromising has its advantages."

The next kiss lasted a long time, and Kelli had to look away, the love light she'd observed reflected in their eyes prompting a wave of renewed grief and pain.

Grabbing her jacket from the hall closet, Kelli quietly let herself out the front door.

She'd wanted to hike along the beach, but it was covered with snow and she wasn't wearing boots, so she headed down the driveway instead and followed the road as it curved down past the lake into the trees.

Even though the afternoon sun felt warm on her face, the water ebbed softly nearby, and the tall pines were lightly dusted with snow, the scene held no beauty for her today.

How was she going to get through an entire week, living in the same house with Kyle and Desiree? Every look, every word that passed between them, even during an argument, showed how much they loved and needed each other.

She'd tried to deny it to herself for the past eight days, but she could no longer ignore it: she missed Grant with an ache so fierce that it threatened to tear her apart.

Kelli wondered what he was he was doing at that moment. It was Saturday. Was he alone at the office, getting caught up

422

on his work? Or at home in his sunny, cheerful kitchen, fixing a late lunch on the set of stoneware that matched her own? The memory of their morning there together came flooding back, and once again she could feel the warmth of his arms around her, could see the glow of affection in his eyes as he said, "I love you. The past two weeks have been the best of my life. I think we'd be good for each other."

Before she met Grant, she'd considered herself a happy person. She had looked forward to exploring her independence and to operating her small business in Seattle. But since he came into her life, everything had changed.

She loved him. She needed him. Now, she realized, she couldn't imagine being truly happy without him.

But how, she asked herself, could they resolve the conflicts that constantly cropped up between them? What did you do when two people both always wanted to have their own way?

Suddenly she saw Kyle and Desiree fighting over the Christmas tree, and heard herself saying, *What you should do is compromise.*

Kelli's heart quickened with excitement. The answer had been there all the time. She'd been so caught up in her need to be strong and self-sufficient that she'd missed the point of what love and life and creative endeavors were all about.

Compromise.

Grant had compromised often and willingly over their work. Every time they'd put their two heads together and combined the best ideas of each, they'd achieved a far better result than either could have accomplished on their own. In some areas he was more knowledgeable than she was, and in others he could learn from her.

What if Grant had kowtowed to her every thought and wish? What kind of a partner would he have made? Yes, his

The Harrison Duet

instinct was to control things; but she was lucky to have found a man who asserted his own opinions, yet was confident enough to know when to give in. He'd apologized for panning her idea about the mural, had gone far beyond the call of duty to prove he respected her ideas. With Grant, she might not get unqualified approval all the time, but she knew she'd get help and unqualified affection.

Yes, yes, she thought, as she turned and raced back up the road. *We can work it out. We can.* She'd get in her car, zip back to San Francisco, and tell him how she felt. Better yet, she'd get on the phone and call him this minute. She'd tell him she loved him and wanted to spend the rest of her life with him.

It seemed to take forever to run home. She hadn't realized she'd walked so far. When at last, panting for breath, she caught sight of the house, a new thought struck her. She'd been so adamant that it was over the last time she saw Grant. She couldn't forget the disappointment and anger in his eyes. What if he wasn't willing to risk being hurt again? What if he couldn't forgive her for walking away?

Please, Grant, she thought, her heart pounding as she ran. You were so right. We *are* good for each other. You have to still care.

Instead of following the road all the way up to the driveway, she took a shortcut across the snowy embankment. Her shoes were soaked through by the time she hurried up the steps to the back porch. She paused outside the sliding glass door, catching her breath and stomping the snow off her shoes. One hand on the door handle, she glanced inside.

On the other side of the glass, she saw Kyle standing near the Christmas tree, laughing. Desiree was sitting cross-legged on the floor, playing with Denise—or was it Darnelle? A man stood next to her, holding the other twin in his arms.

It was Grant!

He said something that made the little girl clap her hands with delight.

Kelli's joy on seeing him was so great, she couldn't move. She watched him for a moment through the glass, wondering what she should say now that he was actually here. He looked up, and his gaze met hers through the window. His smile vanished.

Kelli's heart seemed to lurch to a stop. She could read no message in his eyes. Her worst fears seemed to be confirmed: he was still angry. He hadn't forgiven her. Then why had he come? With a stab of intense disappointment she guessed the answer: he was here to pick up the graphics supplies and equipment from the garage, that's all.

Don't give up, she told herself. Somehow, you have to get him to listen. Taking a deep breath to steady herself, Kelli slid open the door.

"There she is!" Kyle said jovially. "We were going to send a search party if you didn't show up pretty soon."

"We've been entertaining your friend," Desiree said. "Or should I say, he's been entertaining *us*. We just heard how you saved an account for him with that faster-than-lightning drawing arm of yours." She laughed, but Grant didn't join in.

Kelli met Grant's gaze across the room. A long moment passed, the most uncomfortable of her life. What should she say? Do?

Kyle broke the silence. "Well, I guess you two have a lot to talk about. We'll just go on upstairs."

He caught Desiree's eye. She stood quickly, cradling the baby in her arms. "Yes. It's time for the girls' nap."

"Come on, Darnelle." Kyle lifted the other little girl from Grant's arms and kissed her cheek.

The Harrison Duet

"It's all right," Grant said. "You two don't have to leave. We'll go outside." He looked sharply at Kelli and added politely, "That is, if you don't mind."

"No. Of course not." Kelli's voice didn't sound like her own. She backed out onto the porch and Grant followed. Sliding the door closed, he crossed the redwood decking to the far side. She stood a few feet away, nervously clutching the rail, wondering how to begin.

"The house looks great," he said finally. "You must have really worked hard to get so much done in a week."

She shrugged uncertainly. "I didn't have anything else to do." When he didn't say more, she lowered her eyes. "I...guess you came to clear out the studio?"

"No, I didn't."

"Oh." She felt a small burst of hope, but still couldn't look at him.

After a long pause, he said softly, "Kelli, I missed you."

Her eyes flew up to meet his, and she took a sharp breath. "Oh, I missed you, too. So much." *Now,* she told herself. *Tell him now.* "Grant," she began, "I've been thinking all week about—"

"Wait. Don't say anything, not until I've had my chance." He shoved his hands in his pockets. "I've rehearsed this speech about fifty times and you'll probably think I'm too autocratic, too demanding. But I don't know how else to say it, so you'll just have to take it the way it is." He took a deep breath and went on. "I'm sorry for what happened at the office that day, so sorry for what I said. It was inexcusable, and I just hope you can forgive me. This past week has been hell for me. I've been alone a long time, Kelli. I thought I was fine. But I realize now I'd just accepted loneliness as a fact of life. Since we met, you're all I can think about. I love you. You said we're so much alike that we clash, but I don't buy it. All the things we have in common are a plus, a gift. We may have stepped on each others' toes a few times, but we're learning. We both want the same things out of life—to use our creative instincts, to build something from nothing, to do the best job we can. But what's the point of doing great work if you have no one to love, no one to share it with? We've got something special together—you know we do."

Kelli felt a surge of joy. Half whispering, she said: "I agree."

"You do? Then why'd you run out on me? I want you to have just as much say in everything we do as I do. Equal space, equal time. If you don't want to work at the same place as me, fine, have your own business. Just do it in San Francisco. I'll give you a bunch of my clients to get you started, good accounts, and I know they'll be well taken care of."

"You would do that?"

"Of course I would. But that's just a small part of this. I'm talking about our *lives* here. I don't want a life without you in it. I realize this has happened incredibly fast, but your mom had it right: *When you know, you know.* I think *I've* known since the moment I bumped into you outside that elevator. Why do you think I proposed that unorthodox working arrangement? I felt something I'd never experienced before. I had to find out if there was any future in it—and there *is*. I want *you* to come home to, to share with, to care for. I want to make a home together, have children with you." He paused, his voice deep and his eyes brimming with emotion. "Kelli, I love you. Will you marry me?"

Happiness bubbled up inside her and she looked up at him, aware that she could never disguise the depth of love that lit her eyes and her heart. "Yes."

"Yes?" he repeated, unable to hide his delight and surprise.

"Yes. Yes! I love you. I'll marry you!" She couldn't contain her joy any longer and broke out into a laugh, throwing her

The Harrison Duet

arms around his neck. "If you'd given me half a chance, I was just about to ask you."

His arms tightened around her and she both felt and heard his answering laugh.

"I had six more arguments prepared. I thought it might take weeks to persuade you. What made you change your mind?"

"Somewhere along the line, I learned the value of compromise."

"Ah, yes. Compromise. I think we'll be doing a lot of that, and be better off for it, too." His kiss was sweet and tender, his eyes lit with elation.

She smiled. "You know, I never got my night on the town in San Francisco."

"There'll be time for plenty of nights on the town now."

"Should we go in and tell Kyle and Desiree? They must be dying to know what's going on."

"Not yet." He took her hand. "Come with me. I have something to show you."

He led her around to the front of the house, and she stopped short when she saw the car parked next to hers in the driveway.

"I don't believe it!" She ran to take a closer look. It was an old Rover, the identical model to hers, the same exact shade of British racing green. Except that this car had been perfectly restored. It had a sparkling new paint job, the imitation wood inside had been replaced by real burl wood, and the seats were covered with luxurious doeskin.

"Oh!" she said breathlessly, looking in the window. "It's beautiful! When did you get it?"

"About five years ago."

She stared at him. "Five years ago? But then why—" She thought back to the night they'd met, remembered his

428

astonishment when he first saw her car. She'd thought he was making fun of her eclectic taste, but she realized now he'd simply been surprised by the coincidence. She remembered, too, how she'd defended her old car with fierce pride. No wonder he hadn't said anything about *his* Rover. Her car looked like an old clunker compared to his. He hadn't wanted to embarrass her or destroy her illusions.

"I guess I was pretty snooty about the whole thing, wasn't I?" she asked softly, and sighed. "Most men would have put me in my place on the spot and enjoyed every minute of it."

He took her into his arms. "I admired your pride. A good Rover fanatic is hard to find."

"Yours is a masterpiece. How am I ever going to get into my car after this?"

"There's nothing wrong with your car that a little money can't fix."

"You mean we can restore it like yours?"

"Anything you want."

She hugged him. "This is great! I can't wait. Just one more thing we'll have a matched set of." He laughed, hugging her back, and she added, "*Now* I see how you knew which part to get for my car. But how did you get it so fast?"

"I had an extra one on hand, just in case of emergency."

"Good advance planning."

He grinned. "So. Are you going to start your own agency, or come work with me?"

"As creative director?"

"No, as a full partner."

Her eyes widened in astonishment. She could see that he meant it. "I'll take it."

"I'm glad." He kissed her and she responded, wanting to pour into him all the love and happiness she felt.

The Harrison Duet

"There's only one little problem on the horizon," she murmured, "that we'll have to discuss someday."

"What's that?"

"You want four children. I want two."

"A definite impasse."

"What should we do about it?"

"Compromise."

"Three?"

He nodded.

"It's a deal." She kissed him again to seal the bargain. "I predict," she whispered, "a good sixty or seventy years of wedded bliss ahead of us."

"The sky's the limit."

She caught her breath. "I almost forgot to ask! Did we win the Cassera's account, or not?"

His eyes sparkled and he couldn't stop a wide smile. "What do you think?"

She gasped with delight and he lifted her off the ground, spinning her in a circle, their joyous exclamations echoing above the tree-tops.

jane austen's nightmare

BY SYRIE JAMES

Chawton, Wednesday 2 August 1815

An extraordinary adventure which I only just experienced proved to be so vivid and distressing—and yet ultimately so illuminating—that I feel I must record it in its entirety.

It was a gloomy, grey, frigid afternoon, and I found myself traversing a strangely quiet and deserted street in Bath. (Bath! It is indeed the most tiresome place in the world, a visit there surely akin to a descent into Hades.) A low fog hung in the air, dampening the pavements and obscuring the heights of the long rows of limestone townhouses on either side of me.

I wondered how I had come to be there, and why I was alone. Should I not be snug at home at Chawton Cottage? Where were all the residents of Bath—a city generally so filled with crowds, noise, and confusion? Where did I get the (very smart) pale blue muslin gown in which I was attired, and the grey wool cloak with its beautiful lace collar, both too handsome to be seen much less worn? As I shivered and wrapped my cloak more tightly about me, I observed a pretty young woman of about seventeen years of age emerge from the fog and venture in my direction. I could not prevent a little start of surprise, for the newcomer looked exactly like Marianne Dashwood—at least the Marianne that I had envisioned while writing *Sense and Sensibility*.

The Harrison Duet

How wonderful it was, I thought, that a real-life woman and a complete stranger should so closely resemble the character whom I had created entirely in my mind! I was about to politely avert my gaze when, of a sudden, the young woman's eyes widened and she marched determinedly up to me.

"Miss Jane Austen, is it not?" exclaimed she, stopping directly before me.

"Yes," replied I, uncertain how it was possible that this young woman should be acquainted with me.

"Surely you recognise me!" persisted she in an impassioned tone.

"Should I? I am very sorry. I do not believe we have ever met."

"Of course we have! You created me. I am Marianne."

I was at a loss for words. Had I imbibed too much wine at dinner? Was this exchange simply another one of my imaginative flights of fancy? Or could it be that, by some remarkable twist of fate, it was truly occurring? Whatever the cause, I did not wish to appear rude. "Of course," said I, smiling as I extended my hand to her, "I *did* think you looked familiar. How lovely to make your acquaintance in person at last. How have you been?"

"Not well. Not well at all!" cried she with a vigorous shake of her curls as she ignored my proffered hand. "I have wanted to converse with you for *such* a long time, I am grateful to at last have the opportunity." Her eyes flashed as she demanded, "What could you have been thinking, Jane—I *may* call you Jane, may I not?—when you wrote all that about me?"

"When I wrote what?" responded I uncertainly.

"In every scene throughout that entire, horrid novel," answered Marianne, "you presented me as the most selfish and self-involved creature on the face of the earth. I was always waxing rhapsodic about poetry or dead leaves, harshly critiquing somebody or something, or crying my eyes out in the depths of despair! Could not you have given me even one scene where I might have behaved with equanimity?"

This verbal assault, so entirely unexpected and delivered with such depth of emotion, took me utterly aback. "I—I was simply attempting to make you different from your sister," explained I, my voice faltering, "to portray two opposite temperaments."

"By my example then, do you mean to imply that having passionate feelings is a great evil?" cried Marianne.

"No—not at all. My aim was to illustrate the injurious nature of *wallowing* in excessive emotion and the importance of self-restraint."

"If that is so, was it truly necessary to enforce such suffering upon me to get across your point? You made me look ridiculous and pathetic! You humiliated me at a party! You nearly had me die—*literally die!* And the most cruel offence of all, Jane: you broke my heart. You had me fall madly, passionately in love with a man who was akin to my second self, and then you deliberately and remorselessly snatched him away!" Marianne choked back a sob as she dabbed at her eyes with a handkerchief from her reticule. "*All* the other heroines in *every one of your novels* ends up with the man they love, *except me*. You married *me* off to a man nearly twice my age! How could you do it?"

A paroxysm of guilt pierced through me with the speed of an arrow. Every word she spoke was true. Had I indeed sacrificed Marianne's happiness to convey a lesson? But no—no.

"I am sorry, Marianne," murmured I with sincere compassion. "I did indeed put you through a great many trials in my novel—but in the end, everything turns out well. I hope you and Colonel Brandon are very happy?"

The Harrison Duet

"Colonel Brandon is the most loyal, amiable, and good-hearted of gentlemen," retorted Marianne testily. "He loves me, of that I am well aware, and I suppose I love him back. Every day I try to remind myself how fortunate I am to be his wife. But every day is just as quiet, spiritless, and dull as the last! We read. We take walks. We ride horses. We dine. He cleans his rifle and hunts. I do needle-work and play the pianoforte. Oh! Were it not for my mother's and sisters' visits, I think I should go mad! Where is the heart-pounding excitement I felt in every encounter with Willoughby? Am I never to feel that way again?"

"Marianne," answered I solemnly, "the excitement you describe might be thrilling for a moment, but it is not the preferred way to live. A marriage based on affection, respect, and companionship is a more desirable union, and will make you far happier."

"Happier? What do you know of happiness, Jane? Upon what do you base these assumptions? You, who have never married!"

Her brutal and tactless remarks made me gasp—yet I reminded myself that *I* had created her—*I* had made her what she was. "I base them upon my observations of other married couples. I could not in good conscience allow you to marry Willoughby. He was greedy, selfish, and fickle, and would have made you miserable. I thought you understood that at the end."

"You put words in my mouth to show what I had learned—but they were *your* words, Jane, not mine. I know the truth. I know why you stole my Willoughby away: it was because *you* could not have Mr. Ashford. You suffered, so you made certain that *I* suffered, as well!"

At the mention of Mr. Ashford's name, my heart seized and I let out a little gasp. Not a day passed that I did not think of Mr. Ashford. He was the one, true love of my life, but for good reason, I had told no one about our relationship—no one except Henry and my sister. How could Marianne know about him?

"It was most unfair of you, Jane! Most unfair!" Tears streamed down Marianne's cheeks now and she took a quivering breath. "Could not you have given me and Willoughby a second chance? You could have redeemed him at any time had you chosen to, but you did not. I declare, I will never forgive you!" With this last, heated remark, she turned and darted away.

"Marianne, come back!" cried I, running after her. "Have you forgotten Eliza, whom Willoughby seduced, disgraced, and abandoned? I *saved* you from Willoughby! He was one of the worst offenders I ever created! Colonel Brandon is worth a hundred Willoughbys! He is the true hero of the novel!"

But the fog enveloped Marianne's retreating form and she disappeared from my view.

I stopped, catching my breath, remorse and confusion coursing through me. If only she had given me more time to explain! But even if she had, how could I defend what I had done? *Should* I have redeemed Willoughby? I had barely the briefest interval, however, to contemplate these misgivings when, from a tea shop but a few yards ahead of me, emerged two young ladies deeply engaged in conversation.

I recognised them at once: it was Marianne's sister Elinor, walking arm in arm with Fanny Price. I was astounded. How was it possible that these two women from entirely different novels should be acquainted with each other? Moreover, what were they doing in Bath? They looked up, exchanged a brief, surprised glance, and hurried up to me.

The Harrison Duet

"Good afternoon Miss Austen," said Elinor with a graceful curtsey. "How lovely to see you."

"This is an extraordinary coincidence," murmured Fanny with a shy curtsey of her own. "Mrs. Ferrars and I were just talking about you."

"We only just met an hour ago," explained Elinor, nodding towards the establishment behind them, "and already we have become fast friends. We discovered that we have a great deal in common."

"You are indeed very much alike," agreed I with a smile, pleased by the notion of their new friendship. "I have dearly loved you both since the moment of your inception."

"You see?" said Fanny quietly, darting a meaningful look at her companion.

Elinor nodded gravely but remained silent.

A foreboding feeling came over me. "Is any thing the matter?" asked I.

"Not a thing," said Elinor.

"The weather is very cold and damp," observed Fanny, "do not you think?"

I knew them both too well to be taken in by the polite composure on their faces. "You need not keep any secrets from me. If there is something you wish to say, please speak freely."

"Well," said Fanny reluctantly, "we do not mean to complain. It is just that—" She could not go on.

"It is about our characters," interjected Elinor quickly.

"Your characters?" answered I. "But what is wrong with your characters? You are both excellent, intelligent women, with sincere and affectionate dispositions, strength of understanding, calmness of manner, and coolness of judgment."

"Precisely," stated Fanny.

"You made us *too* perfect," said Elinor.

"Too perfect?" cried I. "How can any one be too perfect?"

"I always behaved with the utmost of propriety," said Elinor, "no matter how difficult or oppressive the circumstance. At only nineteen years of age, I was required to be the model of patience, perseverance, and fortitude, obliged to keep my entire family financially and emotionally afloat, and to conceal my pain beneath a façade of complete composure, even when my heart was breaking."

"Yes, and you are *admired* for your strength of character, Elinor," insisted I.

"Admired perhaps, but not *liked.* No one likes a character who is flawless, Miss Austen."

"It was the same for me," remarked Fanny. "How I succeeded in maintaining even a modicum of self-respect in such a hostile, belittling, and unfeeling environment as Mansfield Park is purely due to God's grace and your pen. You made me sit timidly by while the man I loved chased after another woman, had me refuse a charming man who was almost entirely good, and would not even allow me to participate in a private play, insisting that it was indelicate and wrong! How I disliked myself! No one is fond of a shy, priggish, and passive character, Miss Austen. No one!"

"*I* am very fond of you," returned I emphatically. "Edmund likes you. He *loves* you."

"Only because you made him just as good and virtuous as I."

"The book has oft been praised for its morality and sound treatment of the clergy!" insisted I a little desperately.

"That may be so," said Fanny, "and please correct me if I am wrong, but your own mother finds me insipid, your niece Anna cannot bear me, and the reading public at large

The Harrison Duet

finds Edmund and I both annoying and as dull as dishwater."

To my mortification, I could not refute her statement.

"People love strong, outspoken characters," said Elinor, "who will not allow themselves to be trampled on by others—characters who have flaws but overcome them. Yet in *our* books, you imply that by being consistently patient, good, and silent, a woman can rise above difficult circumstances."

"Surely this message controverts everything you told us about life in that *other* book," said Fanny.

"What other book?" asked I.

"Why, the book that is everyone's favorite," answered Elinor with a tight little smile. She then said good-day, and after Fanny made a final comment about the weather, the pair linked arms, turned, and made their way down the damp, grey pavement.

My thoughts were in such a state of disarray that I hardly knew what to think or feel. I strode off in the opposite direction, crossing the road, when a carriage suddenly appeared out of the fog and nearly ran me down. It was some time before my heart returned to its natural pace. How long I walked on in this distracted manner along the nearly deserted streets I cannot say, but at length I passed the Abbey Church and found myself standing outside the Pump-room. A cacophony of voices issued from within, proof that not all the inhabitants of Bath had stayed at home.

As I was cold and thirsty, I hurried inside the Pump-room, where a crowd milled about in spacious elegance, and musicians in the west apse performed a pleasant air. A cursory glance revealed that I had no acquaintance there. Appreciative of the heat emanating from two large fireplaces, I made my way to the fountain where I paid the attendant for a glass of water and drank it down. As I turned, I nearly collided with a handsome young man smartly dressed in the uniform of a naval officer, exactly like that of my brothers Frank and Charles.

"Forgive me," said he with a bow, before purchasing his own glass and moving on.

The naval captain made a most arresting figure, and I wondered what lay behind the sad look in his eyes. My attention was soon diverted, however, by the sight of an attractive, fashionably-dressed young woman who was intently studying all the passersby, as if seeking out some one in particular. She looked strangely familiar. All at once I knew why: it was Emma Woodhouse.

Emma! In my view, one of the most delightful creatures I had ever conceived! Upon catching sight of me, Emma started with recognition, a look that quickly turned to worry as she glided to my side.

"There you are! I have been looking every where for you, Miss Austen. Have the others found you?"

"The others?"

"Word has got out that you are in town. There are quite a few people who are—" (she hesitated) "—most *anxious* to speak with you."

Oh dear, I thought, my heart sinking. This could prove to be a most exhausting day. "Thank you. I will keep an eye out for the others, whoever they may be. But how is it that *you* are here, Emma? My book about you is only just completed. It has yet to be sold or published."

She shrugged. "I suppose since it is written, I therefore exist?"

"I see." I smiled hopefully, praying that, unlike my previous encounters, *she* might have some kind words for me. My hopes on that score, however, were soon dashed.

The Harrison Duet

"I admit, Miss Austen, that I too have been hoping to have a word with you. You know it is not in my nature to criticise. And far be it from me to give *advice*—Mr. Knightley is for ever counseling me on that subject, and he is never wrong—but I believe it my duty as a friend to share certain thoughts which I feel might prove to be of benefit to you."

"Do go on."

"You must be the judge of what is best to write, of course—I would not *dream* of interfering—but I cannot help but think that you presented me in a very disagreeable light in your novel."

"Disagreeable?" I sighed, knowing full well what was coming. "How so?"

"It started out so well. You called me handsome, clever, and rich, and you gave me a happy disposition. You placed me in a comfortable home, I was original in my thinking, and admired by all who knew me. But then you went off in such an unacceptable direction! You made me oblivious to every real thing going on around me. I spent the entire novel completely blind to the truth of my affections, while trying in vain to elevate Harriet's status and procure her a husband. I was dense, obtuse, manipulative—yet all the while firm in my belief that I knew what was best for every body!"

"Yes, but Emma: every thing you said and did, you did from the fullness of your heart and with the best of intentions."

"Not everything," insisted Emma. "I gossiped wickedly about Jane Fairfax, I flirted outrageously with Frank Churchill, and I was unpardonably rude to Miss Bates at Box Hill."

"That is true, but in each instance, you learned from your mistakes—and this ability to learn and change is the very definition of a heroine. Consider your many positive and attractive qualities. Your temperament is cheerful, patient, and resilient. You are not given to self-pity. You are intelligent and have an excellent sense of humour. Your errors are the result not of stupidity but of a quick mind—a mind so necessitous of stimulation that you were obliged to invent interesting diversions for yourself. You are an *imaginist*, Emma—like me."

Emma puzzled briefly over all that I had said, then charged, "Nevertheless, there is one offence so egregious, it negates all the positive qualities you mentioned: you portrayed me as a *snob*."

"Dearest Emma," returned I quietly and with affection, "compare yourself to Mr. and Mrs. Elton. *They* are my shining examples of true vulgarity, self-importance, and boorishness. You, by contrast, are a charming and amusing creature—a *loveable* snob."

"How can a snob be loveable?" retorted Emma sharply. "That is a contradiction in terms. Even *you* admitted that you were writing a heroine whom no one but yourself would much like."

"Perhaps I will be proven wrong. My sister read the manuscript, and she loves you as you are."

"She is hardly the most impartial judge, is she?" cried Emma. Lowering her voice now and speaking with great feeling, she added, "I must take my leave, but please allow me to leave you with two vital pieces of information. First: tell your cook to try gooseberry jam in her Bakewell Pudding, it is quite delicious. And second: I have just been speaking with a Mr. Thurston, a most *interesting*, unattached clergyman with good teeth and a nice living in the parish of Snitterfield. Do you see him standing over there by the great clock?" With a slight inclination of her head, Emma gestured towards a stout, red-faced, nearly bald-headed clergyman who was smiling at me. "I made all your charms known to him and he is hoping to speak to you. No, no, do not even think of thanking me," said she, turning to go. "Just to know that my actions *might* bring you some future happiness gives me great joy. Good-day, Miss Austen, and good luck."

"Wait!" cried I, darting after Emma, as anxious to continue our conversation as I was to avoid the man in question, "may we not return to the earlier topic of our discussion? You are the second person to-day who has alleged that I gave her too many faults, while two others insist that I made them too perfect. How am I to reconcile these opposing points of view?"

Emma glanced back at me and shrugged prettily. "That is for you to decide. I cannot give you an opinion. If you prefer to go on writing flawed heroines who must continually humiliate themselves on the road to learning life's lessons, then be my guest—do not hesitate. You are the author, not I. Not for the world would I think of influencing you either way." With a parting smile, she whirled round and vanished into the crowd.

In a state of great agitation I hurriedly navigated my way out of the Pump-room and into the yard beyond. How could it be, I asked myself, that all the characters whom I loved and had created with such care should prove to be so unsatisfied with themselves? Had I erred in their conception? Was it better to be good or flawed? If neither option was acceptable, what was an author to do?

Half a minute conducted me through the empty Pump-yard to the archway opposite Union-passage, where I paused in great surprise. Even Cheap-street—which was normally so congested with the confluence of carriages, horsemen, and carts entering the city from the great London and Oxford roads that a lady was in danger of losing her life in attempting to cross it—was entirely devoid of traffic. The bleak, eerie stillness was not even broken by the advent of a single female window shopper or a gentleman in search of tea and pastry. Where was every body? The only evidence of life in Bath had been the congregation in the Pump-room. The late afternoon light was quickly fading into early evening. Perhaps, I thought, there was a ball taking place in the Upper Rooms.

I had only just conceived this notion when, to my astonishment, I suddenly found myself halfway across the city, standing immediately outside those very Assembly Rooms, enveloped by an eager, jostling crowd making its way in through the open doors. I had no wish to go within. In my youth, I had greatly enjoyed a ball—I loved music and dancing, and had welcomed the opportunity it afforded for animated association with friends and neighbours or, at times, new faces—but I had never cared for such diversions at Bath, a city of peripatetic visitors of little sense and even lesser education, where young ladies made overt displays of themselves in search of husbands.

Nevertheless, I was pulled along by the crush of people into the hall and the adjoining ball-room. At length the bustle subsided, depositing me at a vantage point from whence I was able to obtain a good view of the dancers. I felt very out of sorts, and was mortified to be standing amongst this well-dressed crowd clad in my day gown and bonnet (although a brief glance in a nearby looking-glass revealed that the bonnet *was* trimmed with the loveliest blue satin ribbon and a very fine spray of forget-me-nots.)

I was fanning my face from my exertion when my gaze fell upon two couples dancing nearby, at the end of a line. Did my eyes deceive me? Could it possibly be? The first couple

The Harrison Duet

looked for all the world like Elizabeth and Mr. Darcy. Dancing directly beside them—I was absolutely certain of it—were Jane and Mr. Bingley. The music ended and I watched in wonder as Elizabeth slipped her hand into the bend of Mr. Darcy's arm and, smiling and chatting, they made their way across the floor. Jane and Mr. Bingley followed behind at a leisurely pace, engaged in a similarly affectionate tête-à-tête.

A great thrill coursed through me. Was it possible that I was actually going to meet those four dear souls with whom, for so many long years, I had been acquainted only in my mind? My initial exhilaration, however, turned to alarm at the thought of another demoralising scene such as the ones to which I had just been subjected. Hot tears threatened behind my eyes. Oh! I could not bear it! Despite my desperate wish to leave, I was frozen to the spot. In moments the first couple stood before me.

"Good-afternoon Miss Austen," said Elizabeth, beaming.

"What a pleasure it is to see you!" exclaimed Mr. Darcy.

Their manner was so friendly and congenial, I could scarcely believe my ears—but I knew better than to expect it to last. "Please," returned I anxiously, "if you have complaints—if you are angry with me or have found fault with any thing I have done—I would truly rather you did not voice it."

"Complaints?" repeated Elizabeth in surprise.

"Faults?" reiterated Mr. Darcy. "We could not in good conscience find fault with you, Miss Austen. And we are hardly angry."

"In fact, it is quite the reverse," said Elizabeth. "We would like to express our most fervent gratitude."

"Gratitude?" said I, astonished.

Elizabeth and Mr. Darcy exchanged a very loving look and then a happy laugh, as he gently clasped her gloved hand in his. "Everything you devised for us was so cleverly thought out," said Elizabeth.

"I shudder to think what kind of man I would have been, had you not thrown my darling Elizabeth in my way," said Mr. Darcy with a warm smile.

"I believe we are the happiest two creatures on earth," added Elizabeth with the liveliest emotion.

"No, you must reserve that honour to us," interjected Mr. Bingley, joining us with a bright grin and Jane on his arm. "I thank you, Miss Austen. You have done us all proud."

"Truly, I do not deserve such happiness!" cried Jane, her adoring gaze meeting Bingley's, where it found an identical response. "Miss Austen, you are a heroine in our eyes. And thank you for giving me your name."

So fraught with emotion and relief was I at this discourse that I was unable to utter a single syllable. All four shook my hand enthusiastically in turn and said their good-byes. When I had at last sufficiently regained my composure to make my way out of the rooms, I was still so consumed with delight that I barely noticed the coldness of the evening air or the grimness of the ever-present fog.

What felicity was this! I thought as I wandered along, heedless of the direction in which I was heading. After such a litany of heartbreaking indictments, to find that I had at least done *something* right! It was in this exultant frame of mind that I approached the wide green lawn of the Royal Crescent, where I suddenly felt a hand on my arm and my musings were interrupted by a feminine voice.

"Miss Austen! Oh! I have been quite wild to speak to you!"

I stopped and looked at the young lady in astonishment. It was Susan Morland! It must be, for she was pretty, seventeen at most, and dressed just as I had imagined her, in a sprigged muslin gown

The Harrison Duet

with blue trimmings (which was bound to fray upon the first washing.) Well, I thought—at least it makes sense that *she* is in Bath, for I did put her here before sending her off to Northanger Abbey.

"I must be quick," exclaimed she, looking about with an anxious expression. "I fear for your safety, Miss Austen."

"My safety?"

"Yes! I will explain in a moment. But first—oh!" (Studying my expression) "I dare say you have forgotten all about me. I would not blame you if you had—I have been sitting so long on the shelf!"

"How could I forget *you*, Susan? You were my very first sale."

"It is that very subject which I long to discuss with you. Oh! Miss Austen—it has been twelve years that I have languished in obscurity at Richard Crosby and Company—twelve years and still I have not seen the light of day! Clearly that gentleman does not intend to publish my story. I understand that £10 is a great deal of money—but you are a successful author to-day. Surely you have the means to buy back the manuscript *now*. Would it be asking too much—could you find it in your heart—please, please, will you rescue me?"

I took a moment to consider her request. I, too, had long agonised over that book's fate—but I had written it so long ago, and much had changed during the interval. Would another bookseller—not to mention the public— still find *Susan* to be of interest? Or would they think it obsolete? Yet how could I voice aloud these thoughts to the sweet, innocent girl who stood trembling so violently before me, gazing at me with such hope and trust in her eyes?

In a tone softened by compassion I said, "Dear Miss Morland. If I am fortunate enough to sell *Emma*, I will use a portion of the funds to buy back your book. You may depend upon it."

"Thank you, Miss Austen. Thank you so much!"

"However, I must warn you, Miss Morland—should I succeed in this effort, there is another problem which I fear may cause you additional distress."

"What is that?"

"It has come to my attention that an anonymous, two-volume novel called *Susan* was published by John Booth some six years ago. Therefore, even if I *do* recover my own manuscript, its title—and your very *name*—will necessarily have to be altered."

"Oh! I would not mind that a bit," replied Susan earnestly. "In truth, I have never much cared for my name. Please feel free to change it. Although I do hope you will not call me Milicent or Lavinia or Eunice—that would be too, too horrid!"

"I promise to give you only the most delightful name."

"You fill me with relief, Miss Austen. And now—" She looked about us with an expression of renewed dread and apprehension. "To that other matter of which I must speak without further delay. I am very concerned about you. You must leave Bath this instant!"

"Leave Bath? Why?"

"A little while ago," confided Susan with rising agitation, "I was strolling through Sydney Gardens when I observed Mr. Wickham engaged in a heated discussion with Mr. Willoughby, William Walter Elliot, and John Thorpe. All four appeared to be very angry about something."

My heart leapt in sudden alarm. I had already witnessed the wrath and disdain of several of my creations whom I *thought* I had portrayed in a most becoming light. What manner of reception could I expect to receive from those

The Harrison Duet

characters whom I had represented in a *less* than favourable manner? Indeed, I could not deny that with the most deliberate of intentions, I had conceived a great many characters who were truly selfish, vain, vulgar, greedy, wicked, stupid, thoughtless, or senseless—or, as in the case of the four scoundrels Susan had described—a combination of most of those traits.

"You say that all four of those men are in Bath to-day?" replied I with unease.

"They are! While strolling by, I overheard some of their conversation. It was dreadful!" (Moving closer now) "I heard Mr. Wickham and Mr. Willoughby mention *your name,* Miss Austen, in the same sentence as the word *murder."*

"Murder? Pray, Susan, do not let your imagination run away with you. Did you learn nothing from your own story?" Despite my brave words, in truth I was growing quite afraid.

All at once I heard the ominous sound of approaching footsteps. Appearing out of the dark fog on the rise of lawn before me came the very four male figures Miss Morland had just named, steadily advancing with torches in hand and no kind looks on their countenances.

I swallowed hard and stepped backward. "Miss Morland—" I began, but strangely, Miss Morland had vanished. I was alone, quite alone, except for the men who were bearing down on me. The heavy trampling of feet began to grow into an ever-louder, thundering din. To my dismay, just behind the angry four, I saw another group of people coming at me through the fog: Mr. Collins, Mrs. Bennet, Lydia and Mary Bennet, Louisa Bingley Hurst, Caroline Bingley, and Lady Catherine de Bourgh.

I gasped in terror. From a different direction, an additional, furious assemblage was descending: Mr. and Mrs.

Elton, Sir Walter and Elizabeth Elliot, Mary Musgrove, Isabella Thorpe, and General Tilney. Behind them strode Fanny and John Dashwood, Lucy Steele, Mr. Price, Mr. Rushworth, Maria Bertram Rushworth, Lady Bertram, Mrs. Ferrars, and Robert Ferrars. Many of them carried pitchforks and flaming torches. Some had guns. All of them were staring at me. The hatred and malice in their eyes is beyond my power to describe.

Panic surged through me. I screamed in horror, but no sound escaped my lips. I turned sharply in an attempt to flee, when I heard Lady Catherine de Bourgh call out in fury:

"Not so hasty, if you please. Unfeeling, selfish girl! I am most seriously displeased!"

Her piercing tone so paralysed me that my feet were rooted to the ground. The fuming horde was getting closer and closer. They were chanting now: "Jane! Jane! Jane!" Again, I tried to scream.

"Jane! Jane! Jane! Wake up!"

Cassandra's voice broke through my consciousness, hurtling me out of that terrifying reality and back to the warm cocoon of my own bed. I awoke to find myself bathed in perspiration, my heart pounding, my sister's gentle hand upon my arm as she looked at me through the moonlit darkness from the next pillow.

"Oh! Cassandra!" I struggled to catch my breath. "I have just had the most horrible dream."

"What was it about?" asked Cassandra softly.

I told her everything, as I always did.

"Well," said she after I had finished my story, "your dream does not surprise me. Your characters have become very real to you—as real as life itself. It is only natural that you should hear their thoughts and feel their emotions as they do."

The Harrison Duet

"Yes, but what does it signify? I can understand why many of my lesser characters would despise me. But my heroines? I love them all! To think that four of them are so unhappy makes me absolutely miserable. Have I done a terrible thing? Am I the most vile and ignorant authoress who ever dared to put pen to paper?"

"Of course not, dearest," replied Cassandra soothingly, as she found and tenderly squeezed my hand. "If all writers were obliged to atone for the portrayals or fates of their creations, think what Shakespeare owes to Romeo and Juliet or Iago and Richard III. Should Defoe and Richardson feel remorse for the trials and tribulations they inflicted on poor Mr. Crusoe, Clarissa, or Pamela?"

"Of course not. Their work has afforded me and the public untold hours of reading pleasure."

"So it is with your books, Jane. You have told me time and again that a perfectly smooth course never makes a satisfying story, that it is an author's job to make his or her characters suffer so that they might learn something at the end."

"True. Although after hearing Fanny Price's complaints, I believe I may have erred in her creation. I ignored my own model! Her suffering did not culminate in a lesson."

"I did *try* to persuade you to let her marry Henry Crawford."

"I know." I sighed. "I have learned *my* lesson. People do not appreciate pure goodness in a character in a novel. Even Fanny does not like herself! Given the complaints of the others, perhaps I ought to strive for a more happy medium in my next effort."

"A happy medium? What do you mean?"

I thought for a moment. "Next time, I will create a heroine who is modest and good, but not *entirely* perfect. She will have made mistakes that she regrets." My mind fixed on one of my greatest regrets in life: the day I was obliged to say good-bye to Mr. Ashford. "Marianne asked for a second chance. Well then—I will fill this new character with longing and regret for a lover she was persuaded to refuse many years past, and I will give her a second chance to make things right."

"A lovely idea. Who will this lover be? A clergyman or a landed gentleman?"

"Neither." New ideas spilled into my brain with lightning speed. "In my dream, I saw a young officer in the Pumproom—a naval captain with sad eyes. Perhaps he was regretting his lost love. I will write about *him*, and thus honor Frank and Charles and all men of that worthy profession."

"A naval captain! I approve of this notion."

"I think I shall set the book primarily in Bath."

"Bath? But Jane, you hate Bath."

"That is precisely why it is the ideal location." I sat up, hugging my pillow to my chest, my heart pounding with rising excitement. "My heroine will be obliged to quit her beloved home in the country and remove with her family to Bath—just as we did when papa retired—and she will despise it as much as I did. Think of the drama! Imagine all the intriguing circumstances which may ensue! And to make up for the odiousness of Bath, I will include a visit to a place I love—" (recalling the precise spot where I met Mr. Ashford) "Lyme, perhaps. Yes, Lyme."

"I declare, Jane, this *must* be the book you are supposed to write next. I have not seen you this impassioned about anything in months."

"Speaking of passion," said I with enthusiasm, "do you recall how Marianne accused me of giving passionate feelings a bad name? This time, I will allow my characters to better express their emotions. And something else occurs to me. In my dream, all my female heroines seemed so incredibly *young*.

I would prefer to write about someone a bit closer to my own age and experience now."

"What age do you have in mind?"

"I don't know, seven-and-twenty perhaps."

"A heroine of seven-and-twenty is very old indeed," returned Cassandra dubiously. "Has such a thing ever been attempted before?"

"Not to my knowledge, but I could be the first to do it. And what would you think if I named her after our dear friend, Anne Sharpe?"

"I should think Anne would be flattered."

"Then it is done! Anne she shall be." I leapt from the bed and threw on my shawl, ignoring the brief, painful twinge in my back which I had been experiencing infrequently of late, clearly a sign of my advancing age.

"Jane, what are you doing?"

"I am getting up."

"It is the middle of the night."

"Do you imagine that I could sleep, with all these ideas spinning in my head?" I lit a candle and strode to the door. "No, I must go downstairs at once, write out the dream I had, and then jot down my plans for this novel, before all these thoughts scatter to the wind."

"Of course you must," said Cassandra with a smile as she lay back upon her pillow. "Do not stay up *too* long, dearest."

"I will not," replied I, although we both knew very well that I would be up until my fingers were stained black with ink and the first light of dawn was creeping in beneath the shutters.

LIKE THE BOOK?
PLEASE POST A REVIEW!

ABOUT THE AUTHOR

Syrie James is the bestselling author of eight critically acclaimed novels, including *The Missing Manuscript of Jane Austen*, *The Lost Memoirs of Jane Austen*, *The Secret Diaries of Charlotte Brontë*, *Dracula My Love*, *Nocturne*, *Forbidden*, and *Songbird* and *Propositions*, books one and two in *The Harrison Duet*. Her books have been translated into eighteen foreign languages. She lives with her family in Los Angeles, California. Syrie welcomes you to follow her on facebook and twitter, and to visit her website at:

www.SyrieJames.com

COMING IN AUGUST, 2014

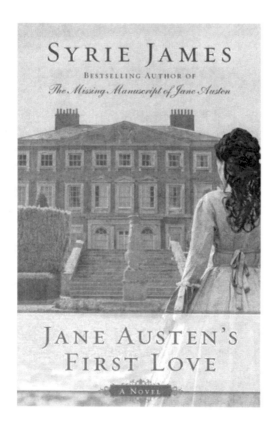

CPSIA information can be obtained at www.ICGtesting.com
Printed in the USA
LVOW10s1606080316

478282LV00019B/674/P